infamous park avenue prince

ELLA FRANK
BROOKE BLAINE

Cover Design: Hang Le
Cover Photo: Ren Saliba
Edited by Arran McNicol

❀ Created with Vellum

ONE

jt

"YOU KNOW, ENDING up in the dean's office before my first day of classes have even started doesn't bode well for my future here," I said, picking at the frayed hem of my jeans, the casual denim a direct contrast to the opulent armchair I lounged in. Everything about the office screamed extravagance, from the designer wallpaper and vintage giltwood frames to the executive desk flecked with actual gold leaf.

I felt like I should be wearing a starched school uniform, for fuck's sake.

Dean Hawthorne sat perched on the edge of the desk, immaculately dressed in a high-waisted pencil skirt and jacket, her auburn hair neatly pinned back off her face. Being the youngest dean in Astor University history meant she needed not only to dress the part to be taken seriously, but present a professional yet tough demeanor as well.

From personal experience, I knew she had the required stern frown down pat. Although at the moment a soft smile played on her lips.

"It's not a crime to want to make sure my only son is settling in okay," she said. "Especially since he wanted to move out and leave his poor mom all alone in a big house."

"First of all, you're not alone; Dad's there. And second, do you really think starting college still living in my parents' house is a good move? Especially when one of those parents runs Astor?" I shook my head. "I'd be a total pariah."

"I'd never let that happen, JT."

"Exactly, which is why you need to give me some space. It'll be hard enough to make friends without them thinking I'm going to run back to my mom."

"Letting you move into a dorm isn't giving you enough space?" A hurt look crossed her face.

"Letting me move into a dorm that you hand-picked."

"What's wrong with that? I thought you'd like the space."

"Mom, how many first-year students get their own private dorm room? Not to mention the biggest?"

"So you'd rather be in a dorm the size of a storage room?"

"Depends. Do those come with armed lobby security and a curfew on the weekdays too?"

"It's for your own safety."

"Seriously? A ten o'clock curfew is going to keep me safe?"

A groan of exasperation left her throat. "JT, please don't start that again—"

"But what if I want to see a late movie? Or the train breaks down and I don't get back in time? I get punished for that?"

"You can go on the weekend."

"What if there's a special showing of *Fight Club* that's only playing on a Tuesday? And Edward Norton is making a special appearance?"

She stared me down like she was wondering if we really needed to have this conversation for the tenth time. "You're here to focus on your studies, not breaking curfew. End of discussion."

A heavy silence descended as I bit my tongue in an effort not to argue the point more. I'd expected more freedom in my college experience, but I should've known better. I'd never really considered going anywhere other than Astor, but maybe that had been my mistake.

When it was clear I wasn't going to be the first to speak, Mom cleared her throat.

"Do you..." She paused, considering her words. "Would you rather switch to a freshman dorm? There aren't any private rooms, so you'll have to share with a roommate or two, but—"

"No, it's not that," I said, running a hand over my hair. "I appreciate your getting me my own room, really I do. I just don't want any special treatment. It's gonna be hard enough fitting in with these people."

"What do you mean?"

"You know how it is with these one percenters. They come from old money and get off competing with each other to be at the top. My getting special treatment is like throwing me in shark-infested waters with a cut. They'll smell blood."

She crossed her arms. "So what am I supposed to do, then?"

"I don't know. Maybe trust me to venture into the water cautiously?"

Her eyes narrowed as she contemplated my words, and really, she had no reason to doubt me. I was a good kid. I excelled in school, got top grades, and always made sure to keep out of trouble.

"Okay, you're right." She got to her feet and walked over to the large window in her office overlooking the main quad. "I just worry about you, that's all. This place does tend to attract a certain crowd, and I want to make sure you're prepared."

It was no secret that Astor University was one of the top schools in the country. Just like it was no secret that it had produced several presidents, some of the top CEOs, and other influential men and women in government and business.

I hadn't been exaggerating when I likened the place to shark-infested waters, because that's exactly what it was, and if you weren't careful you would enter that water as bait. I didn't plan to be eaten on my first day.

I got to my feet and headed over to Mom. I knew she was worried about me—any parent with a child going off to college was. But she also needed to remember that I was her son. She'd taught me to be smart, curious, and brave, and now she had to trust that I could handle myself.

"I know you're worried, but whether I'm here or somewhere else, you have to trust that I can make smart decisions."

She glanced at me, her perfectly shaped brow raised. "Smart decisions, huh?"

"Yeah." I bumped into her shoulder, trying to get a smile from her. "I'm not some delinquent. You know that. I'm going to go to class, study, then come back to my dorm and sleep. What's the worst that could happen?"

She eyed me for a beat, then reached over to tuck one of my unruly curls behind my ear. "I don't like to think about worst-case scenarios. So let's just focus on the positive—that even though you aren't living at home, I'll still get to see you around campus."

"Exactly."

Though her lips were pursed, she seemed satisfied for the moment, and I wondered how comfortable I should get with these office visits. I loved my parents, but I'd been itching for the taste of freedom I'd finally gotten when I moved into the dorm a few days ago. Today was the first day of the rest of my life.

A deep sigh left her as she glanced out the window, and I followed her gaze to a group of guys walking past the main gate.

"Speaking of delinquents," she murmured, her eyes narrowing.

I frowned, wondering if we were looking at the same people. The seven guys she had her eye on certainly didn't look like the kind who'd cause trouble. In fact, the most problematic thing about them was how damn attractive they were.

They were a mix of preppy and flashy, with the exception of one guy dressed all in black like he'd just come off the back of a motorcycle.

"Are we looking at the same people?" I asked.

"Don't let the nice clothes fool you. Trouble comes in all forms. Aren't you the one who just said these one percenters smell blood? You don't think they do anything about it?" She quirked a brow my way.

I glanced down again, studying each guy more closely. They really did look like they'd all just stepped out of the pages of a fashion magazine. I mean, what twenty-something actually wore an ascot to school, for God's sake?

"I don't think you've got anything to worry about." I looked down at my frayed jeans. "I hardly fit in with that crowd."

"Good, because those kinds of men are interested in one thing and one thing only—themselves."

I didn't doubt that for a second, but up until now, I'd never really run across this kind of crowd. Everyone knew about the rich and upper-class society of New York, but unless you were part of that clique, you didn't have anything to do with them.

Here, however, it was a little different, and while money could definitely pave the way into Astor, so could brains, which meant this group of guys had to share classrooms and hallways with the likes of me.

Not saying we were poor or anything, but I didn't hail from some *Fortune* family with enough money to buy a private island.

My eyes drifted over the group again, as I wondered what their families did for a living.

Bankers, maybe? Investors? Oil tycoon? A celebrity?

It had to be something pretty impressive to look and dress like that. I wasn't the only one curious, either. Everyone who passed them by would wave, smile, or sneak a glance at the seven guys who looked as though they belonged in some glitzy, high-end bar, instead of standing in the middle of the quad waiting for their first class to start.

It was fascinating to watch. The way people reacted to them. Like they were royalty, and everyone else were mere commoners. But that was what money did. It gave people power, confidence, a sense of entitlement that was born out of always having what you wanted, or having the means to get it—traits that these guys exuded in spades.

The guy in the pretentious ascot threw his head back and started to laugh at something one of the others had said to him, then he gestured up to the window where I stood beside my mom.

I wasn't sure why, but my first instinct was to duck and hide as the rest of the group turned to look in the same direction. But knowing how ridiculous that would look, I stood my ground and continued to stare down at them.

It wasn't a secret the dean's kid was enrolled this year, and it wasn't like I could keep it a secret for the next four, so it was best to just go with it. If these guys were going to give me shit for it, then my hiding from view wasn't going to help the issue.

Ascot Guy leaned into his friend with the tawny, windswept waves pushed back from his forehead, and like the rest of this group, he was dressed to impress in a pair of grey pants and fitted white polo—and in his hand was a tan jacket that matched his leather loafers.

He looked like he was on some European vacation, not attending his first day of university, and the outfit looked like it cost more than my entire wardrobe.

His blue eyes sought me out and locked on me, and as Ascot whispered in his ear, I swore I caught Tawny's lips crook to one side.

Something about that exchange had my spine stiffening. Call it intuition or call it paranoia, but I knew they were talking about me. I could feel it in my bones.

As quickly as the connection formed, it was severed. Tawny turned back to his group of friends, and they all laughed again.

My mom placed her hand on my shoulder and gave it a squeeze, and I tried not let her show how their attention had affected me. Her apologetic smile told me I wasn't fooling anyone.

"Just steer clear of them and you should be fine."

As she headed back to her desk, I took one last look down to the quad, and all I could hear in my head were my mom's words from minutes ago: *Trouble comes in all forms.*

TWO

THE MERCEDES-BENZ SPRINTER van that chauffeured us to and from Astor hadn't even fully stopped in front of the gates when Daire yanked the sliding door wide and jumped out.

"Jesus, man, what's your rush?" Travis grumbled, in no hurry to move as he leisurely sipped his coffee. At least, I assumed it was coffee. No telling what was in that tumbler.

"Someone's excited about junior year," Preston said, adjusting the strap of his bag as he stepped out onto the sidewalk. "Never thought it'd be Daire."

Daire rolled his eyes. "I don't need anyone opening a fuckin' door for me."

"Speak for yourself." As East joined them, he patted Daire's cheek and smirked. "But thanks for doing the honors. Will you be driving us back later too?"

I shared a look with Gavin and Donovan before we

moved from the back of the Sprinter. Travis was still lounging in his seat, and I kicked at his ankle as I passed.

"You plan on coming with, or is there a leather pants convention in town I don't know about?"

"That was last week," Travis said without missing a beat. He took another sip of his drink and followed me out of the van, just in time for our driver to shut the door after us.

"Thanks, Scotty." I clapped our new driver on the shoulder and gave him a smile. His eyes widened in surprise before he nodded once.

"Of course, Mr. LaRue."

As he took off, East sidled up beside me, batting his lashes. "Anything for you, Mr. LaRue. Fancy a lift? A drink? A fuck?"

I laughed and shoved him away from me. The pompous ass. He even looked the part in a tailored suit he'd paired with an ascot and gloves. It was almost impressive, considering Manhattan would be under a heat advisory today.

But my best friend and roommate considered reputation and style above pretty much everything, and I couldn't deny his wardrobe had rubbed off on me. Except I'd never be caught dead in a damn ascot. As it was, I had the neck of my short-sleeved white polo undone to keep the collar off my neck, but I carried a tan jacket in case of a classroom freeze-out.

We passed through the main gates and into the quad,

where hundreds of students milled in the shadow of the towering red brick building.

First day of school—it wasn't exactly the highlight of my year, but the way I figured, the sooner we started the sooner we'd get the hell out, right? It wasn't like I wanted to prolong my schooling career any longer than necessary, especially after what happened at the end of last year.

We gathered over by one of the benches and dropped our bags and asses down onto it. Daire moved off to the side and pulled a pack of cigarettes from his back pocket, and before he could even get it up to his mouth, Donovan was cursing him out.

"Don't even think about lighting that up around me."

Daire leveled him with a *you shittin' me?* look.

"Unlike you, I care about my fucking body and make a living off it, so if you want to suck on a cancer stick, do it somewhere else."

"Van..." Gavin—Donovan's brother and the youngest of our crew—shook his head.

"What? You telling me you want to smell that shit? I'm getting ready for one of the biggest shoots of my career. I've got to be in tiptop shape, and—"

"Yeah, we got it." Daire rolled his eyes. "No need to get your panties in a fucking wad."

He wandered away from the rest of us to lean up against one of the trees, where he proceeded to light said cancer stick and shoot Donovan the finger.

I chuckled. "Good to see the trip to Milan brightened

12

his attitude. Anyone would think he was the one who'd been sentenced to the summer in New York."

"You know Daire, not happy unless he's unhappy." East smirked. "Hell, he probably scowls when he comes too."

"Not something I ever want to find out, but thanks for the visual."

"What can I say? That's what friends are for." East looked around the quad, tugging at the cuffs of his sleeves. "Speaking of coming, did you manage to find anyone in the city this summer that you hadn't done that particular pastime with? Or did you have to go double-dipping while we were off sampling some Italian delicacies?"

The subject of my absence on our yearly summer vacation was East's favorite topic of conversation since they'd gotten back last week. For years we'd been jet-setting around the globe, living life to the fullest, but this year I'd been grounded by my father and had to make do with Manhattan as my playground for summer fun.

That wouldn't have been so bad if anyone worth having fun with hadn't gotten on a plane and left the city. So to say the pickings had been slim the last couple of months was putting it mildly, and East was right—anyone that had been left, I'd been there and done that, and I wasn't one for do-overs.

"You having fun, basking in my misery?"

East side-eyed me, his lips curling. "Always. So is that a yes, you found someone? Or no, you had to double-dip?"

"It's a 'none of your fucking business.' Since when did you care so much about my sex life?"

"Since you're the only one this summer who didn't have one. You have to admit, that is *very* unusual for you. You're usually the one everyone fights over."

"Ah, okay, so what you're really saying is that you all finally got some because I wasn't there." I looked around the group, who were all rolling their eyes. "You're welcome."

"Fuck off." Travis took a swig—yeah, there was definitely more in that tumbler than coffee—of his drink. "I get plenty whether you're there or not."

"Oh, I believe you. I've seen the calluses on your hand."

Travis flipped me off as the rest of the group laughed and East bumped into my shoulder.

"Hey, check it out. Dean's window, you seeing what I'm seeing?"

Everyone turned then to look up at the main building that towered over the quad, and the large window that looked down onto it. With her arms crossed and a disapproving frown on her face, Dean Hawthorne stared down at us like she could erase us with a blink of her shrewd eyes.

She wishes, I thought, before my gaze landed on the guy next to her.

Well, well, well. What do we have here?

It wasn't the curious expression on his face that caught my attention, but the fact that said face was seriously hot. Unruly brown curls fell across his forehead as he bit down on his pouty lower lip.

East leaned in. "Revenge. And he looks oh so sweet."

My lips curved. Sweet, innocent, *and* the dean's son that we'd heard would be joining Astor this year? Things were looking up already.

I turned away from the window to smirk at my friends. "Hawthorne does owe me, and he looks like a nice gift."

Snorts of laughter met my ears as Donovan lifted a brow. "You think it'll be that easy?"

"I'm sorry, have we met?"

"That's the dean's golden child. She's not gonna let any of us near him with a ten-foot pole."

"More like fifty and a restraining order," Preston said, his eyes shooting back up to the window. "Twenty bucks says she's warning him about us now."

"You call that a bet?" I scoffed. "Come on, preppy."

A wicked grin I knew all too well crossed East's face. "Uh oh, boys. I think Mr. Weston LaRue is looking for a little payback for his summer of abstinence in the city."

"Abstinence my ass."

He winked. "If you say so."

Daire strolled back over, sans cigarette, and crossed his arms over the leather jacket I would've been sweltering in. "Care to make this interesting?"

I cocked a brow. "Meaning?"

"You want revenge. Preston wants a bet..."

"Fuck yes," East said, nodding as he picked up what

Daire was laying down. "What better way to get back at the dean than by corrupting her only child?"

"I hardly think that's fair...for *you*." I glanced back up at the window, but they'd both disappeared from view. "He's not exactly hard on the eyes, and I'm impossible to resist."

A gagging noise came from Travis's direction. "Good God, do you hear yourself? Someone get me a bucket."

"*I* heard him. And it sounds like his cocky ass wants a bet." East tapped his lips with a gloved finger and paced around me. "Hmm. Okay, Mr. Irresistible. You think you're so charming? How about this? If you can make the golden boy up there fall for you by homecoming, I'll pay for your *next* summer vacation."

Hell yeah, now that's a bet I can get behind.

"Location of my choosing? All inclusive?"

"Destination, the family jet, hotel, meals—"

"And drinks," I made sure to add, because the most expensive part of *any* of our vacations was the drink tab we racked up. Our motto being that it wasn't a good vacation if you could remember *all* of it.

"Fine, *and* drinks. But that, of course, depends on whether or not you can manage to keep yourself from being put on probation again. Last time I checked, corrupting the dean's son would probably be considered student misconduct."

"Fuck you. And for the record, it might've been my conduct up for discussion at that student board hearing, but it was all *your* asses I took the punishment for. So again, *you're welcome.*"

East's grin showed no remorse as he stopped in front of me. "So what you're saying is, we owe you the opportunity to go and dip your dick in gold. Tell me, what if he's not into what you've got to offer?"

I looked back up to the window that was now empty, and pictured the gorgeous face of the one who was going to help me get my revenge.

My lips curved into an immoral grin. "Everyone's into what I've got to offer."

"And if he's not?"

"Can't say I don't love a challenge."

Behind me, Gavin sighed and mumbled, "I've got a bad feeling about this."

East shot him a look. "Van, tell your brother not to worry so damn much. Let West have his fun. After all, he's got a reputation to live up to."

THREE

west

DURING THE BREAK between classes I commandeered a spot on a couch in one of the many lounges around campus, my feet kicked up on the chair in front of me. Travis sat on the other end of the couch, scrolling through his phone and glancing up every now and then to scowl at anyone who got too close.

"Who needs a bodyguard with you around?" I said, pulling open a bag of chips from the café.

Travis turned his glare on me. "What?"

"You. Mister Sunshine. There a reason you're grumpier than usual?"

"Yep."

"Care to elaborate?"

He reached over, stole a few chips, and popped one in his mouth. "Nope."

With a shrug, I dug into the bag and nodded. "Sounds about right."

From where I sat, it was a prime position to people-watch, though there was only one person I was on the lookout for. I hadn't seen the dean's son pass by yet, but he wouldn't remain elusive for long. One of the perks of being at the top of the social stratosphere at Astor was being able to get whatever you wanted, whenever you wanted. Guys, information, delivery service in the middle of class, you name it. There was always someone dying to be in your favor, and the lucky underclassman today was running toward me now, his overstuffed bag in his arms instead of on his back.

He was out of breath as he came to a stop a few feet away, smart enough to realize entering our personal space was a bad idea.

"I got the, uh...stuff you wanted," he said, his eyes darting between me and Travis, who barely gave him a cursory glance.

"Good." I dropped my feet from the chair and leaned forward. The kid went to sit in the spot my feet had vacated, and I shook my head. "Not there."

"Oh. Right." He glanced at the other options and took the spot across the table from us, dropping his bag on the floor beside him. As he rummaged through the contents, I shot Travis a look that he answered with a shake of his head.

"Got it," the kid said, a stack of papers in his hand. He glanced around like he was checking for eavesdroppers, and then handed me the top one. "His name is John

Thomas Hawthorne, but everyone calls him JT. Here's his schedule, along with interests—"

"Stop right there," I said, causing the kid's eyes to widen in something that looked like fear. I gave him an easy smile. "What was your name again?"

"Harry."

"You got all that in one morning, Harry?" When he nodded, I added, "You're good at this."

Harry puffed up his chest a little, that fear from seconds ago leaving his eyes. "Thanks. I wanted to make sure I got you as many details as I could."

"And I appreciate that. So, let's see what you've got. Read it out to me."

Harry looked down at the papers in his hands then back to me, seemingly unsure of where he should begin. "Do you want the personal or the hobbies and stuff?"

I sat back, propped one of my ankles up on my knee, and twisted the thick gold band on my index finger. "How about we start with personal?"

"Okay." Harry bent his head back over the paper. "Well, you know his name. He's eighteen years old, his birthday is December ninth—that makes him a Sagittarius. He's an only child, his mother is obviously the dean, and as far as I know, he's a star student. Straight A's across the board."

Shit. This kid really *was* detailed. He even knew JT's star sign. That was almost...scary. In a handy, information-gathering kind of way that we could definitely use later. He just might have a permanent spot on our "payroll."

"That's impressive, Harry. Very impressive."

He shrugged like it was nothing, but the flush on his cheeks told me my praise meant everything.

"Anything else on the personal?"

"Oh, um..." Harry looked back to his papers. "He broke up with his girlfriend just before college. She went to USC and he came here to Astor."

Travis's booted feet hit the ground at the same time my foot did.

"Hold up a second." Travis sat forward in his seat, his phone now forgotten. "Did you just say *girl*friend?"

Harry nodded. "That's right. They were together for, um"—he scanned his intel—"two years."

"Two *years*?" Travis scoffed, and slugged me in the arm. "How you feeling now, Mr. Irresistible?"

I caught Travis's hand and shoved it away. "I feel just fine."

"Did you not hear what the kid just said? Golden Boy is straight."

"No." I shook my head. "He said he was single."

"After breaking up with a *girl*."

"So? He never said anything about him being straight. Maybe he dated a guy before that?" I looked at Harry, whose eyes widened.

"I mean, it's not on my list, but it's, uh, it's possible."

"See? Nothing to worry about. I got this."

"Uh huh." Travis snorted and fell back into his seat. "Whatever you got to tell yourself, man."

"Okay, Harry. What else you got? What's JT like? What's he into?"

"*Girls,*" Travis piped up.

I leveled him with a glare. "Why don't you go back to hate-stalking a certain someone's posts for the day?"

"I'm not stalking anyone."

"Just because you're not physically following them doesn't mean it's not called stalking."

Travis flipped me off but brought his phone back up to "not" stalk the person whose feed we both knew he was now scrolling through.

"Harry?"

"Right." Harry flipped the paper over and drew his finger down the bullet points. "He's a freshman, so he's doing his core classes, but he seems to be looking into the university newspaper, so it seems he's into journalism—"

"Gossip," Travis interjected.

"Like you can talk." I looked pointedly at his phone.

"But I also saw him looking at the creative writing courses being held after school."

"Hmm, interesting." And the complete polar opposite to me. Don't get me wrong, I had nothing against someone who could spin a good story—especially if it got me out of a bind. My father's lawyer was an expert at that. But me, I liked numbers. They made more sense to me, and also helped when it came to counting my money.

"What about likes and hobbies? What's he do out of school?" I needed an in, and so far I had shit.

"It looks like he volunteers once a month at Back on Your Feet NY—"

"Which is...?"

"It's a place people who are struggling can go to get help with finding opportunities. You know, like getting suits for interviews, help with resumés, that kind of thing."

"Jesus Christ, you're dealing with a saint," Travis said, shaking his head. "You're so fucked."

I ignored him and gestured for Harry to continue. "What else?"

"Um. Likes going to bookstores, the theater, even the Off Broadway stuff. He's got a sweet tooth, favorite candy seems to be peanut M&M's, he's a fan of the Frrrozen Hot Mint Chocolate at Serendipity3—"

"Speaking of stalkers," Travis murmured.

"Specifics are great," I said, waving off Grumptastic over there.

Harry sifted through the papers. "I made a list of some of the books on his Kindle app. He doesn't really have a lot going on with his social media accounts, but I can always go back into his emails and poke around if you want."

"No, that won't be necessary." But good to know Harry's hacking skills were on point for future reference. He handed me the rest of the information he'd gotten, and I flipped through the pages, stopping on the one that listed JT's class schedule. A quick glance at the time told me he was about to head to a class with Professor Kingston, the hardass, and even though I had one of my own to get to, I'd always make time for a special appearance.

Priorities and all.

"Harry, you're a good man to have around," I said, grabbing my wallet from my back pocket. I pulled out a couple of crisp hundred-dollar bills and held them up. "One for the intel, one for your silence."

Harry's eyes stayed glued to the money as he nodded eagerly and made a motion of zipping his lips. Once I handed him the bills, he folded them and put them in the front pouch of his bag. As he got to his feet, I noticed the way he carried the damn thing instead of strapping it on.

"Wait. What's the deal with your bag?"

He looked down at the overstuffed monstrosity in his arms. "What do you mean?"

"Why's it not on your shoulder?"

"Oh. The strap broke, and I can't—"

I fished out another bill and handed it to him. "Get a new bag, Harry. Can't have your secrets spillin' out all over the place."

Harry dropped his bag in the chair, pushed up his glasses, and took the additional bill. "Wow. Thanks, um, and hey, if you need anything else, I can get it for you no problem." His gaze shifted to Travis before landing back on me. "Any of you."

"Appreciate that, man. I'll be in touch."

As he hurried off, I balled the empty bag of chips and made a perfect shot into the trash can.

Travis pulled his eyes away from his phone for long enough to ask, "And what exactly do you plan to do with all that useless information?"

"Useless? This shit's a gold mine. Which you'd know if you ever put an effort into your conquests."

"Your definition of effort and mine are vastly different."

"You don't say." I rolled up the papers, shoving them into my bag. "Now, if you'll excuse me, I've got a hot date waiting for me in King's class."

FOUR

jt

SHIFTING MY BACKPACK higher on my shoulder, I caught the door to my next class before it could slam shut, and stepped inside to find a seat. The lecture hall could easily fit a couple hundred people and was slowly filling to capacity. There was no way in hell I was sitting at the front of the tiered seating, but with the back rows already claimed, there weren't many options left.

I moved into a row about halfway down, wondering, not for the first time, how it was that not one of my high school friends was attending Astor. They were spread out all over the country now, something that didn't really hit me until this moment, walking into a crowded room alone. It would've been nice to shoot the shit with a friend on the first day at an intimidating school, where most of the students wore clothes that cost more than my parents' place in Brooklyn.

I dropped into a chair and pulled out my laptop, set it

on the desk in front of me, and opened it up to a blank page. I'd heard rumblings before from my mom's conversations that this particular professor, Professor Kingston, was one of the more difficult instructors at Astor, merciless in both curriculum and personality, which had me glancing behind to see if a spot in the back rows had miraculously opened up.

"What are we looking at?" a male voice to my left asked, and I whipped back around, my eyes colliding with the guy who'd slid into the seat beside me.

Oh shit. I recognized him instantly as the tawny-haired guy from the quad that morning, part of the group my mom had warned me to stay away from. Up close he was even more enigmatic, his blue eyes flashing under the harsh fluorescents as he lounged back in his chair, one arm casually thrown over the back of it. Hell, he even smelled like money, the expensive cologne he wore filling my nostrils as he gave me a crooked grin.

"Uh...nothing." A glance behind showed there were other empty seats in the row, so it was strange that he'd chosen the one right beside me.

"So, you new here?"

I turned back to face my new classmate and offered up a smile. Just because Mom had warned me off didn't mean I should be rude, right?

"Yeah, uh, this is my first day."

"I figured." The guy winked at me. "You've got that deer-in-the headlights look."

"Oh, yeah." I chuckled. "I suppose I do. It's just a lot,

you know. Trying to find class, then getting here on time—"

"Especially for King's class."

"King?"

The guy gestured to the empty podium at the front of the room. "Professor King. That's what we call him."

That made sense, and so did the fact that the professor would be a hardass on time management. Thank God I got here early.

"I'm West, by the way."

I looked at the hand he held out to me and decided there was no harm in making small talk with the guy. He was being nice, and was the first person who'd approached me all day. Everyone else had been giving me a wide berth, and I knew it had to do with my mom. So the fact he didn't seem to care was a relief.

"JT." I noticed several other students in the class looking our way—no doubt gawking at the dean's son.

"Nice to meet you, JT. So, you excited to be starting at Astor? Or are you here under duress?"

The grin he flashed made it easy to relax in his company, despite the dire warning Mom had issued earlier this morning, and I found myself settling back in my seat.

"Not duress, no. I like school and I like learning new things—"

"Wait, wait, wait." West sat up in his seat. "Did you just say you *like* school?"

I shrugged. "Guess it goes hand in hand with growing

up with a dean for a mom and an archivist at the New York Public Library for a dad."

"Are you shitting me right now?"

The look of pure horror that entered West's eyes made me chuckle.

"Nope. You grow up around that kind of academia influence and you end up liking school."

West slowly shook his head. "You poor, poor child."

I grinned. "What about you? Are you here under duress?"

West relaxed into his seat and let out a breath. "Well, I'm definitely not here because I *like* school."

I started to laugh. "No?"

"Fuck no. Parents wanted me to get an education, blah blah blah."

"How horrible of them."

West tossed me that crooked smile again. "I know, right? Assholes."

As more and more students filed in, I noticed them talking amongst one another, some having already made friends and some who clearly knew each other before today. It didn't escape my notice that they were leaving the chairs in front and on either side of me and West free. I'd been dead on in telling Mom I'd be looked at as a pariah. Oh well, at least West seemed willing to take a chance.

I glanced over at my new "friend" to see him pulling a packet of peanut M&M's out of his bag. He opened them up and held it toward me. "You want one?"

"No." I shook my head. "That's okay."

"Seriously?" West looked at the bag. "You don't like peanut M&M's." He said it like it was a crime.

"No, that's not it." I actually loved peanut M&M's. I just felt weird—*yes, I'm going to say it*—taking candy from a stranger.

"Come on, grab a handful."

"Really, it's okay." Although the offer was tempting.

"What's the problem?" Something twinkled in West's eyes as he shook the bag again. "You allergic to nuts?"

Biting back a smile, I shook my head and held out my hand. "You know what? You talked me into it."

As I popped one into my mouth, West's lips twitched. "I can be very convincing."

I didn't doubt that for a minute. He seemed like the kind of guy who could get whatever he wanted. Friendly, rich. It was a killer combination.

"JT, huh," West mused, drumming his fingers along the desk. "Is that short for something?"

"John Thomas."

"What, you didn't wanna go by little Johnny?"

I groaned. "You're not far off. This one kid spent the entire summer calling me Johnny Tommy, and I knew my parents hadn't thought the name thing through."

"I'd laugh, but I think it's a parent's job to give their kids pretentious names." He pointed at himself. "Case in point, Weston."

"Oh, you're right. That's totally pretentious."

"Wanna hear something worse? My best friend's name is James Easton, but everyone calls him East."

It took me a second, and then I burst out laughing. "East and West?"

"Yup."

"Okay, that's terrible."

"Hey now, Johnny," West said, feigning offense.

"Is there a North and South to round things out?"

"I was hoping you'd fill one of those holes, but no such luck."

A snort escaped me. "Yeah, that's too bad. Maybe someone in this room can complete the compass for you."

"Nah, my direction's just fine." He poured a few more M&M's into my hand. "So you staying on campus, or are your parents keeping you under lock and key?"

"Jesus, that was a fight," I admitted. "Yeah, I'm in the dorms."

"Oh yeah? Which one?"

"Uh..." I didn't exactly want to share that I had my own large, private space in the best dorm, but he didn't have to know that part. "Baker Hall. You?"

"Me? In a dorm? God, no." He ran a hand through his hair, mussing up the waves. "I have a place at the Towers."

"The Towers? What's that?"

"At the Waldorf Astoria."

My eyes practically bugged out of my head. "You're kidding. You...live there?"

He shrugged. "Yeah. You should stop by sometime."

This was a joke, right? No one actually *lived* at one of the most famous luxury hotels in the city. Here I was, not wanting to make a big deal out of living alone in a dorm, and West was living on Park Avenue.

The people here were on an entirely different level.

And "stop by sometime"? I didn't even own clothes that would get me past the front door.

"Yeah. Maybe," I said just to appease him.

"That doesn't sound like you mean it."

Hah, busted. "Well, it's not really my scene."

"The *Waldorf* isn't your scene? Have you ever been inside?"

"Sure, all the time. Just a typical Monday night eating three-hundred-dollar ounces of caviar."

"That's your problem right there. Thursdays are the best night for that." West's grin was infectious, and I found myself matching it.

"Guess you've convinced me again."

"See, what'd I tell you? *Very* convincing."

I couldn't help but shake my head, thinking of my mom's words. Maybe she was right. West and his friends probably *were* trouble. His easygoing personality could win anyone over.

"Weston LaRue."

A harsh voice from the front of the room cut the chatter instantly, and I snapped my attention to the man narrowing his eyes in my direction.

Or, should I say, West's.

No doubt that terrifying man had to be Professor

Kingston, but if West was bothered by his tone, he didn't show it.

Instead he gave the professor a lazy grin and said, "Yes, sir?"

"Care to explain why you're sitting in my class when I passed you years ago?"

"I just missed you so much."

Professor Kingston pointed at the door. "Get. Out."

Oh shit. I hadn't even questioned why West was sitting beside me, but he was obviously an upperclassman and didn't belong here. So why—

"Guess that's my cue," West said, scooting his chair back and handing me the packet of M&M's.

"I don't—" I started, but West shot me a wink.

"Keep it. See you around, JT."

West gave a salute to Professor Kingston before making his way up the stairs, taking them two at a time.

Okay, strike that. Maybe there were two people immune to West's charms: my mom and the man they called King.

FIVE

RAIN POURED DOWN as the Sprinter van pulled off Fiftieth Street and into the porte-cochère of the Towers of the Waldorf Astoria later that evening. The rest of the guys had already gotten a ride back earlier, but I'd met up with my grandmother for dinner.

Without waiting for Scotty to get out of the van, I pulled open the door and jumped out. "Thanks, Scotty. Have a good one."

An exasperated sigh left his lips. "Mr. LaRue, I'm supposed to get that for you."

"If anyone asks, we'll pretend you did." I shut the door and grinned at the valet standing by the entrance. "You didn't see that."

"See what, sir?"

"Good man." He met my fist bump, and I strolled past him, the glossy black and white striped walls of the entrance immediately feeling like home, as strange as some found it. I thought back to JT's face when I told him where I lived and the utter shock he expressed that anyone would live in a place like this. Maybe it was a little extravagant, but I'd never known anything else.

How was that for sounding like an out-of-touch asshole?

As I crossed the shiny black and gold floors that led to the lobby, Sofia's bright smile greeted me from behind the reception desk.

"Good evening, Mr. LaRue. How was your first day back?"

JT's curls falling over his forehead flitted through my mind, and I grinned. "Entirely unexpected. You?"

"It's been a quiet day, but I can't complain."

"Quiet? Did the terrors known as my friends not come through?"

She shook her head. "It wasn't raining earlier."

Meaning they'd entered through the Park Avenue entrance and given poor Sofia a break.

"Lucky you. And by the way..." I held up a bottle of Cristal Rosé tied in a bright pink ribbon. "Happy birthday week."

Sofia's eyes widened. "No way. For me?"

"Of course for you. You put up with us."

"I can't accept that."

"And I won't drink it." I shrugged. "Guess you'll have to keep it."

"This is too much," she said, carefully taking the

bottle like it was a precious jewel. "Thank you so much. And for remembering. You know you're my favorite."

I shot her a wink as another resident made his way up to the desk to vie for her attention. "That's what I was hoping you'd say. Enjoy it."

"I will." She hugged the bottle to her chest before putting it away and greeting the other resident with slightly less enthusiasm.

I gave a cursory glance at the towering columns of the marble lobby, which was currently empty, and headed for the elevators. One of my favorite things about the place was the style, a mix of modern with a nod to French Art Deco that screamed opulence, but with a vintage feel. Was it unusual for a handful of college-aged guys to commandeer a place in a building like this? A thousand percent. But with my parents' ties to the adjacent hotel and the insistence of several extremely vocal parents in the Elysium, the social club they all belonged to that practically ran the city, it was all but assured their sons would live in the finest building Manhattan had to offer.

The only downside, if you could call it that, was that we shared a roommate, but with each residence as large as they were, that was hardly an issue. Not to mention East would've been up in my space whether or not we lived together, so it actually worked out well.

Stepping into the entry foyer of the residence I shared with East, I tossed my wallet on the narrow table that lined one side of the hall and my jacket over the bench seat that sat opposite it.

The curtains of the living room had been left open, showcasing the sparkling lights of the city, and I wandered inside, seeking out my friend. East wasn't anywhere to be found in the dimly lit seating area, but the sound of the ice machine on our fridge alerted me to where he was.

I headed through the dining room and spotted East standing in the kitchen vigorously mixing his cocktail in a shaker.

"Bourbon or martini, dear?"

I snorted as I made my way over and pointed to the bottle of bourbon. "I'll take one of those, thanks."

East poured himself his usual martini and then handed me a glass tumbler. "You're later than I expected."

"I'm sorry, *dear*. I got held up. What are you, my fucking wife now?"

East walked to the living room and took a seat in the velvety accent chair, where he rested his arms along the wooden frame and crossed one leg over the other.

"In your dreams. But somehow, I don't think you'd be able to keep up with me."

I took a sip of the bourbon and sat down on the sofa opposite him. "More like I don't want to *have* to keep up with you. You're too high maintenance."

"Says the man who just came home to his private residence at the Waldorf." East arched an eyebrow. "One of these days, West, you're going to realize you're just as high maintenance as the rest of us. Even with that charming smile and polite way you have about you."

"Is that right?"

"It is. Are you or are you not the man who laid down a bet that would win him an extravagant, all-inclusive vacation to anywhere he desired?"

I mused over that for a second then grinned. "Yep, that was me, and guess what?"

"What?"

"I'm gonna fucking win."

East chuckled and shook his head. "Cocky."

"Confident. Also, charming. You just said so yourself."

East's lips twitched as he took another sip of his martini. "So is that where you were tonight? Out being charming?"

"Nope. I was out with my grandmother, if you must know."

"Ah, so you were out being *bored*. Got it."

"Not at all. I showed her how to Facetime with the parentals, since they've been in Amsterdam the past couple of months, so that was nice."

"Nice? These are the same people who made you stay in New York this summer."

"I know, but..." I shrugged. "Maybe I—"

"If you say deserved it, I am revoking your right to be my best friend."

I laughed at that, because that was the last thing I'd been going to say. "Relax over there, Your Highness. I was just going to say that maybe I was a little *sloppy* in my execution of our...escapade, which is why I got caught. It was my own damn fault."

East mulled over that and nodded. "Can't fault that logic. You were particularly slow climbing out that window."

"Hey, fuck you, I was making sure Gavin got out."

"Still, last one out takes the fall."

"Mhmm, I'm well aware." I downed the rest of my drink and placed the empty tumbler on a coaster. "Speaking of deans we played a prank on, I got an introduction with her son today."

East's lips curved into a sly smirk. "Did you now?"

"I did." I leaned back on the sofa, kicked my legs out, and crossed my ankles. "JT, or John Thomas if I'm feeling—"

"Cocky?"

"Confident."

East snorted. "Same damn thing, and you know it. So... What's he like?"

"Gorgeous, sweet, innocent." I turned toward East and rested an arm along the back of the sofa. "And straighter than the pressed pants hanging in your closet."

"Well, well, well, doesn't that make this all the more delicious."

"Don't you mean difficult?"

"That too, but if I know you, that's not going to stop you."

"I respect the word *no*."

"That's assuming you know how it sounds." East brought his glass to his lips. "Has anyone ever *said* no to you?"

I snickered. "Only one."

"That's what I thought. Shit, maybe I should up the bet, seeing as I've got this in the bag."

"Your faith in me is astounding, really."

"Sounds like an uphill battle you won't win, and I have to say, I'm really looking forward to watching you fail."

"This from someone who's supposed to be my best friend?"

"That's the reason I can give you so much shit." East pointed to my empty glass. "Another?"

"Trying to get me drunk to take advantage of my body?"

East got to his feet and bit down on his lip as his eyes roved over me, but then he shook his head. "As tempting as that offer should be, it didn't work out so well for us before, did it?"

"Hey, I wasn't offering, jackass."

"You did back then. Hmm, I kind of like being the only person to say no to you. Makes me feel...powerful."

I rolled my eyes. "It was ten too many shots of bourbon and a raging hard-on. It had nothing to do with you."

"Keep telling yourself that, *dear*."

"You're never gonna let me live that down, are you?"

"No," he called out over his shoulder as he poured another glass.

"That's the last damn 'no' I'll be hearing. The next

words out of your mouth will be 'West, where in the world would you like my private jet to fly you?'"

East leaned back against the marble countertop, mischief sparking his eyes, as always. "So what's this master plan of yours to win this guy over?"

"Like I'd give away my secrets."

"Oh, right, let me guess." He sipped his drink as he crossed back into the living room. "You plan to hide your devious side and rely on the good-guy, lovable aspect of your personality. Befriend JT, make him feel safe, and then act surprised when the sexual tension is too much."

It was a shame the asshole knew me so well. "Maybe you should just watch and find out."

"I will. But can you make it quick? I don't have the best attention span."

"Do you say that to all the guys you bring home?"

A snorting laugh escaped him as he fell back into the velvet chair. "There's a reason they never stay the night."

"Speaking of, you heading out later?"

"Thinkin' about it. Wanna come with?"

Normally I'd jump at the chance to go out at any opportunity, but it'd been a long day. Besides, I needed to figure out when to make my next move with JT. "I'll pass."

East's brows shot up. "Seriously? You lame-ass."

"It wouldn't kill you to have a down night every once in a while."

"And let down my audience of adoring fans? I could never."

Yawning, I stretched my arms up overhead, and then cracked my neck from side to side.

"All right, I'm out. I've got a class schedule to memorize, and I don't mean my own."

East eyed me with a shit-eating grin as I headed to my room. "Good luck with that."

"I don't need luck."

Behind me, I heard him scoff. "Consider this bet mine, playboy."

SIX

THE BEST THING about Astor so far? The high-end coffee bar conveniently located between classes.

As I stood in line, I read over the specials menu, which featured drinks I'd never even heard of. Blueberry matcha latte? Espresso and tonic? Eh, I wasn't quite that adventurous, though something called a cereal milk cappuccino piqued my interest. Whatever had caffeine and tasted decent was good enough for me.

I checked the time on my phone and moved with the line, getting closer to the counter but not by much. Still, I could afford to wait a few more minutes.

"So let me guess. White mocha frappuccino?"

I looked up to see West's lazy grin as he sidled in beside me. I glanced behind him to the glares his cutting in line had earned, but he only crossed his arms over his chest and studied the menu board.

"There's a line for a reason," I said pointedly, pocketing my cell.

"A line?" West's nose wrinkled. "Not sure I'm familiar with the term."

I shook my head. Of course this was new for him. He probably had his coffee delivered in class. "Are you stalking me?"

"What? Two people who go to the same school can't happen to run into each other from time to time?"

"I'm sure they could, but this feels intentional."

"Or it's a double-shot kind of day and I saw you standing alone." West cocked a brow. "Want me to leave?"

I looked around us at all my classmates paired up and in groups and felt that dull pang of loneliness that came with being the new guy. People weren't exactly lining up to be my best friend, but West didn't seem to have the "dean's son" aversion.

"How about this," I said, as the line moved forward. "Tell me what your deal is and you can stay."

"Gonna buy my coffee too?"

"You're the one who lives in the Waldorf Towers. You can buy mine."

West smirked but nodded. "I like you."

"You don't know me."

"I know enough."

"In the whole two conversations we've had?"

"There are other ways to get to know someone."

I cocked my head, eyeing him closely. Something

about that statement sent up warning flags I probably should heed, but... "What do you mean, 'other ways'?"

West chuckled, the sound cool, his smile easy. "Relax, JT. It's not like I'm a stalker or anything."

"You sound like a stalker."

"And you sound paranoid. I just meant that I've seen you a couple times around the halls and you're always alone. You seem like a nice guy, so it can't be that you're an ass—"

"Thanks for the vote of confidence."

"All I'm saying is, you look like you could use a friend."

"And that friend should be you?"

West shrugged and slipped a hand into his pocket. "Could be. I don't see anyone else lining up. And you know why? Not because of you, it's because your mom is—"

"The dean. Yeah, I worked that much out myself."

"Right. But if you're friends with me"—West leaned in a little closer, and Jesus, the guy smelled even better than the coffee—"everyone will like you."

I turned my head to make sure he saw how hard I was rolling my eyes but instead found myself staring into his. They were a cool azure blue, like the clearest lake, and seemed to sparkle at me like the sun was reflecting off the water. It was probably one of the many reasons he got away with everything and anything.

He was too charismatic for his own good.

"JT?"

"Huh?"

"I was saying, if you're friends with me, everyone will like you."

"Because you're that likeable?"

"Let's put it this way, people talk to me for two reasons: they want to be me or want to be friends"—he winked—"or more with me."

I snorted and shook my head. "Wow, you're super confident."

"That comes with having enough money to do whatever the hell I want."

"And is that what you do? Whatever the hell you want?"

"And *who*, if I'm lucky."

I didn't have one damn thing to say to that, because honestly, the guy was good looking enough that he probably *could* get whoever he wanted. I turned back to see we were next in line.

"Oh, come on, JT." West bumped shoulders with me. "Don't you want your college experience to be more than moping from class to class by yourself?"

"I'm not moping."

"But you will be soon. Imagine how much fun you'd have hanging out with—"

"Someone like you?" I raised an amused brow. "Hate to break it to you, but you're literally the one person—or group of people—my mom *doesn't* want me to be friends with."

West's lips twitched, but he didn't seem offended. In

fact, the look on his face said he'd figured as much. "Which would make it all the more fun."

West's eyes definitely sparkled this time, and something about his devil-may-care attitude called to me.

I'd always been a good kid, the one who aced his tests, did his homework, and never broke the rules. I'd had to be with my mom being who she was. But if I were honest, there *was* something fun and appealing about being a little reckless and going against my mom's orders. She would want me to make friends, right? And if I could do that with West and still pass my classes then surely she wouldn't care who it was with.

"I see you thinking about it..."

"I'm not thinking about anything right now except how much I need a hit of caffeine." As the person ahead of us stepped aside, I gestured to the barista. "So, how about you buy me that coffee you promised, *friend*?"

"Oh, I see how it is, using me for my money already."

My eyes widened, and just as I was about to adamantly refute that, he started to laugh.

"Relax, JT. I'm kidding. You want anything to eat? I'm starving."

Hey, if he was buying...

I pointed at the top tier of the bakery case. "I'll take a chocolate muffin and a medium cereal milk cappuccino."

The barista nodded and looked at West.

"Double shot and a guava cheese pastry, thanks."

"Oh, that sounds good too," I said as we stood in front

of the cashier. She took one look at West and waved him off.

"It's on the house," she said, smiling broadly.

"Aren't you sweet." He shot her a wink and slipped a bill into the tip jar, and as we headed to the pickup counter, my mouth fell open.

"You've got to be kidding me."

"What?"

"You really do get whatever you want, don't you?"

West looked like he was trying to hide a smile. "Believe me now?"

"I believe something is incredibly screwed up in the world when the people who can afford to pay don't have to." I shook my head. "But yeah. No one is immune to your charm, I guess."

"Except you."

"I'm still pretty impressed. Is that going to your head now?"

West's bright white teeth bit down on his lower lip as he nodded slowly. "Oh yeah."

He aimed a wolfish look my way, and I felt something in my chest catch. But just as quickly as it had appeared, it was gone and an easy smile curved his lips.

"Do you have lunch plans?" he asked, taking his short cup from the barista. He added a splash of cream and, after a quick mix, downed the entire thing like he was at a bar.

"Uh... I haven't thought about it. I'll probably just grab something quick."

"Something quick doesn't usually mean anything good. If you've got an hour, I can promise you an amazing lunch."

"And why would you do that?" Better yet, why would I? But something about West made me want to know why he'd taken a sudden interest in me.

"Because we're friends. And friends don't let friends eat a stale sandwich between classes."

The offer was tempting. I had no doubt West would know exactly where a killer spot was, but again the warning to stay away flitted through my mind, and I hesitated. Was he actually a decent guy, just a bit spoiled, and that was what my mom had an issue with?

He seemed to know exactly what I was thinking, because he said, "One lunch, you can get to know me, and if you decide you think I'm hideous and don't want anything to do with me, then fine. It'll be your choice, not anyone else's."

I turned his words over in my mind, but I already knew I'd say yes. It wasn't like anyone was beating down my door to hang out, and I *was* curious about him. Him, his lifestyle, his friends.

Couldn't hurt, right?

"I'm free around one," I said, picking up my coffee and pastry.

"One works for me." He grabbed his pastry bag and grinned. "I'll see you then."

I nodded as he walked away, but then it occurred to

me I didn't know where we were going. "Wait, where should I meet you?"

West turned around, walking backward down the hall. "Don't worry. I'll find you."

I frowned, wondering how the hell he'd manage to do that, but before I could say anything else, he was gone.

Well...that was interesting.

The heat of the coffee cup bit into my hand, and I grabbed a collar from the bar, slipping it on before taking a sip. It tasted just like how it'd been advertised—like the milk after sitting in a bowl of fruity cereal.

Not bad.

Beside me, someone reached past to grab the creamer, and as he poured a bit into his cup, he said, "Making deals with the devil. I wouldn't have guessed you for the type."

For a minute I thought he was talking to someone else, but when I looked up, he locked eyes with me.

I blinked. "Excuse me?"

"You're the dean's kid, right?" He stirred his drink, took a sip, then added a bit more cream. "I would've thought you'd know better than to hang out with that guy."

I took in the guy's dark, slouchy beanie, ripped black jeans, and open flannel rolled up at the elbows. He definitely didn't reek of money the way many of the others here did, but he was still bold enough to dole out advice to a stranger.

"You're not the first person to say that. Why?"

He snapped the lid on his coffee and shrugged. "Why

warn you off from making a bad decision? Call me crazy, but I'd rather not see the Park Avenue Princes add to their ranks."

The Park Avenue Princes? Was that an actual thing, title, whatever? Either way, what was going on here? First my mom, now some guy at the coffee bar was warning me off...?

I turned to face him. "How much did my mom pay you to warn me off?"

He smiled. "I didn't know that offer was on the table. You're getting this advice for free."

"And who are you?"

"Caleb." He switched his coffee to his other hand and shook mine.

"JT."

"Yeah, I know. Dean's kid."

Seemed like that label was going to haunt me all the way through college. Hell, might as well get it tattooed on my damn forehead at this stage.

"Well, uh, thanks for the..."

"Unsolicited advice?"

I chuckled. "Yeah."

"But you're not going to take it."

I shrugged my bag up my arm and took another sip of my coffee. "I'm going to think about it."

"S'pose that's all I can ask for."

"Why *are* you asking?"

"Like I said, I don't want to see them add anyone else to their ranks." He reached for the headphones slung around his neck and put them on over his beanie. "See you 'round, JT."

As Caleb disappeared down the hall, I looked around, definitely feeling that paranoia West had mentioned earlier, like I was being watched, and couldn't help but wonder if my mom really had sent Caleb to double down on her warning.

But that was just ridiculous.

She trusted me. Why wouldn't she? I'd never given her a reason not to, and everyone had to eat lunch, right? Right. So I didn't see the harm in making a new friend, and like West said, this way it'd be my choice.

Not my mom's and definitely not some stranger's.

SEVEN

west

HARRY THE HACKER had been worth the money, if only to see the look on JT's face when he walked out of his class to see me leaning against a doorjamb across the hall.

Those brown eyes widened and his whole body went still before he shook his head and made his way over.

"Yep. Total stalker," he said.

"I told you I'd find you."

"And how did you manage that?"

Instead of answering, I pushed off the door and inclined my head for him to follow. We weren't going far, but I wasn't about to chance going through the front and having the dean shut down this little rendezvous before I had a chance to win him over.

The second we were out the doors, the commotion of the city greeted us, the drilling of a construction site and car horns familiar and comforting. I hooked a right toward our destination, and JT jogged a little to catch up.

"Where are we going?" he asked.

"Not far."

"I only have an hour—"

"Skipping a class won't kill you. You're in college to live a little, right?"

When he balked, I let out a low laugh.

"Don't worry, golden boy—I'll deliver you to your next class on time."

As Atlas at Park Avenue came into view, I nodded at the doorman, who promptly let us inside. We were quickly led to a table looking out onto the street.

JT followed my lead, napkin in his lap and washing up with the hot towel we'd been given. He swallowed as he looked around, and I settled back in my chair, following his gaze. Polished wood that gleamed in the light, low-lit chandeliers, and high-backed chairs fit for a king.

"They know you by name here, don't they?" he said.

"You should be glad they do, or we'd never make it back on time."

JT's incredulous expression had me biting back a smile, especially when he glanced down at the menu and choked on his water.

"You all right?"

"Uh...this is nice and all... I mean, better than nice, it's fancy as hell, but I'd be fine with a food truck."

"You've got to be kidding."

"I just..." A flush crept into his cheeks as he looked

back at the menu and lowered his voice. "I can't afford even an appetizer here."

"Doesn't matter. I can."

"I'm not letting you pay for my food, West."

"*Letting* me," I mused, running my finger over my lower lip. "That's cute."

One of JT's unruly brown curls fell over his forehead, and he batted it away, which I didn't mind at all, since it showcased more of his face. And it *was* a gorgeous face. I couldn't deny that. This bet wasn't exactly a hardship on my part, not with this view. Beneath his dark brows were warm brown eyes that reflected an innocence I wasn't sure I'd ever had, and don't even get me started on the pouty lips framed by a smattering of facial hair that I knew would feel fucking amazing on my skin.

"So that's your deal, then?"

I'd been so caught up in checking out my lunch "date" that I'd completely lost track of the conversation. "What's that?"

"That you just do what you want, whenever you want?"

I swept my eyes down over him. "Don't forget who."

JT's eyes narrowed a fraction, and I wondered if he was a) trying to work out my angle or b) whether or not I was flirting with him. But as he lowered his gaze to the menu, the slight flush on his cheeks told me it was definitely the latter.

He cleared his throat, and seeing his skittish reaction had me pulling back a little. It wasn't that he seemed turned off or upset by my once-over, more like...confused. So I decided to ease up a bit, throw him a lifeline, so he wouldn't bolt like some startled animal now that I finally had him where I wanted him.

I leaned across the table as though I was about to impart a secret. "The bone-marrow-crusted beef tenderloin is delicious, if you're into that kind of thing."

JT snorted. "For lunch? Who are you?"

"You already know that."

He held my stare, his bravado back in full force. "One of the Park Avenue Princes?"

Oh, hello, looks like someone has been asking around about me too.

"And you think *I'm* a stalker."

The flush instantly returned.

"I wasn't stalking you. That implies following. You're the one who was outside my classroom—"

"And you're the one who suddenly knows what everyone calls us." I leaned back in my chair and arched a brow. "Been asking around about me?"

"No."

"You sure about that?"

"Yes. Who would I ask? *Why* would I ask?"

I shrugged, running one of my fingers down the condensation on my glass of water. "I would if some good-looking guy was buying me coffee and lunch."

JT's mouth fell open, then he shook his head. "I don't know which part of that sentence to start with first—the fact that you just called yourself good looking or that you're talking like this is a...a..."

"Date?"

"This is not a date." JT shifted in his seat. "It's lunch with a friend. That's what you said."

I chuckled, not put out in the slightest. "I know. I was just making sure *you* remembered that. Since you were asking around about me and all."

"I was *not* asking around about you." When he caught my shit-eating grin, he blew out a breath. "You're an asshole."

"And you're too uptight. Relax, JT. You're having lunch in one of the best places in New York, and I'm paying—as a friend—so enjoy yourself. You do know how to do that, right?"

"I'm sure I can manage."

"That's a no."

"It's not a no, it's just, well, it's hard to step out of line."

"I get that, but what the dean doesn't know won't hurt her or *you*. It's just lunch."

"With a prince, apparently."

The term Park Avenue Princes had been bestowed upon our group practically from birth. That was the way things went in the upper crust of New York. The fact our families all had boys just made the label all the more fitting. So did the fact we were richer than Midas and could get practically anything we wanted.

Which had my eyes wandering back to my new "friend."

"I mean, I don't have my crown on me right now. But if you're nice to me, I might show you later."

"You're ridiculous."

"A ridiculous asshole." I placed my hand over my heart. "That kind of hurts."

"I'm sure you've been called worse."

"I know I have been."

JT let out a loud laugh and looked down at the menu. "God, what I wouldn't give to have your confidence for a day."

"Hey, that's what I'm offering you. The chance to have a fun, exciting college experience, not some boring, run-of-the-mill shit. Confidence comes with fun, exciting stuff."

"Like being a ridiculous asshole?"

"Exactly."

"Okay, then, I'll have the bone-marrow-crusted beef tenderloin and whatever the most expensive, outrageous dessert on that menu is."

I sat up in my chair and gestured for the waiter. "Now that's the spirit."

After we placed our orders, I took a long sip of my sparkling water and licked my lips.

"So, JT. Let's say you got stuck in an elevator with someone for hours—"

"What?"

"Who would be the person you'd choose to be stuck

with?"

A line formed between JT's brows. "I wouldn't want to be stuck in an elevator, period."

"Okay, then a deserted island." The line deepened, and I waved a hand. "An escape room. Whatever."

"You want to know who I like enough to be locked up with, got it. Hmm... A couple of months ago I would've said my ex, but I guess maybe Corey. He's been my best friend since middle school."

"He didn't want to attend Astor?"

"No, he went into the military, same as his dad."

"And this ex—"

"Elise."

Yep, straight as an arrow, this one. "What happened with her? Lemme guess—you broke her heart."

"Why would you think that?"

"You've got a heartbreaker look about you," I said, winking.

"Definitely not." He rubbed at his jaw. "It wasn't anything bad. We just dated in high school, then she went to California for college and I'm here. Neither of us wanted to do the long-distance thing, so..." He shrugged. "What about you?"

"Who would I want to be stuck in an elevator with?"

"Well, that, yeah, and I'm sure you've got a girlfriend or two—"

Booming laughter escaped my throat at his insinuation, and I shook my head.

"What's so funny?"

"The idea of me with a female. Not my thing, golden boy."

"Oh. So then...a boyfriend?"

I chuckled again. "That's almost as funny."

"Why?"

"The idea of a long-term anything doesn't really appeal to me."

"Because...?"

"Why settle for one person when you could settle for one a night?"

JT's brows shot up past the curls that had fallen back onto his forehead. "That's appealing to you? A parade of strangers in your bed?"

"Who said anything about my bed?"

"Okay, *their* bed—"

"Is a mattress absolutely necessary for you?" I said, amusement curling my lips.

"Oh my God, you're killing me."

"If you haven't tried bent over a kitchen counter, you really should."

The scandalized look on JT's face had me laughing again. This was more fun than I'd anticipated.

"Okay, so you aren't a relationship guy. Who would be in that elevator with you, then? Some faceless stranger, or is there anyone you actually care about?"

I ran my eyes over him, down the thin silver chain he wore over a plain t-shirt, and knew exactly who I wouldn't mind being confined with. But I held that thought back for now. It wasn't something I was familiar with, holding back, but putting too much pressure on JT wouldn't get me anywhere. I had to play this one right.

"East is my ride or die, so I guess I'm required to throw his name out. We don't do well in confined spaces, though. He'd probably run his mouth, and I'd either have to strangle him with his ascot or stuff it down his throat, so there you go."

JT chuckled as our food was placed in front of us. "And that's your best friend?"

"And roommate, yeah."

"I thought you didn't do well in confined spaces?"

"A few thousand square feet—and the ability to leave whenever—goes a long way to help with that."

JT let out a moan around his fork as the beef hit his taste buds. *Fucking food truck, my ass.*

"Trust me now?" I said, cutting into my own.

"Oh yeah. Holy shit that's good."

"Better than a hot dog off the street?"

"Hey, don't knock the hot dogs, but...hell yes."

As he speared another forkful, I could feel the wall he'd thrown up around me dipping slightly.

"Out of curiosity, who told you about us?"

JT swallowed and dabbed his napkin at his lips. "Sorry?"

"You didn't hear the nickname out of thin air."

"Oh. Just some guy I met at the coffee bar after you left. Caleb, I think he said."

"Caleb Reeves?"

"I'm not sure."

"Slouchy beanie, always has a rip in his jeans and a camera?"

"Yeah, actually. I didn't notice a camera, though."

Oh, Caleb, that interfering motherfucker. "What else did he say?"

JT seemed to debate whether to tell me, and that was when I knew it was nothing good. Figured.

"He didn't seem to think it was a good idea for me to hang out with you."

"Yeah, I imagine he'd say that. I'm glad you didn't take his advice."

"Is there something I should know about between you? Is he one of your one-night stands that you blew off?"

"Fuck no, I've never touched Caleb Reeves. Trust me on that." I took a long swallow of water, hoping it would cleanse that notion right outta my head. "It's not me he has an issue with. I'm guilty by association, so don't take that advice too personally."

JT gestured to his almost-empty plate. "Doesn't look like I did, does it?"

"See? I'm not that bad."

"Yeah, I guess, or maybe it was just the promise of something better than a stale sandwich."

"Ouch. You've got quite a tongue on you there." One I wouldn't mind playing with mine.

"Someone's got to keep you grounded."

"Oh, I see, and that's going to be you?"

JT popped the last bit of beef into his mouth and shrugged. "What are friends for?"

Indeed. I mean, if I looked at my friends I'd say getting into and out of trouble, partying, and generally getting up to no good. But if JT wanted to volunteer to try to keep me "grounded," I wouldn't shut him down.

"True. I could use a friend like you."

"Wait, I thought this friendship was to help *me* out."

"Why can't it be mutual?"

JT placed his utensils on the plate and took a sip of his water. "I don't know. I've got nothing really to contribute, do I? It's not like I can repay you tomorrow with a fancy lunch."

"We're going to lunch tomorrow?"

JT's mouth parted, and a frown creased his brow. "You know what I mean. I don't have anything to offer. I have no friends, no palatial condo—"

"I thought you were offering to be my voice of reason?" I smirked. "I don't have one of those. So, see, you *do* have something to offer."

"That makes me sound boring as hell."

"Which is why you need me. I'm not boring, and you're not reckless. Maybe we can meet somewhere in the middle."

"At a restaurant I can't even buy an appetizer at? That's some middle ground."

I laughed and tossed my napkin on the table beside my plate. "Okay, then how about this. The guys and I have tickets to see Arrhythmia tomorrow. Why don't you come with? That's pretty normal, right? You have been to a concert before, haven't you?"

"Yeah, I can remember a few."

"Again, this is why you need me. If you can remember the night then you weren't having a good time."

I could see the wheels turning.

"Arrhythmia?"

"Mhmm. You like them?"

"Doesn't everyone?"

"Well, all the cool kids at least."

"God," JT groaned. "You did not just say that." But then he started to laugh.

"Look, I have a spare ticket and it'll be fun. It starts at eleven. You can get away from school, meet even more friends, and, you know, *enjoy* yourself."

I could see he was tempted—it was right there in his eyes as his smile finally caught up to them.

"I don't know, it's a school night, and—"

"Are you kidding right now?"

"No. My mom—"

"Is the dean, blah blah, I know."

"Right, but also, there's security and curfew at the dorms on weekdays."

Such a sweet, naïve boy. It was going to be so much fun corrupting him.

"You think we can't get past a little security?" I winked at him. "I told you, I'm going to teach you how to have fun. The question is, are you going to let me?"

EIGHT

jt

I HAD TO hand it to West. He'd promised an amazing lunch and somehow gone above and beyond my expectations. Though it wasn't just the food that had made the hour enjoyable—West kept things entertaining, that was for sure. He wasn't anything like my usual crowd, and though we didn't seem to have much in common, there was something about the guy that made me want to hang out again.

I eyed the last bite of dessert, a La Madeline au Truffe chocolate that had been presented in a golden tray with sugar pearls on the bottom. It was the biggest truffle I'd ever seen, and from what our server had said, also the most expensive in the world.

Did I want to know how much that meant? No. No, I did not.

But I'd joked to West that I wanted something expensive and outrageous, though to me that meant something more in the twenty-dollar range. The truffle was not...that.

West pushed the tray toward me. "Better not let it go to waste."

My stomach was already full to bursting, but he was right. I'd feel like a shit human leaving so much money on the table.

I scooped up the last bite, and the moment the chocolate touched my tongue, it was utter heaven. Closing my eyes, I savored the taste I'd probably never enjoy again.

"You know," West said, "I've never actually seen anyone climax from dessert before. This is a first."

My first instinct was to deny, but he was right—I'd been moaning with every damn bite to the point of embarrassment.

Grinning, I sat back and rubbed my stomach, content as a housecat. "Can you blame me? That was unreal."

West returned my smile as he slipped his card to the server. "Aren't you glad you took me up on my offer?"

"Hell yes." The words were out of my mouth before I could stop them. How was I ever gonna go back to subs for lunch? I was ruined. Forever.

"See? I can't be that bad, right?"

"True. You didn't poison the food or dump it in my lap. Could've been worse."

West shook his head, but his eyes flickered with mischief. "Yes, it could've. I'd never pull a prank so pedestrian."

"Of course not." I laughed.

After signing the bill—which I didn't dare take a peek at, since I didn't want to throw up such a delicious meal —West checked the time on his phone and rose to his feet. "We'd better go unless you've reconsidered your stance on cutting class."

"Nope." I jumped up and said a quick thanks to the server before following him outside. As much as I didn't want to cut my break short, I also wasn't about to skip out on anything, especially my first week.

The sun beating down on us, combined with the hot pavement, had sweat beading my brow as we made our way back to Astor. I was ready for the heat wave to be over. Tanning by the beach? Sure. Burning in the city? Not my favorite.

"Thank you, by the way," I said, as the back of Astor came into view. "Lunch was unbelievable and way too much, but it was amazing."

West gave me a sidelong glance, his eyes covered by a black pair of Aviators. His tawny hair looked even lighter under the harsh sun, almost dark blond, and when he grinned at me, the white of his perfectly straight teeth was almost blinding.

"We'll do it again."

I knew myself well enough to know I wouldn't let him spend that much on a meal anytime soon, but the fact that he wanted to hang out again... I didn't mind that. It was nice to have someone to talk to, especially a guy as completely opposite to myself as West. I didn't understand all the warnings about him. He seemed likeable enough, just a bit cocky due to his circumstances in life.

Hell, maybe I'd introduce him to a delicious street dog and bring him closer to my level.

We parted ways once we hit the halls, and true to his word, West had managed to get me back in time. I was surprised I managed to keep my eyes open through the whole hour of class—food coma and all—but somehow I rallied, and by the time it was over I made my way to the library and found a quiet corner just in case my eyes did decide to shut for a few minutes.

I settled into one of the empty desks in an alcove of books and put my bag down on the seat beside me, hoping to dissuade any company. Not that there was a line of people waiting to sit with me.

I pulled out my laptop and had powered it up, ready to get some of my reading done for the assignment Professor Kingston had given us on day one, when I felt someone stop by the edge of the desk. Determined to keep to myself, I didn't bother raising my eyes. I'd done enough socializing for one day, and if the person was lost, I didn't know where anything was in here so I'd be no help anyway.

A second later, the chair across from me was pulled out and a bag dumped down on the table. Apparently this person couldn't take a hint.

I let out a sigh, raised my eyes, and locked on to the stranger from the coffee bar—Caleb.

"Good place to make more friends," he said as he slid into the chair.

"Not trying to make friends—"

"Clearly." He looked around the empty space I'd hidden away in. With his beanie and the headphones around his neck, it was no wonder West had known who I was talking about when I mentioned his name. It seemed this getup was Caleb's go-to. "But too bad. I'm bored, and you *need* a friend, so here I am."

Geez, what was it about people here pushing their way into my life? Sure, I didn't have a lot of options going on right now, but we were less than a week in. Friends would form naturally over time, right?

"I have a friend, remember? You saw me talking to him this morning."

"West LaRue?" Caleb snorted. "He's not your friend, trust me."

I sat back and looked over my computer at Caleb. "Trust you, huh? And why would I do that? I don't know you."

"True, but you don't know LaRue either."

"And you do?"

"I do."

Uh huh... Well, West hadn't been wrong—Caleb really *didn't* like him. But what else was it he'd said? It wasn't him personally that Caleb had an issue with; he was guilty by association.

"And what's so bad about West that I shouldn't be

hanging around him? We had lunch today, and he didn't seem all that—"

"You had lunch with him?" Caleb sat forward.

"Yeah. He's my only friend, remember? And I've got to eat."

Caleb's brows slashed down. "You shouldn't be eating with him."

"Why not?" I said, a little harsher than I intended. But I was getting annoyed on West's behalf. I mean, the guy had been nothing but cool with me, and literally everyone I ran into seemed to be warning me off. What the hell was the problem here?

"Because people like West only do things that benefit them, that's why."

I scoffed. "Okay. So having lunch with me and being nice is going to benefit him how? I'm new to Astor and a pariah among my peers. I hardly think he's in this for himself."

Which was exactly what I'd told West. I had nothing to offer to the friendship. Nothing but my moral compass, apparently, and Caleb was making it obvious West was in dire need of one of those without offering up specifics.

I closed my laptop, annoyed all over again that the only two people that had bothered to talk to me in the last handful of days seemed to hate one another. But since I didn't know jack shit about this Caleb guy, I was going to give West the benefit of the doubt.

I reached for my bag, and as I went to shove my laptop

inside, Caleb sat forward again and put his hand on top of it.

"Wait. Wait. I'm sorry." He shook his head. "I'm coming off like a total asshole, and that's not me." He let out a sigh and slumped back in his seat. "Those guys just bring out the worst in me. Stay, seriously. I'll shut up about them."

"Promise?" I eyed him closely, trying to gauge his sincerity when he flashed a crooked smile.

"I'll *try*?"

That was better than nothing, and he was going out of his way to be nice to me. It couldn't hurt to try to make another friend. Even if he did loathe the only other person I knew around here.

"Okay. So no talk about West and his friends—"

Caleb grunted, and I narrowed my eyes.

"Good. So…" I zeroed in on his ever-present head-phones. "You here studying music?"

"Music?"

I gestured toward his neck, and Caleb reached up to touch them.

"Oh, no. They just block out the outside world when I'm trying to be in the zone or, you know, avoid people." He grinned. "You should get yourself a pair."

"Would it have stopped you from sitting down?"

"No. I know better. These are an avoidance technique. Very handy."

I could see that. It wasn't such a bad idea. "You said they help you get in the zone? The zone for what?"

"My photography, writing."

That's right—West asked if Caleb had been carrying around a camera. But I still didn't see one—not on him, anyway. So I focused on the answer that really piqued my interest. Something we actually had in common.

"You write?"

Caleb shrugged. "More like journal, I guess. I love to document things, people. I love to watch."

I nodded, a smile of understanding curving my lips. "I write too."

"You do?"

"Mhmm."

"What do you write?"

"Novels, short stories, but I really love poetry."

Caleb's brows shot up until they almost reached his beanie. "You write poetry?"

I nodded, and Caleb's lips started to twitch, which instantly put me on the defensive. What the hell? I'd finally felt like we were having a good conversation and now he was laughing at me?

"Is that funny?"

"No." Caleb shook his head, but started to chuckle.

"Seriously, what is your damn problem?"

"I'm sorry." He bit down into his lip. "I'm just trying to imagine what you and West have in common, 'cause he sure as shit doesn't write poetry."

I glared at him. "You said you wouldn't talk about him anymore."

"You're right, I did, so I suck for bringing it up."

"Yeah, you do, and we didn't talk about that anyway. We talked about food trucks versus extravagant restaurants, our exes, you—"

"Me?"

"Yeah, he said you hate him because of association, which is obviously true, but I'm trying not to hold it against you, because you seem halfway decent and I need another friend."

"Um, thanks?"

"Well, it's true. All you've done since we've met is warn me off some guy and been all cagey about it. At least with West we joked around and then he bought me lunch."

Caleb opened his mouth as though he was about to say something in response, but just as quickly shut it and nodded. "You're right. You do need another friend, and I need to learn to shut my mouth. Here's my number." He reached for the notebook I had on the table and scrawled his cell number across it. "I'm going to let you get back to work, but text me if you want someone to hang out with at a food truck, because I *know* LaRue didn't take you to one of those."

He grabbed his bag, and as he walked off, I felt a pang of guilt hit me. Maybe I'd been too harsh and he was just trying to be nice by looking out for me. I didn't know. But everything I'd said was true. I'd had fun at lunch today with West. He'd been easy to talk to, friendly to everyone he came into contact with, and, despite his outrageous outlook on life, he intrigued me.

I'd never met anyone like him, and I wanted to know more about him and his friends—something I was going to learn tomorrow night when they picked me up for the concert.

Oh shit, the concert...

I still couldn't believe I'd agreed to go. I wasn't usually the type to buck the system and break rules, but it was tickets to see Arrhythmia. How could I say no to that?

I pushed aside any niggling doubts on whether I still wanted to go through with it and went back to work. If I could get this reading done now then I wouldn't feel half as guilty tomorrow night when I was out enjoying myself.

About twenty minutes later, when the idea of a nap was feeling like a really good one, my phone started to vibrate on the desk. I glanced down at it to see it was an unknown number and was about to ignore it when I saw the words:

> UNKNOWN NUMBER:
>
> Hey Golden Boy. You make it to class on time?

West? No, there was no way the text was from him. We hadn't exchanged numbers. But then again, he had managed to find my classroom without a schedule...

I picked up my phone, and when the next message came through, I knew for certain it was West.

UNKNOWN NUMBER:
Or did you go back to your room and pass out after such an awesome lunch?

I chuckled at how spot-on he was, because that was exactly what I'd wanted to do.

Made it to class. Didn't pass out. But the paranoia is back. How did you get my number, stalker?

UNKNOWN NUMBER:
Isn't much I can't get if I put my mind to it.

I wasn't sure why, but something about that made me smile. Maybe it was that confidence of his? I wasn't sure. But damn if he hadn't told the truth so far. If he wanted to find me, he could. If he wanted my number, he got it. I wondered if there was anything West had ever wanted that he hadn't been able to get.

.   .   .

UNKNOWN NUMBER:

You're not going to punk out on me
tomorrow, are you?

I wanted to mess with him a little.

I'm sorry, who is this?

UNKNOWN NUMBER:

You know exactly who this is.

Mmm, nope. Not ringing any bells.

I chuckled as the three little dots appeared and then his
message came through.

UNKNOWN NUMBER:

I'm your ticket to a good time. Be ready
at 10:30. I'll be coming for you.

Something in my stomach tightened at the message as I wrote back, *I'll be ready.* But I quickly brushed it off as nerves as I added "Stalker" to my contacts.

I read over the messages one last time and then put my phone down. If I had any hope of being ready for a night out with West and his friends, I needed to get the rest of this work done so I could pass out early tonight. The last thing I wanted was to not be able to hang tomorrow past curfew—and that was *if* they managed to find a way to get me out of the dorm.

But if there was one thing I'd learned about West so far, it was that there didn't seem to be much a Park Avenue Prince couldn't do.

west

"IT SHOULDN'T TAKE a group effort to help you win your bet," Travis grumbled, as we snuck around the back of Baker Hall late the next night. "This is fuckin' cheating."

Donovan rolled his eyes at Travis. "No one's forcing you to jailbreak the kid."

"I'm not about to let West get caught again—"

"It was one time," I said with a growl. "Let it go."

Travis shrugged, shoving his hand into the pockets of his black trousers. He practically faded into the shadows with the dark sheer and velvet top he'd left unbuttoned halfway down his chest. The necklaces he wore shimmered faintly with every step he took, and when he caught me eyeing him, his kohl-lined gaze narrowed. "What?"

I clapped a hand on his shoulder and gave it a squeeze. Travis may not have outright admitted it, but his being here was his way of showing he cared—even if he bitched the whole time.

"You're a good man, McKinney. Be even better if you'd keep your watchdog on a leash."

"Excuse me?"

"Caleb's been whispering in JT's ear. I don't like it."

Irritation curled Travis's lip. "Not my fuckin' problem."

"Isn't he, though?"

"The fuck you mean by that?"

Ooh, there went the temper, so quick to rise. "I mean if you could, I don't know, shut him up, stop the interference, that'd be great."

"Again. Not my problem."

Before I could respond with something he'd only deny, deny, deny, Donovan stopped abruptly ahead of us, holding his arm out for us to halt. The lobby of Baker Hall was empty, save the lone security guard.

Beside him, East cursed. "Guess we're gonna have to do this the hard way." He glanced at me over his shoulder. "It's not George working tonight. We could've paid him off, but that's a new guy."

"Guess you'll have to work that charm, then, won't you?" I replied, then turned to Travis. "You've got the cameras once East is in?"

He nodded, holding up the handheld camera jammer. "Be in and out in five minutes so we have enough juice to get his ass back in later."

Donovan snorted. "We'll be back in three."

I shot a message to the rest of the guys waiting in the van, and then nodded at East. "Let's do it."

East straightened the lapels of his jacket and sauntered inside, and once he had the guard's attention, Travis triggered the jammer, scrambling the cameras.

Since Donovan had been the last of us to sneak into Baker Hall for a late-night visit, he led the way. Elevators were too loud and obvious, so we'd have to make our way into the stairwell once East managed to turn the guard's back to the entrance.

Whatever sweet-talking magic he had didn't take long, and we darted inside as quietly as possible, making sure the door behind us didn't click shut. East was showing the guy something on his phone, playing it loud enough that it covered the sound of our breaking into the stairwell. Once we were inside, we raced up to the second floor and down to the end of the hall.

Thank fuck he hadn't scored a room on the tenth. Donovan's ass might've been in shape for that, but I preferred sex as a workout.

He let me take the lead as we stopped in front of 2H, and I leaned casually on the wall and knocked on JT's door.

It opened a few seconds later, and the wide-eyed look JT wore told me he hadn't expected me to actually show up.

"Such faith," I said with a smirk before running my

eyes over him. At least he was still dressed, not sporting a pair of sweatpants or whatever golden boys wore to bed. "Did you really underestimate me? Again?"

JT shook his head before turning to head back inside. "I should've known," he said, grabbing his wallet and phone off the table and shoving them in his jeans pockets. His eyes slid past me, and I realized I'd forgotten my manners.

"This is Donovan. Donovan, meet JT."

"A pleasure," Donovan said, kicking his chin up. "Let's get the hell outta here. I need a drink."

JT grinned. "I'm down. Lead the way."

Instead of going back to the front stairwell, we took the one closest to JT's room. There was no way to get in from the outside, but it made for an easier exit.

Once we burst out into the alley, I looked to the left to see the Sprinter idling half a block away.

"That's us." I winked at JT, and then we all broke into a jog as the van door slid open to greet us.

East and Travis were already inside, and along with the rest of the guys, it was a full house.

As JT climbed into the seat beside me, I could feel the nervous tension radiating off him. No doubt this was an intimidating group, and we sure as shit didn't make it easy on outsiders. I had no doubt they'd all be on their worst behavior, especially once the drinks started flowing. Which, judging by the bottle they shoved Donovan's way, they'd already started without us.

The lights dimmed as we began to move, but the bar light and the dimmable LED lights—currently purple—along the ceiling of the van illuminated everyone just enough that I could start the introductions.

"All right, I guess you should meet these fuckers." I pointed to the back row of the van. "The one with the permanent scowl is Daire. He doesn't hate you; he just doesn't like anyone. Beside him, because he's the most tolerant of the group, is Gavin. And before you ask, yes, his hair really is that color." It was so white-blond it seemed unnatural, and it bugged him to no end when people questioned it.

Gavin gave JT a wave, while Daire narrowed his eyes before looking out the window.

I nodded toward Donovan. "You've already met Donovan, but we call him Van. He makes us go to all his runway shows and shit."

"Makes you?" Donovan flipped me off and went back to pouring himself a glass of Jack on the rocks.

"The shows aren't that bad," I said, lowering my voice so I wouldn't give myself away to Donovan. "You might even like 'em." I cleared my throat and pointed at the dark-headed guy holding tight to a girl in his lap with long blonde hair. "Preston and his girlfriend Serena. Don't be surprised if you see them running for office one day. His dad's a senator."

They lifted their champagne flutes toward JT, who nodded back.

I kicked at Travis's boot and grinned when he raised a brow. "This sexy fucker is Travis. Gives a great lap dance."

He rolled his eyes and kicked my foot away. "There's a reason I don't do Goldschläger. Stop begging for a turn."

Laughing, I turned to see a grin on JT's face, the anxiety starting to melt away.

"And I'm East," my brazen best friend said before I could introduce him, leaning across the aisle to shake JT's hand. "James Easton, but for the love of fuck, don't call me that."

"John Thomas, but I prefer JT, so I get it."

I noticed the way East's eyes trailed down over JT's casual shirt, jacket, and jeans before he pursed his lips. "Nice jeans—they Tom Ford?"

JT chuckled and looked down at the worn denim covering his legs. "Uh, no, the Gap."

East's brow arched as he looked around the van, nodding. "They must've upped their game since I...last looked."

Travis busted out a laugh at the thought of East *ever* visiting the Gap, and I kicked his foot again, much harder this time.

"Yeah, sort of suits me, you know," JT said, shocking me as he chuckled and pointed to East's famous ascot. "Plus, I don't think I could pull off that look. The scarf would feel like it was strangling me."

A boom of laughter left me as I remembered my comment about being stuck with East in an elevator.

When my eyes slid to JT, the sneaky grin there told me that was exactly what he'd intended.

"It's nice to meet you all," JT said. So polite, though once he got to know them he'd be adding on "fuckers" to the end of that sentence.

"Don't worry," I said, throwing my arm over the back of his seat but careful not to touch him—yet. "You're not required to remember any of them."

"No, I think I got it." Starting with Daire, he went around the van, nailing each of the guys—and Serena—along with "the one with the scowl" and "the model" descriptors I'd given them.

Impressive. I wondered how much he'd retain once he got a little alcohol in him. Speaking of...

"Can I get you a drink before we get there?"

"Uh, sure."

"Anything in particular?"

JT looked over at the bottles at the bar and lifted a shoulder. "Whatever you're having."

"I've got it," Preston said. Serena grabbed a couple of glasses while he scooped a little ice and poured some bourbon in each. "This'll have to do, since we don't have all that bourbon sour fancy shit."

Serena stood up and passed out drinks before shooting JT a wink. "Here you go, handsome."

"Thank you," he said, glancing at me before taking a sip. He made a face, but just as quickly it was gone and he swallowed it down.

"We'll get you something better at the bar. This one's just to loosen up a bit."

JT nodded, lifting the glass to his lips again as I grinned and tipped my own back, ready for whatever the night had in store.

jt

WHEN WEST SAID he had an extra ticket to see Arrhythmia, I should've realized he wasn't talking about general seating with the masses.

No, we were taken upstairs, where the entire second floor was sectioned off as VIP, complete with its own bar and couches in the back. It was standing room only along the balcony, which was where West and I had commandeered a spot in the center early on. The rest of his friends had dispersed, some watching the show, others at the bar, and a couple I didn't notice anywhere, but that didn't faze me at all. If anything, I was glad not to have their eyes watching my every move, because that bunch was more intimidating than I cared to admit.

I took another sip of the bourbon sour West had ordered for me, same as his own, feeling a warm buzz running through my veins. The alcohol was doing a decent job of making me a little less self-conscious, and I swayed slightly along the rail, watching the band put on a killer show. Beside me, West was nodding along, and once the song hit the chorus, he shouted out the words with the rest of the crowd.

A feral grin crossed his lips as he punched the air, and as he took another swallow of his drink, he glanced my way, doing a double take as he busted me staring.

Shit. I hadn't realized I was.

I certainly hadn't meant to. He was just so different than anyone I'd been around that I couldn't help watching—charismatic in ways I wasn't, greeting everyone we passed when we walked into the venue, many by name. Bold in ways I wish I could be, like making sure everyone knew who he was, that this spot on the balcony was his and his alone. And then there was the uninhibited way he was moving his body to the music, which wasn't anything I should've noticed in the first place. But damn if I didn't want to learn how to roll my hips like that—though I wasn't sure I'd ever have the guts to do it in public.

What was it like to be that fearless? West seemed to be having the time of his life, not caring at all about what anyone thought.

Not me. I'd need a lot more alcohol to even consider moving like that.

West raised a brow. "Having fun?"

I nodded. "Yeah, this is awesome."

"See?" His shoulder nudged mine. "Aren't you glad

you have a troublemaker friend to show you a good time?"

Yeah, I was. This was what college was about, right?

I pushed my shoulder back against his and grinned. "Thanks for busting me out."

"Anytime," he said, and I knew he meant it. He'd done me a huge favor bringing me here tonight. I never would've guessed I'd be somewhere like this my first week of college. Studying and early to bed had been the plan, but I couldn't deny this night out was a much better alternative.

The energy in the room was contagious, lights flashing over the sea of bodies crammed below us as they undulated in waves to the music. The beat reverberated through the air, a rhythmic pulse that had West moving again. I glanced at him out of the corner of my eye as he pushed his sleeve up with the hand that held his drink, and I almost reached over to help him when I realized what I was doing and dropped my arm.

But West caught it, and he turned his head toward me, a mischievous glint in his eyes.

"You look like you want to dance," he said.

"I am." At least my version of it, pitiful as it was.

West shook his head and reached for my waist, and the moment he touched me, my body went completely still. The heat of his hand scorched through my thin t-shirt, shooting panic through my chest. Why was he holding me there, and why hadn't I backed away yet?

"Relax, JT," he said, his voice low and barely audible over the music. "Just feel it."

Feel what? His hand on my waist or—

Oh.

West tightened his fingers in a guiding motion, trying to get me to move my body in a figure eight instead of the stiff way I moved side to side.

"You're thinking too hard. Close your eyes and let go. Pretend there's no one else in the room."

I bit down on my lip, hesitating, but then shut my eyes and tried to do what he said, to imagine I was the only person in the room, but that was damn near impossible with his hand branding my waist. He was only trying to help, but all I could focus on was how close he was, in my personal space as he tried to get my hips to move the way his did. But there was no way to relax like this, not when something about it felt like it blurred the line between friendly and...more.

My eyes flew open at the thought, and I took a step back, out of his reach. His hand dropped back to his side. "You okay?"

"Uh...yeah." I was overreacting. Just because West was into guys, that didn't mean he was into *me*. It wasn't like I didn't have gay friends, for fuck's sake, and I'd never jerked away from them.

I swirled the contents of my glass and drained the rest of my drink for something to do other than admit I was being ridiculous.

West cocked his head. "Another?"

"Yeah, that'd be great." I reached for my wallet. "Take my card this time—"

"Not a chance," he said, grabbing my glass. "I'll be right back. Save our spot, yeah?"

Nodding, I watched him head to the bar. His confident stride caused the crowd to part for him like he was a hot knife through butter. It was crazy to watch when I'd have to karate chop my way through the same mob of people. How the hell did he *do* that?

One of the bartenders noticed West's arrival immediately and walked over, greeting him with a smile and nodding at his request.

As he waited, West turned to face me, leaning his elbows back on the bar. The white linen shirt he wore, so thin it was almost sheer, had been left unbuttoned at the top, a more casual look than usual. He was always so polished and dressed to the nines, even at somewhere like Astor.

Then again, maybe it was me that didn't fit in with those standards.

I went to turn away, to watch the band again, but my focus shifted abruptly when a guy I didn't recognize sidled up to him. The way he approached, almost touching West, moving his mouth to West's ear—my first thought was that the guy was about to get decked for daring to approach a Park Avenue Prince. But to my surprise, West smirked, then leaned back slightly to take a long, lingering once-over of the stranger. He looked over to me, and I jerked my focus back to the band.

Shit, that was twice now. He was gonna get the wrong idea if I kept watching him, but I couldn't help it that he was fascinating, someone so completely opposite to me and anyone I'd ever met. I gave it a minute before my attention drifted back to West and the stranger at the bar. I told myself it was to make sure the guy wasn't giving him shit or taking advantage of all the drinks West had consumed, but that wasn't at all what was happening.

West must've liked what he saw when he did that not-so-subtle once-over, because he was letting the guy straddle his thigh, rolling his hips against West's to the beat of the drums.

Holy shit. I hadn't expected that, or the way West tugged his lower lip between his teeth as he pushed off the bar and walked the stranger back, keeping their bodies connected. They moved together in sync, grinding against each other in a way that was almost indecent. The stranger ran a hand down the side of West's torso before curving it around to grab a handful of his ass.

It didn't look like West minded that. At all.

In fact, his eyes heated as the guy began to slide down his body, lowering himself almost to the floor before looking up. West speared his hand roughly through the guy's hair before rolling his hips at eye level—

I quickly averted my gaze, my heart pounding hard as I went to take a drink, only to realize West had taken it to the bar.

There was something too intimate about the way they'd moved together, and a part of me wanted to give them privacy, as ridiculous as that notion was in a crowded space.

The other part of me, however...

Out of the corner of my eye, I could see them, and when it was clear they weren't facing in my direction, I chanced a look.

The guy had straightened, rocking against West, his mouth back by his ear and his fingers working the buttons of West's shirt.

Oh shit, he was undoing his damn clothes right there in front of everyone. Did he even realize? I almost found myself starting in their direction when West's eyes collided with mine again, and a wicked smirk tugged at his mouth.

It was like I was caught in a snare, unable to look away and not sure why. All I knew was that my skin was on fire, and it wasn't just my heart that was throbbing. West held my stare, licking his lips, and warning bells sounded somewhere in the back of my head. I ignored them as the music shifted to something slower, more moody, but just as intoxicating.

The stranger lifted his hand to cup West's jaw, to steal back his attention, and it worked—but not before West shot me a suggestive wink.

"He's a good dancer, isn't he?"

The deep voice beside me jolted me back to reality, and I spun to see Donovan shaking his head at the hypnotic display.

I forced myself to answer, though I wasn't sure my

voice would work. "Uh, yeah," I said, before clearing my throat. "He is."

Donovan raised a brow as he glanced at me, and I was grateful he gave me an excuse to tear my eyes away.

"You didn't want to join in?"

My ears went hot, and I shook my head a little too quickly. "No. Not my thing."

"Dancing's not your thing?"

"No." Not dancing. Not dancing with guys. Neither one.

Donovan looked back in West's direction, but I kept my eyes averted, not wanting to see what was happening now.

"Bet he could change your mind," Donovan mused. "He can change anyone's mind."

My stomach flipped at the casual way he said it, the insinuation not just about dancing now. Or was it? The buzz from my drinks had my head feeling more than a little fuzzy, and I ran a hand over my face like I could clear my mind.

There was a lingering unease under my skin, but why it was there, I didn't know. I'd only been keeping an eye on my new friend, after all. I hadn't been the only one watching West dance with a complete stranger. With the way they had run their hands all over each other, moving together like they were in the privacy of a bedroom, I didn't doubt they'd captured the attention of most everyone up here.

"Another bourbon sour for you."

I snapped my head up as West stopped in front of us, holding full glasses. His shirt had been completely unbuttoned and pushed aside so the deep lines of his abs and strong chest were on full display. Jesus. It wasn't enough to be rich and popular—the guy also had to have the body of a god.

I reached for the glass, and my fingers accidentally brushed West's. Even wrapped around a cold drink, his skin was overheated, and I couldn't help but notice the light sheen of sweat on every bare part of him.

West caught and held my eyes when they drifted back up to his face, and that knowing grin had irrational annoyance rising to the surface.

"I thought you'd forgotten," I said before taking a long swallow, letting the tart, cold liquid soothe my burning throat.

"About you? Never." He didn't break eye contact as he nodded toward Donovan. "Van keeping you company or talking your ear off about designer clothes?"

"Aaand I'm out," Donovan said, giving me a salute that he flipped to a middle finger in West's direction before heading to the back where the couches were.

West moved to the rail, resting his elbows along the edge. "Thanks for holding down our spot."

I settled in beside him, nodding absently. "You didn't have to stop."

"Stop?"

"Dancing." I gestured to the where he'd been at the

bar but didn't see the handsy stranger anywhere. "You seemed like you were having a good time."

"It was okay." West shrugged, and before I could say it looked like more than just okay, he winked at me again. "I don't ditch my friends, JT. I invited you out. I'm hanging with you." He lifted his drink to his lips and paused. "Unless you're trying to ditch me."

The tension I'd been unknowingly holding on to drained out of me at the casual ease of his joke—and the way he'd pointedly used the word *friend*.

What had I gotten so worked up over? Nothing like overthinking to ruin the start of a good friendship.

I blew out a breath and cracked my neck from side to side. Then I smiled at West and tapped his glass with mine. "I'd never do that to a friend either."

"Yeah? Well, then. To new friends," he said, the light in his eyes dancing as he took a drink.

I found myself nodding as I lifted my glass. "To new friends."

ELEVEN

"AHH, THE GALLANT prince returns home empty-handed. Tell me, did you manage to sneak the golden boy back into the castle without mother dragon detecting his absence?"

I glared at East where he sat in his velvety chair sipping his usual martini, then toed off my shoes. "Mother dragon doesn't live there, and the golden boy was home before the stroke of—"

"Your hand?"

I snorted and made my way to the sofa, where I grabbed one of the pillows and flopped down at one end, stuffing it behind my head. "You're such a dick."

"Yes, and the only one you're going to be in the presence of anytime soon if you keep playing your cards like you did tonight."

I stretched my legs out along the sofa and placed my hands behind my head. "Oh, I don't know, I think I played my cards just right tonight."

"By avoiding your date and letting some random slip and slide all over you?"

"Slip and slide?"

East gestured to the open shirt that hung off my body. "Don't act like you weren't putting on a show for the guy. Getting all hot and sweaty up in that club."

I angled my head in East's direction. "Seems like I was putting on a show for you, too."

He grimaced and took another sip of his drink. "No thanks. But I'm not sure that 'make him jealous' tactic worked out too well. You know, since you're sitting at home *alone* with me."

I laughed and went back to staring at the ceiling, not worried in the slightest. East was right, of course—I'd definitely been putting on a show tonight for one person in particular, and it wasn't the guy I'd danced with.

I'd made sure to keep my conversation and interactions with JT friendly and, at times, a little flirty. But I'd made it a point to go and dance with some "random," as East was referring to him, in the hopes of sparking some kind of reaction from JT—and boy did I get one. I could still feel his eyes on me now, trailing down over my body, zeroing in on my naked chest where my dance partner had been trailing his hands over every muscle.

I might be sitting here alone with East right now, but I'd done what I set out to—make JT think about me.

"Did you fall asleep over there?"

"Nope. I'm just lying here thinking about where I'm going to go when I win this bet you laid down."

East snorted and pushed to his feet. "Please, you aren't winning anything. That boy is straight as an arrow. He told you as much on your little lunch date, remember?"

I did, but there was nothing *straight* about the heat I'd felt emanating from JT's stare across the dance floor tonight.

"Make yourself useful, would you, and get me a drink?" I said.

"To drown your sorrows?"

"More like to drown you out. I'm busy visualizing here, and you're interrupting."

East grunted and walked off to the kitchen, but I was under no illusion it was because I'd told him to—his own glass was now empty.

"So," East called out. "You have any place in mind?"

"Interrupting again..."

"That means no, and you want to know why?"

"If I say no, will you shut up?"

"It's because you know you're going to lose. Face it, Golden Boy is into girls, and as pretty as you are—"

"Aww, you think I'm pretty?"

"You, my friend, are known as a cocky, seductive bastard for a reason."

I grinned to myself. It was true, I was known as that, but for a good reason—I could back up the claims. Being rich afforded me pretty much whatever I wanted.

Being...well, *seductive* as East said, afforded me *who*ever I wanted, and once I had them, my cock did the rest of the work.

So maybe my equipment wasn't what JT was thinking about at the moment. But by the time this bet was done, it was *all* he was going to be able to think about.

"We need to work on getting you a drink that's easier to make, for fuck's sake. So many ingredients."

I sat up and reached for the bourbon sour. "It's probably the most work you've done all day."

"All week, really, but who's keeping score?" East settled back in his chair, his martini glass refilled, as I crossed my ankles on the coffee table. "So, where are you thinking of vacationing?"

I took a sip. "I thought you said I had no hope of winning."

"You don't."

I arched a brow and then cradled the glass between my hands on my lap. "Then why do you care?"

"*Because* you're such a cocky bastard." East crossed his legs and eyed me. "And you look like that. So on the off chance you do manage to make this kid notice you, I want to know how much money I'm going to have to shell out."

"A lot. I'm working hard for this."

"More like you're working your ass for this."

"What can I say? I like a challenge."

"More like you enjoy a pretty fucking face." East smirked. "Or, should I say, you enjoy *fucking* a pretty face."

"He does have a pretty face."

I looked at the time and groaned as I pushed up to my feet. It was just turning two thirty, and I was more than ready to crawl into bed.

"Doesn't make up for those horrid jeans, though."

"So he doesn't spend a month's rent on a pair of pants." I walked off toward my side of the condo and called out, "It's not going to make a difference when they're on the floor."

"Cocky bastard."

I didn't bother turning as I waved him off, chuckling as I stepped into my room. I closed the door and leaned back against it, draining the rest of the bourbon sour. I felt the warmth of the alcohol running though my veins as I placed the glass on top of the bureau and began to unbutton my pants.

Tonight had been the perfect way to bring JT into the fold without drawing suspicion, and it had worked like a charm. Arrhythmia had been awesome. The vibe, the energy, was exactly what I needed to showcase my attributes, while also acting as a damn good ice-breaker when it came to my group of friends.

I shoved my briefs and pants off my hips and kicked them aside, wanting nothing but to fall into my bed and not move for the next few hours. But the second I pulled the cool, smooth sheets over my warm skin, my brain and dick had other ideas.

I snaked my hand down my body and spread my legs, wrapping my hand around the hottest part of me, and as my cock throbbed, I was reminded of the music that had vibrated through the club tonight.

Closing my eyes, I thought back to the dark space where shadows and smoke hid wandering hands, but pulsing blue lights gave way to secrets—and that was when I saw JT. His gaze locked on me as I touched his waist, and later when my dance partner's hands had traced the lines of my body in a way I wanted JT's tongue to, and my fingers tightened.

I arched my head back into the pillow as the memory replayed—the wandering hands, JT's curious eyes, my aching dick—and my hips jutted up off the mattress. I shoved my cock through my fist, gnashing my teeth together as I imagined JT dancing in front of me. JT's fingers trailing each and every muscle. *JT's* curious eyes begging me for more.

I groaned as the fantasy became clearer, as the feelings coursing through me intensified, and the sticky pre-cum leaking from my cock started to make a mess of my hand.

This wasn't what I'd planned when I crawled in here tonight, but damn if it wasn't where I was going now. I reached for my bedside drawer and grabbed the bottle of lube, and seconds later, my slippery palm was working my dick like it hadn't seen action in years instead of weeks.

I squeezed my eyes shut, once again bringing up the image of JT. Those messy brown curls, slightly sweaty from being in the crowd. That pouty mouth singing and smiling, wrapping around a bottle of water at the end of the night. That body under a simple pair of jeans and a shirt, and how it would look like if—no, not if, *when*—I stripped him out of them.

I began to move my fist faster, the idea of getting my hands on a naked JT spurring on the orgasm I could feel building. I slid my palm down between my thighs to cradle my balls and squeeze, then arched my head back and groaned.

Christ. It'd been a long time since I'd lain in this bed and gotten myself off. Usually I had someone here doing it for me. But fuck if I wanted anyone else tonight.

JT was all I could think about, all I could see in my mind. It'd been less than a week and he was consuming every waking, sleeping, and masturbatory moment of my time.

I widened my legs, working my hand overtime now as I brushed my thumb over the sticky head of my dick.

"Fuck..." I panted into the room, moving my hips at a more rapid pace as I circled back to our lunch date—and yes, it was a date. I remembered the sounds JT made while tasting every bite, and wondered if he'd make the same while tasting me. Those curls brushing my thighs, that eager tongue sampling something new, and those eyes pleading with me to show him everything he'd been missing.

I would, too. I'd show him how good it felt to have another guy take his lips and kiss them until they needed to draw breath. How good it felt to have that rough push and pull. I'd show him how it felt when someone who knew how to work a cock worked his—and that thought was the one to do it.

I clamped my fist around myself and pulled, gripping my throbbing length like I knew JT's tight ass would, and the next thing I knew, I was coming all over myself.

My chest heaved as the rush dissipated, and as my breathing calmed, I let go of my satiated cock and draped an arm over my eyes. As that delicious feeling of satisfaction swept over me, I doubled down.

I would win this bet.

JT would be mine.

I had this, and I never failed.

TWELVE

MY HEAD THROBBED as I parked my ass at one of the tables near the coffee bar the next morning and massaged my temples. I hadn't gotten back to my dorm—and snuck inside—until the early hours of the morning, and my alarm had gone off not long after that. At least, it seemed that way.

"Mocha latte with an extra shot for JT," the barista called out a few minutes later, and I dragged myself to the counter to grab it. I couldn't remember the last time I'd stayed out so late or had that much to drink—

No, wait. Graduation a few months ago had been a pretty wild time. It'd taken a couple days to recover from that.

I sank back in the chair, letting the coffee work its magic. The mocha flavor was perfect, and it felt amazing down my throat, piping hot, the way I liked it.

Even through the incessant pounding in my head, my

thoughts drifted back to last night. West had promised a good time, and he hadn't been wrong about that. The whole thing had been impressive, from the way he'd been able to show up at my door to the perks of watching the show as a VIP. He'd even turned down a sure thing to hang with me. I'd had a great time.

So what was that niggling feeling in the back of my mind?

I shifted in my seat as I sipped my coffee, trying to pin down the source of my unease. West hadn't said or done anything to me at all to make me feel uncomfortable. There was no reason why I wouldn't want to hang out again. He'd been nothing but welcoming since the day we'd met, and I couldn't help but admire the guy's confidence and the way he could get anything he wanted.

Anything and...anyone.

What was that Donovan had said last night? We'd been watching that stranger dancing—or rubbing himself, really—all over West, and he asked me why I didn't want to join in. I'd let him believe it was because I didn't dance, and that was the truth, but Donovan seemed to get the unspoken words there too. I didn't dance *with guys*.

And that was when he'd thrown out that West could change my mind. That he could change *anyone's* mind.

That. That was what the subconscious part of my brain had been focusing on since Donovan said it, since I'd heard it, shoved it into the back of my mind, and locked it up until now.

Why, though? It didn't make sense.

He'd obviously been joking. I mean, it was clear West had the appeal to get whoever he wanted, but it wasn't like he wanted me, and I definitely wasn't into him like that. We'd both made it very clear on that front. That we were friends. *New* friends, yeah, but that was all there was to it. I'd never looked at another guy in my life.

Would I mind being more like West? Sure. Having that self-assurance in spades was something that could be beneficial for anyone, and maybe some of it would rub off on me. Hell, I wouldn't mind the abs on him either. His body was ripped, something I only noticed when he'd come back with our drinks with his shirt unbuttoned.

Couldn't blame anyone for wanting to be like him.

Not *with* him. *Like* him.

As I swirled my cup in circles on the table, lost in thought, my eyes landed on a familiar beanie by the coffee pickup.

"Hey, Caleb," I called out, and he looked up, spotted me, and waved.

I inclined my head to the empty seat across from me, and he nodded before turning back to grab his coffee. When he headed my way, I took note of the camera he wore on a long strap around his neck today, and bit back a small smile. West had been right when he described Caleb.

"Mornin'," he said, lifting the camera strap over his head to set it gently on the table before taking the seat opposite me. His eyes roamed over my face and narrowed slightly. "I hope you don't take offense to this, man, but you look like shit."

A laugh rumbled out of my chest as I nodded and ran a hand through my hair. I probably could've spent more time taming my curls this morning. No telling what state of hot mess they were in right now.

"You're great for my ego, you know that?"

Caleb shrugged and popped the top off his cup. "Nothin' but brutal honesty over here. What happened, someone pull the fire alarm in the middle of the night?"

"No, I went out last night."

Caleb's brow rose infinitesimally while he stirred his coffee. "Really. Anywhere interesting?"

"Yeah, I went to see Arrhythmia with West and his friends."

Caleb only nodded once as he swallowed down his caffeine. The silence was deafening, though, and I shrugged as though it wasn't a big deal.

"If you've never seen them, you should. They put on a great show," I said.

"Arrhythmia or West and his crew?"

I gave him a pointed look. "You know what I mean."

"I'm not sure I do. Both groups are incredible performers."

Rolling my eyes, I sank back into my chair and sighed. "This conversation is getting old. We had a great time."

"Okay. But I maintain what I said before: you need to be careful with that group."

I groaned. "They're not bad people, Caleb. I'm sorry if

they've rubbed you wrong somehow, but it was a fun night out and this is college, for God's sake. We're supposed to sneak out of our dorms and into parties—"

"You snuck out of your dorm? How?"

"Well, technically, *they* got me out—"

Caleb let out a scoffing laugh as he rubbed the back of his neck. "And you don't think that's a problem?"

"No. We weren't doing anything besides watching a band, and let's be real, a ten o'clock curfew in this city is insane."

He watched me, those keen eyes of his assessing, before he dropped his hand from his neck and nodded. "Yeah, I guess you have a point there."

"Damn right I do," I said, glad he was laying off and seeing things my way. I appreciated his opinion, and that even though we barely knew each other, he was still looking out for me.

"Well, if you want to hang sometime without breaking the rules, hit me up. I'm a little more low-key, so maybe leave the fancy shit to your new friends."

I grinned. "I dunno. I'm a little spoiled on private jets and personal butlers bringing me grapes now. I'm not sure how anything else will compare."

"Damn. That's exactly what I'd been planning for the weekend." A grin turned up the corner of his lips.

"Plans for the weekend? Do tell." The legs of the chair beside me scraped against the floor as it was pulled back from the table and West dropped into the seat. He winked at me as he threw an arm around my shoulders before aiming a devilish smile Caleb's way.

Caleb's mouth snapped shut, the easygoing look on his face turning to one of annoyance. "Nothing that would interest you."

"Aw, why not? If JT's up for it, I could be too." West gave me a little, reassuring squeeze, and Caleb shook his head.

"I'm sure you've got better things to do. Terrorize anyone lately?"

West's smile grew wider, but his eyes glinted dangerously. "Would I do that?"

"Wouldn't you?"

A tense silence fell between them, some unspoken communication happening that had me frowning as I picked up on it.

Like he'd felt me stiffen, West dropped his arm from my shoulder and nudged me. "So how's the head?"

He asked it in a way that had the tension instantly dissipating.

"I think it might explode," I said before taking another long pull of caffeine.

"I figured you might say that. Here." West reached into the pocket of his tailored grey pants and slid a Tylenol packet in front of me.

I let out a moan as I ripped it open quickly. "Oh my God, you're the best. Thank you."

"No problem. Might wanna get some water in you too."

"Noted." I threw back the pills as Caleb's brow furrowed.

"So," West said, ignoring the look Caleb was giving him and focusing on me. "No one ratted you out for our escapade last night?"

I'd passed by a couple of students at the vending machine on my floor when I snuck back in, but they hadn't said anything.

"So far, so good," I told him.

"Perfect. Then you're free to come to my party tomorrow night."

My coffee went down the wrong pipe as I swallowed, and I coughed, covering my mouth with my fist.

"You're throwing a party?" I said when it cleared.

"Yeah, it's tradition. The guys and I like to throw one every year, kind of a 'start the new school year off with a bang' shindig at our place."

"Oh. It's at your condo, then?"

"Mhmm. Mine and East's." He turned slightly toward me, his arm crooked and resting on the back of his chair. How was it that he was so put together today? Not a hair out of place, his clothes perfectly tailored to his body, no dark circles under his eyes. Was he just used to going out, or was he some sort of superhuman?

It was unnerving.

West cocked a brow, wanting an answer. "So? You'll be there, right?"

"I, uh..." I wasn't sure what my hesitation was. My head was still aching too much to think.

"Don't worry, the guestlist is exclusive, so none of the riffraff are invited."

Across the table, Caleb snorted, and I could've sworn I heard him say, "Because you *are* the riffraff," under his breath.

West ignored him. "Since it's technically the weekend, you don't have curfew, right?"

I nodded. "Right."

"Good. Then you're coming."

"Well... I don't know." I ran my fingers through the front of my hair, pushing it off my face, only for it to fall back onto my forehead seconds later. "It's just... I was already out last night, and it's the first week of school. I should catch up on homework—"

"You have the whole weekend to do that boring shit," West interrupted. "You're coming. I won't take no for an answer."

When my eyes widened slightly, he held his hands up.

"Only about this. The party won't be the same without you."

"Won't you be busy, like...hosting it?"

West drummed his fingers along the tabletop and glanced at Caleb. "Tell you what. If it'll make you feel more comfortable, you can bring Caleb too."

Caleb's brows shot up to his forehead. "Wait, what?"

Now that *did* make the party more enticing. I didn't want to hang out in West's swanky place by myself, and I hadn't really gotten to know the rest of his friends yet.

Having Caleb there would definitely be a good buffer, considering West had mentioned an exclusive guestlist, and I had no clue what *that* meant.

"What do you think?" I asked Caleb.

"No. No way."

I bit back a laugh at the quickness with which he'd answered and looked back at West. "Okay, I'll think about it."

West leaned toward me, blue eyes shining. "You do that. Make sure to bring this to get through security downstairs." He handed me an envelope, and a quick peek inside indicated it was the invitation.

"Got it," I said.

West nodded once before getting to his feet. "Good. I'll see you tomorrow."

"Yeah, maybe so. But if I don't, I hope you have a great party."

West stopped in his tracks, glancing back at me over his shoulder. "Don't forget I know where you live, Golden Boy." Then he winked and walked away, as Caleb blew out a breath.

"You don't really wanna go, do you?" he asked, but it sounded like he already knew the answer to that question.

"Of course I do." I pulled the glossy black invitation out of the envelope. Shiny golden foil text indicated the location of the party, and there was a barcode of some sort beneath it. Probably something to do with security, if

I had to guess. I slipped it back into the envelope. "I really don't wanna go alone, though."

I could see the debate whirling behind Caleb's eyes, and I gave him my best pleading expression.

"Please come with me. I know you're not a fan of West, but we'll have fun and we can get to know each other better. If the party sucks, we can even dip out and go to... I don't know. A dive bar or whatever you prefer."

Caleb's lips twitched, and I knew I had him.

"Motherfucker," he said, then let out a sound that was a mix between a sigh and a groan. "If you're absolutely set on going, then you're not going alone."

I grinned. "You're the best, you know that?"

He snorted and flicked the empty medicine packet in front of me. "Nooo, West is, remember?" he teased.

THIRTEEN

THE FIRST WEEK of the year was in the bag, and if that wasn't something to celebrate, I didn't know what was. It meant one week less to spend at Astor, and more importantly, one week since I'd started my campaign to win the bet of a lifetime—a vacation to any destination of my choosing.

Tonight's party was essential to my plan, and I hoped that JT would take me up on my invite. All week I'd been going out of my way to ingratiate myself with the guy. Seeking him out to make friends, morning coffee, an extravagant lunch, and the concert... Ah, the concert— that had been the first real inclination I had that this challenge was actually going to be possible, and the memory of JT's curious eyes fixated on me that night was something I saw every time I closed mine.

It was also something I'd gotten off to more times

than I could count, and considering it'd only happened two days ago, it was a shock my dick didn't have some sort of rash with how much friction I'd given it.

But come on. JT wasn't exactly hard to look at, and the more I talked to him, the more I actually found myself coming up with excuses to seek him out—bet or no bet. So it wasn't like this was a chore.

"The bar is going to be over there by the kitchen area." East's voice cut through my musings as he opened our front door and gestured for the two men with dollies stacked high with liquor. "Be careful of the walls and floors. Be sure you don't leave any scratches."

The men gave clipped nods as they pushed the dollies over the threshold and through the foyer, and East shut the door behind them. He strolled into the living room and slipped his hands into his pockets as he looked around the empty space.

Earlier in the day, the staff at the Towers had been by to clear out all the furniture of the main living and dining areas and placed it in storage for the night. They were great like that, accommodating each and every whim we might have no matter how outrageous, and removing half a condo's furniture ranked right up there with outrageous requests.

Or what had JT called me—ridiculous?

Either way, it was one of the perks of my parents running the Waldorf Astorias here and around the world. If I wanted to throw a party I made a phone call, and the staff at the Towers went out of their way to make it happen. I was always sure to be gracious about it, though. I knew this lifestyle was a privileged one, and while I enjoyed every single perk it had to offer, it didn't mean I couldn't be generous with a smile or a handsome tip.

"Please tell me you're planning to get changed before people start showing up tonight?"

I looked down at the navy-blue pants, brown belt, and light blue shirt I'd worn to classes today and frowned. "You got a problem with what I'm wearing?"

"Not if you were strolling along the French Riviera. But since we're hosting our first party of the year on the East Side of Manhattan, I think you could make more of an effort."

"Gee, East, tell me how you really feel."

"Okay. I hate it, all of it. Especially those loafers."

I snorted as the two men finished stacking the boxes of alcohol by the bar and started back toward the door. The staff for the night would be by soon to start unpacking and setting up.

"You're such a fucking snob."

"And this is news since when?"

I shook my head, walked over to where the men were wheeling their dollies out, and gave them each hundred-dollar bills and a wave before turning back to East.

"The day you were born. This outfit is designer, all the way down to the briefs hugging my ass, and you still have a problem with it."

"It doesn't fit the vibe."

"Which is?"

"Corruption of a golden boy." Travis's mocking voice entered the condo, and I glanced over my shoulder to see him saunter through the foyer.

In a pair of black leather pants and a maroon shirt he'd left open halfway down his chest, he was giving off a sexy rocker vibe that very much fit him and the city that was about to come alive tonight. He had several different chains hanging around his neck, and the sleeves of his shirt were rolled up to his elbows, showing off a black leather cuff around one of his wrists. His ink-black hair was styled in a spiked mess that fit him and his broody attitude, and rounding out the look was the dark kohl liner around his ice-blue eyes.

So maybe they had a point. Out of the three of us, Travis looked more like a corruptor than I did, and that just wasn't going to work.

"Dude." Travis eyed my pants and loafers. "You look like you're going to go sailing on a yacht. Not smooth-talk your way into someone's pants."

"No one asked you."

"Travis is right." East shrugged. "No way you're going to win the bet looking like that. If he even shows up."

"Oh, he'll show up, don't you worry. I know exactly what I'm doing. Party starts in an hour. I've got plenty of time to change."

"Sure hope so," Travis muttered, and walked over to the stacked boxes of alcohol. "You managed to find some absinthe last minute."

"Of course," East said as though it were no trouble for him to find anything, and really, it wasn't. "Everything on the list you all filled out is there. So I don't want to hear anyone bitch or moan that they didn't get what they asked for."

My lips twitched. "Daire filled out your form?"

"One line of it." East pulled up the message on his phone and handed it over.

I couldn't help but laugh at the response Daire had written in the *Any special requests?* box:

That you fuck off with these dumbass forms.

That was Daire for you. Blunt to the point of brashness.

"I swear, if I hear one complaint from him tonight—"

"You'll do what?" I laughed, trying to imagine a scenario in which East would go up against someone like Daire. It was ludicrous. East might be able to cut someone off at the legs with his rapier tongue, but when that person didn't give a fuck about anyone or anything, there wasn't much you could say to hurt them.

Not to mention, Daire had a good couple inches on East and was built like a boxer. He was all lean muscles, with a scowl that sent people running. Not to mention the many tattoos that covered most of his body and piercings that showed he wasn't afraid of pain.

So the idea of East getting into it with him? That made me laugh my ass off.

"I was just going to *say*," East interrupted. "I'm going to tell him to shoot one of your poisons. God knows he'll drink anything if it's in a shot glass."

A knock on the door signaled the bar and food staff arriving for the evening, and if I didn't get moving, I wouldn't be showered and ready when people started to show. "You got this under control?"

East shooed me away, and I hurried off down the hall. I headed into my room and the walk-in closet and looked over the clothes hanging there.

Hmm... What to wear, what to wear...to seduce the golden boy.

I looked over the lighter colors I tended to gravitate toward in the summer, but East and Travis were right—it wasn't the vibe I needed. Not for tonight. Tonight was about introducing JT to my world. To the city at night and all the possibilities that came with it.

I zeroed in on a pair of loose-leg black pants with the faintest hint of a silver pinstripe. They molded to my waist and ass like a dream, and anytime I wore them, I got lucky. It was a sign, and I immediately reached for them and a tight black shirt. They were a perfect match.

Minutes later, I was in the shower. The hot water on my body felt amazing as I planned out my moves for the night. I was going to have to play this just right if I had any hope in hell of JT feeling comfortable enough to let down his walls.

So far I'd gotten past the friendship barrier, and considering the dean and Caleb had been sending out warning signals like I was a walking natural disaster, I felt pretty confident I was on the right track.

Something about me intrigued JT. I'd seen the way he watched me dancing at that club, and it sure as shit hadn't been the way my other "friends" watched me.

Sure, I'd made myself difficult to ignore, but at the same time, I had a feeling that if JT didn't want to know me, he'd tell me. Since that hadn't happened, I was feeling pretty confident going into tonight.

My cock stirred at the possibilities and the fantasies I'd been playing out in my head the last few days, but I wasn't going to give in to its demands just yet. If I played my cards right, it would get its turn soon enough.

I stepped out of the shower and dried off, throwing on my clothes for the night and styling my hair. After a final once-over, I was satisfied that if there was a chance JT was even remotely curious about getting closer than friends, then this outfit just might tempt him.

I walked out of my bedroom and saw the rest of our group had arrived, and so had the DJ, who was setting up in the corner. The bottles of alcohol had been unpacked, and the bar was set up like something straight out of an established club. As I moved closer to the guys, Travis's attention shifted from Preston and Serena to me.

"Still look like I'm about to go yachting?"

A wolf whistle filled the room, making East wince, before Donovan clapped me on the shoulder. "Only if we're talking masts and vertical poles. Sometimes I hate that I know you so well."

"What's that supposed to mean?"

"That your pole never stays in one place long enough to make it worth my while."

"Aww." I flashed a grin at Donovan. "You want a safe harbor. A port to call home. I get it."

"Fuck no, I don't. But I also have to be in tiptop health, not wondering where you've...anchored for the night." He snorted at his own stupid joke before I flipped him off.

Preston's brow furrowed. "Can someone please tell me why we're talking in sailing terms?"

"Does anyone care?" Daire's droll voice had me looking at the bar to see him pointing to a bottle of vodka as the door to our condo opened and the first round of guests flowed inside.

Let the games—and shots—begin, I thought, as I wandered over to East in the kitchen.

It was about to get insane real fast up in here, and I had to steal a bite of whatever it was I could smell before they disappeared.

There was a platter of crispy mushroom caps with cream cheese and lox on the counter. I grabbed one up and popped it in my mouth. As I chewed it, I noticed the way East was looking me over.

"You can admit it. I look good, don't I?"

East brushed his hand across my shoulder. "You had a piece of lint, but now"—he stood back and eyed me—

"now I'm rethinking this whole thing. Good-looking bastard."

"I told you. I've got this."

East arched his brow as only he could. "He's straight, West. Don't forget that. You've still got a looong way to go, and that's if he even shows."

I shrugged, not put off in the slightest. JT would show, I could feel it in my bones, and if he didn't, I'd just go and get him.

As a new tray of food was pulled from the oven, my mouth watered at the sight. I grabbed a napkin and one of the cheddar cups with avocado feta mousse, not bothering to let it cool before I bit into it. *Something* had to soak up some of the alcohol I'd be consuming over the next few hours.

I winked at East and then headed back to the transformed space, which was quickly filling with scantily clad bodies and thumping music. The alcohol was being cracked open, and it looked like our annual first-week-back party was in full swing.

I made my way through several of the partygoers, stopping here and there to chat with them, and finally came to a standstill by Travis and his latest hookup.

"Looks like it's going to be a good night," I said, eyeing the door.

"He's not here yet."

"I know." And I did know. Because when JT was anywhere near, it was like my body had a laser that

INFAMOUS PARK AVENUE PRINCE

immediately locked on to him. So far, the target wasn't in range.

Travis took a sip of his drink. "You sure he's going to come?"

I winked at him. "I mean, I'm not one to brag, but I've never had a problem making someone come."

"Too much information, asshole."

"Hey, you asked."

Travis feigned heaving, and *that* was when my radar pinged.

The hair on the back of my neck stood tall and my shoulders stiffened. It was like an electric charge had just filled the air. I turned around and saw JT step inside.

Anticipation began to course through me, making my every nerve ending feel alive. This was it. I'd been playing it cool with JT, friendly, with a little flirtation here and there. But tonight I was going to see if that heat I thought I'd seen at the club was back.

Maybe it *was* the night and vibe that allowed our innermost devious sides to come out and play. But the intense response I was having right now told me I needed a second to rein this shit in.

Don't come on too strong. You'll scare him off.

"The *fuck* is he doing here?" Travis's furious outburst had my eyes shifting to the person who'd just stepped in behind JT, and something about the fact that Travis had given me shit earlier made this little revelation all the more fun for me.

"Oh, did I forget to mention I invited Caleb?" I threw a

shit-eating grin Travis's way that was met with a death stare. "You're welcome."

A distinct "fuck you" was all I heard as I made my way through the crowd, more determined than ever to put my plan for the night into action.

FOURTEEN

JT

THE TOWERS AT the Waldorf...

I thought I'd prepared myself for what I'd find when I stepped out of the taxi Caleb and I had taken from my dorm. But as it pulled inside a drop-off point and a valet opened our door and took care of the fare, I felt as though I'd left reality and entered a new world.

One where money wasn't a factor and ease was the name of the game.

My car door being opened. The entrance at the Towers being held wide. A security guard taking the invitation West had given me and scanning the barcode before ushering me and Caleb inside and sending us up to God knows what floor, because there were no buttons to press. We'd somehow managed to arrive at the right floor, if the giggling girls and whooping guys pumping their fists in the air to the music pounding out of the open door to our left were any indication.

I noticed Caleb hadn't left the spot where he'd stopped after getting out on the floor. I turned to see him eyeing the door like one might a gangplank and felt a slight twinge of guilt over talking him into coming here tonight.

It was obvious he had some kind of beef with West and his crew, but I'd been so caught up in making new friends and getting to know more people that I'd selfishly pushed that aside, figuring Caleb's gripe was probably based around the obnoxious way West threw his money around.

The tight jaw and color blooming high on his cheeks at the sight of the open door, however, quickly changed my mind.

"Caleb?" I walked back to where he stood, his eyes still fixated on the door. "Caleb?"

He blinked and refocused on me.

"Look, we don't have to go. We could leave now and find that dive bar."

A deep frown formed between his brows as he reached up and readjusted his ever-present beanie. "Nah, it's okay. You want to see what West and...the rest of them are about. We should go in."

I couldn't lie. I *did* want to know what a condo at the Towers was like and what kind of party someone like West threw. But I didn't want to do it at the expense of my other friend's feelings.

"Really. If you don't want to be here, we can go."

Caleb's lips tugged into that half-smile of his, and he

shrugged. "We're here now. Might as well go and drink as much of their liquor as we can. Open bars are rare in New York, unless—"

"You're a Park Avenue Prince?"

Caleb snorted. "Yeah, something like that. Everything is open when your mommy and daddy pay."

He had a point. Every time I'd been out with West this week, doors had been opened, tabs had been picked up, and VIP seats had been held. It really was an open-door lifestyle. I couldn't imagine anyone ever telling West—or the rest of them—no, and I couldn't even begin to imagine that kind of lifestyle.

"Come on." Caleb gestured toward the door. "Let's go. The sooner we get in there, the sooner we can get out."

While I knew Caleb was dreading every step he took, I was feeling a different kind of emotion altogether. My heart was thumping and my palms were a little sweaty, and as I gave myself another quick once-over, I realized I was nervous. I'd never been to a party like this. Hell, I hadn't known parties like this existed. So I had no idea what I should be wearing or whether I should've brought anything.

The second I stepped inside the condo, though, the notion that I could contribute anything to a party like this became absolutely laughable.

West's condo looked eerily similar to the club we'd gone to the other night, except this one had VIP views of the Manhattan skyline. The condo's lights were off, and in their place were flashing spotlights that kept beat to the music the DJ was blasting. People bumped and grinded up against each other in the center of the space.

Now, I knew this was where West and his friend East lived, but there wasn't one piece of furniture in the entire area that was currently full of drinking and dancing partygoers, and I wondered where the hell it had all gone. Surely they wouldn't have moved out their entire living room just for a party.

Then again, I was learning never to underestimate these guys—though something about imagining West living in a place like this without a couch had me suppressing a chuckle.

"All right, if we're gonna last more than five minutes, we need drinks and we need them now," Caleb said, pointing out the bar. I nodded, following him through the throng of people, which was harder than it looked. This was where West would've come in handy—he'd make all those people part like the Red Sea.

Speaking of West, I hadn't seen him yet, and that made me grateful Caleb had agreed to come with me. I couldn't imagine navigating the party on my own.

"What's your poison?" Caleb asked.

Bottles and bottles of liquor, wine, and beer were displayed, and though I wasn't new to drinking socially, my mind went blank when I saw all the options.

"Uh. Whatever you're having."

That was easiest, and even if it turned out to be something I didn't like, at least it was something new to try.

Expand my horizons and all, right? Hell, that was what I was doing here in the first place.

A few minutes later, Caleb handed me a bottle of beer with a name I couldn't even pronounce—German, maybe?—and I sniffed at it, frowning.

He laughed and tapped his bottle to mine. "Just try it."

I took a hesitant sip, and pulled a face. Nope. That shit was foul. But I wasn't about to say that, not when the alternative was having to fight my way back to the bar for something else.

"That's...interesting," I said, forcing myself to try it again. What was that I always heard about beer? It was an acquired taste. Just how much was I gonna have to drink to acquire the taste to this one?

"Every bottle of alcohol you can imagine, and you give him a bottle of piss?"

West's voice rose above the crowd as he came up beside us, and relief swept through me. He smiled at me as he approached, and something looked different about him tonight. I couldn't pinpoint what it was, only that he gave off a more magnetic vibe that had your attention falling—and staying—on him.

When West's eyes fell on the beer in my hand, his nose wrinkled in distaste. "Caleb Reeves, I thought you knew JT better than that."

He lifted the beer from my grasp and handed it to Caleb before giving me his own drink, the same cocktail I'd had with him at the concert.

West's hand moved to my lower back as he leaned in to my ear, and my body jolted in response. Whether it was from surprise at his touch, the heat of his fingers, or... something else, I didn't know.

"Hold on to this one and I'll get you something you'll enjoy a hell of a lot more," he promised.

His fingers brushed along my lower back as he pulled away and walked to the bar, and as I watched him go, I realized what was different. Every time I'd seen him, West had been wearing what I'd consider a "rich preppy" style —lighter colors, fitted slacks, and button-ups. But tonight he was in all black, including the pinstripe pants that clung to his hips and ass. The tight black t-shirt he wore showcased the muscular physique he didn't usually put on display, and—

"You're staring."

I blinked, focusing back on Caleb. "No, I'm not. I was just...making sure he was really heading to the bar."

"Uh huh." He studied me as he took a long pull of his beer, leaving my bottle to dangle between his fingers at his side. The crowd only seemed to grow as we stood there, packing into the condo so that no matter where you stood, there was a body bumping into yours.

Someone tripped into me from the side, and I caught her with my free hand, helping her stand back upright.

"I'm so sorry. These heels..." She trailed off as she looked up at me and smiled.

"No problem," I said, still gripping her for balance. "You good?"

Her smile grew as she batted long, dark lashes. "No, I'm Phoebe. And you are...?"

"JT."

"Nice to meet you, JT. You go to Astor?"

"Yeah, just started. You?"

"No, I'm at Columbia. Not too far away for a lunch date." She punctuated that with a wink, and I couldn't hide my surprise at the way she got right to the point.

Phoebe was a knockout, that was for sure—long black hair to her waist and a tiny strapless top that left little to the imagination. There was no way a girl like her was hitting on me, not with the room full of better-looking guys that had several zeroes in their bank account.

"Maybe we'll run into each other sometime," I said, giving her a small smile, along with an out to go hook a bigger fish.

Confusion marred her brow, but she nodded and took a step back. "See you around, JT."

As she disappeared back into the crowd, Caleb said, "Not your type?"

"Huh?"

"She's hot." He gestured with his bottle in the direction Phoebe had just disappeared. "She not your type?"

"Oh, I mean, I think she'd be any guy's type if he had a pulse."

"Not mine."

I narrowed my eyes as Caleb took a swig of his beer, but when he didn't elaborate further, I decided to let it go.

It had been hard enough to get him to come to this party to start with—I wasn't going to start being a busybody.

"I just got out of a relationship," I explained when he didn't say anything else. "Not a serious one, but, you know, a high school thing. She went to L.A. and I came here—"

"Ah, but it was a *her*."

I chuckled and took a sip of the drink West had left me with. "Yeah, why?"

"It's just with the way you were looking after West, and how he's been all up in your business, I thought that maybe..."

"Maybe what?" I'd just been watching him go and get a drink. I knew West was into guys, but *I* wasn't watching him like that. I was just keeping an eye on the only other person I knew at the party.

"I thought you might be into guys," Caleb finally spelled out loud and clear, in case I hadn't picked up on his not-so-subtle line of questioning.

So much for not wanting to be a busybody.

"Nope. Always dated girls. You?"

Caleb coughed around his swallow of beer. "Girls too. But I don't really go for the dark-haired types."

Phoebe definitely hadn't been for him, then. "Gotcha. Well, I'm not really looking to hook up the first week of college anyway."

"Now where's the fun in that?"

I whirled around to see West standing behind us with two glasses in hand. "Of course you'd say that."

132

"Of course I would." He handed one of the glasses to me as he took my empty tumbler and palmed it off to one of the passing staff. "I told you, I'm here to show you how to have fun through college."

I chuckled and took a sip of the new drink. "Mmm, this is good." I licked my lips as the sweet, creamy flavor hit my taste buds. "White Russian?"

"Sure is. You like?"

I nodded and took another sip, and West's eyes fell to my mouth. Not wanting to do anything that might mislead him, I flashed him a friendly grin. "I do. It's one of my favorite drinks."

"You see, Caleb?" West thumped him on the arm. "Friends pay attention."

"A little too much attention," I thought I heard Caleb mutter before a pissed-off voice interrupted the three of us.

"What the fuck do you think you're doing showing up here tonight?"

My eyes shifted past Caleb's shoulder to where one of West's friends—Travis, I think he said his name was—stood with his arms crossed over his maroon shirt, a dark look plastered on his face. Caleb's entire body stiffened, and when he didn't immediately respond, Travis grabbed at his arm and spun him around.

"I asked you a question."

Just as I was about to step up and ask Caleb if he was cool, he spat out, "I was invited. So back the fuck off."

"Bullshit."

"He's not lying. I did invite him." West shrugged and took a sip of his drink.

Travis aimed a fulminating look in West's direction. "You, shut the fuck up."

"Geez, man. Angry much? You might want to work out that...frustration." West grinned around the rim of his glass then winked at me. He was such a shit stirrer, but at the same time I was starting to see he'd been telling the truth about the whole Caleb situation. In less than two sentences it had become crystal clear *who* in this group of "princes" Caleb had a problem with.

News flash—it wasn't West.

"A word," Travis said between clenched teeth, and Caleb glanced over his shoulder at me.

"You gonna be okay for a second here?"

West slung an arm around my shoulders. "He's going to be just fine. I'll take care of him."

Caleb's eyes shifted between West and myself, and I thought it a little odd he was worried about me when he was the one in the middle of a shouting match. "I'll be back."

"Take your time. I'm sure you and Travis have a lot to catch up on," West said.

Travis vibrated with his irritation. "Fuck you, LaRue."

"If only that could solve your problem." West grinned at me. "Come on, do you like cheddar cups with avocado feta mousse?"

FIFTEEN

west

"SHOT! SHOT! SHOT!" the crowd shouted as the bartenders poured liquor into tiny cups to pass around the room. As the last of the partygoers were given theirs, I hopped on top of the bar along with East.

"All right, you fuckers—" East started, but I clamped a hand over his mouth, glancing down to where JT stood below, his brown eyes dancing and a wide grin on his face. He was feeling niiice and happy, and seemed to be having a blast so far. I was on a mission to keep it that way.

The DJ lowered the music just enough that my voice could be heard around the room. "Thanks for coming to our annual 'Welcome back to Astor' party—"

"Coming? I don't see anyone fucking coming yet," East grumbled, sloshing his shot over the edge of the cup as he scanned the room, a pout on his lips. "I expected more debauchery, dammit."

I laughed along with the partygoers, gripping my friend's shoulder to help keep him steady. Couldn't have him falling off the damn bar at his own party.

"The night is young," I assured him, shooting a wink out into the crowd before my gaze landed back on JT. A few of his curls were stuck to the sweat on the side of his neck and face, and fuck me, he looked hot. Especially in that navy button-down shirt I wanted to undo, and a pair of ripped jeans that had tears in places that were practically indecent.

Bet or no bet, I wanted to put my hands all over him, but more than that? I wanted him to enjoy it.

I lifted my shot at him and then managed to force my eyes up. "On behalf of myself and East, we expect you to clean us out of every drop of alcohol in this place." A roar of approval rose, and I grinned. "See? We're nothing if not generous. And if anyone tells you different, they're fucking liars."

"Less talking, more drinking," East said, slinging his arm around my shoulders. "To you, to me, to the bruises on your knees."

The crowd whooped and threw back their shots, East and me along with them, and then I hopped back down from the bar beside JT and his ever-present shadow Caleb. Luckily, the guy wasn't too bad once you got a few drinks in him, but he was still in my damn way.

"Nicely done," Caleb remarked, flagging down the bartender for another beer.

That happy, tipsy little grin on JT's face told me he was feeling just the right side of good without crossing the line into too much. I couldn't help myself, though. I had to reach out and push one of the curls sticking to his skin back behind his ear. The strands were soft and damp, and I wanted to spear my fingers through his hair, angle his mouth to mine, and see if he tasted as sweet as I thought he would.

"I know, I'm all sweaty," he said.

Like *that* wasn't something that was driving me out of my mind, with or without the alcohol flowing through my veins.

"You're not the only one," I said, feeling a trickle down the back of my neck. "All that body heat. Don't be surprised if clothes start coming off..."

"Yours?" he asked, and though he'd probably meant that innocently enough, that one word shot straight to my dick. It stirred impatiently behind the confinement of my boxer briefs, and it was all I could do to ignore it.

Or die trying.

"That wasn't you issuing me a challenge, now was it, JT?" I teased. "I can never resist those."

"No one wants to see that," Caleb said, but I didn't bother looking his way. I hadn't been talking to him.

JT held my gaze. "I dunno, you seem to let others undress you without a challenge, so I'm not sure you need one."

Now *that* had my curiosity spiking. "Do I?"

"Yeah, like at the concert. You let that guy unbutton

your shirt." He gestured toward the one I was wearing—still wearing, for now—and shrugged.

My smile turned feral. "Jealous? There's no buttons here, but if you want it off, you can just take it off."

I waited for the shocked expression, the quick denial, but JT gave me a relaxed once-over that made my impatient cock start to ache.

"I wouldn't want to cause a riot in your condo. Seems like it would be expensive to fix."

That wasn't a no, was it?

I leaned in by his ear and breathed in the salty scent of his skin mixed with whatever cologne he'd sprayed on tonight. While I knew it wasn't anything designer or outrageously expensive, the impact was priceless—my dick went from a delicious ache to an insistent throb.

"Don't forget, I'm rich, Golden Boy. You want to take my clothes off and cause a riot, I'm not gonna stop you."

JT laughed, another sign he was feeling the buzz of the alcohol. "You're crazy."

I fucking was, because all thoughts of bets and dream vacations vanished in that moment until all I could think about was how gorgeous he looked smiling up at me like that. But I had to tread lightly here. I didn't want to spook the guy, and Caleb... Caleb was still lingering.

Luckily, though, I knew a fast way to make Caleb want to get gone.

"So, Caleb." I picked up the drink the bartender had just set down for me—I loved that I never had to ask.

"You look less likely to murder anyone right now. You sort shit out with Travis?"

Right on cue, Caleb's relaxed posture turned rigid and he glared in my direction.

What can I say? I never claimed to be a saint.

"What do you think?"

I shrugged and took a sip of my drink. "I don't know, but it seems like you might've kissed and made up. So I'm just asking."

"You're being fucking nosy, is what you're being."

I was, but when he put his beer bottle down on the bar and turned to tell JT he'd be right back, I almost patted myself on the shoulder. If there was one thing Caleb avoided like the plague, it was anything to do with Travis—talk or interacting in general. So the fact he'd been around when I invited JT tonight was kind of a happy accident. Not only had it meant JT felt comfortable enough to come to the party, it was also a surefire way to make Caleb disappear whenever I wanted him to. I knew his triggers, and I wasn't above using them.

"Speaking of being a sweaty mess, you feel like getting some air with me?" I suggested as Caleb disappeared through the crowd.

"Sure." JT nodded and put his empty shot down on the bar. "Have you got a balcony?" He looked around the crowded living and dining space.

"No, but I've got something even better. Come on." I brushed past him and headed into the dancing crowd that immediately parted, then glanced over my shoulder to make sure JT was following as we made our way through the gyrating guests toward the front door.

When we stepped out into the hallway, I pulled my key card from my back pocket and flashed it under the elevator keypad.

"That thing is *so* cool." JT leaned in close to me—much closer than he probably would have if he was sober—and looked at the small screen that lit up. "How does it know where to go? There's no buttons inside. We just...arrived."

I smirked, then punched in a code. "It's magic."

The elevator door opened, and I ushered him inside then leaned against the back wall and slipped my hands in my pockets as JT looked around the interior for some kind of panel—there wasn't one.

"Wow." He ran his hand over the golden pattern of the wall. "It was packed in here earlier, so I couldn't really see, but there really aren't any buttons."

"Nope. No buttons."

He turned to face me, his eyes sparkling with delight. "So it really *is* like magic."

"I told you."

A grin lit up his features, and it took every ounce of restraint I had not to grab him.

"That fits you." He nodded as his eyes wandered up and around the elevator car, and I couldn't help but notice the sharp angle of his jaw and the light stubble covering it.

"It does?"

He brought his smiling eyes back to mine. "Magic exists in fairytales. Don't you know that, Mr. Park Avenue *Prince?*"

The elevator came to a stop, and as the doors opened I pushed off the back wall. "So do castles." I winked at him. "So come look at the view from the top of mine."

I stepped around him, again careful to let this be his choice, to let JT be the one to decide whether he wanted to hang out with me or head back to find Caleb.

"Where are we?" JT's voice filled the empty corridor I led him down, my key card in hand. When I reached the door, I glanced over my shoulder and waggled my brows.

"Come and find out." I scanned my card under another keypad, and when the door swung open, JT's eyes widened.

"Magic..."

I chuckled as he stepped outside and saw the view of the Chrysler Building and Manhattan's skyline.

"Holy shit. This is... This is..."

"Indescribable?"

JT looked over his shoulder at me. "Pretty much. Jesus. Who lives like this?"

I arched a brow. "A prince."

He scoffed and glanced back at the rooftop patio that was decked out with top-of-the-line outdoor furniture, including lounges, couches, chairs, and tables, not to mention several hanging seats that were suspended from the wooden rungs of the overhead awning. Potted plants and vines grew in lush precision up trellises. There were heaters and firepits for the winters and fans and misters for the summers, and along one side of the roof was an infinity pool that was exclusive for the guests.

But none of that interested me half as much as the man standing directly in front of me.

I gestured to the rail. "Want a closer look?"

"Um, yeah."

"One sec."

I jogged over to the bar that I knew was fully stocked, and grabbed a bottle of bourbon and some ice in a couple of tumblers. I at least knew JT liked this better than a shit bottle of beer.

He took the glass I offered and followed me to the railing, a thick wall of concrete that reached my chest. I swallowed down a bit of bourbon as I leaned against it, looking out over the city. The view never failed to impress, but tonight I imagined seeing it through JT's eyes for the first time.

"Do you ever get tired of looking at this?" he asked, as if he could read my mind.

I shook my head. "No, but it changes."

"How so?"

"Just becomes more familiar. More of a... I don't know. Comfort somehow."

"Must be nice to have the Chrysler Building to keep you feeling all warm and fuzzy." JT winked—yes, winked —as he lifted his drink to his mouth.

My gaze dropped to his lips wrapping around the edge of the glass. So soft, so decadent. I wanted them on my own with a hunger that practically devoured me whole.

Fuck, I wasn't used to having to handle myself with so much restraint. Then again, most of the people who ended up in my bed were pursuing *me*. It didn't take much to have them down on their knees for me.

All this anticipation had me keenly aware of things I probably wouldn't have noticed before. Like the proximity of JT's body to mine, so close as we stood side by side that his arm rested against me.

As the bourbon hit JT's tongue, his eyes widened slightly. "That's strong."

"Oh?" I leaned in a little. "Too strong?"

He cocked his head at me. "Nothing I can't handle."

That look in his eyes was a goddamn beacon, the words he uttered feeling too much like a double entendre.

"You sure about that?"

"Yeah. Apparently I like what you like now."

Fuuuck. "We still talkin' about the bourbon here, JT?" I said, dropping my voice low.

A heartbeat passed. Then two. When he didn't answer by the third, I inched toward him, like his lips were a magnet mine were drawn to.

But JT didn't move. Didn't blink. He just watched me as I leaned in and swept my mouth against his in a light caress.

Will he stay or will he go...

I waited for what was happening to sink in, for him to push me away. But when all I felt was the gentle exhale of his breath, that was all the permission I needed. I moved in, taking his lips with mine, but kept my hands to myself. For now.

I kissed him slowly. Those pouty lips were just as smooth and pillowed as I'd imagined. Nothing too rough or eager, though, nothing that would scare him off. Slow and exploring was the right speed, not my usual hit and run.

I slipped my tongue out to tease the seam of his lips, testing to see just how far he'd let me go, and JT put his hand to my chest and gave a gentle push. The heat from his palm scorched through my shirt, but as I raised my head and stared at his wide-eyed expression, I noted he'd yet to remove his hand.

Interesting...

I trailed my eyes over his windswept curls and flushed cheeks. I noticed they were a little pinker now, and if I were a betting man—which was one of the reasons I was here—that color had more to do with me than the alcohol. He sure was something to look at, and when those eyes dropped back to my mouth there was no way I wasn't going to push my advantage.

"So, JT, you still liking what I'm liking?"

SIXTEEN

JT

IF SOMEONE AT this party pulled me aside right now and asked me how my first week at Astor had gone, and whether or not it was everything I'd expected, I wouldn't have a damn clue how to answer them. Not when my first week of university had somehow led me to the top of one of the most luxurious buildings in the city, where I was currently kissing a guy I'd met five days ago.

Not that there was anything wrong with two guys kissing, even after only meeting one day ago—or hell, at this very party—but I'd never imagined it would be me in that equation.

I didn't kiss guys.

Or, at least, I didn't until a couple of minutes ago. I stared at West, trying to think of a response to the question he'd just asked. My answer should be a no-brainer. A quick denial and excuse should come flying off my tongue. Instead, all I could think about was *his* tongue, and the way it had lightly teased my lip a second ago.

"JT?" West's voice was as smooth as the bourbon and almost as intoxicating. It filtered through all the thoughts bombarding me and settled somewhere below my waist —and my cock jerked.

Oh my God...

A gentle breeze swept through the buildings and across my flushed face, and the cool air felt amazing on my heated skin. I was feeling good and buzzed. Tipsy but not drunk. And that made me hesitate. I knew that whatever I did next I'd remember tomorrow, and while this feeling was a good one, would I still feel that way in the morning?

I lowered my gaze to West's mouth, the same one that had just been coaxing mine to come out and play, and my dick began to throb all over again. I might not know how I was going to feel in the morning, but I knew how I felt right now—I was turned on.

"It was just a kiss, JT. That's all that happened. We can go back inside if you—"

"Do it again." The words were out of my mouth before I realized I was even going to say them. When nothing but silence met my ears, I raised my eyes to see West's lips curve into a wicked smirk that I wanted to feel against my mouth.

"Remember, I'm all about a good time. *You're* supposed to be the voice of reason. So, are you sure?"

I wasn't sure of anything right now except for the way

he was making my cock pound in time with my heart. But still, I didn't move away.

West cradled my face and closed the distance between us, then he whispered across my lips, "That's good enough for me."

My eyes fluttered shut as his mouth once again found mine, and the second we met, it was like a jolt of electricity shocked my system. It sparked and sizzled through my veins, and heat flooded my body as West swept his tongue across my lower lip, seeking entrance.

I could feel the beat of West's heart beneath the palm I had resting on his chest, and when he slipped his tongue inside, I flexed my fingers and dug them into the hard muscle beneath his shirt.

The pulse between my legs intensified as West rubbed his tongue up against mine and groaned. My stomach flipped.

That sound was intense. It was also sexy as hell. To know that someone like West—who could have anyone he wanted at the party—was up here with me was...exhilarating.

Yeah, okay, *that* was the alcohol talking.

Exhilarating? It was insane, was what it was. I had no idea what I was doing, but when West took our glasses and put them down on the ledge beside us, I was done caring.

West took my waist and pulled me in close, his mouth back on mine before I could think too hard. He nipped at my lower lip, and I braced both hands on his chest as he chuckled against my mouth.

"Probably a smart idea..."

My chest heaved as his warm breath ghosted over my lips. "What is?"

"That you brace yourself for what's about to happen next."

Then his mouth crashed down on mine, and this time there was nothing gentle or cautious about what we were doing. I'd given him full permission to go for it, and with the way his tongue stroked mine I couldn't find it in me to regret it.

At least, not yet.

My head spun as he kissed me senseless. I gripped tight to the thin fabric of his shirt, like holding on to him was the only thing keeping me upright.

"Fuck," West murmured against my lips. "You taste better than I imagined."

"You imagined this?" My voice was a breathless whisper that I should've been embarrassed about, but I couldn't find it in myself to care.

Not when one of West's hands found its way into my hair, massaging my scalp with the pads of his fingers in a way that had a shiver racing down my spine.

His sinful chuckle vibrated against my lips. "JT. You have no fucking idea."

I felt his words all the way down to my toes, baffled how I hadn't caught on to the attraction. But why would I? I'd made it clear we were friends, and so had he...

But friends didn't kiss this way.

West shifted, moving us so that my back was against the concrete. He pushed one of his legs between mine as he angled my head to capture my mouth again, drawing me in closer, and with every rock of his hips, I could feel the way he grew hard against me—

Damn. West was hard. For *me*.

The thought lodged its way into my brain as the interest my dick had shown earlier increased tenfold. I didn't have time to think how the hell that was possible, not when he obliterated any thought that wasn't about how good this was.

Feeling bold, I sucked his bottom lip, and his answering groan told me exactly how much he liked it.

He tightened his grip on my hair, tipping my head back. His breath was hot on my neck seconds before his mouth was on me, leaving sexy kisses that trailed down to my collarbone, where my shirt remained buttoned.

But it wasn't my chest that had West's attention. He slid his hand down the side of my waist, over my hips, and then to the rip in my jeans at the top of my thigh. It was dangerously close to my straining erection, and as his fingers brushed over my skin, my hips involuntarily thrust forward. The touch was as effective as a stroke to my dick, but his fingers didn't manage to get that far before the rooftop door opened suddenly and my eyes flew open.

The sight of one of West's inner circle—Gavin, maybe?— with a guy I didn't recognize had reality crashing down, and I found myself shoving West away harder than I intended.

He stumbled back a step, his brow furrowed, but when he followed my gaze to the rooftop crashers, his expression smoothed.

"Hey, Gav," he said, moving slightly to step in front of me. With the new arrivals blocked from view, I adjusted my jeans, but when that didn't do shit to hide my arousal, I grabbed my drink, letting it dangle in front of me.

What a shit distraction. There was no way Gavin wouldn't be able to tell exactly what we were up to, because even if I'd managed to hide my erection, West hadn't hidden his.

"Oh, sorry, West, I didn't know you were out here," Gavin said, before his eyes shifted past his friend to me. They widened slightly, but whereas one of the others, namely East, would've probably started giving him shit, Gavin didn't say a word.

"No problem," West said, smoothly, like all he'd been doing was showing me the view.

Yeah. Of his tonsils.

"We'll get out of your way," Gavin said, inclining his head to the opposite side of the roof, where he was walking backward and tugging his date along. "Carry on."

I didn't move an inch as I watched them disappear behind a trellis, and it wasn't until West turned back to face me that I blew out a long breath.

"All clear." That crooked smile told me he was ready to pick up where we'd left off.

My cock seemed to be on board with that as well, but the fog had cleared from my brain, and I held my hand up.

He stopped moving and arched a brow.

"I, uh..." The rush of what I'd just done hit me all at once, and I shook my head. "I just need a minute."

"Of course." West took a step closer, and I tensed, but he gestured toward the ledge. "Just grabbing my drink."

Right. His drink.

Shit, I didn't know why I felt so jumpy all of a sudden, not when my body had been more than agreeable to West's only a couple minutes ago.

He rested an arm on top of the ledge as he faced me, giving me some breathing room even as fire simmered in his eyes.

I lifted my fingers to my mouth, running them across my swollen lips. It was going to be glaringly obvious if I went back down to the party that I'd kissed someone. And if Caleb saw me, he'd put two and two together.

"JT—"

"Nope." I shook my head.

"Fun's over?"

I blinked at him. "What?"

He slipped his free hand into his pocket, and when I caught sight of his erection standing straight up in line with the damn pinstripes on his pants, I pushed away from the wall.

"I, uh..." I gestured toward the door. "I think I should get back and find Caleb."

West's eyebrows hit his hairline, and I turned on my heel and made a beeline for the door before he said something that might change my mind.

The fact that I knew that he *could* change my mind had me hurrying inside. Luckily for me, going down the elevator didn't seem to require any magic, because the second I stepped in front of it, the doors automatically opened.

I moved to the back of the car, half of me hoping the doors would hurry up and shut and the other half hoping West would catch them just before they did.

So much for being his voice of reason. I'd done nothing out there to steer him away from potential trouble. Instead, I'd raised my hand and volunteered to show him the way.

Ha, what a laugh—that everyone had been busy warning *me* to stay away from *him*. Yet here I was, leading the poor guy on. I felt like a shit. Had I somehow given him the wrong impression? That I was into him that way? I ran a hand through my hair and gripped the back of my neck as the doors slid shut and I found myself alone.

The elevator began its descent, and for a moment I panicked, thinking it was going to deposit me back at West's floor. But seconds later I found the doors opening to the lobby and blew out a sigh of relief.

A taxi automatically pulled into the drop-off area where the door was pulled open, and I all but threw myself in the back seat and rattled off the address for my dorm. As the car pulled out into the busy street, I leaned back, closed my eyes, and felt my head start to spin.

What the hell had I just done?

I reached up and touched my lips again, and couldn't help but wonder if I'd just run off the only real friend I'd made since starting at Astor. But there'd been no way I could stay, not after that. Not when my body was writing checks it couldn't cash.

I liked girls.

Had only *ever* liked girls.

But as the taxi turned off Park Avenue, all I could seem to think about was the prince I'd just kissed on top of his damn castle.

SEVENTEEN

THE PARTY TURNED into one of those epic nights that lasted well into Saturday, giving me barely a day to recover from the rager. Which I did from the comfort of my bed, while our condo was put back into place like there hadn't been an overflowing crowd of bodies crammed inside only hours ago. Then Sunday passed by like all good Sundays do, with nothing planned but whatever the hell I wanted—and what I wanted was to lounge around all day and remember the kiss that had taken place on the rooftop. It might've ended quicker than I wanted it to. But the fact that there was something to end at all was a step in the right direction.

At least, that was what I told myself as me and my crew climbed out of the Sprinter van Monday morning and dragged our sorry asses up through the courtyard of Astor.

God, I was definitely still feeling the effects of Friday night's activities. I might have to sit out anything the guys had up their sleeves for at least another day or two until my system fully detoxed.

"Looking a little sloppy over there today, West. Still crying into your pillow over your failed attempt of seduction this weekend?" Donovan's pearly-white grin gleamed in the sunlight. I seriously fantasized about knocking one of his teeth out.

"Who said I failed?"

East snorted as we stopped under one of the massive trees that shaded the benches lining the entrance. "How about you locking yourself in your bedroom all weekend?"

"That doesn't mean shit." I dropped my bag onto the bench. "I just didn't want to be in the way when our furniture was returned."

"Or be seen red-eyed from crying yourself to sleep," Travis interjected.

I looked over at the phone he was always glued to. "Better than getting carpal tunnel from scrolling and mooning over things I can't have all day."

Travis jerked his head up, leveling me with a *fuck you* glare that rivaled even Daire's. "You don't get to say shit to me after the stunt you pulled this weekend."

Ouch, someone was touchy. But hey, while Travis was causing a scene, the guys weren't focused on me. Again, I wasn't above using someone's weakness to my advantage.

"I didn't pull anything. I merely did what I had to in order to secure myself a win in a challenge you assholes threw down. Don't get pissy with me because the target made friends with—"

"The one person I can't stand?"

"I can't stand either of you," Daire said, glaring between the two of us. "So can you shut the fuck up?"

Travis turned on the scowling shadow that always seemed to be wherever we were despite his caustic complaints.

"For someone who can't stand us, you sure as shit manage to loom over us all the time."

Daire pulled a packet of cigarettes out of his jeans pocket and flipped open the lid. "Not by choice."

"Vice versa, asshole," Travis grumbled to himself as he went back to scrolling and Daire walked off, and suddenly, all eyes were back on me.

"So, you tanked it with the golden boy, huh?" Preston grimaced and shrugged his bag up his arm. "Maybe he really is straight and not wanting to experiment. Some people *are* into girls, you know."

I eyed my friend closely, from his perfect, all-American looks to the light blue collared shirt he'd tucked into his navy pants. "Like you?"

The smile he flashed was so charismatic, I really could see him one day following in his father's political footsteps.

"Exactly." Preston shrugged. "Serena and I get each other, you know? So, there's no point in experimenting and looking around when I have someone who understands me."

"Right, but *JT* doesn't have anyone... Not like you do."

"Oh, right," Preston quickly agreed. "I know. I was just saying—"

"That he's going to fail miserably?" East chuckled, like he'd already won the bet. "I already told him that. But he insisted on jinxing himself by preplanning his great vacation."

"I haven't jinxed shit."

East arched one of those pompous eyebrows. "Did your date not flee *your* party on Friday night without a word to anyone?"

"He wasn't my date."

"Ha, so you admit it."

"I don't admit shit. Except he wasn't my date. He was, however, the guy I took up to the rooftop for a more...*private* party."

I'd been keeping this little nugget of information until a moment when I would enjoy it most—like now.

East's eyes narrowed. "Bullshit."

"Um," Gavin said from his spot at the end of the bench. "It's true, actually."

I smirked in his direction. Donovan's brother might've cock-blocked me that night, but he was also witness to my greatness, so I was willing to forgive him.

"How much did he pay you?" East asked, but Gavin's soft smile was answer enough. "Fucking hell." East turned his attention back to me. "You really got Golden Boy up on the roof?"

I couldn't help it—my shoulders straightened and my chest puffed up like I was some sort of proud peacock, or maybe just a cock. Thinking about that moment on our roof had my dick stiffening.

"I did. Why do you think he left without a word?"

"You persuasive motherfucker."

"I told you, I'm going to win this bet."

"I don't know," Preston interjected. "He did run away."

"He did," I admitted. "But not before he kissed me back."

Gavin nodded. "He was definitely kissing him back."

Hell, I might have to get the kid a gift or something with the way he was corroborating my story. But before I could think of what, a familiar face came into view.

I grabbed my backpack and slung it over my shoulder, more than ready to dip out on this conversation, but East grabbed hold of my arm.

"You coming home tonight?"

I chuckled, knowing he was asking if I had plans around town tonight. But I was exhausted, so I'd definitely be staying in.

"Yes, dear. I'll be home for dinner. Feel free to have it waiting for me."

"In your fucking dreams."

"Not unless you serve it off JT's body it's not."

He rolled his eyes, and that made me laugh even harder as I jogged off in JT's direction.

I tracked his head of curls as he made his way through the morning crowds heading into the halls of Astor before the first classes started for the day. All weekend I'd wrestled with the urge to call or text JT to see where his mind was after the party. But something had told me to give him some space—probably the way he'd fled like it was the stroke of midnight and he was going to turn into a fucking pumpkin.

I was done with that now, though. He'd had two days to curse me out in his head, and now it was time to mend fences and all that "friend" stuff, in the hopes that maybe there was some lingering attraction behind his fleeing the scene of the crime.

If not, the bet would be done, and East was going to be *hell* to live with.

"JT," I called out, not wanting him to disappear inside until we'd at least talked to each other. When he came to a stop and turned to face me, I took that as a step in the right direction.

I hurried over, and as I approached I noticed the way his fingers tightened on the strap of his bag. He was nervous, and the only way he was going to even begin to relax was if I played it cool.

Luckily for me, I was the king of cool. I could sell honey to a bee, or so my father always told me.

"Hey you," I said as I came to a stop. "I was wondering if you'd recovered from Friday night."

He gave a forced smile as he nodded, and I knew I had my work cut out for me. I just had to get him talking.

"Yeah. Took a day or so for my head to stop pounding, though."

"Mine too." I snorted. "Nope, that's a lie—pretty sure it's still pounding right now."

JT's lips eased into a more relaxed grin as he laughed. "I'm not surprised with the amount of alcohol you drank that night."

"Hey now, I wasn't the only one. You were tossing back shots right along with me, Golden Boy."

"God, don't remind me." JT reached up and ran a hand through his hair—the same hair I had twisted my fingers in to angle his mouth closer to mine.

"I get that. Might have to lay off the liquor for a couple days."

"A couple?" JT's eyes widened, and he shook his head. "I'm thinking maybe months."

"Months? Now that's just not right."

JT scoffed and looked away, like his mind was on other things, and I knew it was now or never.

"So, you up and disappeared on me Friday night." JT's eyes darted back to mine. I could see the worry swirling in them, and something twisted in my gut—guilt, maybe? "Everything okay?"

JT worried his lower lip as he toed the ground underfoot. "Yeah, I'd just had a lot to drink and was a little tired, that's all. Thought it was smart to head home before I passed out or anything."

Anything was code for: *continued kissing your brains out on the rooftop.*

"I get that. I was tired as hell too. So, did you catch up on sleep?"

His eyes brightened a little because it seemed I would let that particular line of questioning go.

"I did, yeah. I got home and passed out for, like, twelve hours straight."

"Oh yeah? Have any good dreams?" I lowered my eyes to his mouth. "I did."

I heard JT's breath catch as my meaning hit home, but this beating around the bush shit wasn't for me, and if I had any hope in hell of getting him back to the place he'd been on Friday night, I needed to see where his head was.

"Look..." JT said, and glanced over his shoulder.

Shit, put the nail in my coffin right now. He was clearly about to "let me down easy." I was right back to square one.

"I know what happened on Friday night seemed like I was interested in something happening between us." He swallowed. "And I'm sorry I let it get out of hand, but that's just not for me. The whole kissing guys thing. I'd been drinking, and, well..." He shook his head. "That's no excuse. I'm sorry if I led you on."

Wait, what? He's apologizing to me?

Hadn't seen that coming. But I could definitely work with it.

"Oh..." I tried to remember how to feign regret, and judging by the contrite expression on JT's face, I managed to pull it off. "That's okay. You'd told me, and I should've been stronger—"

"No, no." JT stepped forward and put a hand on my arm. "I feel like a total shit. All weekend I was trying to work out what to say to you because you'd been so nice, and then I went and led you on..."

"JT, stop. It's cool, okay? We just got our wires a little crossed, that's all." And almost our swords, but I wasn't going to push my luck by reminding him. We were finally back on the right track, and I just had to reassure him we were all good. "It was just a kiss, and, well, if you ever change your mind, you know I'm a good time."

A relieved laugh burst free of JT, but he shook his head. "I won't."

I stepped around him, happy to leave well enough alone. But as I did, I spotted Dean Hawthorne across the courtyard, staring at me and her son with an incensed expression on her face.

My, my, she does not *look happy.*

This morning was turning out to be much better than I'd anticipated.

"Okay, so we're good, right? Friends?" I said, placing my hand on his arm.

JT nodded. "Friends."

"Good. Well, you've gotta get to class, and so do I, I guess."

"Right."

"Can I text you later?"

That relaxed *friendly* smile of his was back in full force, the relief from stressing all weekend now gone.

"Sure, I'd like that."

"Of course you would. I'll see you then."

"See you."

With a little extra pep in my step, I walked off across the courtyard. As I got closer to the dean, I couldn't help but smirk and toss her a wink before I made my way to class like the good boy I wasn't.

EIGHTEEN

LATER THAT AFTERNOON, I found a spot at an empty table in the quad and tossed my bag in one of the chairs before dropping down in another. It wasn't quite as hot out as it had been last week, but I was still grateful for the shade from the honey locust tree nearby.

While I didn't mind the downtime between classes, part of me wished I'd had them back to back to knock them all out in a smaller time frame. Something to think about for next semester.

I unzipped my bag, grabbed a notebook and pen, and then flipped it to an empty page. My mind wandered, and I wasn't surprised who it wandered to.

A pair of lust-filled blue eyes seared my memory, and for once I wished I was an artist so I could commit them to a drawing. Instead, all I had were words. Poetry was like therapy for me; it always had been. I'd spent all weekend wondering if it was the alcohol that made me kiss West or if there'd been some desire lying dormant in my brain that had chosen that moment to make an appearance.

But none of it made sense. I hadn't been drunk enough to not realize exactly what I was doing. Even though West made the first move, I'd *asked* him to kiss me again. Why? Because he'd been really fucking good at it, not because I had some kind of simmering attraction.

Seeing him today had eased any anxiety I'd had about the kiss changing our friendship, though, because he hadn't seemed any different. He hadn't made it weird, so I wouldn't either. We were fine. That night could be chalked up to feeling a good buzz and an amazing view. It wouldn't happen again.

Didn't mean I wasn't going to write about it, though.

Lost in thought, I didn't look up as someone loomed over me. Once I had an idea, I had to finish writing it before it vanished.

But the second I smelled the floral musk of my mom's perfume, my head shot up to see her forcing a warm smile.

"Mom, hey." I sat up straight, closing my notebook before she could catch a glimpse of what I'd been working on.

"Your dad and I missed you this weekend," she said by way of greeting, setting my bag on the ground to make room for her to join me. As she crossed her ankles, her astute eyes trailed over my face. As if to check I was still in one piece after my first week at Astor.

"Yeah, sorry, I ended up having more to catch up on than I realized." No way in hell was I going to admit *why* that was the case or where I'd been. Or that my thoughts had been consumed with nothing but analyzing every second of Friday night with West.

Who was I kidding? I'd been replaying every interaction with West and wondering if I'd fucked up royally. But he'd alleviated all that stress in the easygoing way he had, and it felt like a weight off my shoulders.

Even if in the back of my mind I wondered what it meant that I'd enjoyed the kiss—

"JT?" My mom's voice cut through my thoughts, and I swallowed, pushing aside those questions for later. She frowned, crossing her arms. "You seem distracted."

"Not at all." I gave her a reassuring smile. "What's up?"

"I asked why you had so much to catch up on that you couldn't stop by to let us know how your first week went."

"Oh. Just, uh...getting used to everything. It *is* my first time living on my own, you know. I didn't want to run back to you guys so you'd think I'd made a mistake."

The concern etched in Mom's brow eased slightly. "Oh, honey, we know it's a lot to take in. We just missed you, that's all."

How was it moms were so good at the guilt thing? Did it just come naturally, or was there a manual?

"I missed you guys too. I'll stop by soon. Just wanna get settled here first."

"Of course." But the way she drummed her nails along the table told me there was something else she wanted to talk about. I tossed my pen on my notebook and got comfortable.

"What's on your mind?"

"I was just...wondering if you'd made any friends yet."

The question seemed innocent enough, but the last time I'd seen her, she warned me about a group of troublemakers that happened to include West. Had she seen us somewhere? Or was that my guilt talking?

I kept it light, assuming it was the latter, because the last thing I wanted her to know was that I'd ignored her advice.

"You're not worried about me, are you?" I said.

"I'm always worried about you. That's what being a parent is all about." She reached toward me like she wanted to rub my arm, but thought better about it in front of my peers and sat back. "Without Corey and Elise and your other friends here, I was just curious if you've gotten to know anyone yet."

"It's been a week."

"I know. Sometimes it takes a while."

I wasn't running to tell her about West, but I didn't think Caleb would be on her radar. Especially since he was so anti-West's group. "Actually, I did meet someone pretty cool at the coffee bar the other day. Name's Caleb."

At least, I assumed we were still friends after I'd ditched him at the party Friday. Something I'd have to find an explanation and apology for...later.

"Honey, that's great." A genuine smile lit up her face, and she squeezed my forearm.

I chuckled. "You seem so surprised."

"Not at all, I just..." She swallowed as she glanced away, and when she looked back at me, I saw it—the worry that had been written all over her face was back, and this time she didn't try to hide the reason why. "Did I see you with Weston LaRue earlier?"

Oh shit. No wonder she was acting strange.

Heat crept up the back of my neck, but I tried to keep my tone casual. "West? Yeah, I met him at the coffee bar too."

Not *technically* a lie, but not exactly the first place we'd met.

I lifted a shoulder, like it was no big deal. "He seems like a nice guy."

"Weston LaRue?" she repeated.

"Yeah, I think that's his name." God, I was such a shit liar.

"Didn't I tell you to stay away from that group?"

Yes, yes, you did.

"Mom, I'm not gonna be an asshole to someone I don't know. He was friendly, so I was friendly back." Maybe a little more than friendly, but that was the last thing I needed popping into my head right now.

"I know you always come from a genuine place, but West and his friends..." She let out a long sigh. "It's never anything good with that group. The headaches they've given me over the years are only part of that reason."

"Like what?" Curiosity had those words coming out before I could stop them.

"There's no need for us to get into all that," she said, waving her hand like she could swat them away. "Just what rich, entitled boys are sometimes. You don't belong anywhere near them."

"I guess I should cancel the overnight camping trip we planned for the weekend, then," I joked.

An inelegant snort left her, so unlike my mom, and she shook her head. "If any of them have seen the inside of a tent before, I'd die of surprise. Like I said, JT. Not your people."

I could hear that warning nice and clear, but she had it all wrong. Not the rich, entitled part, but that there wasn't anything good that came out of their group. My time with them had been nothing but fun, like the typical college experience I'd expected. Parties and drinking, even with my being underage, wasn't exactly scandalous. Not compared to what I *could* be out there doing.

"Mom, you worry too much. I love you for it, but it's really unnecessary."

As I ran a hand through my hair, I caught the stares aimed our way from some of my classmates, and my cheeks flushed with unease.

"Can I come see you later?" I said, dropping my voice low. "Everyone's looking at us."

A quick glance told her that was indeed the case. She let out a resigned sigh, nodding as she rose from the chair. "Don't be a stranger, JT. And please...just be careful."

"I promise."

She gave me a thin smile before walking off, and as I watched her go, a part of me felt guilty about running her off, while another part had the common sense to panic a little about her warning. Not because I believed West and his friends had bad intentions, but because I didn't like lying to my mom.

But she was wrong about those guys, and I wasn't going to let someone else's opinion of my new friends influence me over what I'd experienced firsthand.

I picked up my pen, tapping it on the notebook before flipping back to the page I'd been working on. Poetry had always been a way for me to get my thoughts out of my brain and into some kind of organized flow that made sense on paper. And Lord knew I had nothing but jumbled thoughts from the weekend that I needed to work out.

NINETEEN

west

"YOU BETTER NOT be punking out on us again tonight." East's voice filtered through my bedroom door before he pushed it open and strolled inside, a martini glass in one hand and a tumbler with amber-colored liquor in the other.

I glanced up at him from my bed with my computer on my lap and took the drink he offered.

"I didn't punk out on you. I took a vow of sobriety—"

"To detox that liver of yours. I know. Well, you've had your three days, and now it's time you confess your sins."

"My *sins*?"

East took a sip of his drink. "Did you or did you not try to corrupt a golden boy through gluttony and lust this past weekend?" He smirked, pulled a rosary from his pocket, and started to swing it around his finger.

I knew exactly where he was going with this. I also

knew the detox after this night was going to take a lot longer than three days.

"I did."

"That's what I thought. And did you or did you not befriend this boy to win a challenge?"

"A challenge *you* initiated."

"I know. That's why it's time we go to Church." East raised a haughty brow as he took another sip. "We've got a *lot* of repenting to do."

I snorted and shook my head. "More like you feel an urge to get down on your knees and—"

"Pray? Yes. I do believe it's time he heard his name on my tongue again."

"Jesus—"

"Nope. I believe 'oh God' might be the more direct route."

"Get the hell out of here." I picked up a pillow and threw it at East's retreating back as he headed to the door. Then I settled back against my headboard and took another sip of my drink.

The bourbon felt good as it warmed a path down my throat and relaxed my body and mind after spending the last couple of hours catching up on school work. But as I saved the last half of my essay and shut down my computer, East's idea of going out became more and more appealing.

The few days I'd given myself to recover from our party had done the trick, and now that I was feeling myself again, I was ready to hit the town and see what trouble we could get into. I pushed my laptop aside and drained the rest of my drink, and then an idea sprang to mind.

East had mentioned going to Church to confess my sins, and maybe, *just* maybe, JT would want to do a little confessing of his own. God knows he'd certainly apologized to me enough over the last couple of days to indicate he might be in need of a little contrition. But I wasn't sure about his stance on the whole Church thing.

Should I or shouldn't I?

Who the hell was I kidding? I was totally going to ask him. We'd gotten past the kiss debacle. I was back in the friend zone, and what kind of friend would I be if I didn't invite him to join us tonight?

I scooped up my phone and opened up a text message to JT.

> Hey there, Golden Boy, what are you up to?

I got to my feet and headed into the closet, looking for an appropriate outfit. There was a pretty specific dress code for the congregants of this establishment, and as my eyes trailed over my choices, I grinned to myself, realizing that if JT did show then this might just work out in my favor.

You know, God's plan and all? Because despite JT's

protests that he wasn't into the "kissing guys" deal, I remembered the way he'd reacted the first time he spotted me at the party last week. I'd worn black on black that night, and there'd been a distinct shift in the air as he looked me over. Not to mention a very *intense* reaction later that night.

So yes, this could definitely work in my favor—*if* JT answered my damn text.

I grabbed a black coat, shirt, and pants, and then my phone vibrated. I picked it up, swiped open the message, and shook my head at his response.

GOLDEN BOY:

Hey. Was just getting into bed until my phone went off.

Getting in bed? Seriously?

GOLDEN BOY:

Yes, seriously. It's 10:30 on a weeknight. What else would I be doing?

I shook my head as I walked into my en suite and flicked on the light.

Do you really want me to answer that?
Because I will, in great detail.

I could practically see him frowning at his phone, trying to decide how to answer. I put my cell down on the counter and stripped out of my shirt, and as I tossed it in the laundry basket, my phone vibrated again.

GOLDEN BOY:

Thanks, but I'd rather be spared the nightmares ;)

Ouch... I was just going to say that you should be working on your homework, JT.

Lies. All lies. And he knew it. But hey, two could play at this game, and if he wanted to be "friends" then a friend I would be.

BUT since you're not doing homework, I have a better idea instead.

GOLDEN BOY:

I'm almost afraid to ask….

> Then I'll spare you the trouble. Get up.
> Get out of bed. And get dressed.

I shoved my sweats and briefs to the floor and kicked out of them.

GOLDEN BOY:

Ok, bossy much? Clearly I'm up (thanks for that) and not in bed yet. I said I was getting there.

> And dressed? Don't forget that. Are you dressed?

He sent back an eyeroll emoji.

GOLDEN BOY:

I'm up, of course I'm dressed.

I smirked and leaned my bare ass up against the counter.

. . .

> I'm up too, but I'm completely naked. So I just thought I'd check.

Three dots appeared and then disappeared, and as I let him think about that for a couple of minutes—and yes, it *was* minutes, not seconds—I turned on the shower.

Finally, a message popped up that had me grinning from ear to ear.

GOLDEN BOY:

> Again with the nightmares. Now I need to go and scrub my eyeballs out.

> See, great minds think alike. I'm about to take a shower too.

Hmm, think about that a little bit...*friend*. And when it seemed he was, a little longer than normal, I added—

> Then I'm going to get dressed, go downstairs, and head to your dorm.

. . .

That got a response.

GOLDEN BOY:

You're going to what? No, you can't.

> What have I told you about the word "can't," JT? It doesn't exist for me, and since we're friends, it doesn't exist for you either. It's Wednesday night, which means it's time to go out.

I held my breath for a second, wondering if he'd push back some more, decide to take a stand.

GOLDEN BOY:

That's what Wednesday night means?

I knew I had him.

> That or hump day. I mean, I am naked...

GOLDEN BOY:

Where are we going?

My cock throbbed at knowing I was going to see him tonight, and I reached down to give it a firm squeeze.

Can't tell you.

GOLDEN BOY:

What are we doing?

Can't tell you that either. All you need to know is I'll be there in twenty. Dress up, and in black.

GOLDEN BOY:

Uh...this isn't a cult, is it?

It's not a cult. Trust me?

I held my breath and stared at the phone—knowing I didn't deserve his trust but wanting it all the same. Then his message came through and I blew out a sigh of relief.

GOLDEN BOY:

I trust you. I'll see you in twenty.

I put my phone down and stepped into the shower, and as the warm water sluiced down over my body, I thought that while I might be going to Church tonight, I had feeling it wasn't going to do shit to keep me out of hell.

TWENTY

THEY PICKED ME up in a limo. A fucking limo.

To go two miles across town, which, even with traffic, hadn't taken more than twenty minutes. If ever I needed a reminder that money was no object to these guys, things like this proved it.

West hadn't told me where we were going, but as I stared up at the towering Gothic Revival structure we'd pulled up to, I knew this couldn't be the right place.

"You got me all dressed up to take me to church?" I joked, because there was no other explanation for what this place was. Even the stained glass of the window depicted a set of wings and other art that could only be described as holy.

I tugged at the collar of the black dress shirt I'd had to unpack from a box in the back of my closet as West turned to give me a sly grin.

"Feeling a little...on edge?"

"No," I said too quickly, causing him to chuckle. He didn't need to know I hadn't set foot in a church before. My parents had been on the morally upright side, just not the religious side. Was I even allowed to go inside?

More to the point, how were *they*?

The exterior of the church remained dark except for a couple of low spotlights along the ground. Enough to light our path to the front entrance—

Which, apparently, as the group veered off to the left, was not where we were going.

Oh shit... "Are we breaking in?" I whispered to West, keeping close in the dark.

"You think I'd wear these shoes if we were?"

I couldn't see a thing in the utter black, but I knew for a fact he wasn't in a pair of sneakers. Not when the rest of him was decked out in a suit jacket and slacks.

Not that I'd noticed what he was wearing other than in relation to what I was.

At the front of the group, Travis rounded a rail on the side of the church, the only indication anything was there at all, and led us down a short set of stairs, lit only by a couple of lanterns hanging along the wall. As he came to a stop in front of the arched wooden door, he pulled a beaded necklace over his head, and one by one I watched the other guys do the same—some from their pockets; others wore them on their bodies.

Like he could see the question written all over my face, West lifted his arm to show me the black and silver rosary wrapped around his wrist, the cross dangling between his fingers. Only it didn't look like just a cross, it looked like...a key of some sort.

By the time I looked back up, a couple of the guys had already disappeared inside. Gavin inserted his key into a panel on the wall, and the door inched open enough for him and his date to squeeze inside before shutting again.

"You're with me," West murmured in my ear, and something about his breath on my neck and the proximity of him in the darkness had me remembering exactly how he'd felt against me the other night. I repressed a shiver as he added, "You don't mind, do you?"

I shook my head, even as I wondered what that meant. What *was* this place? Some kind of secret society? Would they be doing blood rituals and sacrificing goats? Or worse?

Finally it was West's turn, and we entered a small, low-lit chamber that was a little too reminiscent of a dungeon. Even the smell reminded me of something dark and damp. It didn't seem at all like a place a group like the Park Avenue Princes would ever be caught dead in, but there they all were, Travis and the others who entered before us, waiting for the rest of the group in silence.

When Donovan pulled up the rear, he nodded at Travis, who again took the lead by walking over to what looked like a simple stone wall. He felt around the stones with his hand before finding what he was looking for, and once he inserted his key into a hole I couldn't even see, a door popped open on the right. And with that, the sultry sounds of slow jazz with a heavy bass filtered into the chamber.

Based on the music alone, I didn't have to be religious to know whatever was happening inside was definitely *not* a church service.

"You have got to be kidding me," I said under my breath when the first thing I saw was a tremendous, glittering chandelier hanging over a small circular bar, looking like something out of *The Phantom of the Opera*. The second thing was the smell—it was fucking amazing, luxurious and sexy, and I took in a deep inhale as I tried to place what it was. Sandalwood? Some bergamot or citrus? Whatever it was, I wanted to bottle it up and bring it home with me.

"You gonna keep sniffin' the air, or do you wanna have some fun?" East's shoulder knocked against mine as he passed, causing West to throw him a curse.

As I took in the view, I realized why we were all dressed in our best—and in black.

Because everyone else was.

"What is this place?"

"You already know." West winked. "Welcome to Church. Come on, I'll show you around."

The burlesque dancers putting on a show in the middle of the room explained the music choice, but they were the least shocking thing about this place.

Far dirtier deeds were happening in the green velvet booths lining the perimeter of the room, which wasn't nearly as large as it looked from the outside. A flash of skin to my right had me averting my eyes, but the next table over wasn't any better. That sure as hell wasn't powdered sugar on a silver platter being snorted.

"So this is an anything-goes kind of place," I said, putting my hands in my pockets as West continued to give me a tour.

"Everywhere can be anything goes if you want it to, but this one caters to a certain clientele."

"A rich one."

"A members-only one." His hand moved to my lower back as he switched direction toward a row of nondescript black doors. "Have any sins you need to confess?"

"What do you mean?"

"Those are confessional booths. Although I suppose they're better suited to commit sins in rather than confess." West leaned in close. "Want to see?"

I swallowed, taking a small step back. Like everything else in this room, the air of sex and depravity was overwhelming, and I had no clue what I was doing in a place like this.

"Relax," West said, closing the space between us. "It's a bar first, and whatever you desire second." He gestured to the bar, where several of his friends already had drinks in their hands. "Come on, let's get something that won't make our heads a throbbing mess tomorrow."

I tamped down the hesitation that came from feeling entirely out of place and agreed, letting West order me a white Russian. That would be safe enough, as long as I didn't throw back shots along with it.

It was amazing what a little alcohol could do for getting rid of your nerves. A couple of drinks in, and I was laughing along with the rest of them. The music had changed over to a faster, harder beat, and the burlesque dancers had been switched out for the crowd to get in on the action.

"I have a question for you," I said to West as he leaned against the bar beside me. "What do you guys do when you're not partying?"

"Sleep. Sex. Eat. Sex. Occasionally grace Astor with our presence."

I laughed. "You're obnoxious."

"I prefer charming."

Rolling my eyes, I shoved his bicep, ignoring the way it flexed under my hand. "Seriously, what about normal people stuff. Do you go to the theatre? Venture into Central Park? Do your own damn homework?"

"I'll have you know I was finishing up an essay before East interrupted."

"Really?"

West narrowed his eyes. "You don't think I know how to string a few sentences together?"

"It's not that, I just figured you could pay off someone else to do it."

"You're right. I could." He twisted the gold band on his finger. "But I don't. Can't just be a pretty face."

When I chuckled, West feigned offense.

"What? You don't think I have a pretty face either?"

In the back of my mind I knew he was taunting me,

wanting me to tell him he was as attractive as he already knew he was. West didn't need me to say it. He just wanted to hear it.

I could see it now that I really looked at him. I could respect when a guy was good looking, but I'd never really noticed beyond that. But I'd kissed *this* guy. What was it about him that had made me do that?

His sky-blue eyes certainly grabbed attention. They were both warm and inscrutable at the same time, and you were never quite sure what he was thinking.

Maybe it was the cocky way he smiled, or the confident way he carried himself in clothes that fit his body to perfection. My fingers could attest to that, having felt the solid muscle of his chest and abs when I asked him to kiss me.

I'd also felt something else rock solid, but I'd tried not to think that about for days now.

It had all been a drunken mistake, one that wouldn't be repeated. That didn't mean I couldn't appreciate how very attractive West really was.

He just wasn't my type, was all.

I sucked down another swallow of my drink, glad I'd gone with something that wasn't too strong. I needed to keep my head on straight tonight—something that had never been a problem in the past.

"Earth to JT?"

I blinked West's face back into focus. "Sorry, what?"

"See, my face is so pretty, you're daydreamin' about it."

"Actually, I was just trying to avoid hurting your feelings."

He gave a knowing look. "Sure you were."

God, some people were just too good looking for their own good. But that was the last thing I needed to focus on tonight. It was time to change topics.

"So how'd you hear about this place?"

"Hear about it?" West shook his head, his eyes twinkling with mischief. "We didn't hear about it. We launched it."

"Launched it? What do you mean?"

West turned and rested back against the bar, looking out at the sea of people mingling with one another, and I did the same. There were men and women dancing in any and all combinations, but the one glaringly obvious thing was that these people were not your everyday crowd.

They were too beautiful, too glamorous. They wore clothes worth more than all of my belongings put together. Diamonds and crystals glittered on their wrists and necks, the bling sparkling under the enormous chandelier, and they handed over black credit cards with cash tips—minimum a hundred dollars.

They were unlike any people I'd ever associated with. Yet here I was, standing with one of them.

"The owners of the bar approached us, knowing if we showed, so would the rest of Manhattan's upper—"

West cut himself off, and I arched a brow. "Upper *class?*"

"Uh, yeah."

"Sounds obnoxious, right?"

"Only when you point it out."

I pursed my lips. "Yeah, but I didn't this time."

"Shut up."

I chuckled as he turned back to the crowded dance floor, enjoy myself a little too much at his expense. It wasn't his fault he'd been born with a silver—hell, probably gold—spoon in his mouth. But sometimes it was nice to remind him of his elitist take on life.

Hey, he'd been the one to tell me to ground him.

"You gonna dance tonight?" West said, gesturing to the crowd. "Or you going to be a wallflower like you were at the club last week?"

"I wasn't a wallflower."

He scoffed. "Please, you practically melted into the damn thing."

"Says the man who was gyrating all over his dance partner."

As soon as the words left my mouth, I wanted to take them back. But it was too late, and when West winked at me, the heat in my cheeks intensified.

"Glad you noticed."

I rolled my eyes, doing my best to play it off. "Oh, get over yourself."

He downed the rest of his drink, and just as he was about to speak, I heard, "LaRue?" from somewhere behind us.

West turned, that magnetic smile flashing bright enough to replace the light overhead. "Blake? I didn't know you were back in town. Where the hell have you been?"

"Oh, you know me, here and there."

My eyes tracked the newcomer—Blake—as he made his way around the small bar. Just like the rest of this crowd, it was clear the man was rich as Midas. The black choker surrounding his neck with a large diamond at the center of it told me that much. As did the gorgeous lace bustier that showed off his leanly muscled shoulders.

Now, I wasn't one to stare, but when I trailed my eyes down to the leather pants that were glued to his trim waist and long legs, and got to a pair of six-inch heels, I winced.

Blake pointed a toe in my direction. "Aren't they gorgeous? Brand-new Jimmy Choos. They were worth every penny, and if West here tells me he's going to dance with me, they'll also be worth the pain."

I looked between the two men staring at me and then shook my head. "I don't know that *anything* would be worth the pain those would inflict."

West put his empty glass down on the counter and leaned in to bump arms with mine. "That's because you've never danced with me."

A shiver raced up my spine, and I couldn't be sure if it was from the contact, or what he'd said. But before I could overanalyze it, West pushed off the bar and reached for Blake's waist, then leaned in to kiss his cheek.

"Blake?" West looked back at where I stood frozen in place, and I imagined what it might be like to— *Nope, not going there.* "This is my new friend, JT. He just started at Astor this year."

Blake cozied in to West's side and ran a hand down his chest, a lighthearted laugh floating out of his mouth.

That laugh was annoying.

"Nice to meet you, JT." Blake looked between West and me. "*Just* friends?"

I almost wanted to refute that, if only to get him to go away. We'd been having a good time before he interrupted.

Before I could answer, West smirked at the intruder. "I do have platonic friends, Blake."

"Not sure where the fun is in that. But it does make it easier to steal you away." Blake's eyes flashed to mine. "You don't mind, do you?"

Hell yes I did.

But I didn't say anything at all, because Blake didn't wait for a response before wrapping his arm around West's waist and pulling him away.

"One dance," West called out to me before disappearing into the crowd with the interloper.

"Another," I said to the bartender after I drained the rest of my drink and pushed the empty glass his way. There wasn't much I could do besides wait. Around the room I could see the others we came with, but I didn't feel like joining anyone right now. Not when Blake, a full head above the dancers, could be seen all over West.

Was that his type? Arrogant guys in heels? Or did West prefer them like the one from the concert? Did he even *have* a preference, or was he into everything and everyone?

Whatever—if dancing or gyrating or getting naked with someone in a club was what he was into, then it wasn't my business. I didn't care. I just thought he'd invited me to come hang out with him tonight, and here I was, standing alone at the bar.

I finished off one drink without him.

Then two.

By the time the bartender handed me the third, I was past the point of impatience.

Grabbing my drink, I pushed off the bar and headed toward where I'd last seen them. I stopped at the edge of the crowd and looked around, but I didn't see them anywhere.

What the hell? West wouldn't have left me here. Maybe he'd gone back to the bar and I'd somehow missed him—

I did a double take as I caught sight of them heading toward one of the confessional booths. Blake pulled open the door and turned to West, a seductive smile on his face, one that, even from a distance, I could see West returned.

My heart pounded harder as I realized what was happening. What those private rooms were for.

West's hands were low on Blake's stomach as he said something, and Blake shook his head, that smile never dimming. He gripped the back of West's neck, pulling him into the booth. As the door slammed shut behind them, my stomach dropped to my feet.

All of a sudden it was too hot, too loud, too not my scene. I couldn't believe West had invited me here only to ditch me to go hook up. Why bother inviting me at all?

I had to get out of there.

Did I leave the way I'd come in or what?

"Where's the exit?" I shouted to the bartender, setting my half-full drink aside. He pointed to where another couple was slipping out a hidden door, and I followed, knocking into people in my hurry to leave.

Turned out I wasn't much of a fan of Church after all.

TWENTY-ONE

west

BLAKE TUGGED ME inside the confessional, a favorite haunt of mine on my visits to Church, and the door shut behind us, making everything pitch black. I couldn't see Blake anymore, but I could feel his hand on the back of my neck as he pulled me closer for a kiss. Any other night I might've welcomed this little interlude, but I'd left JT at the bar a while ago. No doubt one of my friends had joined him for a drink if they saw him standing alone, so I wasn't worried about JT finding a girl to spend his time with. And maybe I'd been gone long enough to have him wonder about me. If he was still feeling even a bit of the connection between us at the party, then maybe a little jealousy would serve its purpose.

So unfortunately for Blake, this wasn't going to happen tonight.

I pushed against his chest as I leaned back.

"Playing hard to get?" he said.

"I am, but not with you." I found the door latch and popped it open. "Maybe another time."

Blake let out a groan as I kissed his cheek, and then I stepped out of the confessional, leaving him inside. The man was a great dance partner, but my cock wasn't interested. Not with JT only a few feet away.

I headed to the side of the bar where I'd left him—

But JT wasn't there.

Frowning, I scanned the bar, the dance floor, the booths. Nowhere.

Maybe he'd gone to the bathroom.

I'd started in that direction when a hand landed on my shoulder.

"He left," Gavin said as I turned to face him.

"What?"

"JT. I saw him leave—"

"When?"

"Just now."

"Why the hell didn't you stop him?"

Not that he needed to tell me why. The reason was standing right behind him, a finger looped through Gavin's belted pants—his boyfriend, Joey.

He tried to explain anyway. "Sorry, we were busy with—"

I held up a hand and cursed. Why the hell had JT *left*?

"You can probably still catch him," Gavin offered.

I ran out the door into the muggy night toward the front of the building. The limo we'd taken idled nearby, but if JT had ditched the bar, he wasn't above ditching a ride too.

This late at night, the sidewalks weren't crowded, especially in this stretch of avenue, and I instantly spotted his lean body about a block away. I took off at a run, not letting JT leave without an explanation.

"JT," I called out when I was several feet away.

His head snapped toward me and he stopped.

"Leaving without saying goodbye?" I tried to keep my tone light, but I couldn't help that a sliver of annoyance crept in.

"You disappeared. I figured you wouldn't care."

Oh, he was pissed. The bitter edge of his words told me that, and if they hadn't, the fire in his eyes would've.

"You knew where I was. You could've come and joined in."

JT gave a curt shake of his head. "I don't think so."

"I guess asking you to come back is a waste of time, then."

"Yeah. I'm just gonna go."

I could feel the tension in the air between us. "Let me give you a ride," I said, shooting a text to our driver.

"No thanks."

I pinned him with a look. "I wasn't asking."

"And I'm done following your orders. I can find my own way."

This attitude wasn't one I'd seen from him before. While a small part of me was irritated as shit, this was also pretty fucking hot. JT's handsome face was set in a scowl that set off his pouty lips, and I knew I could harness the energy radiating off him into something much hotter.

If I could just get him in the limo.

"While I appreciate a stubborn ass from time to time, you have two options here. You can either get in the car or suffer the long walk home with me. I can assure you, there's only one reasonable choice here." As the limo slowed to a stop beside us, I lifted a brow. "So what'll it be?"

"I don't need you to do me any favors," he grumbled.

I rolled my eyes and opened the door. "Just get the fuck inside, JT."

JT narrowed his eyes on me and I could see that one part of him wanted to tell me to go to hell, but the other part...

He muttered something under his breath as he walked to the door I held open for him.

"For the record, I'm only doing this because it will get me home faster."

Someone was definitely in a mood, and it was time to find out why.

I leaned in until only a few inches separated us, and it didn't escape my notice the way JT's breath caught and held. "For the record, I don't care why. I just care that you get in—*now*."

Those usually warm eyes of JT's shot daggers at me as he finally climbed inside. I followed and shut the door behind us, and decided to sit on the opposite side of the limo to give him his space.

I knocked on the divider between myself and the driver, and as the car slowly pulled away from the curb, I settled back and eyed JT, who was busy staring at anything and everything we passed by.

That just wouldn't do. I had approximately two miles to get him talking to me again.

"So, you gonna tell me what crawled up your ass between the moment I left you at the bar until now? Or would you just like me to look instead?"

JT's eyes finally locked on mine, and his pissed-off expression had my cock standing up to take notice.

"I'll pass, thanks."

"You sure?" My lips crooked into a smirk that made his scowl darken even further, but hey, at least I was getting a reaction. "I'm told I'm helpful with that kind of thing."

"Looking at asses?" JT fired back. "Why am I not surprised?"

I lounged back and stretched my arm along the seat, and when I let my legs fall wide open, JT's eyes automatically shifted to them.

Ah, there it is... I'd been hoping to see if there was a chance that all this posturing and frustration was stemming from jealousy.

I raised a brow. "You seem very worked up tonight, Golden Boy. What's going on with you?"

JT rolled his eyes so hard I was surprised they didn't fall right out of his head.

"I'm not worked up. I'm just... It's just... Is this what you *do* all the time? Go out, party, hook up with random strangers?"

"We've already had this conversation—well, part of it. So how about we just skip to that last part, which I think is the real reason you're so fired up?"

"I'm not fired up."

"If you were any *more* fired up, I would be a pile of ashes right now. You're pissed off, and I want to know why. But since you don't want to talk about that, let's start with my random hookup."

"I don't want—"

"First off, Blake is not random. He's a good friend who, at times, I've had benefits with."

"A *friend?*"

"Yes."

JT frowned as I ran my eyes down over him. The message I'd just delivered was received loud and clear: *The door is wide open for you here...*friend.

The question was, would he be brave enough to walk through?

"And second, I didn't hook up with him tonight. Something you would've known if you'd bothered to wait for me. Instead, you ran away like you were fleeing a crime scene."

JT swallowed and angled his chin up a fraction. "I didn't *flee* anywhere. I just decided to leave. I usually do that when I've been ditched and left at a bar to hang out on my own."

"Hmm." I tapped my fingers along the back of the seat. "So what you're saying is, you didn't have a good time tonight."

JT let out a long-suffering sigh as the fight seem to drain out of him. "It was okay."

"Just okay?" I cocked my head to the side, studying him, then decided to dig a little deeper. "You seemed to be having a good time when *we* were talking."

"I was," he snapped. "But then you left."

"Ah, I see." And boy, did I. "That explains everything."

"What does?"

"The reason your night was just okay. The *reason* it wasn't good." I leaned forward in my seat and whispered, "I left."

A look of confusion entered JT's eyes.

"*I'm* the good time, sweetheart. I already told you that."

JT scoffed. "Do you think before you talk, or do you just say the first thing that comes to mind?"

"I didn't say it. You did."

"I did *not* say that."

"Yeah, you did."

"No I didn't."

"Did you or did you not just say, 'I was having a good time and then you left'? Hence, *I'm* the good time."

JT opened his mouth to refute that, then shocked the

hell out of me by busting out laughing. All of his anger and annoyance left him as he shook his head.

"Admit it," I said.

"I'm not admitting anything."

"Eh, well, at least you're smiling now—and looking less like you want to kill me."

"It wasn't you I wanted to kill." He bit down on his lip as soon as the words tumbled out.

"JT—"

"Forget I just said that." He rubbed a hand over his face, and the tension from seconds ago started to vibrate between us all over again.

"I don't think so."

"West..."

"Who did you want to kill? Blake?"

He looked to the ceiling of the limo, anywhere but at me. "I don't even know Blake."

"That's not an answer."

JT swiped his tongue over his lower lip and brought his eyes back to mine. "I'm sure he's very nice."

I grinned. "He is. But that's still not an answer."

"Well, maybe I don't have an answer."

"You know..." I ran my eyes down over his messy head of curls, heated cheeks, and slick lower lip, to where his dress shirt was tucked into his pants—and the distinct outline of his cock. "I might believe that if you could look me in the eye longer than five seconds and your dick wasn't hard."

JT cursed and went to cover himself.

"I wouldn't do that if I were you. I hear rubbing it just makes the condition worse." JT snorted despite himself, and I scooted to the edge of my seat. "Why did you want to kill Blake?"

He bit down into his lower lip, and I nodded.

"You can say it."

"Say what?"

I winked at him and reached out to draw a circle over his knee. "That he stole your good time."

JT's eyes lowered to my mouth, and I could see the battle with what he thought he wanted and what he *really* wanted playing out right in front of me.

He whispered, "Well, looks like I just stole it back."

TWENTY-TWO

WEST'S EYES HEATED at my words, and his hand went still on my knee.

"You wanted me all to yourself," he said, his voice coming out in a low growl that had my dick reacting. "You have me. Now what?"

My pulse stuttered as the realization of what my body wanted clashed with my mind. There was no two ways about it: I'd gotten jealous. *Jealous.* Of West's attention being anywhere but on me.

And now that he was here, close enough to touch but somehow still too far, I didn't know how to be honest about what I wanted.

I sucked in a shaky breath. "You...promised me a good time."

The hand on my knee gripped a little harder. "I did," he said carefully. "But I need you to be specific here. What is it you want from me, JT?"

I licked my lips as my cock throbbed insistently, then dropped my gaze to the way it strained beneath my pants.

"I see." West dropped his hand from my leg, but before I could tell him not to stop touching me, he slid off the leather seat...and onto his knees.

The sight of him moving in between my thighs made me swallow hard.

"Do me a favor, JT." He rose so that his hands were planted on the seat on either side of me, his face only inches from mine. I had a feeling I'd do whatever he wanted in that moment, but then he said, "Hit the call button beside you."

I did it, pressing the button that connected us to the driver.

"My guest wants a tour of the city," West said, his mouth curving up on one side as held my stare. "Keep driving until I say otherwise."

Oh shiiit.

As soon as the driver confirmed, West didn't waste another second to close the space between us and take my lips in a kiss so possessive I felt it through every nerve ending in my body.

If I'd thought the night of the party was a fluke, that my reaction to kissing West was somehow related to anything other than the man himself, this proved it wasn't. No, his mouth covering mine was electric. Hot and demanding, his tongue swept along my lower lip, and I opened for him, craving another taste.

It was better than I remembered, at once settling the envy that had coursed through my veins, but replacing it with something even more dangerous: a shit-ton of lust.

West cursed as I fisted his shirt, tugging him closer. The friction of his hips rubbing against mine as we kissed didn't do a thing to ease the ache in my dick. In fact, it only made it worse, made me want more than just his mouth on mine.

I thrust my hips up, greedy for more as I gripped West's ass with one hand, causing a low rumble to leave his chest.

"Fuck, JT," he breathed against my lips as he moved his hand down between us to cover my cock. His fingers tightened around my length through my pants, massaging me into a frenzy. "Tell me you want more than this."

He punctuated the question by sucking my lower lip into his mouth, and I answered with a groan.

"Say it." His hand was insistent, driving me out of my mind with need. And that's exactly what it was—I fucking *needed* him to touch me.

"More," I managed to say, squeezing his ass to make my point. I wanted West's hands on me. His mouth. I wanted him to forget all about his almost-hookup in the club, and I wanted to sate the last bit of jealousy riding me. In that moment it didn't matter that I'd never done any of this with a guy before. The desperate need pumping through me overrode all of that.

"You got it." He winked, and before I could change my

mind, West lowered his head and his lips found my neck. The heat from his mouth as he began to kiss and suck on the skin there had my head falling back against the seat of the limo. I was burning up in this damn shirt he'd made me wear tonight, and like he could read my mind, he reached up and popped a button free.

The blood rushed around my head, making my ears ring, as one by one, he started to release the buttons.

Oh God... were the only two words racing through my head as West began to make his way down to my collarbone. When he reached the waist of my pants, he tugged the shirt free, and two more buttons later, my shirt was undone.

West raised his head. "More?"

I had a feeling that while being with a guy like this was a first for me, West stopping to ask if someone wanted what he clearly wanted to give was just as groundbreaking.

"If I say no?"

"I'd move back to my side of the limo and probably cry."

My courage shoved aside whatever lingering doubts I had, and I reached for the lapels of his jacket and pulled myself up against him.

"Well," I said against his lips. "I wouldn't want to make you cry..."

West shoved me back on the seat, then he smoothed his palms up my chest and parted my shirt. He hummed in the back of his throat as he took in my half-naked body, and while I knew I wasn't half as ripped as West was, the heat from his stare was doing nothing to help cool my skin. "I know you don't want to make me cry," he said as he drew his fingers down and flicked one of my nipples. "But I just might with how fucking bad I want you right now."

Jesus. I thought I'd had a pretty good understanding of sex and desire and all that kind of stuff after being with Elise. But as West lowered his head and put his lips to the base of my throat, a bolt of lust shot straight to my balls.

I reached for the back of West's hair and speared my fingers through it, and as he began to kiss and suck his way down my torso to my abs, I was shocked at the sounds rumbling out of my throat.

Half growl, half groan, I sounded exactly how I felt—like a damn animal—and the need to claw, bite, and tear the clothes off West wasn't so much a shock now as it was a need.

"West," I said between gritted teeth as he circled his tongue around my navel and pushed my legs further apart.

"Yeah, Golden Boy?"

My fingers automatically tightened in his hair, and his rough chuckle made my entire body vibrate.

"Always wondered if you liked that name."

Liked it? According to my dick, I was in love with it.

"You wanted something?" he said like this was an everyday conversation and not one of the hottest sexual moments of my entire life. I glanced down to where my hard-on was close to bursting through the black fabric of my pants. "I know. I want that too. But haven't you heard?" He winked at me. "Good things come to those who wait. And I'm really fucking good, so you *will* come for me."

He ran one his hand down past my waist and circled my length. His eyes were on mine, his warm breath was on my skin, and as he began to squeeze and stroke my cock, I pumped up into his fist.

A smug grin crossed his mouth as I moved in time with him, then he lowered his head and mouthed the fabric covering my zipper.

A harsh shout—mine—filled the limo as he let go of my dick and followed the outline of it with his lips. The damp heat of his breath seeped through the material to my sensitive skin, and I bucked up against his face.

West planted his hands on my legs to keep me still then sucked on me like there was nothing in between us. I wasn't sure if the inside of my pants were wet from his mouth or my excitement. If I had to guess, I'd say both.

"More." I threw down the challenge, knowing it would get West's attention, and the hand on my left leg moved to my waist. Seconds later the button was free, and seconds after *that*, the zipper was down. All the while, West hadn't lifted his head.

Well, I knew one thing—he hadn't been lying. He *was* good at this, if his skill at getting someone naked was anything to go by.

His fingers curled around the waist of my pants and

boxer briefs as he lifted his head, his swollen lips looking entirely too fuckable.

As if he knew what I was thinking, he said, "Lift your hips for me, sexy."

My body complied of its own accord, and as West stripped me naked to my ankles, freeing my rock-hard cock, my breath hitched.

This was really happening. Pre-cum coated the head of my cock, telling both of us exactly how much I wanted his mouth on me. It would've been embarrassing if it hadn't been for West's nose flaring in desire at the sight.

"Fuck, JT," he said. "It's almost a damn shame no one gets to enjoy this but me."

West lowered his head, licking my underside from base to tip. He flicked his tongue along the head, tasting me, and I couldn't tell whether the moan between us came from him or me. Maybe both. It didn't matter, because when he began to suck down my entire length, the noises I made covered any that were coming from him.

Holy fuck. My head hit the back of the seat and my eyes rolled to the back of their sockets at the full force of my dick inside West's hot, wet mouth. He took me farther than anyone ever had, his nose skimming the cropped curls surrounding me, and I reached for him, not sure whether I wanted to hold him there or push him away. It was just too good.

As he moved back up my length, his eyes collided with mine, the lust there reflecting exactly what I was feeling.

In that moment, I would've done anything he asked of me.

I wanted to please him.

I wanted to make him beg.

But more than anything else, I wanted him to keep going.

That must've been reflected in my eyes, because he took me deep into the hot recess of his mouth until his nose was again nuzzling into the short curls. This time I knew exactly what I wanted as I held him there, reveling in the euphoric sensations making my toes curl and my brain detonate, as the head of my cock brushed over the back of his throat.

"Fuuuck." I loosened my grip as West's head began to move under my hand and I could do nothing but stare.

The erotic sight of him bent over my lap had me clutching at the back of the seat with my free hand, as I propelled my hips up to chase his retreating mouth. When he wrapped a strong fist around the base of my dick and sucked on the tip, I squeezed my eyes shut and hissed out a breath.

"Open your eyes." West's low voice floated around me, and I immediately did as he asked. He seemed to have infiltrated every single inch of the limo, from the air I was breathing, to my field of vision, to the sensations coursing through my body and the reactions I was having to them. He was everywhere all at once, and still it wasn't enough.

But then that arrogant smile lit up the limo like a beacon as he swiped the tip of his tongue across the head of my dick and hummed in a way that made my balls tingle.

"I figured you'd be sweet." He shook his head. "But not this fucking sweet."

He'd figured? As in he'd *thought* about this?

I knew he'd wanted to kiss me—he'd said so the night of the party. But he'd thought about *this*? He'd thought about getting me naked and tasting me?

But before I could say anything in response, his mouth was back around me, obliterating any hope I had of thinking, leaving me nothing to do but hold on for the ride. He cupped my balls as they pulled tight against my body, sucking me in like I was his next breath.

I couldn't take much more, but I never wanted him to stop. My thighs trembled from holding back as I tightened my fingers in his hair. West looked up at me, watching me fall apart under that menace of a mouth. It was torture and ecstasy, and when West's cheeks hollowed out as he swallowed me, I slapped the seat and cursed.

"I'm gonna come," I gritted out, jerking as the orgasm began to barrel through me. "West—" I tried to pull him off me, to warn him in case he hadn't heard. But West only raised a brow, those blue eyes full of sin, telling me in no uncertain terms he wasn't going anywhere.

He hadn't just wanted a taste, he wanted the whole goddamn meal—and that was all it took for the little resistance I had left to crumble.

My shout was primal, almost unrecognizable, as West

greedily consumed every last drop of me. It was the hottest thing I'd ever seen, this confident, powerful guy on his knees and enjoying my cock like he never wanted to let go.

As I tried to get my breathing under control, I released his head, dropping my arm on the seat as every part of me turned boneless and satiated beyond belief.

"Holy...fuck," I managed as West drew off my cock, giving the head one final lick before it too collapsed onto my stomach.

West smiled as he leaned back, and I reached down to pull my pants and briefs back up. As I lazily fumbled with my zipper, West moved back to his side of the limo, throwing open the flap of his jacket as he shifted to a comfortable position. He propped an ankle on his knee as he swiped the corner of his smirking lips with his thumb and then, nonchalant as you please, winked at me.

"See? Told you I was a good time."

TWENTY-THREE

west

THE FRONT DOOR slammed open, and I glanced over my shoulder to see East marching inside the foyer to toss his wallet and rosary down on the table. A scowl twisted his regal features into a pinched expression as he scanned the dark living room, searching me out.

"You took the fucking limo?"

I'd been expecting this, had known the second I demanded JT get in the back of the limo tonight that I'd incur East's wrath. But had it been worth it? Totally.

"I did."

East pointed at me. "Fuck you." He walked into the kitchen, and I got to my feet to follow. The fact that this was the second person I'd managed to piss off tonight—well, third if I counted Blake—was not lost on me. I was on a roll. But there was no way in hell I was about to suck East's dick to make shit better. Lucky for me, I had something he might like even more—gossip.

"What's the matter? You have to stand on the curb like regular folk waiting for a cab?"

East opened the freezer and pulled out a bottle of vodka, then leveled me with a look that would kill most men. To me, it just felt like a warm hug.

"I don't *wait* for anyone. We sent Gavin out there instead."

I scoffed as he poured a finger of vodka into an icy tumbler then looked to me.

"I'll pass. But if you're over this little shit fit of yours, I've got some news that might cheer you up."

East's eyes narrowed a fraction, his fingers pausing on the screw cap of the alcohol. "I'm intrigued."

"Thought you might be." I gestured to the vodka. "Put that away and come sit."

East joined me a few seconds later, the irritation from when he arrived gone as he propped his feet up on the coffee table and we stared out at the glittering city that was our playground.

Manhattan. We'd been born and raised here a couple months apart, and while East liked to lord over me the fact he was older and therefore wiser, I knew the day would come when the tables turned and I would have the advantage.

Maybe around the time he started to have a mid-life crisis. Though East felt like he was in a constant state of life crises, so how I would tell the difference, I wasn't quite sure.

"So this news," East said, cradling his glass in his lap.

"It wouldn't have anything to do with a certain dean's son, would it?"

My lips crooked as I stared out at the Chrysler Building, something that suddenly reminded me of JT and kissing him on the roof.

"Why would you say that?"

"Because when you and the limo disappeared, so did he."

I turned back in East's direction. "Maybe."

"Maybe my ass."

"No, it definitely wasn't *your* ass he was squeezing as he kissed my brains out. But it was mine..."

"Un-fucking-believable." East shook his head, then took a sip of his drink.

"Oh, that isn't even the best part."

"If you tell me Golden Boy let you fuck him in the back of the limo, I'm going to throw myself off the roof."

I was tempted, so very tempted, to mess with East's head. But I didn't need to *lie* to win this bet, not when I knew I'd be able to win for real. It was only a matter of time.

"That won't be necessary. But let's just say things are...*coming* along very well."

He arched a brow. "No way."

"Actually, all the way—down my throat. Kind of why I don't want a drink." I got to my feet. "I'm rather enjoying this sweet taste of victory on my tongue."

"You know, you're not half as good looking when you're—"

"Winning our bet?" I walked behind East and leaned down to say by his ear, "Fuel up that private jet. I'm going to need it real soon."

East said nothing as he flipped me off and downed the rest of his drink. I chuckled and headed for my room.

I shut the door, and as soon as I was alone, I closed my eyes and leaned back against it. I wasn't sure why, but my stomach suddenly felt a little off, all twisted and uncomfortable.

Thank God I hadn't said yes to a drink. Maybe this was my body's way of giving me a heads-up to give it a rest. I thought I'd recovered from Friday night, but clearly I needed a little longer.

I washed up in the en suite and stripped out of my clothes, ready to fall in bed and *hopefully* asleep. But an hour later I found myself staring at the ceiling wide awake.

Damn it. There was nothing I hated more than when I couldn't sleep. I'd tried everything, from counting back from one hundred, turning on the white noise app on my phone, to getting up and doing a couple sets of push-ups, and still sleep eluded me.

The one saving grace? My stomach seemed to have settled.

I climbed back into bed and shifted under my covers. The rustling sheets were nice and cool against my warm skin, and suddenly my cock decided it was an insomniac too.

Huh, maybe *that* was my problem. I'd gotten JT off in

the back of the limo but, not wanting to scare him away, I'd denied myself. Then, by the time I dropped him off, my...*situation* had been back under control.

It sure as hell wasn't under control anymore, though.

I reached down under the sheets and wrapped a hand around my thick shaft, and the ache between my thighs intensified.

This was exactly what I needed. I was wound up, my body still on edge after not getting the release it wanted. I thought back to those hot moments in the car and started to stroke.

I pictured JT with his shirt open, his cock hard, and those full lips shouting my name—and suddenly, I was reaching for my phone.

I glanced at the time—three forty-five a.m., a ridiculous time to text or call anyone. But if I wasn't able to sleep because I hadn't gotten off tonight, maybe there was a chance JT couldn't sleep because he had.

This experience had been a first for the both of us.

Deciding a text was slightly less invasive than a call, I quickly typed out a message and sent it before I could change my mind, then lay there staring at my screen, willing the three dots to appear.

Finally, they did.

GOLDEN BOY:

Do you have any idea what time it is?

. . .

I grinned as I pictured JT frowning at his screen with his curls spread out all over his pillow.

> I do. But I couldn't sleep. And it's your fault.

GOLDEN BOY:
My fault?

> Yeah.

I stared at the message I was about to send back, wanting to add more, but again finding myself hesitating, something I never normally did.

Jesus, when did I start overthinking shit? Just write what you want to write. He obviously enjoyed what you did to him earlier.

> Yeah. I can't stop thinking about the sounds you made in the back of the limo tonight. It's making it HARD to sleep.

My dick jerked, remembering exactly how he'd sounded, and I wondered if he'd write back. After several minutes and no reply, I was starting to think I had pushed too hard —but then my phone started to vibrate in my hand.

JT was calling me? This was either going to go really well or he was going to tell me to leave him the fuck alone.

I hit answer. "Good morning..."

JT's answering laugh was deeper than usual, but a good sign he wasn't going to end the call. It was also sexy as fuck.

"Early, *early* morning. I can't believe you texted me at three thirty."

"Three forty-five, if we're being specific. But like you have any room to judge—you called *me*."

"I know. It's just, I didn't want to write all that stuff in a—"

"Text? Hmm..." I shifted on my mattress, already liking the direction of this conversation. "What kind of stuff were you going to write to me, JT? Must've been juicy if you're afraid someone might see."

"That's not what I meant."

"It's not?" I rubbed my palm over my abs. "That's a shame. I was getting excited."

JT snorted. "According to your message, you were already excited."

"So you decided to call me and, what? Calm me down? 'Cause I gotta say, it's not working."

A soft gasp met my ear, and I immediately remembered the way JT's breath caught when he was nervous. It was delicious.

"I told you, that's not what I meant. I wasn't going to text you dirty messages. But if *you're* going to bring up earlier, then I'd rather talk about it. I like to keep my private life private, and you always see these horror stories of messages and photos being leaked."

He had a point. I couldn't remember the amount of times me or one of my friends ended up on a gossip site, our latest outings or sexual escapades entertainment for the nosy masses.

But if JT wanted to talk me to sleep instead, I had no problem with that.

"Is that what we're having? A private life?"

Silence met my ear for several seconds, and then, "Well, I don't usually do that kind of thing in public."

"What kind of thing?"

JT chuckled, and the sound made my stomach flip. A much nicer sensation than I'd been feeling earlier. "You just want me to say something dirty."

"Wow, it's like you're really starting to know me. But you *are* the one who offered to talk."

"After you brought it up."

"No, actually, *you* brought it up. And it's been up ever since you grabbed my hair and fucked my face in the back of the limo tonight."

"Oh my God... I can't believe you just said that." JT's whisper in my ear was both scandalized and proud.

I ran my fingers down my treasure trail to where my

cock was standing at attention. "Yes, you can." I wrapped my fingers around myself and squeezed. "I even think you like that I said it. Don't you?"

"I..."

"You?" I lowered my voice and drew my hand up my length. "It's just us listening, Golden Boy. Remember? That's why you called."

"I didn't call to have phone sex."

"Yeah, but you owe me."

"What?" JT's disbelief was mingled with a curious undertone.

"Well, if you remember, earlier tonight—"

"Uh, I do."

"Me too. Anyway, if you remember, you got to come. All down my throat."

"Fuck, West..."

"Don't I wish," I said as I rolled my hips up, sliding my dick through my hand. "But since you're not here and I didn't get to come down *your* throat, you owe me."

If I'd been worried about JT ending the call earlier, the harsh breathing in my ear told me I had nothing to worry about now. He was turned on. He was enjoying this. Maybe not as much as I was going to, but enjoying it just the same.

"And, um, how exactly would I pay you back?"

I kicked the sheet off, knowing I had him. Then I looked down at the glistening head of my cock where it was poking out of my fist.

"Maybe you could tell me how you felt tonight."

"I... I don't know if I can."

"Sure you can. Just close your eyes, think back to my mouth and how it felt, then start to talk."

JT coughed. "Just like that?"

"Yep, just like that."

"And what are you going to do while I...talk?"

I widened my legs on the mattress and closed my eyes. "I'm going to lie here naked in my bed and fuck my hand, wishing it was *your* mouth."

JT cursed, and a shiver raced down my spine.

"You're naked?"

"As the day I was born." I drew my hand down to the root of my cock. "You're thinking about it, aren't you?"

"No. Yes. I... Okay. Yes. You saw me tonight and—"

"Now you want to see me." I released myself to fondle my balls. "That could've happened, but you wanted to talk instead. So talk."

"I am talking."

"Come on, Golden Boy. Tell me how you liked the feel of my tongue tangling with yours."

"Jesus, you're way better at this than me."

"Yet here I am, *hard* for you."

JT's breathing came a little faster. "The second you got on your knees in the limo tonight, I wanted your mouth on me."

Damn, where did that come from? I had no idea, but I wasn't about to interrupt him now that he'd started.

I closed my eyes, propped the phone on the pillow by

my ear, and listened for whatever he was about to say next.

"I knew you'd be good, you said so yourself, and after the kiss on the roof Friday night, I wanted more."

Oh hell yes.

JT might've started out shy, but he was picking up fast.

"I wanted to kiss you more. Touch you more. And I wanted *you* to touch *me*."

"Fuck, JT." I tightened my fingers around the head of my dick, not wanting to explode three sentences in.

"Sorry, am I doing this wrong?"

A strained chuckle left me as I rolled over and reached for the lube in my top drawer. "Definitely not doing it wrong. Please tell me you're touching yourself." I poured some liquid into my palm.

"I think you know I am."

"Good. Keep going. And tell me about how you wanted me to touch you?"

JT let out a moan, and I could've sworn I felt it against my neck, or maybe that was my own skin heating up.

"I wanted you to kiss me. Like you did up on the roof. I wanted to see if it would make me—"

"Hard?"

"Yes. And it did, and when you wrapped your hand around me—"

"Yeah?" I moaned in the phone.

"I went out of my mind a little bit. Your hand was

strong, and you knew exactly how much pressure to use, and fuck, West, I almost came just from that kiss."

Jesus Christ. My climax was a hair trigger from firing.

"I didn't know that."

"I know." He panted in my ear. "I was trying to hold back."

I understood that feeling real fucking good. "Why were you doing that? Holding back."

I licked at my lips, drew my hand up to the crown of my cock, and swiped my thumb across the sensitive head.

Come on, JT, be brave, say it...

"Because I wanted to feel your mouth around me."

Fuck. Yes. That was what I wanted to hear.

"And did you like it?" I demanded through gritted teeth as I shoved my hard-on through my slick fist. "The feel of my lips around you."

JT moaned, and the familiar sound had me cursing and craning my head back into the pillow, pushing me closer and closer to the edge.

"JT?"

"Hmm?" The breathy question told me everything I needed to know. This phone call might've started out with JT owing me, but right now, we were about to reward one another.

"Did you like the feel of my hot mouth sucking your cock?"

JT grunted, and when he finally said, "I loved every fucking second of it," that was it.

I squeezed my eyes shut. "God, your fucking mouth."

I wasn't sure whose curse hit my ear first, and didn't much care. But the second it did, my orgasm slammed into me and my dick pulsed, and the next thing I knew I was making a hell of a sticky mess all over my stomach and hand.

Fuuuck. Fuck. Fuck. Fuck.

I couldn't remember the last time I'd had phone sex, let alone phone sex that blew my damn mind. As I reached for the box of tissues on my bedside table, I said into the phone, "You didn't fall asleep over there, did you?"

JT had obviously come right along with me. But someone had to break the ice, and I had a feeling he was probably busy getting up in his head again.

"Uh, definitely not asleep."

I chuckled and tossed the tissues in the trash by my bed.

"I figured." I stretched back and pulled the sheets up over me. "So... If my calculations are correct, you've enjoyed yourself *twice* now tonight."

"Shut up." JT chuckled, and I laughed along with him.

"Not a chance of that happening. But if you're nice to me, I might let you get away with this acting as your IOU paid in full."

"*Might?* You totally just came."

"And so did you. So the way I see it—"

"Okay, okay. I'll be nice to you."

"Aww, see, is that so hard?"

"It isn't now," JT shot back, and it was so unlike him that I laughed.

"Did you just make a sex joke?"

"I'm ending the call now."

I could feel my eyes growing heavy and my body melting into the mattress. Finally sleep was coming, even if it would be more like a power nap.

"Just tell me one thing before you go."

"One thing."

"Hilarious." I closed my eyes. "Tell me you liked it. Not Friday night. Not the limo. And not now. Tell me you liked *all* of it."

I could feel myself drifting off as JT's sleep-sexy voice whispered, "Let's put it this way. I have a feeling I'll be *up* for a 'good time' again, real soon."

That was good enough for me. "See you soon, then, Golden Boy."

TWENTY-FOUR

I COVERED MY yawn with my sleeve as I practically sleepwalked into class the next morning. My late night had made me hit my alarm a few too many times, and I'd barely made it here on time.

But hey, the important thing was that I was here. Not still in my bed running through the events of last night that I couldn't stop thinking about.

West's mouth around my dick. West getting himself —and me—off on the phone.

I couldn't believe the way my body responded, the way it reacted even now. It made shit for sense, but I couldn't deny the way I wanted him to touch me again. Hell, it was making me half-hard as I dropped into an empty seat in the back of the room and set up my laptop. Without a way to release the ache that was building, I reached for my trusty notebook, flipping it to the page I'd started on last night. I'd scrawled a few lines about the way I was feeling when I couldn't sleep, something that always helped when I was confused or the emotions were too much.

As I read them back now, it did nothing to help the pulsing of my cock, only served to remind me of the hot-as-hell moments with someone I'd never expected. I couldn't even blame any of this on West, not when I'd been the one to ask him to kiss me, to touch me. To blow my fucking mind. I'd fully expected to wake up with nothing but regret, but to my utter shock, all I could think about now was wanting to do it again.

Who the hell was I?

I shifted uncomfortably in my seat before having to reach down to adjust my dick in its confines. Shit, maybe getting out of bed had been a bad idea after all.

Or maybe you shouldn't have gone out partying, a voice said in the back of my mind.

I ignored it.

As I added a couple more lines to the poem, I didn't notice the shadow that fell across the paper from someone standing over me.

"If English class had included reading poems like that, maybe I would've paid more attention."

I quickly covered my page. "What are you doing here?" I whispered as West sat down beside me like he had nowhere else to be.

"Oh, come on. Don't act like you aren't thrilled to see me."

I glanced at the front of the room, where my professor

was still getting his notes together for the lesson, and then back at West. Shaking my head, I couldn't help biting back a smile, because damn, the guy was relentless, and too bold for his own good.

"You can admit it, you know," he said, keeping his eyes on mine as my face heated.

I couldn't help the blush, not when seeing him here felt like a continuation of last night. When I could still hear his ragged breathing in my ear. I'd been able to picture the way he looked when it happened, but my imagination was shit compared to having him here right in front of me.

West broke our eye contact to lean in closer and whisper, "You're thinking about it now, aren't you? The limo. *After* the limo…"

Swallowing, I absently watched my professor lower the video screen, and as he dimmed the lights, I said, "You need to leave."

"Why? You don't want me here?"

"It's not that—" My hand knocked against my pen, sending it clattering onto the floor, but before I could reach for it, West bent down to grab it. With his head down by my thighs, my cock took notice, which was absolutely ridiculous, considering where we were.

I should've known that wouldn't matter at all to West.

As he moved back up, the hand holding the pen trailed along my leg, up to my thigh. It lingered there as West angled his body toward mine, and then he ran it up the outline of my dick. It twitched, liking the attention, but wrong place, wrong time.

I grabbed West's wrist, stopping him, but he only raised a brow.

"Something wrong?"

"Don't you have somewhere to be?"

"Nowhere near as fun as this."

I glanced back at my professor giving the lecture and shook my head. "Somehow, I don't think this is gonna be your thing."

"No, but *this*..." His fingers replaced the pen on my cock and I tightened my grip on his wrist.

"West." His name rolled off my tongue on a hiss, and he responded with a low chuckle.

"You said you were up for a good time *soon*. Your wish is my command."

My mouth fell open. "Not right now. Are you crazy?"

"Sometimes." His hand moved insistently over the bulge growing steadily under his palm, regardless of the grip I had on him. "Now's as good a time as any, don't you think? Your professor even set the mood lighting."

He was certifiably insane. The room may have been darker for the time being, but there were well over a hundred people in there, and the last thing I needed was West's hand on my dick.

But I couldn't deny that my body wanted it. That it responded to his touch with an eagerness that made the fit of my jeans painful.

I loosened my hold on his wrist, and a triumphant

smile crossed West's face. He unbuttoned my jeans and then slowly pulled down the zipper, and I held my breath the whole damn time.

He couldn't do this. *We* couldn't do this. Right?

I glanced around, looking for anyone who was paying us any attention. But their eyes were all focused on the screen. At that moment I was beyond glad I'd been running late, because the seat on the other side of me was empty except for my bag.

I reached over, propping it up more to cover my lap before sliding down a little in my seat.

"Just keep your eyes on your lesson and your mouth shut, handsome, and let me take care of the rest," he said in a seductive murmur.

My pulse kicked up as I nodded, and *fuck oh fuck*, this was happening.

West pulled something out of his pocket, quietly tearing it open, and then poured a little in his palm before slipping his hand beneath my boxer briefs. I jolted at the contact of the cool liquid in his warm grip as he wrapped his fingers around me and began a slow, measured slide.

The struggle to remain focused on what was happening in the front of the room was real, but practically impossible as West brushed his thumb over the head of my cock in leisurely circles, like he had all the time in the world to tease me. I bit down on the tip of my thumb, resting my elbow on the arm of the chair in another attempt at blocking what he was doing.

Shit, we were so gonna get busted. And when we did,

the word would spread around campus like wildfire, surely getting back to the one person I didn't want to know—

No. I wasn't thinking about that right now. West wasn't the type to get caught. He was audacious to the extreme, but he seemed to get away with it, didn't he?

And damn, he could work a cock.

It wasn't only his mouth that was talented. Those fingers... He stroked and squeezed, varying the pressure, the speed, until my whole body tensed with need.

West's words were barely audible in my ear as he said, "You feel so fucking good." I grabbed his thigh, digging my fingers in so hard I had a feeling they'd leave bruises.

That only seemed to turn West on, because he squeezed me tighter. "I can't wait to taste you again."

It didn't matter that he wouldn't be getting his mouth on me today—his words still hit their mark.

"Fuck," I panted, biting down on my finger again to keep quiet. It wasn't easy, not when all I wanted to do was rock into his hand and groan out how damn good it felt.

I pictured him between my thighs, remembering the way he watched me as he took me all the way down his throat. It made my breathing come out ragged, and I could only hope it wasn't as loud as it sounded to my ears.

West kicked his foot up under mine, connecting our legs and giving him more access to me. He angled my laptop a little to the left as he scooted in closer and gripped the base of my cock.

"Try not to shout out my name," West said under his breath, seconds before he began to work my dick at an unrelenting pace. I lifted my arms to clench the sides of the desk to cover what he was doing a little better, and also because I still needed something to hold on to. My teeth tugged my lower lip between them as I quickly glanced around, making sure we didn't have an audience before I succumbed to the pure pleasure of his working me over.

Holding my breath wasn't an option for long, and I struggled to breathe through my nose as he jerked my dick like a pro. Opening my mouth for any reason, even for air, only caused an involuntary groan or noise that would draw attention, so I kept it shut as much as I could manage.

My toes curled and my body went hot and tingly as my climax reached its inevitable peak. I couldn't hold back anymore, and I prayed that West's magic fingers sending me over the edge wouldn't cause me to shout his name.

The sharp, sudden burst of pleasure that roared through me had my vision going white as I came in a trembling mess. My release coated West's hand, filling my boxer briefs. I could feel his eyes on me as he rocked me through it, pulling every last ounce of tension out of my body.

I relaxed my grip on the desk, but there were marks where the edges had dug into my palms. I didn't care. Not with the blissed-out feeling of my orgasm still coursing through me.

"So...damn...hot," West said, pulling his hand out from under my briefs. He wiped it against the front of them, but my cum still lingered on a couple of his fingers as he brought them to his lips. I sucked in a shaky breath as he licked them before sucking the digits.

Fuck me, that move was so sexy. I couldn't tear my eyes away from his as he reached down to adjust himself.

"Told you I wanted another taste," he murmured, a cocky smile on his lips. Lips I wanted to take with my own.

What was happening to me? What was it about West that had me acting so reckless?

The bright fluorescent lights were flipped on, and I squinted at the sudden change before quickly and carefully zipping my jeans back up. My release had caused a seriously sticky situation happening in my briefs, but it had been worth it.

Especially when I saw the way West's pupils practically covered the blue of his irises, his desire evident for anyone to see.

Desire for *me*.

West leaned in, so close I thought he was about to kiss me right here in front of everyone. But his lips never touched mine. "That's three. See you soon, JT." And then he crept out of the room like he'd never been there.

TWENTY-FIVE

IF I'D KNOWN the classroom handjob would be the last time I'd get my hands on JT's dick for a while, I might've taken things a little slower. Life had just been so damn busy over the last week that I'd barely even seen him. With my parents having stopped in Singapore after Amsterdam, they'd asked if I'd handle some of the smaller jobs at their office, so between classes and work, my priorities had been forced to shift. No hardcore partying, which was killing me—and East—to no end, though I'd managed a couple of nights at the hotel bar next door. My invites to JT had been declined, a damn shame, but he'd insisted it was only because he needed some time to settle into his new place and get ahead on his studies. Not because he was avoiding me for any reason.

I put that to the test, of course, by showing up at the library a time or two when JT was there studying. Sneaking him into one of the alcoves for a hot make-out session served as a reminder that I hadn't forgotten him or those delicious lips and would be back for more once things had settled.

And with my father now back in the office, my patience had finally worn thin. Whether he liked it or not, JT was mine tonight. After all, the clock was ticking, and I had a bet to win.

I strolled out of the elevator and past my father's secretary, smiling at him as he greeted me and made no move to stop me from going wherever I wanted. A perk of being the owner's son—you almost never heard the word no.

After knocking on my father's office door as a courtesy, I walked inside, carrying a to-go bag.

Jacques LaRue was a formidable presence in the world of luxury hotels, but the tall, lean man with tawny waves the same as mine had a carefree smile that he flashed as I entered.

"Weston," he said, crossing the room to greet me by taking hold of my shoulders and kissing both cheeks.

"Welcome back." I lifted the bag and grinned. "I brought dinner."

"Oh, you sweet child of mine," he said, taking the bag from me. With his hand on my shoulder—my father was a tactile human, always leading with touch—he walked us over to the circular table he used for meetings.

"I figured you deserved something good after an eighteen-hour flight."

As he opened one of the containers of spicy rigatoni

vodka and took in a deep inhale, he shook his head. "Carbone? Weston, you're my favorite son. I'll leave you everything in the will."

I snorted out a laugh as I unloaded the rest of the containers. "I'm your only child. I have to be your favorite."

"Still. You're so good to me." His French accent had faded a little over the years, but it always returned full force when he was excited about something. Carbone was his weakness, and with so many dishes he loved on the menu, I'd ordered several of them to tide him over a few days. The love for my father was mutual, so a place that didn't offer to-go services made an exception for him.

His eyes grew wide as I pulled the top off the long container that held a whole branzino, and I smirked.

Favorite child indeed.

"Sit, sit," he said, grabbing a bottle of wine off the wall. His display was impressive and also included expensive bottles of liquor given to him and my mom as gifts. Definitely one of the perks of the job.

I loaded my plate with a bit of everything as he opened the red wine and poured it into a Waterford Crystal decanter.

"So how was the trip?"

"Productive," he said, laying a napkin across his lap. "Your mother decided to stay and visit a little longer with the couple that lived next door when you were young. You remember the Kims?"

"Not really."

"Ah, well." He waved his fork with a shrug and scooped up a bite of fish. The second it hit his mouth, he closed his eyes and moaned.

"Sounds a little indecent. Should I leave you two alone?"

"This. I would sell a hotel for this."

"You might not want to let it slip you're willing to let it go for a hundred-dollar branzino. I imagine you'd get a few offers."

My father grinned and scooped up another forkful. "How is school? I hate I missed your first few weeks."

I shrugged. "You haven't missed anything. Astor is Astor."

"You've been behaving?"

I waggled my brows, because he knew me better than that. Probably because I was practically his mini me, which should've scared him, but he found it amusing. "Define 'behaving.'"

He chuckled and shook his head. "You know I enjoy your creativity and imagination. I just hope you haven't started off the year with another suspension. Or worse?"

"That suspension was bullshit, and you know it."

His brow arched. "Perhaps. Although if someone had broken into my office and overturned everything..." He shrugged. "Perhaps it was a justified punishment."

"It was a prank. It's not like we broke or stole anything."

"Pranks are harmless, Weston. Maybe Dean Hawthorne didn't find your sense of humor amusing."

I speared my rigatoni with my fork. "That sounds like more of a her problem than a me problem."

"It's still breaking and entering on school property. Have you apologized to the dean yet?"

Had I *apologized?* Why the hell would I do that? She'd gone overboard in her punishment, wanting to use me as an example, as if to say, "The Park Avenue Princes aren't above the rules." It had been a simple prank, a bet the group of us had dared each other to do, but only I'd gotten busted for. That only happened because Gavin's fucking foot had gotten stuck as he climbed out the window, and I'd done a good deed by helping his ass out instead of saving mine.

If it had been anyone else other than Gavin, I'd probably have thrown them all under the bus with me, but taking one for the team didn't matter to me so much as long as I didn't get expelled for it. Which the dean had probably wanted to do, but wouldn't, considering who my parents were.

So...apologize? Absolutely not.

Get revenge on her by corrupting her golden child? *That* was my sort of apology.

My thoughts turned to JT, all of them wicked as hell, causing me to bite back a grin as I poured the decanted wine into my glass.

"Weston?" My father looked at me as if waiting for an answer, and that was when I remembered his question.

"Oh. No, I haven't gotten around to that. I've been a

little busy with my folks jetting off around the world," I said pointedly.

"You should do it soon. We want your last two years to be good ones, end them on a high note."

"Does that really matter out in the real world? It's not like anyone is gonna look at my college transcripts and see the dean had it out for me."

My father lifted his napkin, pressing it to his lips, and as he laid it back across his lap, he gave me *that* look. The one he gave when he wanted me to really listen to what he was saying.

"Life is all about relationships," he said. "The good, the bad. You think the world is big, that you'll never see someone again, but it's just not true. You never know if your next deal could be affected by an argument you had over a taxi. Or if not making amends with a certain dean could harm a future negotiation. You must always be mindful, even about your silly pranks."

I twisted my ring, the one that had belonged to my father's father, and nodded. What he said made sense, but damn if I didn't still feel annoyed every time I looked up at Dean Hawthorne's office.

I'd think about it.

"All right, enough with the serious talk," he said, pouring his own glass of wine. "Your mother wants to know if anyone has caught your eye lately?"

I practically choked on my wine. "My *mother* wants to know?"

"Okay, fine. Your mother and *I* want to know."

"That's what I thought." I added a little branzino to my plate and took a bite as I thought over what to say.

Had I met someone? Well, yes. In a mastermind revenge sort of way. That shit wouldn't fly with my father, though, no matter how laidback he was about most things. He wanted me to apologize to JT's mom, for fuck's sake, not make her son the subject of a bet.

I had an uneasy feeling in my gut and sat back in my chair to rest a hand on my stomach. My eyes were always bigger than my appetite. When would I ever learn?

"Not really," I finally said. "Just the same old crew as always."

"Ah. And still none of your friends...appeal to you?"

My burst of laughter echoed through the room. "No. Absolutely not."

"Not even East?"

"*Especially* not East."

"I understand," my father said, a small grin on his lips. "A little high maintenance, that one."

"I think that might be the understatement of the year."

"Okay, so we find a low-maintenance handsome man." He lifted a shoulder, like finding such a thing was no big deal. Then he pointed at his plate with his fork. "Must like Carbone. What else?"

I traced a finger along my twitching lips. "I don't exactly have a list."

"We'll make one. Law of attraction. Build a man." He snapped his fingers like he could summon a fairy godmother to take notes of our order. *Just place the order and he will come.*

How the hell I hadn't turned out to be a romantic with parents like mine, I had no clue.

"How about this instead? I have fun in college, get to know as many hot guys as I can. Maybe that'll last for a few years after that. A decade or so, who knows. And if I decide having someone to warm my bed every night sounds like a good idea, and I meet a guy that keeps my interest, I'll consider it."

My father shook his head as he slid a forkful of fish past his lips. "That is not how love works, Weston."

"Who said anything about love? You're getting way ahead of yourself, old man."

"Oof." He grabbed his chest like I'd aimed an arrow there. "Old man. You're no longer my favorite."

"Aw, come on. I'll always be your favorite." I reached for his hand and gave it a squeeze.

"I suppose I'll keep you," he finally said. "I wouldn't mind keeping a son-in-law, too."

A COUPLE HOURS later, after we'd chatted some more and I went over some of the work I'd done in his absence, I headed down the walkway that connected the hotel to the condos. I wasn't ready to go home for the night, though. Thinking about JT over dinner had only made me impatient to see him again, and not for a five-minute sneak-away between classes.

I pulled my cell out of my pocket and shot off a text.

> I want to see you.

GOLDEN BOY:

Straight to the point. Hello to you too.

> You should know by now I'm anything but straight... And hi ;)

GOLDEN BOY:

Hi. :) You've made that clear, promise.

> I dunno. Sounds like you need a reminder.

GOLDEN BOY:

Do I?

> You do. Care to join me?

I'd send my driver his way in a hot minute if he said yes. *When* he said yes.

GOLDEN BOY:

Not really in the mood for the club scene tonight.

> Then you can come to my place.

JT seemed to write and erase his message a few times.

GOLDEN BOY:

You do know it's almost curfew.

When the hell had that ever stopped me before? Not even once.

I rubbed my jaw as I debated the options. If JT didn't want to go out, that meant he should be fine with staying in...

> I'll come to you, then.

GOLDEN BOY:

You want to hang out at my dorm?

> No, I want to hang out with you. And if that's where you are, that's where I'll be.

GOLDEN BOY:

If you can manage to sneak inside, I'll let you into my room. Deal?

. . .

I slowly smiled. JT really should know by now not to underestimate me. If I could sneak him out multiple times, I wouldn't have a problem getting in. This wasn't even a challenge.

Deal. Keep an ear out, Golden Boy.

TWENTY-SIX

I GLANCED AT the time on my cell phone's screen. It was only five minutes since the last time I checked. I tossed it on my mattress and got to my feet to pace my room.

I needed to chill out. West would be here. He'd only texted ten or so minutes ago, and he had to get across the city and somehow—if he was able to—sneak up into my dorm. The guy was good, but even he couldn't bypass the peak-hour traffic that came with a weeknight in the city.

I stopped at the window that overlooked the entrance to the building and bit at my thumbnail, my stomach a jumble of nerves and excitement.

It'd been a little over a week since I'd had any kind of alone time with West—not counting the helping *hand* he'd given me in class last week—and I was secretly hoping he'd work out a way to get past security and get up to my room, because damn if I didn't miss the guy.

I'd seen him around campus, of course. West took every opportunity he could to remind me that my brain and body were feeling things they'd never felt before—stealing kisses between coffee and classes, and finding private nooks in the library to take those kisses further. I was long past believing my attraction to him had anything to do with drinks and a party atmosphere, and was well aware it had everything to do with West himself. He was intoxicating in a way that was much more dangerous than any kind of alcohol, which was why I'd made the decision I had. I'd told West that I needed to refocus on my school work for a little bit.

I wasn't used to crazy nights out like him and his friends, and I knew if I wasn't careful I'd get swept up in not only him but the insane world he seemed to inhabit. Where it was easy to forget everything but where you were going out that night and how you'd feel by the end of it—and so far, I'd felt pretty damn good.

West's world was new and exciting.

West was new and exciting, and this need to be near or around him was stronger than anything I'd ever felt before. It would've been embarrassing if he wasn't always seeking me out too. But it seemed the feeling was mutual, so at least I didn't feel like some kind of clingy, obsessive boyfriend.

Boyfriend? Really?

Where the hell had that thought come from? I ran a hand through my hair as I continued to stare out the window, the word *boyfriend* now on an annoying loop in my head. That sure as hell wasn't how I saw myself in relation to West—was it?

No. We were friends. Friends with *benefits*, which was totally unexpected. But we weren't boyfriends. We hadn't even gone on a real date.

Knock. Knock. Knock.

I spun around so fast the room began to spin, but a quick look at the digital clock on my desk told me it'd been fifteen minutes since West's text.

Okay, maybe I was bordering on obsessive. But what West didn't know couldn't be used against me, right?

My heart pounded as I somehow made it across my room to the door, and as I reached for the handle I sent up a quick prayer it wasn't some kid on my floor needing to borrow something, or worse...my mom.

Please be West. Please be West.

I cracked open the door, and when West's lopsided grin came into view, my heart wasn't the only thing pounding.

He was here. At my bedroom door. How had I missed him sneaking into the building?

"Hey there, Golden Boy. Gonna let me in?"

Sweet Jesus. West's voice acted like a live current through my body, making it spark to life, and I was pretty sure I would've let him do anything right then.

I stepped aside and opened the door a little further, and as West slipped inside my room, I poked my head out to make sure no one was outside in the hall to see.

"You can relax," he said as I closed the door. "George let me up the fire stairs. No one saw me."

I turned and leaned back against the door. "George?"

"Yeah, he's a pal, and one of the security guards at this building."

"Ah, so that's how you did it."

West slipped his hands into his pockets, and for the first time I allowed myself to check him out. As always, he was put together in a way that I never could—or would—be.

He was in a stylish light blue suit jacket, and his designer jeans fit him in a way that drew attention to his long legs and muscled thighs. His immaculate white shirt was tucked in to show off his trim waist, and the few buttons he'd left open at the collar made sure the ensemble was sophisticated but not stuffy.

He looked sexy as hell, and not even the white handkerchief in the jacket's pocket could take that from him.

"Did what?"

"Huh?" I brought my eyes up to West's, which were sparkling with mischief, and that did nothing to restore my brain cells, because damn, the guy was hot.

"You said, that's how I did it. I was asking, did what?"

Oh, that's right. Think with your head, JT. The one on your shoulders.

"Snuck into the building. I was watching for you—"

"Were you now?" His lips kicked up into that crooked grin of his.

"I was. But you must've gone a different way."

West nodded. "George let me in the side entrance. I wasn't sure if it was just security you wanted me to avoid when sneaking in, or your dormmates too."

I knew what he was saying, what he was wondering: whether I cared if anyone knew what we were doing. Truth be told, I wouldn't have given a flying fuck if this had been any place other than Astor.

The problem was, this *was* Astor, and my mom *was* the dean—and for that reason alone, I was glad for his discretion.

"Normally I wouldn't," I said, wanting to be honest. But when the tips of his polished shoes bumped my bare toes, I lost my train of thought.

"But your mom might find out?" he finished for me, and I nodded. "I understand."

He was close now, close enough that the lapel of his jacket was brushing against my arm and his warm breath teased my lips.

"Then you better lock this door, don't you think?"

Think? I couldn't think about anything with him standing so close to me again.

What was that saying? Absence makes the heart grow fonder? According to my body, it also made my dick harder and desire stronger.

But when West was near, it was like my brain would shut down. Everything about him called to me. His clothes, his smile, his sexy-as-sin voice, and don't even get me started on the way he smelled.

I swallowed and flicked the lock on the door, and the second I did, his mouth was on mine.

Our lips met in a fierce kiss that bordered on brutal, and he cradled my face to angle me for better access. He had no need to worry about that, though—I was more than willing to grant him entry.

West slipped inside, teasing and tasting every inch of my mouth like I was his favorite meal, and maybe it was that that made him so potent, so difficult to resist. That he had the ability to make a kiss all-consuming. That he could make something I'd done with several other people feel like a whole new experience, all because it was *his* mouth on mine and *his* tongue tasting me.

I moaned and pulled him closer, wanting more of him. West nipped at my lower lip and rested his forehead against mine, and I couldn't stop myself from flicking my tongue along his lips.

West chuckled then released my face and took a step back, running his eyes down over my white t-shirt and grey sweats that did nothing to hide my hard-on.

"I was going to ask if you missed me this week, but clearly..."

I eyed the very clear outline in his jeans. "*Clearly*, I'm not the only one."

I moved around him, and as I did I realized for the first time that the only real furniture in my room was my desk and bed.

Fuck.

"You're definitely not," West said as I perched on the

edge of the desk, deciding that was the safer of the two options, even with some of my clothes piled on top of it. "I just wasn't sure when I texted you if you'd tell me no, since you've been blowing off all my invites lately."

"I haven't been blowing you off."

West's eyes immediately lowered to my kiss-swollen mouth. "Would you like to?"

Yes. The thought hit me from out of nowhere. But now that he'd said it, my mind spun with the possibility, and like he could read it, West groaned.

"Fuckin' hell, JT."

"What?" I said, eyeing the way he reached down to adjust himself. "You don't want that?"

West let out a loud boom of laughter. "Have you met me?"

"Hmm, let me think. Cocky charmer who does whatever and *who*ever he wants, right? That's you?"

West narrowed his eyes and shrugged out of his jacket, tossing it over the end of the bed. I sucked in a breath, taking in the visual in front of me, and if I thought he'd looked sexy before, that was nothing compared to the way that white shirt fit his broad shoulders and built chest like it was tailor made for him.

Hell, it probably was.

West unbuttoned the cuffs of his sleeve and began to roll them up his arms as he walked over to the desk, and then he moved right between my spread thighs. He placed a hand on the desk on either side of my hips and looked down at me, a smirk curving his irresistible lips.

"Yeah, that's me. But who are you? Because the JT I know sure as hell wouldn't have just boldly eyed my dick and offered to suck it last week."

He was right. There was no *way* I would've done that last week, maybe not even an hour ago. But as soon as he'd stepped inside my room and that door was locked, it was as if all of the pent-up sexual tension I'd kept in check during our make-out sessions finally had permission to be free—and I was done holding back. I was ready to explore.

I wrapped my legs around his ass and tugged him in closer, then reached up to wind my arms around his neck. I craned up like I was going to kiss him, and at the last second dodged his mouth to put my lips by his ear.

"You don't like *this* JT?"

West grunted as I flicked my tongue over his lobe, and when he trembled, my cock jerked. Damn, I did that. I made Weston LaRue shiver.

"You didn't answer me," I said, taking a page from his book. "You don't like this version of me?"

West turned his head, and the teasing mischief from earlier had been replaced with a much more intense expression. His blue eyes had been engulfed by the black of his pupils, and the strained look on his face made my thighs tighten around him.

I knew that look. I'd seen it that night in the limo when his mouth had been full of my cock, and it seemed the idea of my returning the favor was just as appealing to him.

"If I like you any more right now, you're going to end up naked and bent over this desk."

Holy. Fuck.

I wasn't sure I was ready for *all* of that just yet, but maybe some of it? One thing I knew for certain: I didn't want to stop. I didn't want just another kiss and then to say goodnight. My body was aching for West's hands, his mouth, and the body between my thighs—and judging by the look on his face and erection pressing up against mine, he was aching for me too.

It was time to be brave. Time to take what I wanted, and in this very moment, I wanted West.

"How about this?" I said. "I'll get naked if you do too."

TWENTY-SEVEN

west

FOR ALL MY confidence in my ability to persuade anyone and everyone into my bed, I had to admit there'd been a few moments over the past week that I wondered if JT was distancing himself from me. But as the throb of his cock matched time with mine through our layers of clothing, I realized that wasn't the case at all.

If anything, it seemed our time apart had made him eager for more than the brief kisses we'd shared during his "study time." Something I wasn't about to complain about. Not when he was sitting on his desk with his legs wrapped around my ass, offering to get naked.

I reached up to where JT's fingers were playing with the hair at the back of my neck, and as I brought them down, I nipped at his knuckles. "You want to see me naked?"

JT sucked in a breath and nodded. The fevered look in his eyes made my skin heat.

"Then you're gonna have to let go of me."

"Oh. Right." He looked down my body as he loosened his thighs, and his gaze zeroed in on the outline of my dick when I straightened to my full height. He shifted on the desk and went to reach between his legs, but hesitated.

"Don't stop," I said, pulling my shirt from my jeans. "The idea that you want to get off to me is sexy as hell."

JT raised his eyes to mine as I unbuttoned my dress shirt. "It is?"

"Fuck yes. I'm not even naked yet, and you can't keep your hands off yourself." I shrugged out of my shirt and winked at him. "I can't wait to see what you do when you actually see my cock."

JT groaned and wrapped his fingers around the bulge between his thighs. That response was all I needed to keep going with my strip show.

I toed out of my shoes and tossed my shirt on the desk beside him, then I popped open the button of my jeans. Not wanting to startle him—or send him running from too much, too soon—I decided to leave my boxer briefs in place as I took my jeans off and tossed them alongside my shirt.

JT whispered a curse, and now he had his hands *inside* his sweatpants.

Fuckin' hell.

"JT?" My voice was rougher than usual as I watched his hand move behind the grey material of his sweats.

"Yeah?" His response was absent-minded, his attention solely focused on the distinct outline my erection made behind the last scrap of material covering me.

"Still want me naked?"

He didn't bother looking up at me, just bit down into that plump lip of his. "Yeah."

Christ. This was going to take every ounce of self-control if he kept looking at me like that, and I wasn't about to come before I got to see him naked too.

I grunted and pushed my briefs off. Then I pulled off my socks and kicked all of my discarded clothes aside.

"Holy shit..."

JT had widened his legs, and that hand in his sweats was moving a little faster now. But that wasn't going to work for me. I moved back to between his parted thighs, and his attention finally moved back to my face.

My lips curved at the hungry expression swirling in his eyes. They were glassy and dazed with his obvious arousal, and when I took his chin in hand and bent my head, he parted his lips for my kiss.

I brushed my mouth over the top of his, my tongue flirting with his top lip and then teasing the bottom. "I believe the deal was, if I got naked, you would too."

JT moaned as I kissed my way along his jaw to his ear.

"Not sure if you noticed, but I'm pretty fucking naked."

JT's hands moved to my hips, the temptation of touching me outweighing his desire to touch himself, and he slipped off the desk.

"I noticed," he said, trailing his fingers around to my abs. "It's pretty hard not to."

I clenched my fists by my side as JT's eyes came back to mine.

"And getting harder by the second."

That sweet fucking smile of his curved his gorgeous mouth, and when he lowered his eyes back to where his fingers were playing over my taut skin, I groaned. "Are you trying to drive me crazy?"

"No. Just hoping I'm good at this."

"This?"

Color bloomed on his cheeks, and he shrugged. "You know, sucking your..." He gestured to my throbbing erection.

"Cock?"

He nodded. "Yeah."

"Only one way to find out."

JT's eyes flew back to mine, and the curiosity there was coupled with worry. "Have you ever had a bad blow job?"

"Is there such a thing?"

"So that's a no."

JT went back to looking at my dick, and it seemed to stand up a little taller, as though trying to impress him. It must've worked, too, because without another word, JT moved to his knees.

I swallowed back a shout of triumph as JT settled in front of me and circled the base of my shaft with his hand, his face directly in line with my hard-on.

This was it. This was the moment where he'd either follow through or call it quits. Up until now, all JT had done was share a few kisses with me and let me get him off. But if he did this, if he actually decided to—"Oh my fucking *God*"—taste me, everything would change.

I glanced down at the messy brown curls covering his head, and wondered if I'd just imagined what I'd felt. But when JT leaned in and flicked his tongue over me a second time, I threaded my fingers through his hair and punched my hips forward.

JT raised his gaze up my body, opened his mouth, and sucked the tip of my cock between his lips. He placed a hand on my thigh, and as he took me in a little further, he shifted up on his knees. That gave him more height and a better angle for me to work with, as I pushed in a little deeper and his fingers dug into my leg. I stretched his mouth wide, and when JT began to draw his lips off me, my toes curled into the hardwood.

"Jesus, JT..."

He sat back on his heels and looked up at me from under his lashes. I could see the thick outline of his erection beneath his sweats and the damp spot from his arousal, and wondered what it was that had really set him off.

Seeing me naked? Touching me? Or tasting me for the first time?

But when he licked his lips, any thought other than getting back between them left my mind completely.

"So, um, that was okay, then?"

"Okay?" I trailed my fingers down his jaw. "It was a hell of a lot more than okay. But maybe you should do it again, so we can make sure it wasn't beginner's luck or anything like that."

JT chuckled, and the sound was like a warm stroke up my spine.

"I mean, I wouldn't want it to be a fluke."

Now that was interesting. "No? Why not?"

JT moved back into place and ran his fingers down my thigh—and my cock lurched in response.

"Because I'm an overachiever. How else do you think I ended up at Astor on my parents' salaries?"

I gripped his chin then and tugged it down, and this time when JT's mouth parted, I was the one directing my cock onto his tongue. "I don't care how you ended up here. I'm just glad you did."

I pushed inside his mouth with a little more force this time. He dug his short nails into my thighs and started to suck on me, and my eyes slammed shut from the sheer pleasure of it.

I grabbed a handful of his hair and slowly pulled out. Then I tunneled forward, again and again and again. JT went about learning the shape and size of my dick like it was going to be a question on his next exam.

He traced the veins and grooves, tasted the sticky excitement coating the tip, and when the ache in my balls threatened to overtake me, I shoved in deep, and JT took as much of me as he could until he started to cough.

"*Ah* fuck." A ragged sound escaped my throat as I

shoved him away and gripped my cock, giving it a vicious squeeze.

I stared down at his gorgeous face as I fought back the orgasm threatening to explode. Unable to take any more of the sweet torture that was his mouth, I reached for his arm and urged him to his feet.

"Take off your clothes," I said in a voice full of pent-up sexual frustration. "I want to look at you. I *need* to fucking look at you."

JT nodded and reached for the hem of his shirt, and as he pulled it up over his head and his leanly muscled body came into view, I started to work my length.

This wasn't the first time I was seeing his naked chest. But it sure as fuck was the first time I was seeing it after he'd had my dick in his mouth. JT wasn't as built as I was, but the light dusting of hair that trailed from his navel down to the drawstring of his sweats had me remembering just how good he'd tasted on *my* tongue.

"Who's eye-fucking who now?" he said.

My eyes flicked up to the bold ones roving all over me, and hell if this golden boy was turning out to be one surprise after another.

Unable to stay away any longer, I reached for the low waistband of his pants. I pulled him in until my bare cock was rubbing up against the soft fleece of his sweats, and low groans of pleasure rumbled out of both of us. JT slid his hands over my shoulders and around my neck, and when those flirty fingers started to play with my hair, I whispered against his mouth, "Then let's get you naked so I can do more than just eye-fuck you."

I pushed my tongue between his lips, stealing his answer. But the moan that followed was confirmation enough. I squeezed his ass with one hand and began to tug the material down with the other—and fuck, the sweats were all that was covering him.

I'd figured he'd had a pair of boxer shorts on at least. But nope, he was butt-ass naked under those things, and I was about two seconds away from embarrassing myself.

JT ground his hips against me as I continued to slide the pants off him, and when my palms were finally cupping his bare ass, I thrust forward, connecting our naked dicks.

At the first contact, JT gripped the back of my neck, and I dug my fingers into his ass to hold him still, letting him get used to the feeling of me.

"Oh God..." His heavy breathing by my ear was warm as he rocked a little harder, using my body to pleasure himself. "That feels... You feel..."

"Really fucking good?" I chuckled as he started to move his legs, shoving the sweats the rest of the way down and letting go of me long enough to kick them out of the way. Then he was back, arms around my neck, mouth on mine, and that long, hard cock bumping up alongside mine.

"Damn, JT," I said as I eyed the bed beside us. "Please tell me you have some lube in this room."

He nodded. "Yeah, I have lube." He opened his desk

drawer and pulled out a bottle. "I'm a nineteen-year-old guy who had the hottest person on campus give me a handjob last week in class. You don't think I've gotten off to that a time or two this week?"

I liked the sound of that.

I took the bottle from him and walked him back toward his bed, then shoved him down onto it. "Only a time or two, huh?"

As I uncapped the lid, JT scooted up his bed until his head was on the pillow. "Maybe a few more. Can I have some of that?"

I eyed the bottle where it landed and shook my head. "Nope."

"Nope?"

"That's right." I put a knee on the mattress and moved down over him, and as I wrapped my slicked-up hand around JT, understanding dawned.

"West..." He pressed his head back into the pillow and bucked his hips up. "That feels so good."

"I know." I rested one of my forearms on the pillow beside his head as I slowly started to stroke him. "But what I do to you next is gonna feel even better."

He groaned as I crushed my mouth down on top of his, and I swallowed the raw sound as I tasted every delicious part of his mouth.

I knew he was sweet. The samplings I'd had of him over the last few weeks had told me that much. But nothing could've prepared me for this adventurous, eager side of him. It was a potent combination, one that had my dick making a sticky mess all over his thigh.

JT speared his fingers through my hair and angled his head for a deeper kiss, and as he propelled his body up to fuck my fist faster, I moved over him to give him something to really rub up against.

JT gasped, the sudden weight pinning him to the mattress and shocking his brain out of the euphoric space it had been caught up in. I rested both arms by his head and lined my cock up with his, and with our eyes locked and our lips inches apart, I slowly started to rock my body over his.

JT panted as his hands came up to my hips and he smoothed his palms over my ass.

"Mmm," I moved a little faster. "You like that?"

JT nodded and squeezed tighter.

"Want to keep going?" *Please say yes. Please say yes.*

"Yes."

Thank fucking God. "I was hoping you'd say that."

I brought my slick hand down between us and trailed my fingers along the underside of his cock to his balls. JT shot up off the mattress.

"Kiss me," I said, wanting to distract him with something that was familiar.

As our tongues dueled, I began to gently play with the sensitive sac between his legs. I fondled and teased him, making him tremble under my hands, and when I slid a finger further down to his virgin hole and pushed inside, I muffled his shout with a kiss designed to obliterate any and all thought.

The next thing I knew, one of JT's legs was moving around my waist, and he pulled himself up in an attempt to get closer. Closer to my mouth, closer to my cock, and closer to the hand that was burrowed between his thighs. I could feel his ass pulsing around my finger in time to his throbbing dick, and as I started to slide it out, I found the exact spot to make him lose his damn mind.

JT tore his mouth free, his eyes glazed, and as I continued to massage that magical bundle of nerves, his breathing started to come fast.

"*There* it is..." I winked at him. "Now, to get the most out of this, you're gonna want to use me. Rub yourself all over me, Golden Boy. Make a mess of me."

JT groaned and hooked his leg a little tighter at my waist, and I grinned.

"Yeah, just like that."

I gave him my tongue to suck on as I went back to driving him wild. I wanted this first experience of his to be something mind-blowing, something he'd never forget. I wanted him to come out on the other side of this wanting and craving more.

More kissing. More sex. More me.

JT punched his hips up against me, grinding his slick, sticky length all over mine. As I fingered him to an orgasm that made cum shoot out of him so hard it caught on our chins, my balls clenched and I exploded all over his cock and stomach.

It was hot as hell and messy as fuck, and as I stared down at JT's kiss-swollen lips and blissed-out expression, I felt something shift—and it wasn't the mattress.

Usually after a moment like this I'd be working out the easiest way to get up and get gone. But as I brushed a sweaty curl back from JT's face and pressed a gentle kiss to his lips, I was trying my hardest to think of a reason to stay.

Fuck. That wasn't part of the plan at all. Not even a little bit. This was a bet. Nothing more. But when JT closed his eyes and whispered, "Don't leave yet," I knew I wouldn't be going anywhere.

After all, the night was young, and if he wanted to explore some more, I was more than happy to offer myself up to him.

That was what I was telling myself, anyway.

TWENTY-EIGHT

I WAS DREAMING. I had to be. That was the only explanation for the pure fucking ecstasy of West's mouth on my cock as I rocked my hips up, dying for more of what he was so damn good at. There was no way this could be real, because I didn't do things like this. I didn't crave getting another taste of a guy's velvet-smooth dick down my throat. Or wish it hadn't been just West's fingers exploring my ass. I couldn't deny that I wanted more, though, wanted him, as crazy as it seemed.

My head rolled on the cloud, looking down at—

Wait. *Cloud?*

My eyes shot wide open.

"You moan in your sleep." A voice thick with gravel came from my right.

I turned my head—on a pillow this time—to see · West's heavy-lidded gaze on me.

I rubbed my eyes, not sure what I was seeing was reality, because the idea that West had spent the night in my bed, not to mention stayed the whole time, didn't seem true. Everything I knew about him told me he wasn't the type to wake up with his one-night stands the next morning, but... I wasn't considered a one-night stand if we hadn't had sex, right?

Shit. That dream hadn't been far off.

The memory of last night came crashing back in vivid detail, every damn bit of it, and my cock stirred to life beneath the sheets.

Holy hell, that had been... Well, the hottest night of my life. One I may not have believed if West weren't lying beside me.

"I don't moan in my sleep," I said, moving to my side to face him.

"You do. You also talk."

"Really. And what did dream me say?"

West's lips curved, his blue eyes lighter than usual this morning. "Something about 'fuck me harder, West, yeah, right there—'"

I reached behind me for an extra pillow and slapped it over his head. "Liar."

He chuckled, tossing it aside. "I have a feeling it won't be for long."

The challenge in his eyes, as if he were daring me to say otherwise, was doing something to my dick.

"You seem awfully confident about that," I said, tucking my arm under my head.

"I am. Look how far you came last night."

"How far? Or how many times?"

"I mean, I'm not one to count, but..." As he waggled his brows, my eyes drifted down his body. His very naked, very *aroused* body. He didn't even bother covering himself with a sheet, so his morning erection was on prominent display. It was somehow even more impressive in the daylight.

"Pretty sure I lost count after four," I murmured, eyes locked below his hips.

West chuckled as he ran a hand down over the ridges of his abs, then further, until he had the base of his cock in hand.

"There something you want, JT?"

My cock lurched beneath the sheets in response, and a sexy smile crossed West's lips. He scooted in closer, reaching up to take the cover at my chest between his fingers, and then he drew it down slowly, unwrapping me like he would a present.

"Aren't you a stunning thing to wake up to?" He brushed his fingertips lightly across my skin, and I shivered under his touch.

I couldn't resist the urge to kiss him with his hands on me like that. His lips were soft and pliant under mine, and the thought crossed my mind that it had to be from the hours I'd spent kissing him last night.

That memory did nothing to help the ache in my dick, and neither did West's hand massaging my ass. He knew exactly where to touch, how to wield the right pressure, to drive me out of my mind.

Our kiss grew hungry as I pushed my leg between his and felt the insistent throb of his cock against my hip. I reached between us and—

A loud knock on my door echoed through my room.

We both pulled away from each other at the same time, bodies going rigid as we stared at the door.

"Who is that?" I whispered.

"You're asking me?"

I waited another heartbeat, and when the knocking stopped, I shrugged. "Probably someone who ran out of shampoo. They'll go away."

West didn't waste any time wrapping an arm around me and hauling my body up over his. His skin was on fire, which was probably why he didn't bother with the sheet. I let my legs drop down on either side of his hips and groaned at his stiff cock rubbing up against mine.

The knocking started again, and this time, the voice calling out behind the door had my heart stopping.

"JT, are you awake?" my mom said, pounding a little louder.

"Fuck me."

I sprang up like my ass was on fire, and West's eyes widened, though he couldn't help joking, "Now's not really the time."

As I got to my feet, I looked around the mess on my floor and grabbed my boxer briefs. "Get up," I mouthed to West, who wasn't moving at nearly the pace I was.

The knocking continued, almost frantic, and I took a

deep breath, forcing my words to not come out shaky. "Mom, I just woke up. Gimme a second."

"Oh. Okay, sleepyhead," she called back.

I tugged on my underwear as West searched around for his. Amusement was written all over his face, but I didn't know what he found so funny about this situation. If my mom had a key, we would've been so screwed. And not in the way I'd been dreaming about.

As I reached for my crumpled shirt, I stubbed my toe on the edge of the bed frame and cursed. Pain lanced through my toe, and I clamped a hand over my mouth, hopping around on one foot.

"Is everything okay?" my mom asked.

I bit back a hiss. "Fine," I said through gritted teeth. "One sec."

I threw on my shirt as West grabbed his blazer, whirling around to find the rest.

"You have to hide," I whispered.

"I can't find my boxers."

"Too bad—you'll have to hide without them."

West pinned me with a look and ran his hand through his disheveled waves. I didn't even have time to enjoy the way he wasn't so perfectly put together as usual, but still somehow managed to look hotter than ever.

Damn, I was really over here calling another guy hot and checking him out.

"Honey, are you sure you're okay? What's taking so long?" Impatient was my mom's middle name, and her voice snapped me out of my perusal of West.

I reached for his jeans and then threw them his way. "The closet," I mouthed, pointing.

With his arms full of his clothes, a naked West took off for the closet, but not without scanning the room one more time for his underwear. I didn't see them either, but the bottle of lube on the nightstand was a dead giveaway of what I'd been up to. I shoved it in the top drawer and threw the covers over the mattress in a shoddy attempt at making the bed.

"West." I kept my voice low, and he opened the closet door a crack. "Call me later?"

He grinned and winked at me. "To be continued," he said, before closing himself inside.

Even in my mad scramble, my stomach flipped at his words. There would be a next time. Only maybe it could happen somewhere my mom wouldn't be able to just pop by.

The small smile stayed on my lips as I yanked on my jeans. Then I checked my face in the mirror as if she would be able to see where West's mouth had been, then headed to the door.

My heart was beating out of control, and I sucked a deep breath in through my nose and ran my fingers through my curls for some semblance of order. One last check over my shoulder to make sure West was hidden in the closet, and then I swung the door wide.

My mom stood in the hallway, looking perfectly polished in a navy sheath dress and pointed heels. The pointed look she gave me was punctuated by the further rise of her already arched brow.

"Sleeping in?" she said, not waiting for an invitation before slipping inside.

"Uh, no." At least, I didn't think so. "What time is it?"

"Eight o'clock."

"I don't have class until nine thirty today."

With her hands clasped behind her back, she strolled around the room at a leisurely pace, looking every bit the dean. Her sharp eyes were narrowed as she looked around, taking in everything, and I found myself glancing at the closet to make sure not even a peek of West could be seen.

Did she suspect something already? Was that why she was here? She'd never just popped in unannounced before, not without a phone call or text—

Shit, where *was* my phone?

"I haven't seen you lately," Mom said, coming to a stop at the center of the room. "I thought we could have breakfast. Catch up."

I almost let out a sigh of relief. Yes, getting out of my dorm was a fantastic idea, and I nodded eagerly.

"I'd love to. Let me just, uh, brush my teeth and we can go."

She smiled. "Great. I was thinking that new spot on the corner—"

"Yeah, yeah, that works." Wherever she wanted to go to give West time to get out of my dorm was fine with me.

I didn't even want to think of how he'd manage to get out without attention, but that wasn't my problem.

My mom waiting in the middle of my room with his boxers unaccounted for somewhere? *That* was my problem.

I finished rinsing my mouth, then wet my fingers and ran them through my curls. Some deodorant and a spritz of cologne and I was ready to get the hell out of there.

"Ready," I said, grabbing my bag from beside my desk, along with my phone hiding underneath, and slinging it over one shoulder. "I'm starving."

Mom frowned as we headed to the door. "Are you eating enough?"

"Of course I am. Why?"

She gestured to my jeans. "You look like you've lost some weight. Those are big on you."

As she headed into the hall, I glanced down at the dark denim sitting low on my hips—much lower than where I normally wore them. The legs were too long by several inches and slightly baggy, and for a moment I wondered if I *had* lost weight and didn't notice.

I glanced back at the closet before shutting the door, and—

Oh shitballs.

I'd put on West's jeans by mistake.

TWENTY-NINE

WHEN THE DOOR to JT's room clicked shut, I let out the breath I hadn't realized I'd been holding. I didn't *move*, but I allowed myself to finally breathe.

Jesus Christ. That had been too close for comfort, because if Dean Hawthorne had caught me crawling out of her son's bed this morning, she would've killed me. No if ands or buts about it. I mean, there'd definitely been a cute butt involved—JT's ass was phenomenal. However, I didn't think pointing that out to his mom would've won me any points.

After counting back from one hundred, and hearing no one come in or out of the dorm, I cracked open the closet door and popped my head out. When I saw the coast was clear, I stepped out into JT's room with my clothes clutched to my naked body. I scanned the floor, looking for the boxer briefs I knew I'd kicked off somewhere, but still I couldn't see them.

Oh well, it wouldn't be the first time I'd gone commando, and it wasn't like I could stay here all day, so it looked like I was going to have to collect those some other time. I grinned to myself as I put the clothes on JT's desk and reached for my jeans. That would just give me a good reason to come back for round two.

I stepped into the denim, and as I tugged them up over my legs and thighs, it was like pulling on jeans after stepping out of the shower. They were tight, tight as hell, and when I finally got them up over my ass, it felt like the material was trying to suffocate my boys, not to mention my dick.

What the...?

I glanced down at the skintight fit of the jeans and frowned, knowing damn well they hadn't been like that last night. But as I looked closer at the color and quality of the material hugging my thighs, it hit me—these weren't my jeans.

Great. That was just great.

JT must've grabbed mine by mistake during the chaos his mom's appearance had created. That was just fine for him. He was leaner than I was, so while my jeans might've been a little baggy on him, at least they weren't indecent. These things were cradling my jewels like they were precious fucking artifacts, and while they were to me, I doubted the whole building wanted to see that.

Scratch that—most probably would want to see it, but not like this. Like *this*, I looked ridiculous.

I searched out something else I could wear, and when

my eyes locked on JT's sweats on the ground, I cursed. Of course the one option that might've been slightly looser than the denim clingwrap I was currently in was covered in last night's...activities. They'd been the closest thing to grab when I wanted to wipe us down before sleep finally claimed us, and now I was paying for my thoughtful deed.

Should've just used my tongue.

I shook my head and picked up my dress shirt from the desk, and as I slipped my arms into the sleeves, I was happy to note it was long enough that if I left it untucked it would cover up what I was packing below.

I quickly buttoned it, and debated whether I should throw on the jacket. But at the last second I decided it would be smarter to hold it, just in case I needed an extra barrier between the outside world and my dick.

Ha, now that was a laugh. I couldn't remember the last time I'd ever worried about modesty, and I wasn't all that concerned with it now. What I *was* concerned with was how utterly absurd I looked in skinny jeans.

Could some guys get away with them? Sure. Travis lived in leather pants and jeans that looked as though they were painted onto his legs. Me, however, not so much. My thighs were too muscular, and it just looked... strange. But I couldn't hide in here forever, so it was now or never.

I shot off a text to our driver, and when he messaged back that he was nearby and to head downstairs, I sent up a quick prayer that my walk of shame really only had to be a mad dash out the side door of JT's dorm building—and true to his word, there he was.

Having a driver was one of the best perks of living at the Towers.

I shut my eyes and tried to relax for the drive across town. But with these jeans trying to cut off circulation to my legs, it wasn't easy to get comfortable. I didn't have a class until later today, and since I wasn't about to shower in a dorm block communal setting, I was feeling much less put together than usual.

Thank God no one had seen me. If I could keep it that way until later today, that would be A-okay with me.

As we pulled up at the Towers, I glanced at my phone, wondering if JT's morning was going as well as mine. Sure, I could do with a good shower and something a little less constrictive than a python squeezing my ass, but at least I didn't have to go anywhere.

JT was currently at breakfast with the *dean*, for fuck's sake. Sure, it was his mom, but still, there was no way he couldn't smell me all over his skin after the things we'd done to each other last night.

My dick jerked as I thought back to the way JT had explored my body after that first go-around, when the initial shyness wore off and was replaced with curiosity. He'd kissed and touched me all over, and when he ventured down to my cock and sucked on it for the second time, the only thoughts on my mind had been about soft brown curls, malleable lips, and eyes that were full of arousal and trust.

I winced as the zipper pressed against my newly awakened hard-on, quickly shoved aside thoughts of sweet smiles and naïve charm, and climbed out of the van. I needed to get upstairs and somehow peel these the hell off me before they caused irreparable damage.

With my head down, I booked it through the lobby to the elevator, not wanting to stop and talk with anyone, and seconds later I was stepping off onto my floor. I twisted my ring around my index finger as I walked down the hall to the door, and just as I was about to pass the key card over the pad, the door opened and East and Donovan appeared in the entrance.

Fuck.

"Well, would you look at what the cat dragged in." East ran an assessing eye over my disheveled state, and I almost wished I was back in JT's dorm room closet. "And 'dragged' seems rather polite with how you look this morning."

I rolled my eyes and shoved in past them, and Donovan chuckled as they stepped aside.

"Nice jeans, or are they those jegging things?"

I threw my jacket over the couch and turned on the two morons standing in the foyer looking me over with shit-eating grins.

"Weren't you just leaving?" I pointed out, but unfortunately for me it seemed my luck was up, because East shut the door and they wandered back into the living room.

"We were, but I'm willing to risk being late if it means

finding out where you decided to sleep last night. If I were to take a guess based off your horrible ensemble right now, I'd say you woke up in a GapKids store."

Donovan started to laugh as I leveled a glare in their direction.

"Since I know you won't shut up until I tell you, I spent the night at JT's."

"And woke up in his *jeans?*" Donovan's eyes widened as East's narrowed.

"You said it, not me."

East strolled over, running his eyes up from the unforgiving denim to my crumpled shirt. "Bullshit."

I shrugged. "It's the truth. You think I'm walking around in these dick stranglers for fun?"

"I have no idea how you're walking at all. But that still doesn't prove anything."

"Oh, so I just happened to put on his pants for shits and giggles? I don't think so. We took our pants off last night, and when his mom knocked on the door this morning—"

"No she fucking didn't." Donovan laughed.

"—JT gave me his jeans by accident while shoving me in his closet."

East blinked at me once, twice, and then his lips twisted into an immoral smile. "You dog."

"I told you." I winked. "Straight or not, they all fall for me in the end."

East slapped me on the back and shook his head, and

the horrified expression from earlier had morphed into that of a proud parent.

He was such a fucking reprobate.

"Now let's not get ahead of ourselves." East eyed me, a fiendish spark in his expression. "The bet wasn't that the golden boy would let you kiss him. That would be too easy, and you would've won already. The bet was that *you* could corrupt him. That you could make him fall for you and do anything to have you. So, what has he done to you?"

I knew exactly what the bet was. I'd been working every angle I could to win it since I'd seen JT that first day of school. But as East reminded me why I'd been in his room last night, and I remembered the way JT's lips had felt against my bare skin, I found myself reluctant to spill the details.

East scoffed. "Oh, so our little ray of sunshine *did* go down in the West last night."

I shook my head. "Shut the fuck up."

"Wait, so he didn't?" Donovan asked, shrugging his bag up over his shoulder.

"I've gotta get out of these jeans." I stepped past East and headed toward my room, dodging their questions and suspicious looks. "I'll catch up with you assholes later this afternoon."

"Don't think this bet is over, Weston." East's voice echoed up the hall. "To win you have to have solid proof, and so far all I see is a denim mold of your ass. You're going to have to be more convincing than that to win your dream vacation."

I flipped him off as I entered my room, knowing full well I could've given in-depth descriptions of what JT and I had done last night. But spilling those details to my friends didn't sit quite right with me.

Maybe it was the shock of everything that had happened this morning, or the lack of blood flow to my brain from these fucking jeans, but the idea of laughing with East and Donovan about my night with JT made my stomach turn. Not because I was worried they'd make fun of me—hell, they'd likely high-five me and pour me a drink after East bitched about forking over his private jet for me to use—but because last night hadn't gone the way I'd thought it would.

I'd thought I'd show up at JT's, we'd have some fun, and afterward I'd peace out and go meet up with my friends. Instead, I'd stayed the night, and no matter how hard I tried to tell myself it was just so I could get another taste of him, I knew deep down there was another reason —I hadn't *wanted* to leave.

What the hell was I doing? I wasn't the kind of guy who caught feelings, and I certainly wasn't going to start now. So if I could stop thinking like some lovesick fool with a crush, that'd be fucking awesome.

I was doing this for a bet. I was with *JT* to get back at his mom, and once I had it in the bag, I'd tell my friends.

I locked my bedroom door and headed into the en

suite, and when I caught a glimpse of myself in the mirror, I grimaced.

Jesus, East was right. I did look like something the cat had dragged in, and maybe that was the problem. The reason my head was all over the place. I wasn't feeling myself right now.

Well, it was time to change that.

I put my phone down on the vanity and stripped out of my shirt. Then I popped open the button of the jeans and let out a sigh as I finally removed the torturous garment from my body.

When they were finally in a heap on the floor at my feet, I shook my head. What a fucking morning. If I hadn't actually been there myself, I wouldn't believe everything that had happened. But as I thought back to the rude awakening, the closet, and this damn pair of jeans, I snapped a photo of them, laughing, wondering if JT was feeling the same, then I sent a text.

> BTW, I have your jeans. If you want 'em back you have to come and get them. Otherwise I'm torching the motherfucking things.

THIRTY

"YOU SURE YOU don't want to try my eggs Florentine?" Mom lifted one half of her English muffin topped with a poached egg, spinach, and I didn't know what else, and I shook my head.

"I don't know if I'll be able to finish what's on my own plate." I'd ordered so much that it'd taken three plates to bring it all out. But hey, I'd been ravenous on our walk here, having worked up quite an appetite after the hours I'd spent with West...doing things the woman across from me would die over if she knew.

But she didn't know. And she wouldn't. Not until I figured out what West and I were doing.

Christ, what *were* we doing?

"I'm just glad to see you eating," Mom said. "If we had time, I'd take you shopping for some new jeans."

"Nah, that's okay. I must've just...stretched these out or something."

Mom frowned, and I speared my stack of souffle pancakes, making sure it was an extra-large mouthful for her benefit.

Appeased for the moment, she thankfully changed the subject.

"How are your classes going so far? Anything giving you trouble?"

"Am I supposed to believe you haven't already asked each one of my professors how I'm doing?"

She at least had the grace to look offended. "I promised you I wouldn't speak with your professors unless there's a problem, and I haven't."

"Really?"

"Yes, really. I'd expect you to come to me if there was any issue."

Huh. That was a first. Even my high school teachers had gotten an earful if they so much as assigned home-work on a holiday weekend. "Everything's fine. Honestly. It's been an easier adjustment than I expected."

"Good, that's good." She held up her glass as the waiter refilled it with grapefruit juice. "And you're still happy with the living situation? Because you can always come home—"

"No," I said a little too quickly. "I mean, uh, the dorm's great. I know I complained about it before, but it's actu-ally nice to have my own space."

"See? I knew you'd settle in just fine and want some privacy. And you feel safe there too, right?"

"Yep. Security's great." Other than the fact West and

his friends could get by them anytime they wanted. A serious flaw for sure, but one that was working in my favor at the moment.

"I'm glad to hear it. The last thing we want is some troublemaker breaking into your room." Mom jabbed a little harder than necessary at her sliced fruit.

Had she... Did she know? Surely not. She would've led with that and not waited until now if she'd heard West had been caught sneaking in my dorm.

Still...

I tried for indifference. "I haven't given anyone a reason to want to break into my room. Nothing of value in there anyway."

"You're my son. That's reason enough."

I frowned. "What are you saying?"

She stopped stabbing at a grape, and when she looked me in the eye, her expression softened a little. "Nothing. I'm sorry. I suppose I'm just being cautious. That's what parents do, you know. Worry."

"Yeah, you've mentioned that a time or two before," I said, winking at her to lighten how tense she'd gotten all of a sudden.

There seemed to be something else on her mind, though, and I sent up a prayer that she hadn't installed any cameras in my room without my knowledge.

"You haven't been bothered by Weston LaRue again, have you?"

Ah, there it was. No doubt she'd been dying to ask that since she knocked on my door.

"Are you really bringing him up again?" I said.

"Yes."

"Why?"

"Because I don't trust him. I don't want you mixed up in anything he and his friends are doing."

"I barely know the guy." A pang of guilt settled low in my stomach at having to lie to her, but she seemed to have it out for West, and from everything I'd learned about him, it felt unjustified. And what she didn't know wouldn't hurt her...or make her stay up all night worrying.

Mom's lips pulled into a thin line, and she nodded. "Okay. But...if he asks you to do anything—even if it seems innocent—just say no. All right?"

There hadn't been a lot of the word "no" when it came to West so far, and I was doing pretty okay. Better than okay, actually.

But I reached over to gently squeeze her arm. "I hear you. Now stop worrying. You've got enough on your plate at Astor without stressing over me."

She gave me a small smile and put her hand over mine briefly before popping a grape into her mouth. "Speaking of worriers, your dad was hoping you'd get a chance to stop by the library one of these days, since you're close by. Maybe you two could have lunch?"

The New York Public Library was practically my dad's second home, especially now that I was out of the house and Mom worked such long hours.

"Yeah, that's a great idea. I've been meaning to call him."

As I filed that on my mental to-do list, Mom's phone went off, and she reached into her purse to check the screen before quickly silencing it.

"Shoot, I need to take this, honey." She gave me an apologetic look. "I'll only be a sec."

"Take your time," I said, gesturing to all the food I had left to scarf down.

Mom answered the call as she scooted past the tables and out the front door, and I waited until she was out of view to grab my own phone.

Speak of the devil...

There was a text from West waiting, and my mouth fell open when I opened it and there was a photo of my jeans in a heap on the floor.

STALKER:

BTW I have your jeans. If you want 'em back you have to come and get them. Otherwise I'm torching the motherfucking things.

Oh shit.

I wanted to slap my damn forehead. I hadn't even thought about the fact that even though *I* was wearing West's jeans, he'd be forced to wear mine home. I could only imagine him having to squeeze into a pair that were too short and too tight and having to walk-of-shame it. I'd pay to see that view, though, and I chuckled to myself.

> I'll definitely be coming for the jeans. They're my favorite. Btw, I think I stole something else in addition to your jeans…

I hadn't meant to, but I must've grabbed his boxer briefs thinking they were mine. But I hadn't been wearing any last night...

STALKER:

> Tell me you're not wearing my fucking underwear.

Laughing, I sent back a zipped lips emoji.

STALKER:

> Thanks for that. I'm going to use that image in my shower right now.

. . .

That was seriously hot. But it was also doing things to my body I'd rather not happen right now.

> You do remember I'm sitting at breakfast with my mom, right?

STALKER:

Yeah, but I'm not, and all I can think about is your dick in my boxers and jeans.

> Speaking of my jeans, it's too bad you didn't snap a pic of yourself in them. I could use a good laugh.

I glanced out the window to make sure Mom was still occupied before l looked back at my phone.

STALKER:

Does this inspire a laugh or make you want to bite it?

A few seconds later, a photo popped up, a shot of West's bare ass, still outlined in pink from the stitching of the too-tight denim. I'd expected to laugh at an image of him encased in tight jeans, but the photo he'd sent me was hot, seriously fucking hot, made even better by the fact that he'd been wearing something of mine. No doubt West had probably managed to pull off looking amazing in jeans a couple sizes too small, because I was beginning to wonder if there was anything he couldn't do.

That in and of itself would be annoying as hell if my body didn't have specific memories of *other*, more intimate things he did just as well...

My face heated as I tried to push those delicious thoughts to the back of my mind, because now was *not* the time to think about all the things I wanted to. My mind was a mess I needed to sort out, and not at breakfast with my mom. I sent back a fire emoji.

> Bite it. Definitely. I think I might let you keep the jeans after all.

STALKER:

> Nah, I'd rather you come in them. I mean, for them. ;)

Good God, I needed to shut this down before the grin on my face grew any wider. How was it West could have such an effect on me? I'd known him for a few weeks and already I could feel this massive shift in my life. Opening up sexually to a guy hadn't been on my radar, and if I went back and told pre-Astor me the things I'd done, he never would've believed it. The me *now* could still barely believe it.

But kissing West was as natural as breathing, only with the full-body flutters that were normally contained to my stomach. Was that a normal reaction?

He was just so...different. His body was rock hard under my hands. He took what he wanted, no hesitation, just desire, hot and intense. West's complete lack of self-consciousness made it easier to want to try new things, and last night, I'd certainly checked a few off.

I squirmed in my seat, getting hard just thinking about it. There was something to be said for new experiences, though I wasn't sure if it was something I'd be open to if it weren't with West.

Even now, scanning the room for an attractive face, my eyes didn't stop on any of the guys, though there were a few that would be considered conventionally good looking. Would I be as open to kissing any of them, or more, if the chance arose? Or was it just West's magnetism that had my stomach in knots?

Biting down on my thumb to keep from smiling so hard, I read over West's texts again, careful not to scroll up to the photo of his ass as I heard my mom approach.

"You look happy," she said, pulling out her chair and

looking at me with a pleased, but curious, expression. "What's got you grinning so big?"

I quickly shut off my cell and shoved it deep into the pocket of West's baggy jeans. "Nothin' much. Just a funny meme someone sent me."

"Oh, you'll have to send it to me."

Send my mom a photo of West's ass? Only if I wanted to give her a coronary.

Nodding, I rubbed my jaw, needing a subject change and fast. "That wasn't work calling already, was it?"

"Yes, I'm so sorry. We've had an unexpected expense, which has sent the budget into disarray..."

As she went into all the reasons she was dealing with incompetence, I let out a thankful breath that she'd taken the bait. I'd already had too many close calls this morning, and I needed to keep the focus on her.

The rest of breakfast passed uneventfully, thank God, and by the time I'd walked with her back to Astor, it was time for class. It wasn't lost on me that I hadn't gotten a chance to shower or change before starting my day. That meant West's scent would linger on me, driving me crazy —in a good way—for hours, and like he knew I was thinking of him in that very moment, my phone buzzed.

STALKER:

Don't make plans for Friday night. You're mine.

THIRTY-ONE

"HMM. CENTRAL PARK at night. Should I be worried?"

JT grinned at me as we made our way through the park, but we were far from the only ones.

"You should. This is where I dump the bodies of all the guys I'm done with after they've sucked my dick."

There was a low gasp, followed by a rough shove that knocked me off balance. I laughed as JT cursed my name, his curls scattering as he shook his head.

Did the couples around us hear me? Sure. Did I care? Not in the slightest.

JT groaned. "Please say that a little louder next time."

If it hadn't been dark, I was positive I'd see a blush on his cheeks.

"Is that a dare? 'Cuz I'll do it." I brushed my hand along the back of his as we walked. The urge to hold his hand hit me out of nowhere, but I held myself back.

"Nooo, not a dare. I don't think there's anything you *won't* do."

"You might be right about that," I murmured as the makeshift movie screen came into view. There were two lines of food trucks on either side, and between them, string lights crisscrossed over the fifty or so small round tables set up for dining.

"What's that?" JT asked. "It can't be where we're going. You'd never eat from a food truck."

"Maybe I wanted to bring you somewhere that would make you feel a little more comfortable." I didn't grab his hand, but I did place mine on his lower back to guide him toward the entrance. All the while I watched him, his eyes bright as he took in every detail. It was rare I spent my Friday night somewhere other than partying, but I thought JT might want to do something a little different.

"Movie by the Mouthful?" he read off the sign, and looked at me.

"As we watch the movie, they bring out food and drinks based on what the characters are eating."

"No way. What movie?"

"Ever seen *Chef?*"

JT's mouth fell open. "Shut up, I love that movie."

I grinned. "Get ready for some molten fucking lava cake."

The excitement on his face was contagious, especially once we were sat at a table in the center and he read off the menu for the night.

"Oh my God, we even get beignets. This is the coolest thing ever."

"I'm glad you think so."

JT set the menu down and looked at me curiously. "You like this kind of thing?"

"We'll find out. I know I like the movie." It had been pure luck JT did too. But who didn't love Jon Favreau and John Leguizamo?

"Hmm." That was all he said as he rested his chin on his fist and watched me.

I wiped at my face, looked down at my shirt, but I didn't see anything out of place. "What?"

"This is a date, isn't it?"

My mouth opened to utter a denial, because I didn't go on dates. I never had.

Instead I focused on moving my silverware a few inches to the right. "Do you...want it to be?"

"I asked you first."

I met his eyes. "What do you think?"

"I think you're trying not to answer." A smile began to spread across his lips. "It's totally a date. You like me, West, you can admit it."

"Maybe I just like the way you—"

JT clamped a hand over my mouth before I could say something that would have him blushing again.

"Admit it," he said softly.

It was hard not to want to give him anything he asked for when he looked at me like that. After a long moment, I nodded. JT's grin grew wider, and he pulled his hand away.

"Thank you."

Whether he meant that as a thank you for admitting it or for the date itself, I didn't know. Maybe both. Either way, I shoved down the strange feeling in my chest and looked around for a waiter to get me a damn drink.

I didn't have to wait long. Soon the lights overhead dimmed and the movie began, and not even two minutes in, our first dish was being set in front of us.

With the opening scene being one featuring a pig, we received a tasting dish of spicy honey pork belly, and not three minutes later, at the mention of New Orleans, a hurricane cocktail to wash it down with.

If that was the kickoff, we were both gonna leave here more than happy, because that shit was damn good.

"You know," JT whispered, "I seem to remember you giving me hell over liking food trucks."

"So?"

"So it looks like each of these trucks is in charge of one of the meals or cocktails. And from the way you just forced yourself not to lick your plate, I'm thinkin' you liked it."

"Me? Lick my plate?" I scoffed. "Unless you're being served up on that plate, I'm not licking anything."

JT choked out a laugh, muffling it with his napkin. "I'm not on the menu tonight. At least not here."

Great. Now that was all I was gonna be able to think about—getting JT naked and laying him out on this table in front of everyone to devour the way I wanted to. My dick was completely on board with that plan, if the sudden tight fit of my pants was any indication.

I tried to focus back on the movie and only succeeded when the next dish was brought out. Molly's Post-Sex Pasta, otherwise known as Aglio e Olio.

"This is my favorite part," JT whispered, scooting his chair a little closer to mine as Jon Favreau's Chef Carl Casper ripped into a food critic bashing his meal. I wasn't even sure if JT noticed he'd done it, or if it was a subconscious move. I didn't mind. If he wanted to straddle my damn lap, I would've been okay with that too.

Miniature chocolate lava cakes were passed around as the chef onscreen yelled about the insides being fucking molten, grabbing it up with his bare hand as evidence. Luckily, we were given forks instead of having to use our fingers.

I didn't even hesitate as JT cut into his cake and the liquid inside came spilling out. I swiped some of the chocolate with my finger and held it up in front of his mouth, painting his lips as I waited for him to open up.

When he caught my wrist, I thought he'd pull away.

But JT never did what I expected him to.

His brown eyes smoldered as he sucked my finger deep into his mouth, licking me clean in a way my dick was getting jealous of by the second. The urge to reach down between my thighs to better position my growing erection was strong, but I didn't want to get us kicked out of here.

JT gently nipped at the tip of my finger before letting go, and I raised a brow.

"How'd I taste?" I said, keeping my voice low.

He leaned in like he was going to kiss me. "So good I'm tempted to ask for another mouthful."

His words and his sugary-sweet breath on my lips had me thinking, *Fuck it.* It hadn't been my plan for PDA, not when anyone could see us, but in that moment I just didn't care.

"You're right," I said, brushing my mouth against his before leaning back. "I do taste really fucking good."

JT let out a bark of laughter. Without thinking, I threw my arm over the back of his chair, noticing the way he went still for a heartbeat. But then his shoulders dropped and he relaxed against me, his curls brushing against my arm.

I liked that, liked the way he went along with anything, like he trusted that his curiosity and attraction wouldn't lead him wrong.

Like he trusted me.

He shouldn't, a voice in the back of my mind said. *You'll only end up hurting him.*

Oh, fuck off, I thought, shoving the guilt somewhere I didn't have to hear it. For the past few days, all I'd heard from the guys were taunts about JT and when was I going to close the deal already.

I was about ready to throw them all out a goddamn window.

With my arm still over the back of JT's chair, I focused

on the movie and finishing my lava cake. Each portion of food was small, but I could feel myself getting full, and we weren't even halfway through yet.

It might be a good idea to cancel the car service and walk off the meal later. Unless we needed rolling out of here, in which case, I wasn't canceling anything just yet.

As Chef Casper headed down to Miami, JT nodded at him at a club dancing salsa.

"Can you do that?"

"You've seen me dance."

"No, not the club stuff. Like that."

I watched their moves. "I've never tried. You?"

"Nah, I don't think my hips could move like that."

"Trust me, Golden Boy, your hips aren't a problem."

"Oh really?" JT rolled his head on my arm, looking up at me. "So what's my problem, then?"

I shrugged. "Maybe you just need a good partner."

"Yeah? Someone knowledgeable to teach me the moves?" A teasing glint sparked his eyes, or maybe that was the dim string lights reflected in them.

"You seem pretty self-motivated to learn already. Not sure you need a teacher."

"Just another willing participant, then?"

I smirked. "We still talkin' about salsa, JT?"

"I honestly have no idea," he said, shaking his head. He rested his neck back on my arm, and his curls tickled my skin in the warm breeze.

The movie, and tasting, continued, a round of Miami mojitos up next, followed by Cubanos. And just when I thought there couldn't possibly be more, a final course was served, beignets topped with what seemed like an inch of powdered sugar.

They were decadent and just the right amount of pillowy softness. You devoured two before you realized you'd done it.

"I didn't even need that dipping sauce," JT said, licking the sugar off his fingers, but when he saw me watching his mouth, he dropped his hand. "You can't look at me like that."

"Says who?"

He shook his head and murmured, "Trouble."

"Me? Trouble?" I gave him my most tempting smile. "Who would ever say that about this face?"

"Lots of people."

"And it bothers you what people say?"

"I don't need other people telling me who they think you are."

He said it so matter-of-factly that it caught me off guard. I knew his mom and Caleb probably hadn't been the only ones telling him I was bad news. And while maybe I deserved it, I was glad JT hadn't listened.

The string lights overhead brightened as the movie credits began to roll, and we both finished off our drinks before getting to our feet.

"That might be one of my favorite things I've ever done in the city," JT said as we strolled out of the park alongside other moviegoers. We headed in the direction of his dorm, and I shot a text to my driver, keeping him on standby for later.

"You know what? I might agree with you." Or maybe it had more to do with the person I was with.

"At least a nice change from clubs every night, right?"

"Are you saying you don't like a wild party?"

He ran his hand through his hair as we stopped at a crosswalk, letting it fall back at his side as the signal turned white. "Not *every* night. Don't you get tired of them?"

"Not really. I'm not crazy about the hangovers, but..." I shrugged. "It's what we do."

When we stepped back up on the sidewalk, my hand automatically went to JT's lower back, moving us out of the way of a couple who weren't paying attention to where they were walking.

As we passed them, I dropped my hand, and we walked in silence for half a block before JT said, "Do the guys know you took me to a movie in Central Park tonight?"

"I could ask you the same. Does your mom know?"

We both looked at each other at the same time, the answer to that one clear.

Hell no.

If the dean had a clue, JT would be behind a padded cell door, not walking the streets with me.

"I just realized something," he said, stopping to look around. "Where's your driver?"

"I do know how to use my legs on occasion."

"Bullshit," he said, laughing. "You're just trying to walk off all that food we ate."

"For good reason. If they'd served me another beignet, I think my stomach would've combusted right there on the spot."

"Ugh, it was so good, though. I wonder if they taste like the real thing."

"As opposed to…what, fake ones?"

"Yeah, like the ones in New Orleans. Those are the real ones."

"This is New York," I said, gesturing around us. There was an intangible buzz in the air here, there always was, and I could feel it in my veins no matter where in the city I went. "Everything is better here."

"Some might say that's a close-minded opinion," JT teased.

"Then those people would be wrong. I've been everywhere. Seen everything. There's no place like this."

"I'm not disagreeing with you. I love that there's always something new happening, like what we did tonight. It's never boring."

No, it was definitely never boring.

The backs of our hands grazed each other's as we walked, every touch forcing my focus to the one spot we connected. We'd been closer than this before, but something about it felt intimate in a different way. Like if I laced my fingers through his, it would mean more than just holding a random guy's hand.

Not to mention that the likelihood of one of our peers

seeing us like that was greater the closer we got to his dorm.

I kept my distance, not wanting to risk it, but as his building came into view, I found myself not wanting to let him go just yet. The guys were all going out—were probably already at the club—but I wasn't ready for my time with JT to be over.

I chewed on the inside of my cheek as he turned to face me.

"Did you wanna come up?" he asked with a nervous smile.

Did I? Fuck yes. But I didn't want an unexpected visitor popping in unannounced like last time. And truth be told, I wasn't sure overnight would be long enough...

"I have a better idea," I said before I thought too much about it. "East is out of town this weekend. Why don't you stay with me?"

JT blinked, his forehead furrowing like he didn't understand my request.

"You want me to...stay with you? All weekend?"

"Yeah, why not? We'll have the place to ourselves. No one has a key, so they won't know you're even there."

I could see the war in his eyes, that he wanted to do it, but something held him back.

"That sounds amazing. But I do actually need to study this weekend—"

"Then you can do it at my place."

He snorted. "You think you can manage to keep your

hands off me long enough for me to get some work done?"

"Hey, I *can* show some restraint. Besides, I'm sure there's something school-related I need to catch up on. You can inspire me."

When I winked, JT bit back a smile and looked down, and I knew I had him.

"Pack your shit," I said, lifting his chin. "And come home with me."

THIRTY-TWO

THE GENTLE SPLASHING sound of water had my eyes opening the next day, as it washed away the haze of sleep and sunlight crept in through the window to dapple my face.

It wasn't my usual wake-up call, but as I rolled over and caught sight of the Chrysler Building greeting me, I wasn't about to complain. It sure as hell beat my alarm clock.

Wow...

I pushed up on my elbow and rubbed a hand over my face as I stared out at one of the most spectacular views in the city—hell, the world, some might argue—and still couldn't quite wrap my head around the fact that West lived here.

It was so outlandish, so pretentious, and while parts of that fit West and the person I'd first met when I started at Astor, last night he'd shown me a totally different side of himself.

The sound of running water found me again, and I glanced over my shoulder to see West's side of the mattress was empty. It'd been late last night when we got back to his place, and even *later* when we finally fell asleep. But after our delicious dinner date in the park and last-minute packing for my impromptu weekend getaway, I'd passed out the second my head hit the pillow.

Some date I was. I'd barely had the energy to kiss him goodnight. But it was his own fault. He'd filled my belly, walked me through Central Park, and by the time we got back to his place, I'd drifted off into the best damn sleep of my life.

I mean, who wouldn't? His mattress was so luxurious and soft it was probably made up from royal goose feathers or something just as outrageous.

I swung my legs over the edge of the bed and realized I was in nothing but my boxer briefs. I glanced around the floor, looking for the clothes I'd stripped out of, and frowned when I couldn't see them. Maybe West had put them somewhere?

My bag was out in the living room. I remembered leaving it there when he'd given me a tour now that the place had actual furniture, and if I'd thought his condo was impressive the night of the party, *with* furniture it was like something out of a movie. It didn't seem real.

He'd told me all about how their group lived in the

building—hence the nickname Park Avenue Princes—and how each of them were paired up with another friend because their parents thought it was the best way to keep their kids out of trouble. Clearly that hadn't worked, judging by the reputation that seemed to follow West and his crew around.

As I got to my feet to go and grab my belongings, I decided at the last second to take the sheet with me. West had assured me that East was out of town for the weekend. But in the unlikely event he decided to cut short whatever jet-setting trip he'd taken, I didn't want to be caught by West's roommate wandering around his living room in my briefs.

I wrapped the sheet around my waist and hiked the remaining material up off the floor. I glanced inside the open entryway of the en suite at the marble floor and walls, and saw the wide bathroom vanity up ahead, its full-length mirror running along as much of the wall as I could see.

From the tour last night I knew that there was a shower to the left and a bathtub overlooking the same view I'd woken up to on the right. But judging from the sound of rain falling, I knew exactly where West was.

My cock kicked at the mental image of him standing in the shower all slick and wet, and I stared at my reflection in the mirror, wondering if I was brave enough to go in and see the real thing.

Holding the sheet in place, I stepped inside the bathroom and was immediately hit with the scent of West's soap or shampoo as it swirled around me. Damn, that was why he always smelled good. Whatever he was using in there was crisp yet creamy, sweet and a little spicy, and as it wound itself around me, I felt intoxicated. It was sexy and sophisticated, just like the man himself, and no doubt helped with the "I get whoever I want, whenever I want" part of his life.

He'd gotten me, hadn't he? It wasn't like I stood in naked men's bathrooms every weekend for fun. But as that delicious scent beckoned me closer, I knew there was no other place I'd rather be.

I walked into the center of the en suite and realized that my imagination had nothing on the reality of West naked and wet, standing under a shower spray. Steam swirled around him, fogging some of the glass, but the peekaboo way it hid parts of his body only added to the sexy overall effect.

West's head was tipped back and his eyes were closed as he ran his fingers through his hair and the water sluiced down over his neck to his chest. I greedily followed the droplets of water as they ran in rivulets along the hard ridges of his body, and as they disappeared behind the fogged part of the glass and fell to the shower floor, I licked my lips.

Jesus, talk about feeling thirsty. West made me feel as though I'd been in a sexual drought my entire life, and he was a goddamn oasis. He almost seemed too perfect to be true. Like a mirage that was going to disappear from sight, just when I reached the heart of it.

"JT?" West swiped the water from his eyes and moved his head out from under the spray.

"Hi, um, morning."

"Morning?" While the polite thing was probably to turn away and give him some privacy, he didn't seem all that concerned I was staring at him. "It's probably more afternoon at this stage."

I frowned, wondering just how long I'd slept. "Really?"

"Really." He slicked a hand through his hair, and dear God, I didn't think I'd ever seen anything hotter. "When I left you, it was almost noon."

My mouth fell open in disbelief. "No way."

"Guess I wore you out last night with my quick wit and conversation. That's a first—usually it's with my body."

My eyes immediately dropped to the body he was referring to, and I didn't doubt him for a second. Not when I'd been on the receiving end of what he could do with it.

I cleared my throat. "I guess you did. But for the record, I enjoyed every minute of our conversation last night."

"Me too, but now I'm starting to feel a little self-conscious..."

Shit. Had I overstepped by coming in here? As soon as the thought crossed my mind, West chuckled.

"Not because you're in here, JT. Because I'm standing here naked, and we're *still* just talking."

"Oh."

"You're starting to give me a complex."

"Yeah, right."

"It's true," West said, turning around so the front of his body took the brunt of the spray. "Here I am, naked and vulnerable, and you still have a...sheet? Wrapped around you?"

"Vulnerable?" I grinned and bit down on my lower lip. That was the last word I'd ever use to describe him.

"Yes." West swiped his hand across the fog on the glass, and when his thick erection came into view, it was all I could do to keep my tongue from rolling out of my mouth. "I'm at my *most* vulnerable right now. Can't you see?"

I could see, all right. It was pretty hard to miss now that he'd cleared things up for me.

"Why does the word 'vulnerable' sound a whole lot like 'powerful' coming out of your mouth?"

"I don't know." He flashed an arrogant smirk as he circled his cock. "You tell me."

God, if I had one ounce of the charisma West did, I'd feel invincible too. "You're good looking to the point it's ridiculous?"

He eyed me through the glass. "How about good looking enough to have you dropping the sheet?"

Knowing I wasn't naked underneath, I felt the devil on my shoulder urging me to have a little fun with West. It was time for some payback. Time to tease him a little.

He was always the one who had the upper hand, so maybe it was time to play with *him* for a change.

I reached for the spot where I'd tucked the sheet in by my hip. "You want me to take this off?"

West licked at the condensation on his top lip. "More than my next breath."

I swallowed and moved so I was standing in front of the glass. Then I flattened my hand and slid it down to where my hard-on ached between my thighs. "I can do that."

"Yeah, you can."

"And then what?"

West moved in the shower stall until he was leaning back against the marble wall, and when he widened his stance and pumped his shaft, I curled my fingers around the material covering me.

This plan to tease West sure felt a lot like I was teasing myself.

"Then..." West's voice was gravel rough. "We can see if I can wear you out with more than just my scintillating conversation."

"Did you really just use the word *scintillating* while stroking your dick?"

"What can I say, your scholastic ways are rubbing off on me."

I snorted and reached for the tucked-in edge of the sheet.

"Then maybe you're right." I dragged my teeth over

my lip as I let my eyes linger on his flexing fingers. "And I'll find other ways to rub off on you too."

"Hell yes." West nodded and pushed off the wall. "Do it. Drop the sheet and get in here."

"Yeah?" I said, bolder than I'd ever been as I angled my chin up. "That's what you want?"

I wasn't sure why, but something was pushing me to get him to admit it. To get West to admit that he wanted me as much as I wanted him. Talk about feeling vulnerable.

"JT?"

"Yeah?"

"Drop the fucking sheet."

There was that cocky arrogance again, and it was all I needed to decide to follow through with this little game and give him a taste of his own medicine.

I took a step back, and as the sheet fell to the floor and he caught sight of my boxer briefs *still* covering me, his eyes narrowed.

"You better take them the fuck off."

I chuckled and ran my thumb inside the edge of my underwear. "What? These? No, you just said the sheet, and, well, anything more and I might start to feel...vulnerable."

"JT..." West said as I started to walk backward. "Don't make me chase you."

My dick lurched at that threat, and I was starting to discover things about myself I never knew.

First: I liked bossy, arrogant men.

Second: I also liked the way West looked at me like he wanted to devour me.

And third: I apparently liked the thrill of the chase.

Because the second he turned off the water and I saw him reach for the towel, I turned and made a mad dash for the bedroom. My heart pounded almost as hard as my cock, but when there was nowhere for me to hide, I ran out of the bedroom door and down the hall.

I heard the sound of his feet on the marble floor behind me, but didn't look back. It wasn't until a large hand gripped my arm and drew me to a halt in the middle of his living room that I glanced over my shoulder.

West's warm breath was harsh by my cheek, his wet chest pressed up against my back, and as he wrapped his other arm around my waist, my entire body trembled.

Jesus. I couldn't remember the last time I'd been so turned on. But when West's hard-on bumped up against my ass, I moaned.

Without a word, he walked me over to the wall of windows flanking the living room. Then he slid his hand down inside my briefs and curled his fingers around me.

"You little fucking tease," he said, and flicked the tip of his tongue over my lobe.

A shiver raced up my spine as I leaned back into him, and never had I felt more aroused than I did right then.

"Feeling *powerful* right now, JT?"

I wasn't sure what I was feeling, but it was good. I rolled my hips back against him, making him groan.

"Then how about this?" West moved his lips to the

side of my neck and sucked. "We both get each other off. Right here, on top of the fucking world..."

In that moment I would've given him anything, handjob included.

Minutes later, I did.

And when West bit down into my shoulder and came all over me, I realized what it meant to feel truly powerful.

"YOU'RE STARING AGAIN..."

I glanced up from my laptop and looked at where West sat opposite me in a velvet accent chair. He had his feet propped up on the coffee table and a book in hand, and while I'd been trying my hardest to ignore the heated stares he was aiming my way, the flush on my cheeks was becoming more and more of a distraction.

"You're cute when you concentrate. It's difficult not to."

"Cute?" I scrunched up my nose and directed my attention back to the essay I'd been trying my hardest to write for the last hour or so. Not an easy feat when I was in the same room with a personality that dominated the space just by its presence.

"Yeah." West laid the open book over his thigh. "Your brow furrows, and you get this little V right here." He rubbed a finger between his eyebrows. "Very cute."

I'd never been called cute before, and especially not by a guy, so I wasn't quite sure how to take it. "Um, thanks?"

West chuckled. "It's a compliment, JT. I like how you

look, and I like looking *at* you. You're so different from the people I know. I find myself watching you to see the way you'll react to things."

"You mean to see if I'm going to be all wide-eyed and impressed by your money and charm?"

"Don't forget my amazing body."

I picked up a Twizzler from the packet I'd been munching on and tossed it at West's head, and when he caught it and bit down into the candy, I forced myself *not* to look at his mouth.

"Well, it doesn't matter *why* you're looking at me— you need to stop. I'm trying to work, and it's distracting."

"Because you *want* my amazing body."

"Wessst." I groaned and pretended to beat my head on the back of the couch. "I have to get this done. You promised if I stayed here this weekend you'd let me work."

"I know, I know, but isn't it break time yet?"

I let out a sigh, doing my best to feign annoyance. But my grin was a dead giveaway that I was more than happy to stop.

"Okay, you get"—I looked at the time on my phone— "fifteen minutes."

"Fifteen minutes? We've been working for hours."

"*I've* been working for hours. You've ordered lunch, eaten lunch, listened to your headphones, and read some of that book—is that for class or fun?"

"It's a book about how 'a small group of Wall Street

iconoclasts realize that the U.S. stock market has been rigged for the benefit of insiders.' What do you think?"

I chuckled and shook my head. "It's definitely not my idea of fun. But I've never been very good at math and numbers."

"But JT, how are you going to count your millions if you aren't good at numbers?"

"Millions?" I scoffed. "Yeah, somehow I don't see myself counting wads of cash from whatever career I go into."

"No? Why not? You got a thing against money?"

I laughed and looked around his lavish condo. "No. But I highly doubt my poetry or writing is going to land me a condo at the Towers."

"You don't know that."

"Says the man reading books about Wall Street for *fun*."

West shrugged, his smile a little sheepish. "It is fun for me."

"Really?" I didn't believe him for a second.

"Well, not Wall Street per se, but finances in general. That's my major. I'm good with numbers, they make sense in my head, and if I want to take over the family business one day"—West winked at me—"then it doesn't hurt to know how the world of money works."

I wasn't sure why, but the idea of West majoring in finances seemed so out of character for him. It was too low-key. West was so charismatic, and numbers were just...boring.

"You look horrified."

I really needed to get better at keeping a neutral expression. "Not horrified, no. I was just... I guess I was just wondering if that was your idea or your parents'?"

"To run this place?" West looked over his shoulder at the magnificent view, then back to me. "Do I look crazy? Running the Astoria would be a privilege. But it's one I'm going to have to earn. So while I'm positive my parents are happy with the direction I decided to take, they definitely didn't force it on me."

"That makes sense. I just figured with your parents owning such a massive company that they might—"

"Force me into a job I don't want? Nah. Some of the other guys are in that situation, but mine, they're pretty cool. What about you? You into all that poetry and creative writing because of the librarian and the dean?"

My eyes widened at West's recollection of what my dad did for a living, because as far I could remember, we'd only ever talked about it the first time we met.

"Ah, no. Like you, they pretty much gave me the option to pick my own path. And while I love writing poems and going to slam poetry nights in the city to watch others perform, I can't imagine that's going to work out for me."

"Why? I've read some of your stuff. It's great."

"You've read three lines of my stuff."

"And those three lines were great."

"Yeah, but the odds of making anything off it? Not high. I'm too shy. I much prefer to be the person behind the words than up there saying them. So I don't know where that leaves me, which I know freaks my mom out." I gave him a crooked smile. "But as long as it leads to some sort of career that will feed me, I think she'll be just fine. My dad, on the other hand, just wants me to be happy."

A slow smile curved West's lips and when it reached his blue eyes, they all but sparkled. "And *are* you happy?"

My stomach flipped at the question. "I am. Are you?"

West picked up his book and nodded. "Yeah. I really am." Then he pointed to my computer. "Break time's over. Stop trying to distract me from my studies."

I laughed and grabbed up my laptop, and as I reopened my essay and began to write, I heard West say, "I'd like to hear some of your poetry one day."

My eyes flew to his, and he shrugged.

"Sorry." His smile said he wasn't sorry in the least. "I just wanted you to know."

THIRTY-THREE

west

TRUE TO MY word, I gave JT the study time he asked for. Long, torturous hours, as a matter of fact, where all I could do to pass the time was come up with different ways of getting him naked later.

"I swear I'm on the last paragraph," JT called out from the living room, as if he could sense my impatience.

Not that it took a genius to see it. I was never good at waiting. Hell, I was never good at *hiding* that I hated waiting.

Even now I paced the length of the kitchen, a bourbon sour in hand as I counted down the minutes until we could begin playing a little game.

Would I have the upper hand in this game I'd devised? Yes. Would JT know that when he agreed to it? Not so much.

But all was fair in sex and...sex, right? Or something like that.

"Done." JT shut his laptop and stretched his arms up over his head. He cracked his neck from side to side before pushing up off the couch, and I was only too happy to play bartender. I poured a little vodka, Kahlua, and a splash of cream over ice and rounded the counter.

"Your reward," I said, handing him the glass.

"Thank you." He took a long, grateful sip. "I have to admit, I assumed my reward would involve something with a lot less clothes."

"Really? And why's that?"

"Because it's you."

It seemed like Golden Boy knew me already, because that was exactly what I had in mind.

I tapped my glass against his and winked. "Is that what you want? To get naked for me?"

JT's eyes heated over the lip of his glass, and I smirked.

That's what I thought.

"So I was thinking we could play a game," I said, reaching for his fingers as I walked backward toward my room.

"Oh yeah? What kind of game?"

"A sort of...getting-to-know-each-other kind."

JT's brow wrinkled, and I laughed.

"Not what you expected?" I asked, kicking my door open wide.

"No, but I'm open to new experiences. Didn't I tell you that?"

I let go of JT's fingers and backed up to one side of the room. When he started to follow, I held my hand up.

"The way this works is, you stay over there. No cheating."

JT mimicked my pose, leaning back against his side of the wall.

"I'll start things off by telling you something about me. You can decide if it's true or false. If you guess correctly, I'll take something off. Guess wrong, and *you* have to take something off."

"So you *are* trying to get me naked." JT set his drink on my desk and spread his hands. "I think I can take you, though."

"We'll see about that. True or false, my favorite actor is Al Pacino."

"Ooh..." JT tapped his lip as he studied me. Like my face would give away the answer. "His movies seem up your alley, so I'll say true."

"Wrong. That would be Denzel." I looked over JT's body, at my options for what to take off. He wasn't wearing shoes or socks, just a pair of jeans, a shirt, and underwear, which meant it wouldn't take long to get him naked. Perfect. "Lose the shirt," I said.

JT reached for the hem of his shirt and pulled it up over his head. As he tossed it on the ground, he said, "My parents nicknamed me Michelin Man because I was such a fat baby."

Ding, ding, ding. I remembered reading this one in the

many files Harry had given me about JT. "I'm gonna go with true." He cursed. "Lose the pants."

His lips tipped up as he met my eyes and unzipped his jeans slowly. He took his time pushing them down to the floor before kicking them aside and looking at me expectantly.

I was getting closer to what I wanted, though JT leaning back against the wall in nothing but a pair of navy boxer briefs was a hot visual. He knew just how to make me crazy, because he fingered the waistband, drawing my eyes there before sliding his hand down over his growing erection.

My own dick jerked, impatient, but it'd already been hours of denial, so what was a few more minutes?

"True or false," I said, my words coming out a little rougher as JT continued to massage his cock through the thin cotton. "I wanted to fuck you the first time I saw you."

A knowing smile crossed his lips. "True." When I nodded, he said, "Your pants."

I didn't feel the overwhelming need to draw things out, so I unzipped and shoved out of them in record time.

JT panted as he worked himself, and I was ready to call the damn game.

"True or false," he said, desire etched in every line of his face. "I want you to fuck me right now."

I sucked in a breath, partly because that wasn't something I'd ever expected to hear out of JT's mouth. And partly because if it wasn't true, I had a feeling I'd die right here, right now.

"Please, fuck, let that be true," I said as I bolted across the room, crashing my lips down on his before he had time to utter "true." Our tongues tangled as he grabbed fistfuls of my shirt.

"Take it off," he breathed across my lips, and I leaned back just enough to rip it up over my head. JT was staring at me with a wild look in his eyes, and I knew if I went back in for another taste right now, this would all be over before it even started.

I forced myself to take a step back and waggled my finger at him. "Don't think you're going to win this game by seducing me, mister."

JT's eyes scorched a red-hot path over every inch of my naked chest. "Is that what I'm doing?"

"Who got the freebie out of this conversation just now?" I aimed my eyes down at the briefs barely containing him. "As I recall, you were supposed to be losing those."

"Oh, I see." JT slipped his thumbs into the edge of his briefs and tugged them down his hips. "So I *forced* you to take your shirt off."

"No, you seduced me into it with your soft lips and—" My words left me as JT's cock sprang free and he shoved the material the rest of the way down his legs.

"And what?"

"Huh?"

JT stepped away from the wall, naked as the day he

was born. He placed a hand on my chest and angled his face up until our mouths were only inches apart.

"I seduced you with my soft lips and...?"

"If you think for one second I can think about anything other than your being naked right now, you don't know me at all."

I reached for JT's hips and smoothed my hands around the curve of his naked ass, then, before he could say another word, I hiked him up off the ground until his legs were around my waist.

A shocked sound left JT as he speared his hands through the back of my hair and slammed his mouth down onto mine. He shoved inside like it'd been days, not minutes, since our last kiss, and the throb of his cock against my naked body told me he was done thinking too.

I took a step back until the mattress hit the back of my thighs, and sat down on it. I dug my fingers into the curve of his ass and hiked him up high on my lap until not even a breeze could get between the two of us. I could feel his hard-on rubbing up against mine through the last layer of material between us, and while I cursed its existence, it also felt really fucking good.

Something JT must've agreed with, as he tightened his fingers in my hair, clenched his thighs around my hips, and began to rock on top of me.

I closed my eyes and concentrated on not coming, knowing that if JT really wanted me to fuck him then I would do anything he asked for, give him anything he needed, to get him to that place where he was comfortable enough to take what he wanted.

"West..." JT panted against my lips as my fingers flirted with the crack of his ass.

"Yeah, gorgeous?"

JT bit my lower lip and kissed me hard, then he trailed a hand down between our bodies until his fingers found the edge of my briefs.

"I want these off."

I took his hand and brought it back up to my lips, nipping at his daring fingers. "Say please."

"*Please...*" He batted his lashes at me, and the flirty move was so unexpected and so unbelievably hot, my fingers tightened around his.

"You should come with a warning label."

"Oh yeah?" JT rolled his hips over the top of me, a taunting smirk playing on his lips. "And what would it say?"

With a hand around his waist, I surged to my feet and turned, laying him out flat on his back. "*Caution: contents are seriously fucking hot.*"

JT might look all sweet and innocent, but I was quickly discovering that looks could be deceiving, because the image he made right now, naked and spread out, mine for the taking, had me tearing the last scrap of material from my body like it was a matter of life and death.

I walked up the side of the bed, and JT's gaze followed me, his hand wrapped around his cock as he tracked every step I took. "Not going to join me?"

"Not yet." I pulled open my side drawer, grabbed out a bottle of lube, and tossed it on the bed. Then I held up a condom between my fingers. "The next time I have my hands on you, I don't plan to stop."

I tore open the packet and suited up, then placed a knee on the bed. As I climbed up onto it and was about to move between JT's thighs, his eyes caught on my erection and I paused as a slight frown furrowed his brow.

It was the first sign of indecision I'd seen from him, and though I knew I could make him forget it with a few strategic kisses or touches, I didn't want to do that.

I moved up alongside him, instead of between his legs, and when JT turned his head on the pillow, the frown was gone. He'd either shoved it aside or schooled his expression for my benefit. "Is everything okay?" I asked.

JT's cheeks turned scarlet as I reached over and brushed one of his curls back from his face. "Yeah. Why'd you stop?"

I wasn't quite sure the best approach to a situation like this because, well, I'd never been in one before. But I knew I needed to work out what had just happened without making him feel self-conscious in any way.

"You had that cute little frown you get going on here." I rubbed my finger between his brows. "And I want to make sure you still want to do this."

"Oh." He gave a nervous little laugh. "I definitely want to do it. I just saw how big you are, and then it hit that... You know, and, well, I just got up in my head a bit."

So he wasn't about to run away from me, just wondering how I would fit. That was a massive stroke to my ego—and my cock.

I rubbed my thumb over his lips. "I'll make you feel good," I said, leaning in to kiss him softly. "I promise." I licked inside his mouth, long, languid strokes that soon turned heated. I wanted him ready for this.

As I ran my hand down to his cock, it jerked under my touch. Hard and ready.

I drew my mouth away and moved between his thighs, hovering over him as I waited for him to look at me.

"Remember to breathe for me. We'll go slow."

JT swallowed as he nodded, but whatever nerves he was feeling were overshadowed by the lust swirling in his brown gaze.

I bent down to lick the pre-cum beading at the head of his dick, and when his breath hitched, I looked up at him and winked.

"Gonna have you screaming my name before this night's over," I promised, before diving down for a mouthful of his cock. I took him all the way to the back of my throat, then pulled off a little, sucking on him as I made my way back up.

The sounds JT was making were indecent, a mix of moans and curses. Making this good for him was my only objective tonight, because he only got this first time once. I knew I'd be able to come just looking at him writhing beneath me. Those brown curls spread out against my pillow; his hands grasping the sheets at his sides.

So damn gorgeous.

As I sucked on his cock, I reached for the lube, popping it open and pouring a little on my fingers.

"Gonna get you nice and stretched for me," I said, pressing against the heat of his entrance.

JT's breath came out in a heavy exhale the moment my finger penetrated his hot hole.

"That's it," I murmured, sliding deep inside him, loving the way he clenched around me. He was so tight his ass was gonna strangle my dick, but it would be worth it. The only problem I had now was keeping my overly excited cock from blowing before I got inside him.

"Another." JT rocked his hips against my hand. "I'm not gonna break."

No, but I fucking might.

I added a second finger, scissoring them inside him as he focused on breathing like the good little bottom he was. So eager. He wanted everything I gave. As I continued to stretch him, I flicked my tongue over the head of his dick.

"Shit, West. That feels...so good." His words were music to my ears. I wanted him crazy for my mouth, my fingers...my dick.

And when JT grunted out, "I want you inside me," I knew I was halfway there.

THIRTY-FOUR

WAS DEATH BY orgasm a thing? Because if it was, I had a feeling West would be driving me to the brink of mortality before all was said and done.

His mouth sucking my cock while his fingers teased my ass to get me ready for what was coming? This was stimulation overload in the best possible way.

"I want you inside me." The words were out of my mouth before my brain caught up, because if I'd been using it, I might've hesitated again at the sheer size of him. His dick was huge, a perfect pink that was now turning a deep shade of reddish-purple as he ignored it to focus on me.

And that? Having West's attention solely on me?

Hottest. Thing. Ever.

He withdrew his fingers and sat up on his knees, reaching for the bottle of lube again. His cock was already sheathed in a condom that looked like it was choking him, and as he poured the lube in his hand and then wrapped it around his length, the mixture of relief and torture played out across his handsome face.

Handsome... I could admit that now. West was attractive in a way that made people stare, and now I was one of them. He made my dick hard and made my body want to explore its limits, and tonight I'd find out just how far that desire went.

I could feel the absence of him inside me as he lubed up, but he wasn't in the mood to draw this out either. He spread my legs a little wider and lined his cock up against my entrance, his tip nudging the hole like it was asking my body for permission.

But he had it. Even with the nerves coursing through me, wondering if it would hurt, if I'd like it, if *he'd* like it... I still wanted this with every fiber of my being. Lust was a powerful thing, and I needed the release I knew West would give me.

He'd make it so, so good. I just needed to breathe.

"Let me inside you," West said, tension cording his neck as he drove his hips forward enough to breach the first ring of muscle.

I blew out a breath as he slowly made his way in deeper, and the feeling was so unfamiliar that my body wanted to reject it. God, he was just so thick and long, there was no way he'd fit. I clenched my teeth together at the burn, but West's hands soothed over the tops of my thighs, my hips.

"Relax. I promise it gets better."

Swallowing, I nodded and tried to do as he said, relax my body as he pushed inside me, tearing me apart—

"I'm there."

I opened my eyes to see West above me, his jaw tight, his eyes glassy with desire. His hips were flush against mine, balls deep inside me. I could feel the way his cock pulsed, and it was such a new, sexy discovery that the burn lessened with every second that passed and the hunger for him ramped up again.

"I think..." I sucked in a breath. "Do that again."

West shook his head a little, and as his waves fell into his face, I reached up to push them back. "Actually, I need a second," he said, surprising the hell out of me. It must've shown on my face, though, because he lowered his mouth down on mine. "It's your fault you're the hottest, tightest body I've ever been inside."

Desire, hard and fast, crashed through me, and I arched my hips up into him, causing him to rip his mouth away and curse.

"Oops." I grinned, not sorry at all as he narrowed his eyes.

"Trying to kill me, Golden Boy? You're gonna have to do better than that." He withdrew from me, giving me just enough time to mourn the fullness of him, before driving back in. Still slowly, but this time I felt myself relaxing a little more.

I tangled my fingers in his hair, pulling him down to kiss me. "Again."

West was more than happy to oblige, stretching me

with every push inside, and it wasn't long before my need began to take over. I brought my legs up around his waist, crossing my ankles over his ass, and when I used them to help propel my hips up off the bed, West growled and tunneled inside me.

I craned my head up to take his lips with mine, and he met me halfway. His tongue thrust into my mouth, and when I began to roll my hips under his, West started to move.

He gripped the pillow under my head, gently urging me back down to it, and as his hips pistoned back and forth, my eyes rolled to the back of my damn head.

Wow... I had no idea. No idea what I'd been missing all this time.

The pleasure of being filled so completely was definitely new. But the toe-curling lust that followed was utterly mind-blowing, as West plunged his cock in and then slowly withdrew.

He was all over me...

All around me...

And one hundred percent all up in me, as he took over my body and demanded it give in to the sexual satisfaction that only he seemed to be able to give.

I held on tight, my fingers twisted in his hair, my legs twined around his waist, as West kissed his way along my jaw to my ear.

"I was right," he said. "You do need to come with a warning."

Me? He was the one destroying me an inch at a time.

"But more like: *might cause self-combustion*."

I turned my head on the pillow, and his dark eyes swirled with desire.

"I've never had so much trouble *not* coming in my life."

"Never?" I breathed across his lips.

"Never."

My dick pulsed at his confession. The idea that I was affecting West in a way he'd never experienced before excited something deep within me. I'd known going into this weekend that I wanted him, but I'd also known that meant stepping outside of what I'd known all my life. So the fact that he was having a moment too made this step we were taking feel all the more special.

"JT..."

"Hmm?"

"If you don't stop clenching your ass around my dick the way you are right now..." West shook his head like he was in total agony. But I knew the truth now. He was in total ecstasy, and nothing was going to stop me from taking him with me into oblivion.

"You'll what?" I said, and did it again. But this time I made sure to bow my hips up, rubbing my sticky shaft across his abs.

His eyes flashed, the heat in them incendiary, then he pushed up from the pillow and slid out of me. I cried out at the loss, and was about to beg him to come back when he grabbed my wrist and tugged me up until I was sitting.

"Turn around and get on your hands and knees."

I blinked at the order, even as my cock stood up, ready to obey.

When I didn't immediately move, West arched a brow.

"You just asked what I'm going to do," he said, and reached down to fist his length. "But this is one time that words aren't going to be nearly as impactful as what my dick is gonna say."

Oh God, am I really going to do this?

But one look at his arrogant smirk and I knew the answer. He did too. So before I could talk myself out of it, I shifted until I was facing his headboard and moved into position.

The second my palms were braced on the mattress, West's strong hands gripped my hips. I sucked in a breath but had little time to think it through, as he nudged my legs apart and came up behind me.

West stroked the broad tip of himself down the seam of my ass, and as the hands on my hips pulled my cheeks apart, I closed my eyes and dropped my head.

This time when he entered me, it was a lot like the first, in that it was a completely different angle and my body took a minute to adjust. But feeling West's hard body against my back, the slickness of the sweat on his chest rubbing against me with every thrust, had my hands gripping the top of the mattress.

"Still feel like being a smartass?" he said in my ear, and I couldn't help it—I glanced over my shoulder and winked.

"Still dying to come in my ass?"

West cursed, sending a stinging slap to my rear, but his reaction only made me chuckle.

Until West lifted off me and took my hips in a punishing grip before thrusting in deep.

"Oh fuck," I cried out as his cock hit a spot inside me that had me almost blacking out. My arms began to shake as I tried not to face-plant on the mattress. Before I could tell him to do it again, he did.

Of course he did. Because somehow West seemed to know my body better than his own, teasing and claiming every part of me in ways I'd never imagined.

He kept one hand on my hip while the other skated up my spine, threading through my hair and tugging my head back. His body covered me again, and then his mouth was on my neck, sucking at the sensitive skin beneath my ear.

It was like he'd set off a string of tiny explosions, and the sensations coursed through me, firing under my skin, making it tingle. But he wasn't done with me just yet. He reached around me and wrapped sure fingers around my aching shaft.

"West, Jesus, I can't—" I bit my words off as he drove in deep and bottomed out, my brain using what little function it had left to keep me upright.

His growl by my ear did nothing to keep my orgasm at bay. My balls tightened as West scraped his teeth along my shoulder and nipped at the skin.

"Yeah, you can." He slowly pulled out of me, one deli-

INFAMOUS PARK AVENUE PRINCE

cious inch at a time. "I'm gonna make you come now, and I wanna hear you scream my name when you do."

His hand started to pump up and down, setting the rhythm as he drove back inside of me with such force that I almost lost my balance.

I loudly cursed as he picked up the pace, delivering several hard, fast thrusts that made the room begin to spin. Lights started to flash and fire off somewhere in my periphery.

Fucking hell, had I been living under a rock my whole life? Here I'd thought I knew what it was like to have good sex, and maybe I did. But this was pass-out-blind, phenomenal sex, and I never wanted it to end.

My body, however, had other ideas.

West hit that magic spot inside me again, and combined with the rough stroke of my dick, I had no chance of holding back. My climax slammed into me so hard and fast that I was grateful there was no one else around, because West's name on my lips echoed off the walls.

"So...fucking...hot." West's strained words were each punctuated with a jagged pump of his hips. He was so close, his movements no longer steady as he continued to stroke my cock, wrenching every last bit of cum from me.

A loud curse met my ears seconds before West bit down on my shoulder.

I memorized the groans coming out of him as his orgasm hit, and the way my own name fell so easily from his lips. His dick throbbed inside me, and I wished I could feel what it would be like to have his hot rush of cum spilling into me.

But I wasn't complaining. Not when it already felt perfect. Not when he'd worked me over so thoroughly that I was sure I was ruined for anyone else.

I collapsed in a heap on the mattress, West's heavy body on top of me. I liked it, the weight of him. And when he went to move off me, I reached behind me to hold him there, just for a minute longer.

West dropped his forehead on the back of my neck and pressed a kiss between my shoulder blades. "I'm gonna suffocate you like this—"

"No, I like it." My voice was muffled by the mattress, but he heard it anyway. "Feels good."

"So you like my cock in your ass." He nipped at my earlobe, and I turned my head to the side.

"Have I ever told you you're obnoxious?" I said.

"You might've mentioned it once or twice. But like I told you before, I prefer 'charming.'"

THIRTY-FIVE

"LOOK AT YOU picking me up for a date night." West smirked as he strolled out of the Towers, hands in the pockets of his charcoal plaid pants, and looking entirely too irresistible.

I supposed he was wearing what he considered casual, along with a fitted black polo shirt, but he'd swapped out his fancy shoes for a pair of black sneakers. A good call, considering what I had planned for tonight.

"I didn't think you owned anything other than loafers." I grinned as I walked his way.

"I think you'll find I own at least one of everything."

I shook my head. "Snob."

West reached for my waist, pulling me in close. "Tight-ass." He brushed his lips over mine, greeting me with a kiss I felt through my entire body. After spending last weekend with him, it didn't occur to me that he was claiming my mouth in the open. Not when he'd been inside me. Something I was hoping would happen again sooner rather than later, but school and studying had gotten in the way the past few days.

"So. You gonna tell me where we're going?" he asked, his arms still wrapped around me.

"Nope."

"Well, at least tell my driver—"

"Oh no, no, no. It's my turn to surprise you with a night out, and there will be no chauffeur."

"That's a joke, right? He can take us anywhere in the city you want to go—"

"So can the many other modes of transportation, and probably faster." I ran my hands over his arms, pulling them from my waist. As I did, our fingers interlaced, and I wasn't sure if it was me or him that had initiated the move. But there it was—the two of us holding hands on Park Avenue and heading out for a date night.

How was this my life?

"Come on, we can't be late if we want a good seat." I tugged him along, heading toward the train station across the street.

"You're lucky you're hot," he grumbled, but the teasing lilt to his voice told me he was curious about what we'd be doing.

West had planned several surprises and nights out in the time I'd known him, but I hadn't gotten the chance to reciprocate until now. We'd done the lavish meals, the extravagant clubs and parties, and those had all been things he enjoyed that I was open to. But now it was time for him to take a walk on my side of the city.

This was either going to be the best night ever or a total disaster. Either way, it'd be entertaining as hell to watch his reaction.

"I should've known you'd make us take the train," he said, as we headed down the stairs.

"The fact that you call yourself a New Yorker is shocking, you know that?"

"So I shouldn't admit I don't own a MetroCard?"

"Oh my God. You poor little rich boy. You don't need those anymore." I pulled out my debit card, and as we approached the turnstile, I tapped it on the screen. "Go on through, Mr. LaRue."

West's answering laugh had me grinning as I tapped again for myself.

"Getting me out of my element. I see how the night's gonna go."

"Do you? Any guesses?"

"I can only imagine." West's nose wrinkled as he sniffed at the air. "Why does it smell like someone died?"

"In this heat? Someone probably did."

"Lovely." He turned to face me where we stopped to wait on the platform, and when he reached for my hands, I took a step toward him, lacing our fingers again. Something about it felt so right but also sent a wave of butterflies to wreak havoc in my stomach. "You know this means I must like you."

"To brave my idea of a date night?" I teased.

He brushed his thumbs along my skin. "That too."

I looked down at where we were connected, and the thought crossed my mind that it wasn't just me experiencing something new here. West may have always been into guys, but he told me he'd never had a relationship, and I had a feeling even something like holding my hand was foreign to him.

I squeezed his fingers. "Yeah," I said. "I think you do."

"I HOPE YOU'RE hungry," I said as we stepped out into the hustle and bustle of Second Avenue.

"For your cock? Fucking always."

A few nearby pedestrians turned to stare, and I ran a hand over my face. "I set myself up for that one, didn't I?"

"You did, but I was serious."

"Yeah? Wanna drop to your knees right here on the sidewalk? Or maybe that alley over there?"

West took in our surroundings. "Not sure I want to get up close and personal with any needles tonight."

"Well, shit. There go my plans."

"I knew it. We're getting tattoos from some burly motorcycle guy named Axel, aren't we?"

I grinned. "You wanna get my name on your ass, we can do that later. For now?" I nodded toward East Village Pizza. "I'm stuffing my face." Before West could open his mouth, I put a finger over his lips. "And not full of your dick. *Yet.*"

Then I winked and swung open the door, inhaling the

scent of tomatoes, dough, and pepperoni. I wasn't sure anything smelled better.

As West passed me, entering first, I suddenly realized that was no longer true. *He* had taken the top spot of the smell I couldn't get enough of.

We both ordered massive slices of pepperoni at the counter, carrying them on paper plates as we headed back outside.

"You want to grab that table?" West nodded at an empty two-seater along the sidewalk as I bit into my slice. I had to pull at the melty strings of never-ending cheese before answering.

"Nah, we can walk and eat. The café's not far."

"A...café?" West folded his pizza and shook his head as he took a big bite. "Not what I expected."

"It's something you mentioned wanting to see, and I thought since we're getting to know each other..." I shrugged. "I know it's not your thing, but I figured you showed me yours, now I'll show you mine."

West raised a brow as he swallowed. "I do like that game. And this slice is damn good."

"Yeah?" I said, pleased he'd liked my choice. "Next time we'll have to get one of their double stacks. It's a pizza on top of a pizza." I kissed my fingers. "*Eccellente.*"

We continued eating, and I led us in the direction of the Poet Café, a place I knew for sure he'd never been or would ever think to go. I'd kept our destination a secret for obvious reasons. If I told him, he'd assume it was some quiet literary place where we'd have to whisper and consume extra-large cappuccinos. It definitely wasn't that. It also wasn't a club or bar atmosphere like he was used to, but I had a feeling he wouldn't hate it.

At least, I hoped not.

I finished off my slice and tossed the paper plate in the trash, along with West's. As the café came into view, I felt some nerves, but I shoved them aside. It wasn't a big deal if he didn't love this place as much as me, because it was my thing. The same as West going to... Well, *Church* was more his thing.

I still wanted him to have a good time and not end up running out of the place the way I had at Church. Although the aftermath in the limo had more than made up for the entire night.

Murals and graffiti covered the exterior of the unassuming Poet Café, and when West walked right by it and kept going, I called out his name. He turned around, looking at where I'd stopped and then up at the sign overhead. When comprehension dawned, I said, "We're here."

"Huh," he said, heading back. "I was looking for a coffee shop or something."

"Yeah, the name kinda throws you off, but it's more like a bar."

"And we'll be...writing poetry in this bar?"

I laughed, taking his hand. "As much as I would love to see that, no. It's slam night. We'll just be watching."

The all-brick interior was a lot like many of the spaces in the city—long, dim, and not all that wide. A random assortment of benches and chairs tightly packed the space, leaving only a path to walk in front of the bar.

Music blasted from the DJ spinning before the slams started, and already the place was packed. Usually I didn't bother to hit up the bar, not while being underage, but West had managed to get me a better-looking fake ID than the one I'd been trying to pass off before, the bad influence. The alcohol selection wasn't much at all, and what they did have was the bottom-shelf stuff guaranteed to give you a hangover, so we both grabbed sodas and squeezed through the crowd to find a couple of seats.

As we waited for the bottlenecked crowd to move, West flattened his hand against my stomach possessively as he pulled me back against him from behind. He rocked us from side to side to the beat, his breath tickling my neck as he said, "Feel like dancing?"

I shook my head. "I think your moves might get us kicked out of here."

"Might be worth it..." His hand dipped lower, and I grabbed his wrist before things could turn indecent.

"You really are a troublemaker, aren't you?"

"Never promised to be anything less. Besides, I think you like that about me."

As he took my chin in hand, I murmured my agreement that soon got swallowed by his kiss. It never failed to ignite something hot and fiery in my gut, which was a smart reason to keep the PDA down when we were out. It made me want to do bad things to his body, and as a few of those visuals crossed my mind, my cock jerked behind my jeans.

"Dammit," I said when I pulled my mouth away. I moved my hand over his and drew it down over the bulge in my pants to show him just why kissing him was dangerous. But West gave me a rough stroke, and I groaned and forced myself to shove his hand away as the crowd began to move again.

It wasn't my fault I was greedy for his touch, not when we had to keep our distance at Astor. So many prying eyes, so many opinions. I was still getting used to whatever this was between us, and I wanted to keep it private a little longer, a want that West seemed to share. I didn't know how much he'd told his friends about us, but I got the feeling it wasn't much. He hadn't asked me to go out with them for a group night lately, and had told me how much shit they'd been giving him for blowing them off. Surely they had guessed where he was spending his time?

Or maybe not.

I managed to snag two seats on the end of a row, giving West the aisle to stretch his long legs a little. His arm automatically went to rest on the back of my chair as he leaned in toward me.

"So how does all this work?"

I popped the tab on my soda, then reached over to do the same to his. "They let a certain number of people sign up to perform their slams and choose a few people in the audience to act as judges. They all get ranked, and the top five get to go again at the end of the night to narrow it down to a winner."

"Does that mean I get to watch you perform tonight?"

I almost choked on my drink. "Uh, no."

"Why not?"

"Because I don't perform my poems. I just write them."

"So no one gets to hear them? Read them?"

"Nope. Just me."

West's eyes shifted between me and the small stage at the front. "That hardly seems fair. They share with you, but you don't return the favor?" The impish look in those blue eyes had me shaking my head.

"Whatever you're thinking, just don't. There's no way I'm getting up there."

"What if—"

"No."

"You don't even know what I was going to say."

"Still not happening."

"Not even for me?" He moved his mouth toward my ear. "My very own private show?"

I groaned. If that turned out to be something West really wanted, I knew it would be hard to deny him. It would require a lot of alcohol on my part, and many assurances on his that there were no cameras or recording devices, but...maybe one day. Like one day far, far off in the future.

Lucky for me, the lights at the front of the stage flickered, and as the music shut off, the roar of the crowd gave me a reason not to answer West. He probably already knew he could wear me down anyway. No one could resist him when he put his mind to something.

As the host for the evening took to the stage, I felt West's fingers playing with the curls at the nape of my neck and hid my smile behind my soda. For all his expensive tastes and giving me hell, he didn't seem to hate the night too much so far. That could always change, but maybe it didn't matter where we were if we were together.

Wow, I thought, taking a long swallow of my drink. *That might be the sappiest shit I've ever thought.*

THIRTY-SIX

west

IF SOMEONE HAD told me last month that I would be voluntarily spending a weeknight in the East Village in some dungeon-looking poetry café, I would've called them fucking crazy.

I didn't do shit like this. Ride the train. Eat my pizza standing. Walk up some dodgy alley where I may or may not get mugged. Or sit in *seriously* uncomfortable seats for hours and listen to people pour out their emotions in energetic bursts of words that, if I were being honest, made me feel like running for the door at times.

But as I looked at JT, whose attention was riveted to the latest contestant of this slam poetry competition, I knew exactly why I was there.

Or did I?

The thought taunted me as I ran my gaze over the gorgeous man seated beside me. The line between bet and reality blurred more and more with every day that passed by—that much was obvious by my current surroundings. If I'd just told the guys I'd sealed the deal with the golden boy this past weekend, then I wouldn't be sitting here wondering if I was going to have to make an appointment with my chiropractor later this week.

But here I was, in a building I'd paid fifteen whole bucks to have the privilege of sitting in, and despite all of that, I was enjoying myself.

Which raised the question... Why?

The bar was a plus, I hadn't expected that when JT had said it was a poetry "café." I'd imagined a quiet little group of creative types spouting limericks and sonnets in some coffee house that would bore me to tears. But I'd been really fucking excited when I learned that wasn't the case at all. This place served alcohol and even had a DJ.

But still, that was hardly enough for me to deem this a good time.

The three-minute buzzer went off, jarring me out of my thoughts, as the latest poet concluded her monologue and JT began cheering and clapping along with the rest of the crowd. His eyes were bright and full of excitement, and there it was—the exact reason for my good time.

JT Hawthorne. Who fucking knew?

I sure as hell hadn't seen that coming. But he was making a mess of my head, not to mention my revenge plan, which apparently I didn't give a shit about anymore with the way I had been skipping out on my friends and dodging their calls.

Or maybe I just wanted to enjoy the fruits of my hard

labor before handing him over to the rest of those vultures. But as I ran my eyes over JT's soft curls, the joyful expression on his face, and the tight, compact body I'd had under mine last weekend, my heart thumped a little harder, and I knew that for the lie it was.

Fuck.

This was not good. I mean, it *was* good. JT was good, and so were the conversations and hours I spent with him. It was easy, comfortable, and for the first time in my life, I felt as though the person I was hooking up with was actually in it for me. Not the prestige, not to ladder-climb, and not for my money.

I ran a hand through my hair, frustrated where my thoughts were taking me. Since when did I care why someone was with me? As long as we both had a good time and got what we came for, why did it matter?

JT glanced at me, no doubt sensing my attention had shifted from the stage.

"You're supposed to be watching them." He grinned and gestured toward the front of the café, where the next poet was moving up to take their spot.

I leaned over to place my mouth close by his ear. "I thought I was here to watch poetry."

"You are."

"Then don't you worry, I'm getting my money's worth."

JT snorted then leaned back to look me in the eye. "Did you seriously just say watching me is poetry?"

I shrugged, flashing him a smile. "I don't know—will it get me laid if I did?"

JT's eyes widened and then he shoved me in the arm. "West."

I grabbed his wrist before he could pull it away. "You didn't answer the question."

People moved in and out of the rows surrounding us, and when someone bumped into the back of my chair, I winced.

JT bit back a laugh. "I'm not sure you're up to getting laid. How's your back doing?"

"My back is just fine, and getting *up* around you is never a problem."

JT's breath caught, and when the lights flashed, signaling the next slam session was about to begin, I made a decision.

"Come with me."

"What?"

I took his hand, and the second our fingers touched, JT entwined his with mine.

"Come with me," I said again as I moved to my feet, and when someone behind us called out, "Sit down or move," JT quickly followed.

I led him toward the back of the seating area, making sure not to step on anyone that was huddled on the floor —yeah, people were sitting on the *floor*.

"Did you want another drink?" JT asked, but as we by passed the crowd gathered around the bar, I kept on going.

"No, just a little quiet, that's all." That wasn't it at all, and judging by JT's smirk, he knew it. Since when had I, Mister Playboy Party Guy, ever needed a little quiet?

What I needed was to taste JT's lips, and I wanted to do it without someone's impassioned poem about religion being the root cause of indifference.

I scanned the crowded café, searching for anywhere that wasn't shoulder to shoulder with people, and finally spotted it. An escape from the main floor. A narrow brick hallway that had a sign hanging above it with an arrow that read "Viewing Balcony."

A second-floor balcony overlooked the stage area, but it was empty tonight, completely shut down, and that seemed like the perfect place to steal a moment alone with my date.

I steered the two of us down the hall, but the stairs had a rope across them and a sign that read "closed."

JT moved in behind me and placed his chin on my shoulder. "Now what?"

A smile tugged at my lips. "You don't think that's going to stop me, do you?"

JT frowned. "But it's closed."

I stepped away from him and reached for the rope holding it up. "It's not a locked door, JT."

He eyed my hand then looked back down the hall to check no one was coming, and when the coast was clear, he shook his head. "Why do I get the feeling that a locked door wouldn't deter you anyway?"

He ducked under the rope, and I followed. "Because you know me."

"Uh huh." JT started up the stairs, and I couldn't stop myself from swatting his ass, making him chuckle.

When we reached the balcony, I was happy to see the space wasn't all that big, and with the lights downstairs the only thing illuminating this area, the shadows danced over the two of us as we crossed the floor.

About halfway across, JT turned to see if I was following, and I was so close behind him that he almost stumbled. I reached out to steady him, and when he placed a palm on my chest and looked up at me, something inside of me snapped.

I slammed my mouth down on his in a fierce kiss, making him moan. The sound was better than any damn poem I'd heard tonight.

His fingers curled into my shirt, and I walked him backward across the floor. When his back met the brick wall, I moved my hands to the belt loops of his jeans and tugged his hips forward. JT slid his hand around my neck and angled his head to let me in deeper. I tasted every corner of his delicious mouth, and the faint hint of the soda was more intoxicating than the bourbon sour I'd finished before coming out tonight.

Jesus, it was like he'd cast a spell over me, the way I craved him. One taste and I wanted more. And with the way my cock stood up and took notice the second he was in a room, I wasn't sure I'd ever be done.

I moved my hands to his denim-clad ass and squeezed

as I wedged one of my legs between his thighs. JT stared up at me, his eyes searching my face as his chest heaved against mine.

"What are you doing?"

I did it again, pressing a little harder this time, and JT moaned and rubbed his hard-on against my thigh.

"I think you know exactly what I'm doing."

His gaze shifted over my shoulder, then back to my face. "We can't. Not here."

"Says who?" I lowered my head and pressed teasing kisses up his neck.

JT shivered. "Says... What do you mean, says who?"

I smiled against his skin, not missing that even though he was protesting, he was still rubbing himself off on my leg.

"I mean..." I brought a hand around to the button of his jeans. "Who's gonna stop me? You?"

I popped the button open. A shard of light showed enough of JT's eyes to see his pupils were dilated with arousal.

"Want me to stop?" I slipped my hand inside the denim and his briefs, and when my fingers brushed the head of his cock, he shook his head.

"No."

I nipped at his lower lip as I curled my fingers around him. "Are you sure?"

JT's head fell back on the wall, and he twisted his fingers in the back of my hair. "Don't you dare stop."

That was all the permission I needed.

I took his mouth again in a scorching kiss, and when JT shoved his dick through my fist, I knew we were set to burn. The flames were licking through my veins as I dragged the denim off his ass to give myself better access. I could hear the faint sound of someone speaking on stage down below. But the blood rushing out of my head to my cock was much louder.

JT licked into my mouth as he rode my thigh, fucking my fist like it was a matter of life or death. I swiped my thumb over his sticky head, then brought my hand to my mouth, licking my thumb clean. JT's hungry expression had me reaching for my own pants. There was no protest this time, but before things got completely out of control, I grabbed my wallet from my back pocket and pulled out a condom.

JT made a soft scoffing sound.

"You laughing at me?"

He eyed the condom and shook his head. "More like marveling over your preparedness."

I held it up for him between two fingers. "I told you, I'm always up around you, so it's best to think ahead."

JT plucked the packet from my hand, his lips twitching. "Or *of* your head."

"That too, if we're talking about the one you rode all weekend."

"Fucking hell." He groaned and tore open the packet, and as he rolled it down me, he looked to the wallet. "I suppose you have a packet of lube too?"

I pulled one free before putting my wallet away. "Don't tell me you're mad about it. I won't believe you."

JT moved to his toes, his mouth grazing mine. "You really think you can get away with everything, don't you?"

I grunted and walked him back to the wall, where I spun him around and bumped my cock up against his bare ass. "Well, I'm about to fuck you in a poetry café full of people. So yeah, I do."

JT braced his hands on the wall and pushed back into me. "And if someone comes?"

I tore open the packet of lube and squeezed it down the crack of his ass. "*Two* someones are going to come."

"You know what I mean."

I did, but he didn't need to worry. I kissed the top of his spine, and a shiver raced through his body as I stroked a finger up and down the shadowy cleft, getting him nice and slick.

"Money, JT. It'll get you out of practically everything—including public indecency."

I spread him apart and nudged the entrance to his body with the tip of my cock, and he grunted. "Got plenty of experience with that, have you?"

I nipped at his shoulder. "Why, jealous?" JT turned his face toward mine, and though his eyes said yes, he stayed silent. "I fucking would be," I added.

He gasped as I pushed forward, whether from my words or the feel of me breaching that tight ring of muscle, I wasn't sure, and I crushed our mouths together to take his mind off the initial pain.

There was no time to fool around here. No time to slowly get him ready. Not with the very real risk of being caught only a dozen or so stairs away. I might've done a good job at reassuring JT nothing would come of us being caught. But I knew he'd still be mortified if we were, and I didn't want that. I wanted him to look back on this and remember how fucking hot it was.

When his body started to relax, I slid in further, and when I was balls deep inside of him, I stopped. I could feel every breath he took as his back rose and fell against my chest, and his body's hot hold around my cock was exquisite torture.

"Jesus, it feels like weeks since I've been inside you." I nipped at his ear and wrapped an arm around his waist to take hold of him. "Not days."

JT hummed—fucking *hummed*—in his throat as he wriggled his ass on me. It seemed I wasn't the only one needing this contact.

I squeezed my slippery fingers around his pulsing shaft and gave him several slow pulls, and when he started to shove through my fist then push back onto me, I knew it was time to move.

I gripped his hip with my other hand and began to pump my hips in time with the hand stroking him. JT dug his fingers into the brick for leverage, and the sight of him letting go and chasing after what he wanted sent another wave of adrenaline rushing through me.

Never did I expect JT to be this responsive. Never did I expect him to be all in this fast. But it seemed the more time we spent together, the more eager he was to explore —and being the greedy motherfucker I was, I wasn't about to turn him away.

I was all about enabling.

I bent my head and dragged my tongue up his neck, and when he whimpered, I started to suck. I sucked and fucked him with every part of me I could—and JT went wild for it. The sounds coming out of him made my dick throb and my balls tighten, and my patience flew right off the fucking balcony as that damn buzzer went off somewhere down below.

The sound of the raucous applause followed right behind it, and as JT's cock pulsed in my palm and he shook, about to detonate, I let go of his hip and threw a hand over his mouth.

I smothered his shouts as I buried my face in his curls, letting out an almighty growl as the two of us came with thunderous force. The impact was earth-shattering, the implications even more so, as the man in my arms collapsed back against me and I worked him to completion.

It was *definitely* like he'd cast a spell over me.

That was the only explanation for why I was standing in a poetry café in the East Village thinking about limericks and sonnets and how in the hell I was going to be able to keep JT and what we had to myself for a little bit longer.

THIRTY-SEVEN

I SMOTHERED A yawn as I hopped out of the Sprinter van Friday morning. The lack of sleep was catching up with me, and for once, it wasn't from partying my ass off every night.

No, I'd been giving my late-night attention to something else entirely—or should I say someone. Texting and talking into the early-morning hours with JT when I wasn't sneaking into his place or hiding him away in mine was a new thing for me, but one I was slowly becoming addicted to. The more of him I got, the more I wanted, and even though I knew it was a dangerous game I was playing, I couldn't seem to stop. I needed a hit of him more than I needed caffeine this morning, and that was fucking saying something.

Behind me, Donovan was giving us shit for missing his show. I felt a pang of guilt at that, considering I'd never skipped out on supporting him at New York Fashion Week, but it had completely slipped my mind.

Maybe I'd bring JT to his next show—

A hand clapped down on my shoulder. Preston.

"Hey, West. Are you coming out tonight?"

Was I? I hadn't figured out plans with JT for the weekend yet.

I shrugged. "Maybe."

Preston looked at me with an incredulous expression. "Really? It's opening night for Bassiani. East didn't tell you?"

Oh shit, that's right. I'd completely forgotten about the new nightclub opening up in Chelsea. I vaguely remembered East telling me about it, but along with apparently a lot of other shit, I was letting it slip through the cracks.

There was no way in hell the guys would let me skip out on opening night, not when we'd all be expected to be there.

"Like I'd miss it," I said, hoping that was enough to get him to lay off and not ask me where I'd been all week. Well, longer than that, if I were honest.

Preston squeezed my shoulder. "Good. It's not the same without you."

Well, that was a boost to my ego—and had me feeling like a terrible friend times two already this morning. "Sorry, shit's just been crazy."

"Uh huh." He gave me a look that said he didn't completely buy it, but unlike my pain-in-the-ass BFF, Preston didn't run off at the mouth about it.

Thank fucking God.

Across the courtyard, Serena waved at him to join her, and as he walked off, I caught sight of a familiar head of brown curls disappearing through Astor's front door.

"I'll catch you guys later," I said to the rest of the guys over my shoulder before following JT.

It seemed I wasn't the only one in need of a caffeine fix, because he was standing at the counter of the coffee bar ordering the largest mocha latte they had when I found him.

"And a double shot for me," I said, sidling in beside JT.

He smiled, bumping his arm gently against mine in greeting. "Hey, you."

"Morning." I nodded toward the large cup with his name on it. "Late night?"

"You would know."

My eyes flashed in the direction of the barista, warning JT of the potential eavesdropper, but he only raised a brow as if to say, "So?"

Interesting...

I pushed my card forward on the counter before JT could even reach for his, and he shook his head.

"Don't you dare."

"Oh, but I dare. What are you gonna do about it?"

JT licked his lips, his eyes falling to my mouth. "I can think of a few things."

Out of the corner of my eye, I saw the barista's eyes widen, and wondered when this innocent man of mine had gotten so damn ballsy. He seemed to give no fucks about who heard him or the fact that it could get around... back to a certain someone I knew he didn't want to find out.

As I pocketed my card, I pushed him toward the pickup counter and said under my breath, "You're being reckless."

"Guess that means you're rubbing off on me."

"Not in the way I want to right now."

The way JT's eyes heated had me wanting to drag him into a dark corner, like I had the night at the Poet Café.

Actually...

Once our orders came up on the bar, I grabbed mine and subtly inclined my head for JT to follow. We didn't need the prying eyes and nosy assholes knowing our business, or watching me steal the kiss I was dying to take. There had to be an empty classroom or storage closet we could slip into for ten minutes. Hell, maybe five with the way my body reacted every time he was near.

I tried the handles of several doors we passed, all of them locked. That didn't usually stop me, but I didn't have time for breaking and entering before our first classes.

Instead, I curled my finger into the belt loop of his jeans and tugged him into a small nook. He chuckled at my obvious impatience as I backed him against the wall, quickly glancing over my shoulder to make sure no one was around before slamming my lips down on his. He groaned, arching into me, but voices heading in our direction had me ripping my mouth away before I wanted to.

I took a step back, putting some space between us, and that was when I noticed the reddish-purple bruise low on the side of his neck. I remembered exactly how that mark had happened, and JT's upturned lips told me he did too.

"That," I said, trailing my fingers over it, "is fuckin' hot."

"And really hard to hide. Maybe next time mark me in a place where I won't need to wear a scarf to cover it," he teased.

"All I'm hearing is that you want me to mark you again. You like when I suck on you, JT?"

He dropped his head back against the wall, and just when I thought he was about to answer, I heard the clacking of heels and looked out to see—*shit*—the dean heading down the hall.

I jerked back into the nook, putting a finger over my lips and blocking JT the best I could. Catching us in a private moment with her son sporting a hickey? I didn't personally give two shits, but JT would. And for that reason, I'd keep him out of sight.

She passed by, deep in conversation with a professor, and once they'd rounded the corner, I straightened.

"Was that my mom I heard?"

"Yep."

"Oh, I see how it is. Hiding me away, huh?"

"Well, it's not like you've told her you have a boyfriend. That changes things."

"A boyfriend?" JT cocked his head, a twinkle in his eyes. "Is that what we are? Boyfriends?"

I opened my mouth to respond, but for once, I didn't know what the hell to say. I'd just called JT my *boyfriend*, for fuck's sake, and the reality was...it was true. All the bullshit I'd tried to tell myself about my interest in him being limited to a bet or some stupid payback on his mom was just that— bullshit. If I were honest with myself, it hadn't been about those things for a long time. Not once I'd gotten to know how damn amazing he was. How open and curious, captivating, and so damn sexy. He made me want him with an ache in my chest that I knew was dangerous. JT was the last thought I had before I went to bed and the first when I woke up every morning. And that was whether or not he was *in* my bed, and when he wasn't, it drove me crazy. I hated it.

Somehow this golden boy had slipped in past my defenses and made me so territorial that I wanted to stamp the word *mine* on his chest.

So, yeah, I settled for a hickey. Fuckin' sue me.

"You got a problem with calling me your boyfriend?" I challenged, my voice low as I stepped in closer.

If he did, I knew myself. I'd haul us out of here and into my place so fast, and I wouldn't care how long it took or how many different ways I could show him that this thing between us was happening. It was real.

But JT only tugged his lower lip in between his teeth

and reached for my hand. "I think that's something I can get used to."

Relief like the weight of a pile of bricks being lifted off my chest had me breathing easier. "Yeah?"

"Yeah. I think I'd like calling you my boyfriend. You know, instead of stalker."

I smirked as I brought his hand up to my lips, kissing the tips of his fingers. "You better be sure. I don't plan on letting you go."

One of his brows arched, challenging me right back. "That a promise?"

I leaned in, angling my head toward his. "That's a goddamn guarantee."

A glimpse of a smile was all I saw as I took his lips with mine, forgetting where we were as I sealed our relationship with a stroke of my tongue against his. It was too damn bad there were so many hours to waste before I could see him again later.

Oh shit. Later.

A moan left me as I reluctantly pulled away. "I'm supposed to go to this club opening tonight. The guys are giving me shit, and I told them I'd be there."

"And that sounds like a problem because...?"

I gave him a bewildered look. "Why the hell do you think?"

He laughed and shook his head. "You could just ask me to go."

"You hate that shit."

"I don't *hate* it. I just hated watching other guys steal your attention away from me."

I fucking knew it. And damn, that admission was hot.

"You don't have to worry about that happening," I said. "But...as long as we're keeping this quiet, it's probably not a good idea to hang around the guys until we're out with it. Mouthy fuckers." Plus, I had some explaining to do before admitting I'd gone and fallen for the very person I wasn't supposed to. It was one thing for JT to go out with us when the plan was corruption and deception, but I knew I wasn't a good enough actor to hide that I'd caught feelings. Or that he had. My friends would pick up on it in a second.

But this sneaking around shit? I was over it.

JT nodded and squeezed my fingers. "That's okay. You go, and we'll do something this weekend."

"I'll think about it. Tonight, I mean."

"You can always come over after—just let me know. I've gotta get to class. *Boyfriend*." He pressed a quick kiss to my lips and grinned before sliding past me into the hallway.

I ran a hand through my hair and blew out a breath as I watched him go, and when a voice came up from behind me, I flinched.

"What the hell was that?" Travis crossed his arms.

Schooling my face into nonchalance, I said, "What?"

Travis looked pointedly in the direction JT had gone. "*That*. You were supposed to wrap shit up with him by now."

"You have a problem with the way I handle things?"

"Only when it seems like the dean's golden boy has been the one doing the corrupting here. Not you."

"You don't know what you're talking about."

"Then tell me. Have you won, or do you just not want to admit defeat?" Travis's eyes glittered wickedly. "Or is it something else entirely?"

Irritation rose inside me. I didn't appreciate being questioned. Or told that I was not in control of a situation that had, admittedly, gotten out of hand.

So I did the only thing I knew would shut him up. I turned that shit back on him.

"You wanna talk admitting things? Go right ahead. We'll start with you."

Travis glared at me before turning on his heel and stalking off, exactly as I expected.

But the confrontation had me feeling like shit. I didn't fight or hide things from my friends, and I sure as hell didn't want to hide JT anymore, either.

My gaze fell on the dean as she crossed the hall, and our eyes collided for a moment before she looked away.

That was the source of all our complications. And I didn't know what I was supposed to do about it.

THIRTY-EIGHT

"I'M STUFFED." I slid my empty plate onto the coffee table, where platters of pastry, fruit, and cooked items littered the surface, and fell onto the couch beside West, rubbing a hand over my belly.

"Hey, you're the one who told me you were starving." He reached over and twirled a finger through my hair. "I was just trying to accommodate you."

"By ordering everything on the room service menu?"

"It wasn't *everything* on the menu. Just the items under the 'breakfast' section." He winked. "It's one of the perks of dating the owner's son."

"Five-star meals at your beck and call?"

"Five-star meals at *your* beck and call." West grabbed my wrist, lounged back into the end of the couch, and pulled me down with him. "Me? I'd settle for having *you* at my beck and call."

I shifted in between his legs, almost sad he'd pulled on a pair of blue and black checkered lounge pants, then cuddled into his bare chest, kissing the warm skin there.

"Lucky for you, that's one of the perks of dating me."

West brought his arms around me, kissing me on top of my head, and something about the gentle move made my heart flutter.

"Really?" he murmured, stroking a hand down my back. "Well, that's good to know. Because I really would love it if you rode my—"

I quickly lifted my head and pressed my mouth to his, cutting off whatever outrageous thing he was going to say. West's lips immediately parted for mine, and without a moment's hesitation, I dove in for another taste.

I wasn't sure when I'd turned into such a tactile person. But the more time I spent around West, the more I found myself needing to touch, taste, and have some sort of connection with him.

I'd never felt anything like it. That kind of relationship was not something I'd ever been drawn to. But I was now. I had a *boyfriend*. A boyfriend that I found myself craving more and more with every day that passed by, and not just physically. I found myself eagerly awaiting the next time he would call or text. The next time we could hang out and just...be.

West slid his hands down my back to the elastic of my sweats, his fingers flirting with the edge of them and then dipping underneath. I raised my head to tell him to behave, but one look at his sleep-disheveled hair, that talented mouth, and his stubble-covered jaw line, and my resolve quickly started to fade.

West was the kind of man that you wanted to *misbehave* with, but my mind wasn't that far gone that I'd forgotten West's roommate and best friend, East, was due home sometime today. The last thing I wanted was to be caught bare-assed naked on his living room couch. East didn't seem like the type of guy to let something like that go. In fact, he reminded me of someone who'd use anything and everything to his advantage. So I'd rather not give him any kind of leg up here, especially not my naked one.

West rolled his hips up, rubbing his hard length along mine, and the temptation to throw caution aside was a difficult one to ignore.

"Come oooon," he said, nipping at my lower lip. "I'll be quick."

I chuckled. "Gee, how could I pass that up?"

West slipped his hands under my sweats, smiling up at me as he waggled his brows. "I'm just trying to—"

"Get laid?"

"*Reassure* you we won't be caught."

"By promising to make it quick?" I pushed up over him and rocked my hips against his. "Do you really want to rush this?"

West leaned his head back on the arm of the couch, closing his eyes and digging his fingers into my ass as he guided my movement. "No, but you're the one who said you were at my beck and call, not me."

"That's true." I leaned down to graze my lips over his, and West's gorgeous blue eyes opened and locked on mine. "But not when your roommate might bust in and catch us."

West frowned. "He's seen *and* done worse. I promise."

"I believe you. But he doesn't even know we're together, so..." I pushed up and moved back from him, settling on my knees between his legs. "I'd rather not announce that with my bare ass."

"No?" West ran his eyes down over me, then offered up a crooked grin. "But it's such a nice ass."

I snorted and moved to get up, knowing it would take very little to persuade West to move this to the bedroom, but then my phone alarm started to go off. I glanced over at where it sat on the coffee table and scooped it up. "Shit."

"What?" West sat up as I silenced my alarm and dropped it back on the table.

"I'm supposed to meet my dad for lunch today. In, like, twenty minutes." I got to my feet and shoved a hand through my hair, wondering how in the hell I was going to get ready and get across town in twenty minutes. "I'm totally going to be late."

I hurried down the hall and heard West follow, but didn't have time to stop. I needed to find my jeans and shirt, hope they weren't rumpled to hell, then pack my shit and get going if I had any hope in getting to the restaurant on time.

How the hell had I forgotten about this?

"JT? Slow down, would you? Why don't you just call and change the day, or tell him you'll be a little late?"

I glanced over at the sexy man eyeing me across the bed and knew exactly how I'd forgotten. When I was around West, everything else vanished from my brain. Something I wouldn't generally mind if I knew my mom wouldn't grill me for my tardiness the next time she saw me.

"You don't get it. Mom set this up for me and Dad thinking it'd be perfect for father and son time, since she's going to brunch with her friends. If she finds out I bailed or was late, she's going to ask why. You really want me to tell her I was late because I spent the night here?"

West's mouth fell open, but when nothing came out, I nodded.

"Exactly."

I pulled on my jeans, and when I located my shirt, I groaned. It was a crumpled mess, just as I'd feared.

West crossed over to me and took the shirt out of my hands. "Go and pick something out of my closet."

One of his shirts was probably worth more than everything I owned combined. "No, that's fine. I'll just tell him—"

"That it spent the night on your boyfriend's floor?" My cheeks flushed, and West chuckled. "I mean, maybe that could be a good icebreaker."

"Seriously?" I shook my head. "You're crazy. I need to ease my parents into this, not announce that I spent the weekend in your bed."

West kissed me quickly. "With me inside you."

I swallowed and shoved him away. "You're not helping."

"I just offered you the clothes off my back—well, hanger." He gestured to the closet again. "Go pick something, and I'll have this cleaned and back to you the next time we hang out."

I bit down on my lip and finally gave in. "Okay."

I darted into the closet and picked out the first shirt I spotted, a black button-down with a subtle pattern that I was hoping my dad wouldn't look too closely at, because it was unlike anything I would pick out for myself.

I shrugged into it and tried not to think about how damn good it smelled—just like the man it belonged to—then headed back out to the living room, where West was waiting for me with my bag.

"Thank you." I took it from him and pressed a quick kiss to his lips, and just as I was about to slip out of his arms and head for the door, West grabbed my waist and pulled me in to deepen the kiss.

I melted into his arms, my mouth going pliant, my willpower zero against the hunger he always inspired in me. When I found myself contemplating how I could get out of lunch again, though, I started to pull away.

But *not* soon enough.

"Oh, Weston *dear*? Is your motherfucking ass finally at home?"

West's arms stiffened at the sound of East's voice, and he pushed me away.

I frowned even as I took a step back, knowing we were keeping this a secret from his friend. But something about West's sudden dismissal of me cut deep. Much deeper than I'd expected, given how close we'd become over the last month.

East stepped out of the foyer, and when his eyes shifted between the two of us, I found myself reaching for the strap of my bag. God, this was awkward. West was standing beside me, still and silent as a statue. It was completely out of character for him, but I didn't have time to analyze it. Instead I had the insane thought that maybe we should just rip the Band-Aid off and tell his friends and my family we were together. Because this feeling I was experiencing right now? It sucked.

"Hi," I said, deciding the best thing I could do was get the hell out of there.

"Hello." East's eyes narrowed a fraction, reminding me of a hunter stalking its prey. "Fancy meeting you here, JT. Though I'm not sure why I'm so surprised. I haven't seen my boy West here in days. I should've guessed you were the reason."

"East..." West finally said, walking around the couch toward his friend.

"What? From the minute I saw you two together, I

had a feeling it would end up this way. Hell, I should've *bet* on it."

I grinned, almost relieved that he was joking about it. Maybe if I got out of there West could finally tell his friend everything, and the next time we all hung out it'd be much less awkward.

"Look, I've got to get going."

"So soon?" East said.

"Yeah, I've got to meet my dad for lunch."

"That's sweet." He looked over at West. "You're not going with?"

When West merely glared at his friend, I took that as my cue to get out of his hair. "Okay, I'll see you two later."

West gave a nod as East waved me goodbye, and I quickly headed for the door. Great, now I was running even later. I was about to make a dash for the elevator when I reached for my phone in the pocket of my jeans and realized I'd left the damn thing on the coffee table.

Shit. Today was not my day.

I turned around and luckily caught West's door before it shut, and I hurried back inside, about to make my apologies for barging in.

"So you finally fucked the golden boy, huh? Guess you won the bet after all."

I froze as East laughed, my entire body paralyzed by the words I'd just heard.

"I told you I would." West scoffed, the sound caught somewhere between a chuckle and a cough. "You're the one who doubted me."

"My mistake for sure. We were starting to think you'd ditched the bet altogether, but we should've known better. You never give up on a challenge. You've just been busy sealing the deal."

My mind began to spin, and the rush of adrenaline from seconds ago instantly drained away as I tried to comprehend what I was hearing.

Bet...?

Deal...?

They'd all been waiting for West to...fuck me?

No. There was no way I'd just heard what I thought I had.

My stomach roiled as I blinked, trying to focus, trying to reason away what these two guys had just said, but nothing was making sense.

Nothing except the fact that I was a bet. A sick and twisted *bet*. How low could someone go?

My legs shook and the room started to sway, and when my bag fell off my arm and hit the floor, East and West both stepped into view.

East's smirk was like that of a snake—cruel and cunning and not at all sorry for the venom he'd just spewed out of his mouth.

West, on the other hand, looked like he wanted to vomit. His face had turned ashen, his eyes glassy and wide, as he tried to swallow back the revolting things he'd just said.

"JT... I—"

"Don't," I said quietly.

West walked around the table scattered with our left-over breakfast, and my eyes welled as I thought about what a difference a handful of minutes could make. Minutes ago, I'd felt happy and hopeful, like my entire world had been turned upside down by the possibility of falling for someone so completely unexpected.

And now? Now I felt like my world was crumbling down around me—or maybe it was just the castle this Park Avenue Prince had lured me into.

"JT, it's not what you—"

"*Think?*" I spat out, the word so harsh that West had enough common sense to stop by the end of the couch. "Are you really going to stand there and tell me I didn't hear you just call me a *bet?*"

"Technically"—East shrugged—"*I* said you were the bet. He just said he won."

"By fucking me."

"Yes. I hear he's quite good at it, so you're welcome."

"Shut. Up. *East,*" West ground out.

But it was too late now.

I was done listening to him.

Done looking at him.

Done with him.

Humiliation washed through me like ice-cold blood in my veins, and if I didn't get out of there and soon, I wasn't sure I'd make it out alive. With my eyes on East, because it was much easier to feel hate and loathing than heartbreaking disappointment, I said, "I left my phone on the coffee table."

He turned to eye the cluttered space and picked it up, daring me to come get it. Not about to give these two assholes another reason to laugh at me, I forced my legs to move.

I stormed over to East and snatched the cell from him, and as I turned to get the hell out of there, the last thing I heard was West saying, "It's not what you think..."

THIRTY-NINE

I HIT IGNORE on my phone for the tenth time already that morning as I hid out in my usual corner of the library. I'd positioned myself so I could see any unexpected asshole "princes" that walked through the front door, but I hoped that wouldn't happen.

I didn't want to see West. I didn't want to talk to him. And I sure as hell didn't want to think about him, though that one was a little harder to make happen.

All I could think about was how stupid I'd been. Of course West had an ulterior motive. He'd slid in beside me in a class he didn't belong in just to meet me. That should've sent up massive red flags from the get-go, but I hadn't been able to see past the alluring exterior he wanted me to see.

The whole thing made me want to vomit.

My phone buzzed with a message, and I looked down to see it was from "Piece of Shit."

I'd changed West to something more suitable in my phone. He'd gone from *Stalker* to *Boyfriend* to *Piece of Shit*. What an evolution.

PIECE OF SHIT:

I just got to Astor. Can we talk? Five minutes.

Why, so he could try to justify being an asshole? I could just see him now, walking through the courtyard with his gang of dicks laughing about how he'd fucked the dean's son for a bet. Who did something like that? I knew my mom didn't like those guys, but I'd given West and his friends the benefit of the doubt, and look where it'd gotten me.

The worst part about it all, though? That I'd opened up and started to fall for someone who never had any intentions of being with me.

Not even Elise moving across the country had hurt this bad.

Gripping the back of my neck, I sighed and forced myself to look over my notes for my next class. I hadn't managed to get shit done after running out of West's place yesterday. I knew I'd met up with my dad for lunch, but that and everything after was just a blur of avoiding calls and feeling numb.

. . .

PIECE OF SHIT:

Where are you?

I picked up my phone, hit the button to clear the screen, and slammed it down on the table with a little more force than necessary.

"Whoa, take the beatdown outside." Amusement laced Caleb's voice as he pulled out the chair across from me. "Where've you been? I haven't seen you around for a —" His words cut off as he took a look at my face. His smile dimmed. "Everything okay, man?"

"Fucking perfect. You?"

"All good here." He cocked his head. "You wanna talk about it?"

"About being fucking perfect?"

"If the sarcasm didn't tip me off, your face would. You look like shit."

"Wow, you're really great at this cheering-up stuff."

"I would be if I knew what I was cheering you up from."

My phone buzzed again, and as the name of the messenger flashed on the screen, Caleb's brows shot up.

"Well, that explains it. What did West do?"

"Who's that?"

"Oh, sorry, what did the piece of shit do?"

The fact that he knew straight off exactly who my hurt and anger was focused on only confirmed what he and my mom had tried to warn me about. Why the hell hadn't I listened? All the excuses I made for someone I assumed was just being friendly... What an idiot.

I sighed and looked up at Caleb. "You mean you didn't hear?"

"Hear what?"

"That I was a bet."

I expected more of a reaction than a slow blink and the pursing of his lips. But maybe that was worse. Because Caleb didn't seem at all surprised.

"A bet, huh? Would it make you feel better to know I expected worse?"

"What could be worse than those assholes all sitting around waiting for an update on whether or not King Dick fuck—"

Caleb's eyes widened as I bit off my words. "Look, I don't need all the gory details, but if you *want* to talk to someone about it—"

"I don't." I glared over his shoulder, humiliated all over again. How long would it take for news of my "corruption" to spread through Astor? Even worse, how long until it reached my mom? Talk about mortifying.

What a gullible moron I'd turned out to be, to believe that someone like West—oh, my bad, Weston *LaRue*—would be interested in me. I was nothing like him. Nothing like the guys he no doubt fucked on rotation, and here I'd been all hearts in my eyes, thinking he was falling for me.

"I gotta be honest, I'm not at all upset by that murderous gleam in your eye right now," Caleb said. "You need someone to help you hide a body?"

I shook my head. "Don't tempt me."

"Come on, you can't let these guys win. That's what they thrive on."

"Yeah, I kind of got that from the delighted sneer on East's face when he informed me of the exact reason West had ever bothered with me."

"Pompous fucking prick. Someone needs to take him down a peg or two." Caleb leaned back in his seat, tapping his finger on the table. "That whole group is bad news."

"You keep saying that, but not telling me how you know," I snapped, knowing my anger was misdirected but unable to control it.

"It doesn't matter how I know—"

"Really? That's what you're going with?"

"Yeah, it is. It's water under the bridge, and let's just say I'd rather not jump in and drown."

I couldn't fault him for that. Not when that was exactly how I was feeling. It was like West had swept me up in a riptide and pulled me way off course, and no matter how hard I tried, I couldn't get my head back above water. I'd been drifting, flailing around, ever since I heard him admit to the disgusting challenge, and I couldn't seem to work out how to save myself.

"Guess I learned my fucking lesson, then, didn't I?"

"Wouldn't have been my choice on how you found out about them. But it's better to learn their true colors now so you can start fresh and forget about them the rest of your time here."

I wasn't sure how easy it was going to be to forget West or what he'd done to me, not when it was all I could seem to focus on at the moment. But I could see Caleb was trying to help, and the last thing I wanted was to lose the only friend I had left in this stupid place.

"I should've known JT was hanging around you this morning..."

West's achingly familiar voice had my entire body stiffening. Caleb glanced over my shoulder, and his lips twisted with contempt.

"And why's that? Because he finally got a clue and ghosted your sorry ass? Fuck off, LaRue. No one here wants to talk to you."

Thank you, Caleb.

I closed my eyes and did my best not to breathe in West's intoxicating scent, more than aware that something over the past month had woven a spell over me, and I was scared to fall under it again.

"I'm not going anywhere," West said, clearly not about to do anything he didn't want to. Why would now be any different? "Do you speak for JT now?"

"Pretty sure I speak for anyone that has a brain and knows the best way to deal with you is to *not*."

I could feel my anger vibrating through me the longer

West lingered, and when a hand touched my shoulder, it was like something exploded inside of me.

I shot to my feet and whirled around on him. "Don't touch me."

West jerked back a step. "JT, come on."

"Come on? You have a lot of fucking nerve."

"I just want to talk to you."

"I've made it clear I *don't* want to talk to you. I don't want anything to do with you."

A few shushing sounds came from those seated around us, and I quickly apologized before grabbing my phone and my bag and shoving past the piece of shit. I stormed off out of the library, not caring where I went as I crossed the courtyard, only that it was far away from the guy calling out my name behind me.

"I wouldn't do that if I were you," I heard Caleb say seconds before West grabbed my elbow and spun me around to face him.

"I said don't touch me." Glaring, I ripped my arm out of his hold.

He held his hands up but didn't back away. "Look, I know you're angry, and I get it. If I'd walked in on you saying what I did, I'd be pissed. But I can explain."

I could only stare at him, the guy I'd once thought was so attractive and charming, but now could only see for what he was. Repulsive.

"Explain how you went after me to win a bet? I don't think that needs an explanation."

Was I aware of the crowd gathering around us,

listening to what was going down? Yes. Did I plan to censor myself? No. They would all find out anyway, if they didn't know already. I'd suffer through the humiliation, though, if everyone could see once and for all what motherfucking assholes their beloved Park Avenue Princes were.

"I was going to tell you about it—" West started, but I burst out into a scathing laugh.

"Wow, really? How sweet of you to want to give me a heads-up. But see, *Weston*, that's one of the many differences between us. I don't make bets about sleeping with people. Only the lowest of shitheads would do something like that."

West sighed, running a hand through his waves that I noticed weren't as perfectly styled today as usual. "It may have started out that way, but I swear all of it was real once I got to know you."

"But I never got to know *you*. Not the real you. Not the one laughing behind my back with all your friends about how to fuck over the dean's son. I don't know why you did it, and I don't care. You took advantage of me. Made me believe you were someone else entirely. But this guy?" I motioned toward him, my fists clenched tight. "I don't know him, and I sure as hell don't want to."

I went to turn away, but West grabbed for me again, and this time I'd had enough. I shoved him with every ounce of strength I had, sending him stumbling back into a couple of bystanders.

"Leave me the fuck alone." My shout came out raw,

and I hated the way my voice broke a little at the end. I didn't want to be upset about this. I wanted to keep the rage inside longer, so that the look of hurt and guilt on West's face didn't affect me at all.

My chest heaved with adrenaline, and as I looked around at all the faces watching us, many of whom I didn't even recognize, I felt another surge of anger.

"Go ahead," I said, addressing them all. "Bow down to your fucking prince."

Mouths dropped, gasps of surprise met my ears, but I didn't care. They wanted to hold these fuckers up to a different standard, then they should know what the hell they were worshipping.

I looked at West, ignoring the apology written all over his face.

"I hope whatever you won, it was worth it."

I picked my bag up, and as I stalked away, Caleb joined me, the awe in his voice clear when he said, "You are my fucking hero."

FORTY

west

FUCKING HELL.

I couldn't remember the last time I'd had my ass handed to me so badly, but as JT stormed off through the courtyard, and the crowd around us dispersed, I couldn't help but feel a little proud of him.

Don't get me wrong, I also felt like the complete and utter piece of shit he'd just called me. But something about his fiery response gave me the tiniest sliver of hope that maybe, just maybe, he still felt something for me.

Even if it was homicidal in nature.

I let out a sigh and ran a hand through my hair, and when I caught sight of several stragglers gossiping amongst each other, I leveled them with my best "get the fuck out of here" glare and was happy to see it still had some punch to it.

God, talk about a shit show. Who knew the golden

boy had such a temper on him? I'd figured he'd be pissed off; of course he would be. East hadn't exactly broken the news gently. But in my defense, this bet had turned into something I'd never seen coming. How could I? I wasn't the type who fell for a guy within a month of knowing him. They weren't usually around longer than a night for me to feel anything other than horny.

But JT? I was pretty sure part of me fell the second I sat down next to him that first day in class.

Fuck.

Annoyed at myself for letting this situation get out of hand, I grabbed my phone from my pocket and headed out of the courtyard. I wasn't about to stick around here all day and have everyone stare at me.

I called our driver and headed out to wait for him in our usual spot, and as the van pulled up at the curb, I went to open the door, but it slid open instantly.

"Shit," Donovan said when we almost butted heads. "Hey, man, you leaving?"

I moved aside so he could step out. "Yeah. Let's just say today can fuck right off."

Donovan grimaced and, instead of getting out, moved back to his seat and gestured for the empty one beside him. "Okay, get in. Sounds like you need some 'van time.'"

I snorted and shook my head. Donovan's "van time" was legendary, like therapy on wheels, because despite all the crap we gave him about his model reputation, Donovan was a really good listener. He was also one of two out of our group of friends who'd ever actually been in a real relationship.

I slid the door shut, and before the van even began to move, I was reaching for the bourbon.

"So, Mr. LaRue, what brings you by my office this morning?" Donovan's pearly-white, million-dollar smile was difficult to ignore as he lounged back in the leather seat.

I took a sip of my drink and rested my head back against the seat, wondering where the hell to start, then I just blurted out, "I fucked up."

"Well, yeah." Donovan nodded. "I gathered that much. You're drinking before noon, and that's excessive, even for you."

I looked out the window at the taxicabs and cars that came to a stop alongside us at a red light. "Have you seen East this morning?"

"No. I had a fitting and was just getting to school when I ran into you. Did you two have a lovers' spat?"

I turned, frowning. "There was a lovers' spat, all right, but not between me and East."

Donovan's blond hair fell across his forehead. "JT?"

"Yeah."

"Oh, hell, he found out about the bet, didn't he?"

I downed the rest of the bourbon in a long swallow, welcoming the burn, and nodded. "Yeah."

"Fuck." Donovan let out a sigh and shook his head. "I'm guessing he didn't take it too well?"

"That might just be the understatement of the

century with the way he reamed me a new one in the courtyard a few minutes ago." When Donovan's mouth fell open, I nodded. "Give it an hour. I'm sure it'll be all over social media."

"Holy shit, West. That means the dean is going to—"

"Find out what we did? Find out what *I* did to her precious son? I know. I'm fucked. Or, incidentally, not fucked anymore. That was out of the equation the second East opened his big mouth and threw me under the bus."

"Threw you under the bus?" Donovan's lips quirked. "Weren't you the one *driving* the bus?"

I opened my mouth to deny that, but I was the one who'd accepted the bet, and I was the one who'd been adamant I could win. So I didn't really have anyone to blame but myself. My intentions had been shit from the get-go.

Eyeing my empty glass, I debated having another, but that wouldn't do shit to help me figure out how to get out of this mess. Though the temptation to numb everything was strong.

Donovan seemed to sense my internal debate and reached for my glass, setting it back on the bar.

"So what's bothering you the most?" he said. "The fact that you have another strike against the dean coming down the pipe or that JT called you out in front of everyone?"

I needed that second glass.

Sighing, I rubbed a hand over my face and admitted, "Neither."

Donovan was silent for a long moment. "What does that mean?" he finally asked.

"It means..." I didn't know what to say. I didn't have the words to explain that spending time with JT had only made me want to be around him all the time. That I missed him when he wasn't around. That I checked my phone constantly in case he called or sent a message.

"Oh my God," Donovan said quietly. "You fell for him, didn't you?"

I didn't have to say anything. I knew it was written all over my face. The reason I didn't give a shit about who'd been watching or what they were going to say during my character assassination was because no one else's opinion mattered but JT's.

"It doesn't matter. He hates me."

"West, if you like the guy, it sure as hell does matter."

"Did you miss the part where I said he hates me? That I fucked him over and he won't even look at me now?"

"I did. But I can only assume that if you were falling for JT, he was doing the same for you, and that's why he's so upset. Did you apologize?"

I shot him a look. "I didn't exactly get a chance to do that."

He shrugged, crossing his ankle over his knee. "Then you didn't try hard enough."

"Excuse me?"

"You heard me."

"I've left him a thousand fucking messages and voice-mails, I tracked him down to the library—"

"West, if you really care about the guy, beat down his goddamn door until he listens to you. Grovel on your knees—which I'd pay to see, by the way."

I rolled my eyes, but there was no malice when I said, "Piss off."

"Ever heard of a grand gesture? 'Cuz you're gonna need to do that."

"Fuck, now you're just speaking in gibberish. I thought you knew what to do about relationships, considering you've been in one."

Donovan let out a low whistle. "Wow. Weston LaRue and the dean's son in a relationship. Sorry, you've just shocked the shit out of me. And probably everyone else at Astor."

"No one is more surprised than me, trust me."

"Do you mind if I ask how it happened? Because the last I knew, you were still looking at JT like a bet—"

"Stop saying *bet*."

"Okay, as a...piece of ass? Is that better?"

"Van—"

"I'm kidding. Don't give me those crazy eyes. I'm on your side, whatever it is."

I scooted forward to rest my elbows on my knees, dropping my forehead on my palms. "You shouldn't be. I'm a dick."

"The first step to forgiveness is acknowledgment of bad behavior."

I lifted my head. "I thought that was the first step to recovery."

"My van talk, my rules."

Staring down at the ground between my feet, I couldn't stop picturing the pure rage on JT's face. But behind all that had been disappointment. Hurt. It made me sick to my fucking stomach.

"He didn't deserve that," I said. "I never should've made that bet. And the second things changed, I should've called it off."

"And when did they change?"

I thought back over the last few weeks. Like the night on the roof when we'd first kissed and I hadn't been able to get it out of my head. All the times after when he'd opened up to me with a vulnerability and curiosity that was not only surprising, but stoked my own interest. So many moments where it would make sense that I started to look at JT differently. But it was none of those.

It had been the first day at Astor when I crashed King's class. The moment I'd looked into his big brown eyes, I was fucked.

"Daaaamn, you've got it bad."

"You know, these van talks used to be more helpful than judgmental, if I recall."

"That's because you've never cared enough before to *feel* judged. That fact that you do now is a step in the right direction, if you ask me."

"Yeah, I'm starting to wish I hadn't." I scrubbed a hand over my face.

"Aw, don't be like that. Think of it this way, you could be sitting here with East or Daire..."

"I thought you were trying to cheer me up. The last thing I want to do is hang out with the guys—any of them. I've already been subjected to one round of public humiliation. I don't really feel like listening to them laugh their asses off at me."

"I hear you—well, maybe head somewhere quiet and think about what you're going to do next?"

"You mean other than throw myself out of the van and into oncoming traffic?"

Donovan laughed. "Yeah, other than that. Because if I had to guess, JT's probably fond of that pretty face you have there."

"I doubt it. With the way he was raging at me, I think he was about one punch away from rearranging it."

Donovan brought his phone up and started scrolling. "Damn it, it's still not up."

"Seriously? You're looking for a video?"

"I know you said give it an hour, but we all know the way gossip hits about us. Especially gossip like this. I figured five minutes, maybe— Oh, oh, there it is..."

I glared at my friend, though I was seriously reconsidering that title now, as the sound from the video filled the van.

"I was going to tell you about it—" Yep, there was my voice, just as pathetic and desperate as I figured I'd sounded. JT's scathing response was next, and it was just as brutal the second time around as it had been the first.

"Buuuurn," Donovan said, earning a glare from me, and

at least the fucker had the good grace to look somewhat apologetic. "Sorry, but that was harsh. Oh no," he said, looking back to the phone. "Don't do it, West. Don't...touch him," he ended lamely as JT's final words rang through the van. I snatched the phone out of the asshole's hand.

"Give me that." I switched the damn thing off and tossed it back at him. "I told you he hated me. I don't need a reminder."

"On the plus side, it really helped me understand the situation."

I flipped him the bird, and Donovan laughed.

"Dude, quit with all this woe-is-me crap, would you? We already have Daire to darken our day—we don't need you to as well. The way I see it, this can all be fixed with a few simple steps."

I rolled my eyes. "This I'm just dying to hear."

"You do want to win him back, don't you?"

"Of course I fucking do."

"Then first, you need to go and grovel. Just like I said. None of this 'I'm sorry' in a voicemail. Go to his dorm, get down on your knees, and use your mouth for something other than—"

"Yeah, yeah, I get the point."

"Do you? I mean, have you ever said you're sorry before?"

"I'm sorry I got in this van with you right now. Does that count?"

Donovan shrugged. "Baby steps. But you have time;

we'll work on it. Second, you're going to apologize to the dean—"

"Wait, what? Are you out of your fucking mind? If I even set foot near her office after she hears about this—and she will hear—it won't just be my ass a Hawthorne has handed me this week, but my balls. When she cuts them off and *gives* them to me."

"Don't care. You have to do it. You have to apologize for the suspension and for fucking her son, but maybe don't put it that way."

"You think?"

"*Then* you'll be one step closer when JT finally comes around."

"One step closer to what? My ultimate demise?"

"Nooo, winning him back. JT will be happy, his mom will be happy—"

"And what about his guard dog Caleb? You think he's not going to be there barking bullshit in JT's ear about what a piece of shit I am?"

Donovan opened his mouth, but nothing came out as a deep V formed between his brows.

"You didn't say anything about Caleb."

"Yeah, well, I am now. Asshole is determined to keep a five-mile West-free zone around JT now that shit has hit the fan."

Donovan tapped a finger to his chin. "That's a fucking pickle you've got right there, my friend. I got nothing on how to get rid of him, unless Travis moves to Siberia and you personally pay for the ticket."

"Fat lot of help you are."

"I solved two out of three of your damn problems. I can't fix everything. Now it's up to you to go and show JT you aren't the total douchebag he thinks you are."

If only it were that easy. I had a feeling it was going to be anything but that.

FORTY-ONE

THE SUN WAS just starting to set as I stared out over the East River from where I sat on a bench at Brooklyn Bridge Park. Behind me, the sounds of laughter and the music from Jane's Carousel painted a happier picture than the one brewing inside me.

It'd been a full forty-eight hours since the bomb exploded, and two since I'd finished my last class of the day and caught a train to my parents' house. Only, I never ended up there.

I glanced down at the text I'd sent to my mom, telling her where I was and that we needed to talk. I had no doubt she'd heard about what happened yesterday, not if the million calls were any indication, but I wasn't ready to talk to anyone last night.

I couldn't put it off forever, though, and even though it felt like my insides were being clenched in someone's tight fist, it needed to happen. Not inside the confining walls of my parents' place, but out in the open, where I could get some fresh air to help me not pass out.

I absently rubbed my thumb across the screen of my cell. West had apparently gotten the message after our blowout in the courtyard yesterday. He hadn't tried to call again. Hadn't messaged, emailed, tried to show up anywhere I was. And while I knew that was what I'd wanted, what I'd asked for, I couldn't help wishing he cared enough to try to explain. No matter how much of a fight I'd put up saying otherwise.

Somewhere deep down, I guess I'd been hoping I had come to mean more to West, the way he had to me. That what I overheard was a mistake, because the man he'd been with me would never do something like that.

Getting to my feet, I brushed off the back of my jeans and stretched out my legs before heading to the railing. There were more people out and about than usual, probably because the last of the sweltering heat had passed, replaced by a warm breeze that practically begged you to be outside.

At least no one here stared at me the way my classmates did. When I first started at Astor, they looked at me with wary eyes because I was the dean's kid. Now they looked at me with a kind of acceptance that I knew only came from watching me go off on someone I cared about, and that wasn't any better.

"I'm surprised you haven't commandeered Gus already," my mom said, joining me along the rail. Worry crinkled her eyes, but she gave me an affectionate smile as she nodded back at the carousel. "Or have you gotten a new favorite?"

"Nah, I'm still a Gus loyalist," I said, my eyes automatically seeking out the horse I always chose as my own on our visits down here. "Just didn't feel like riding today."

Mom didn't say anything, but her hand rubbing along my back sent pinpricks behind my eyes.

She knew.

And she didn't rush me to say anything else as I wiped away a stray tear. I thought I'd gotten all that out last night after the anger subsided, but her gentle reassurance was unexpected, and welcome.

"I'm so sorry, honey."

I couldn't look at her, keeping my focus on the setting sun gleaming off the water.

"I'm sorry too," I managed. "That you had to find out this way. I was going to tell you..."

She pulled me into her arms, holding me tight. Something inside me eased, all the stress from worrying about her finding out and what she would say gone with her embrace.

She pulled back a little, giving me a sad smile as she pushed my hair from my face. "Let's go sit, and you can tell me all about it."

We made our way back to the benches, and I forced in a few deep breaths. Doing this outside had been the right idea.

"Start at the beginning," she said, squeezing my fingers.

I told her everything. From the way West had crashed King's class to the time we'd spent together—leaving out the salacious details, obviously—and through it all, she listened patiently, no judgment on her face. It wasn't until I mentioned being a bet that I saw her react, a slight twitching of her jaw.

"And I'm sure you heard about what happened yesterday," I said.

"I didn't have to. I saw it."

"Who sent you the video?"

"I didn't need a video, JT. It happened in view of my office."

Oh shit. I'd been so busy trying to get away that I hadn't even thought about the fact that we'd been in the courtyard. So I'd basically given my mom a front-row view?

Now I was going to be sick.

"While you know I don't condone violence, I'll say I was proud of the way you handled yourself," she added.

"Why? I lost my temper."

"You don't think you deserved to? You stood up for yourself. That's exactly who I raised you to be."

"But I lied to you." I trailed figure eights on the bench between us with my finger and shook my head. "You warned me, and I didn't listen. I got what I deserved."

Mom lifted my chin firmly between her fingers. "You do not deserve to be treated as anything less than the magnificent man you are."

"You're not gonna say I told you so?"

"No. I think you've learned your lesson. I know exactly how persuasive people can be, and you're someone who wants to see the good. Even in those who don't deserve it."

"I really thought West was different. Misunderstood. I thought you were wrong about him. He seemed interested in getting to know *me*. Like he wanted to know what I cared about, about my poetry... I even got him to sit through a slam night, if you can believe it."

Mom's brows rose in surprise as I continued.

"I mean, he didn't need to do all that to win the bet, so why did he? Why did he bother?"

"I don't know, sweetheart," she said gently.

"Does it..." I bit down on my lip and tried again. "Does it bother you that I fell for a guy?"

She shook her head before the words were even out of my mouth. "It doesn't matter to me who you love, as long as they're good to you. As long as you're happy."

"I thought I was," I murmured, rubbing my forehead. "It felt right, like I was becoming the person I was always meant to be, and that somehow West had brought that out in me. That sounds so stupid, doesn't it?"

"No, it doesn't." Mom seemed like she wanted to add something to that, but snapped her mouth shut.

"What?"

"Nothing."

"No, tell me."

She gazed over at the carousel. "I could see it," she said quietly, before turning back to me. "That you were happy. A little too busy for old Mom, perhaps, but every time I saw you, you had this energy about you. I wish I'd asked why, but I could see you didn't want to talk about it. Maybe that was wrong. Maybe I could've saved you the heartbreak."

"It's not your fault. You told me that whole group was trouble, and I didn't listen. I doubt I would've changed my mind once I was deep in it."

She gave me a tight-lipped smile. "Maybe not. It's just my instinct as a parent, I guess. Wanting to put you in a bubble so nothing and no one can hurt you. I know it's not possible, but it doesn't mean I won't try to do anything and everything in my power to keep you safe and happy and healthy."

"Two out of three ain't bad."

Lifting my chin again to force me to look her in the eyes, she said, "You'll be okay, kiddo. You've got all the time in the world, but maybe focusing on your studies for a while is a good idea. Although there is something I could do to speed up the process..."

"I'm scared to ask."

"Would it help you if a few of your peers were expelled for bad behavior?"

My mouth fell open. "Mom. No way."

She waved a hand, like she knew I'd say that. "Just thought I'd offer. Let me know if you change your mind."

I had no doubt it would sting every time I passed West in the hallway or heard the jokes his friends would no doubt tell about me loud enough to hear, but that wasn't enough for me to want them expelled. Besides, their high-powered families would have a field day with my mom over it. No thank you.

"I appreciate the offer," I said, mustering up a small smile. "But there is something you could tell me."

"What's that?"

"What happened to make you hate those guys so much?"

"Ah. Besides the pranks they like to play on their classmates and professors that get them sent to my office?" Mom stretched out her legs, crossing them at the ankles. "Let me just tell you..."

BY THE TIME I got back to my dorm, I was spent. The conversation with Mom had definitely helped ease the weight off my shoulders, but pouring my heart out always left me feeling drained.

It'd felt good to finally share with her everything I'd been going through over the past few weeks. But after hearing all of the crap West and his crew had pulled over the years to earn her bad opinion of them, I wished she'd maybe divulged some of it. That way I would've at least known why I should stay away.

Would I have listened? Maybe. Maybe not. But at least I would've known what I was getting into instead of choosing to believe it was just a case of misunderstanding.

Geez, how naïve am I?

I pulled my key out as I reached my room. All I wanted now was to get inside and shut the door on this day—and the whole world, really. I was done dealing with peopling and talking about emotions, and all I wanted now was to lock myself away, close my eyes, and be by myself.

That had felt impossible after everything that happened. But as the darkness of my room enveloped me, I welcomed it—along with the silence that followed. This was what I wanted, peace and quiet, a moment to forget how spectacularly my life had been turned on its head. Then I would wake up and somehow work out a way to move forward.

It was the only way I was going to be able to survive the rest of my time here at Astor. I needed to file this first month under "colossal mistakes" then do my best to try to learn from them. In other words, steer clear of the people I was told to.

I shut the door and leaned back against it, letting out a sigh of relief that there was no one else here. I flicked the light on, and the sight of West sitting on the end of my bed scared the shit out of me.

My hand flew to my chest, and as he slowly got to his feet, I reached for the door handle.

What the hell is he *doing here?*

"Hey," West said, as I tried to locate my tongue, my words, my *brain*. But seeing him there in my room, sitting on my bed, immediately transported me back to the first night he'd stayed with me. The first night I'd fallen asleep in his arms.

He didn't look half as put together as he had that night: his pants were crumpled, his shirt half hanging out at the waist as though he'd slept in it, and his usually styled hair looked a mess, as though he'd been pulling at it—or someone else had—and that thought made me want to throw up.

"I was hoping you'd be home tonight." He continued on as though there was no gaping hole where he'd ripped away any and all trust that had been built between us. "But I have to admit, I was starting to have my doubts after the sun went—"

"What are you doing in here?" I cut him off, finally finding my words. "*How* are you in here?"

West slipped his hands in his pockets and gave a small shrug. "George."

Of course. I wasn't sure why I was so surprised. If he could get in the building, my room would be a breeze.

I shook my head and curled my fingers around the handle. "Well, allow me to show you out." I pulled open the door.

West looked past me and out into the hall, then brought his eyes back to mine.

"Thanks, but I'm not quite ready to leave yet."

I blinked, not sure I'd heard him right. "You're not quite *ready*?"

"Right. You see..." He took a step forward, but when I stiffened and straightened my shoulders, he stopped. "I came here to do something, and I'm not going to leave until I've done it."

Unbelievable. The arrogance of him. The gall. After everything he'd done, everything he'd put me through, he had the nerve to tell me what he was going to do in *my* dorm room?

I didn't think so.

I opened my mouth, about to blast him, but before the words could come out, he said, "I owe you an apology."

Excuse me, *what?*

All of the anger that I'd been preparing to once again unleash on him slowly fizzled out at his words and earnest stare. But I was well aware of what a good show West could put on when he wanted to, and I wouldn't believe him just because he was looking at me with eyes I wanted to lose myself in.

No, sir. Not this time. I was not going to fall for his smooth tongue and pretty lies.

"Please, JT." West's voice was soft, as though he were trying to soothe a wild animal. "Let me talk to you. Let me apologize."

"And why would I do that?"

"I don't know." He shook his head. "Because you're a better person than I am."

"That's true."

West nodded and looked to his feet, and for the first time since I'd known him, he looked unsure of himself.

"I know I don't deserve any of your time"—he had that right—"but please, JT, let me say this."

My heart warred with my brain as I looked at him, and though every instinct told me to throw him out and lock the door on this chapter of my life, I couldn't find it in myself to be that cruel.

I let out a breath and slowly shut the door, then crossed my arms. At least that way I had something between him and my chest if he aimed at it again.

"Okay, I'm listening."

West nodded, and when he raised his head, I was shocked to see his eyes were a little glassy—probably from lack of sleep.

"Everything you said to me in the courtyard yesterday was true—"

"I know."

West's teeth clicked as though biting back a response, and I arched a brow, waiting.

"What I mean to say is, I'm sorry my friends and I are such dickheads. That we even thought of or came up with the stupid..." He trailed off, waving his hand through the air, but I wasn't about to let him weasel out of it that easy.

"Bet."

West's eyes locked on mine, and I took a step forward.

"You came up with a *bet* to fuck me." When he just blinked at me, I added, "If you're going to apologize, you need to acknowledge what it is you're apologizing for."

He swallowed, and color bloomed on his cheeks. Good —he should feel humiliated about the way they acted, the way they treated me, because that was exactly how he'd made me feel.

"I'm sorry we came up with a bet for me to fuck you. Corrupt you, actually."

I forced myself to breathe. "*Corrupt?*"

"What better way to get payback on the dean for my suspension than to bring her golden child to our dark side?"

I could barely hear him over the blood rushing in my ears. "From what I heard, you earned it. You broke into her office and trashed the place."

West opened his mouth to respond, but then snapped it shut.

"What?" I said. "Going to deny it?"

"No. We flipped over all the furniture as a prank, but *trashed* is a strong word."

"And that's supposed to be a joke to you?"

A sigh left him as he ran a hand through his hair. "Look, I know she's your mom, but she'd had it out for us since we started at Astor. We're privileged assholes she has to put up with; I get it. Did we pull some stupid shit to liven things up around campus because of it? Sure. But it was all harmless stuff."

"So what you did to me," I said slowly. "That was harmless?"

He swallowed. "No. It was thoughtless and cruel. The kind of thing selfish, bored, rich shits do because they can. But just because I can do something doesn't mean I should, and I *never* should've let them—or myself—do what we did to you. "

I bit the inside of my cheek, trying not to give him the satisfaction of seeing how his words affected me. But with the way I could feel my chin shake, I knew that would be a losing battle.

He approached me slowly. "JT, you got caught up in something that had nothing to do with you, something stupid and impulsive. Something I'll regret every fucking day of my life. I'm sorry. I'm so damn sorry."

West's face blurred as I stared at him, and I realized I was fighting back tears. But hearing him admit it, hearing him say all that I was to him out loud, hurt more than I'd ever thought possible.

"I never meant for it to get this out of hand," he said.

"Out of hand?" I shook my head, and as a tear slipped free, I quickly reached up to brush it away. "How does a bet get out of hand, West? You had a mission, a goal. You came after me, befriended me, made me fall for you, and you won. It didn't get out of hand. Everything worked out exactly as it was supposed to—"

"Except my falling for you."

"No. I can't... I can't do this." I put up a hand, and West took hold of it, closing the distance between us.

"But it's true. Somewhere between the moment I saw you in your mom's office to the second I sat down beside you that first class, you had me. I was expecting some naïve kid who was determined to play by the rules in case his mommy found out. But you were nothing like that. You were sexy and fun and were willing to risk your ass by sneaking out of your room just to hang out with me, and the more time we spent together, the more I realized how much I want to be around you. How much I care about you. *You*, JT, not some stupid fucking bet."

I shook my head and pulled my hand free. "I don't want to hear this."

"But I need you to hear it. I need you to know that I miss having coffee with you, talking to you, kissing you... Nothing replaces that, especially not winning something so stupid."

"You hurt me," I whispered.

"I know. I'm sorry. So fucking sorry I hurt you—that was the last thing I ever wanted."

I nodded. "I believe you. But it's not enough." Then I bit down on my lip and reached for the door handle. "Goodbye, West."

"But..." His face fell as his gaze roamed over me, but I was careful to keep my emotions to myself.

I was too vulnerable. Too close to caving.

Then he stepped out the door, and I closed it behind him and finally let the tears fall free.

west

I WALKED DOWN the familiar hallway that led to the last place I wanted to go, or frankly, was even allowed to be anywhere near. But if I ever had a chance in hell of proving myself to JT, it was necessary.

I'd heard his "no" last night, but Donovan was right—I needed to make my apologies to not only JT, but the woman whose opinion mattered more to him than anyone else's.

His mom's.

Her secretary looked up from her desk as I approached, then did a double take. She shot to her feet with surprising speed, rounding her desk to step in between me and the door to Dean Hawthorne's office.

"Mr. LaRue, you know you've been banned from this office. Don't make me call campus security."

I held both hands up. "I need to speak to the dean," I said. "Please."

"I'm afraid that's not possible."

"Could you please check with her and see about making it possible?"

"Why?" The woman's eyes narrowed, her disapproval of me evident behind her thick lenses. "So you can disrespect her again by trashing her office?"

"I—"

"No," she said, raising her voice. "You need to leave."

Sighing, I shoved my hands in my pockets in an attempt to show her I wasn't a threat. At the moment. "I'm not leaving until I speak with her. Can you just tell the dean I'm here?"

"Unless she calls for you directly, I can assure you Dean Hawthorne doesn't want you or any of your—"

The door to the dean's office flew open, and she stepped out. "What's going on out here?"

The secretary gestured toward me. "I've told him several times to leave. We need to call security—"

"You don't need to do that," I said, focusing on JT's mom. "I'm not here to start trouble. I just want to talk to you."

"I'll call security right now." As her secretary reached for the phone on her desk, Dean Hawthorne held her hand up.

"That won't be necessary," she said. "Weston and I have a few things to discuss."

"But ma'am—"

Dean Hawthorne's eyes cut to the woman, whose mouth snapped shut. When she set the phone back into its receiver, the dean turned toward me and inclined her head for me to follow.

I stepped inside her office for the first time since I'd gotten busted in it last spring. "Shut the door," she said.

The air in the office turned icy as I slowly closed the door, and when I turned to face the dean, I noticed she was already behind her desk, immediately establishing who held the power in this room.

"Take a seat, Mr. LaRue." She gestured to one of the chairs opposite her. "Unless you'd rather I flip it over for you first?"

I deserved that, and whole lot more, if I was being honest. But I kept my mouth shut. I was here to apologize.

"This works fine." I took a seat as she took hers, and when she clasped her hands on the desk, I swallowed.

I'd been in plenty of situations where I was summoned to my father's office to be reprimanded over the years. But knowing the dean had likely caught wind of what had gone down between me and her son had my balls scrunching up and hiding somewhere in my body.

Jesus. I could feel the sweat popping out on my brow. This apology had been a long time coming.

"Well, Mr. LaRue? I'm waiting."

I shifted on the seat, tugging at the collar of my shirt, as I tried to decide how best to start. "I just wanted to stop by today and apologize for what I did to your office back in spring of this year."

The dean's eyes narrowed, and for the first time ever I

noticed a resemblance between mom and son, as an image of JT glaring at me the same way the night before flashed before my eyes.

"And you chose today, of all the days between the beginning of school and now, to do that?"

"Um—"

"*Um* is not an answer, Mr. LaRue."

"Yes," I said, wishing the floor would just open up and swallow me whole. This apology tour was tanking. "What I mean to say is, I've realized that what I did to your office was immature and juvenile—"

"Don't forget illegal."

Illegal? She couldn't be serious. "We didn't steal anything. It was just a prank."

"You broke into my *office*, Mr. LaRue. That is breaking and entering, which is, if I'm not mistaken, illegal. You're lucky I didn't press charges."

Oh fuck. She was pissed. But unlike her son, who got fiery in his rage, she aimed to kill with an arctic fucking blast.

"Of course. I wasn't thinking."

"A problem you seem to have more often than not, from what I've witnessed lately."

"Agreed. I won't deny I've done some things I regret lately. And I'm sorry."

God, I'd said that word more times in the last twelve hours than I had my whole life. But when you finally realized you were a shit, it was time to come clean.

"Anything else?" she said.

I wiped my sweaty palms on my pants. It wasn't like me to be this nervous, but if the dean didn't accept my apology when it came to JT, then I had no hope at all of winning him back. And I couldn't accept that.

I took a deep breath and forced myself to meet her stare head-on. "I care about your son, Dean Hawthorne. More than I've ever cared about anyone—well, except myself. And I know I fu—messed that up and hurt him"—another deep inhale—"but I swear I'll never do it again."

She leaned back in her chair, hands crossed over her stomach and those assessing eyes unblinking.

"Why?" she finally said.

"What do you mean?"

"Why do you care about him?"

I blinked at her like she was asking me for the codes to the nuclear missiles.

"Weston?"

"Huh?"

"*Why* do you care about JT?"

I thought back to his easygoing smile, the way he blushed whenever he got nervous or flustered, and the way he was able to take me down a peg or two without making it feel like an insult. He'd made me look outside the glitz and glam of my life, beyond the glass walls of my condo, to what else was out there, and the shocking thing was, I liked it—as long as it was with him.

"He's good."

The dean opened her mouth as if to respond, but I got there first.

"JT is *good* and I'm not. Trust me, I know. I'm probably your worst nightmare for him." She lifted a brow, not disagreeing, but also not interrupting me, so I figured my best bet was to just keep going. "I get it. I'm a delinquent. I run with overprivileged snobs who don't really need an education to further their careers, but who attend your university because our parents know it looks better to have some sort of degree. Nepotism and all that. But here's the thing. When I'm with JT, I find myself stepping away from that crowd and looking at other possibilities beyond what is sitting on the platter at home."

Dean Hawthorne let out a breath and shook her head. "I see how you might think that's a compliment—"

"It is. I rode the *train* last week for the first time because I wanted to go on a date with your son. Do you know how monumental that is? I've never set foot on a subway platform in my life, and I was born in New York."

The dean's lips twitched, but beyond that, she didn't move a muscle, and I was starting to wonder if ice queens needed to breathe.

"What I'm trying to say is, I'll do whatever it takes to hang out with JT. I want to be good enough for him. I want to be better than some punk who breaks into your office and tosses it."

I clamped my teeth down into my bottom lip in the hopes of shutting the hell up. I'd said what I'd come to say—I'd apologized and done my best to try to convince the dean I wasn't a total shitbag.

Now it was up to her.

Dean Hawthorne pushed back from the desk and got to her feet, and I looked around, wondering if I should do the same. But I decided to keep my ass exactly where it was. I'd move when she gave me permission to.

"You know the one thing I love the most about my son, Weston?"

Oh God, was this a trick question? Could I phone a friend?

Dean Hawthorne leaned back against the edge of her desk, crossed her arms, and stared down at me.

"Uh, no, dean."

"The thing I love most is that I trust him."

I winced, and she nodded.

"Yes, and can you understand how his recent involvement with you might make me slightly uncomfortable about that?"

I swallowed around the sudden burst of frosty air coming my way, then cleared my throat. "I can, yes. But in JT's defense, nothing he did was his idea."

"Except the part where he fell for you."

Nothing, and I mean *nothing*, she could've said then would've shocked me more.

"You look surprised."

"I, um, yeah. I wasn't expecting that."

"For him to fall for you or for me to know?"

"Both?"

She shifted to her feet. "Let me be very clear about something. You are not who I would choose for my son. You are arrogant, reckless, and, more often than not, the cause of many complaints that get sent to my office, at least by association. But for some reason or other, my beautiful boy sees something in you, and...I trust him."

Holy shit, what? JT had told his mom about me? That he had fallen for me? Why did she make it sound like there was still a chance?

The dean looked down at me, a confounded expression on her face. "Far be it for me to be the one to stand in the way of my boy's happiness. You are who he wants, Weston, so prove me wrong."

If I hadn't been staring at her so intently, I might've missed what she'd said with the blood ringing in my ears. But I caught it, and fucking hell, that sure seemed like a blessing—or at least as much of a one as I was going to get from her—so I sprang to my feet, giving her a genuine smile.

"I'll try my hardest."

"Don't try, just do."

Not about to stick around and have her change her mind, I stepped around the chair and made a mad dash for the door.

Just as I was about to open it and get the hell out of there, I heard, "Oh, and Mr. LaRue?"

I stopped with my fingers on the handle and glanced back over my shoulder, waiting for one final threat, but she gave a small smile instead.

"If you're serious about him...it's Wednesday night. You know where he'll be."

FORTY-THREE

"WELCOME TO SLAM night, everyone!" The usual host jumped up on the elevated platform that served as a stage, the lone spotlight following her. "We've got our judges for the night all set, but a couple of spots are still open for slams, so sign up at the bar if you'd like to share with us tonight. First up, let's make some noise for Ramona."

The crowd whooped and cheered as Ramona took the stage, and I popped the tab on my soda. I was ready to hear some poems other than my own pages of heartbreak. Something angry would be nice, but I was open to anything. I just didn't want to sit around my room moping or secretly hoping for another West break-in. It was pointless to even entertain a second chance when I'd shut him down so completely.

Cutting ties was for the best, though. I needed to focus on school and figuring out what I wanted for my future. I didn't need to think of a certain someone's blue eyes or the confidence he possessed that I wanted to rub off on me.

And I certainly didn't need to think of any other part of that someone rubbing off on me. Or in me.

One day, West would be a blip in my memory, just a fun, wild moment in time that I wasn't emotionally attached to in any way. One day, thinking about him wouldn't hurt so much. I'd forget all about the worry I had that maybe it was a mistake not to give him a second chance. He'd shown me his true colors, after all. No matter how sincere he seemed, no matter how much I wanted to believe his apology...

This *was* for the best, right? And time was supposed to heal...right?

Then why was I sitting here with my gut twisted up like *I* was the one who'd messed up somehow?

I took a long swallow of my soda and tried to focus on what Ramona was saying. Something political, exactly the kind of thing that would get me out of my head. If only I could manage to pay attention.

She finished off her piece, and the next performer was introduced, this time an older guy with an attitude that promised something fun. And raging.

"Is this seat taken?" came a quiet whisper above me, and I shook my head, not paying any attention to the late-comer. It wasn't until he sat down beside me, squeezing in at the edge of the aisle, that I realized who it was. His cologne filled my nose, causing my heart to stop dead in my chest.

"*West?*" I said, disbelief making my voice go up an octave or two as he flashed a grin and put a finger to his lips.

"Shh..." He gestured to the stage. "They're about to start."

He turned to face the stage as though the fact that he was there, in the East Village, sitting in the Poet Café, was a regular occurrence for him. Not one I'd forced on him during his imposed fake dating of me.

Edwin, the next performer, greeted the crowd, but I couldn't seem to tear my eyes away from West. What ulterior plans did have this time around?

"What are you doing here?" I said under my breath, my eyes boring a hole into West's handsome profile.

No, not handsome. Arrogant.

His arrogant and close-to-perfect profile.

Damn it.

He didn't look my way, focusing instead on the performer. "Oh, I just thought I'd take in a little poetry for the night."

"You thought... *What?* This isn't your thing," I protested, my words coming out a little louder than I'd intended, if the people behind us shushing me were any indication.

West couldn't be here. Not in *my* space, a place I'd gone to escape him.

"Says who?" West's eyes met mine. "I like what you like. Remember?"

I swallowed, trying not to get lost in the crystal-blue depths of his gaze, and jerked my attention back to the performance. As I silently fumed, I did my best to focus on the words Edwin was saying, but no matter how hard I tried to concentrate, all I could think about was West's audacity.

"You don't like what I like." I couldn't seem to stop the words from leaving my mouth. "You like hundred-dollar caviar, limousines, and five-star hotels with chandeliers dripping from the ceiling."

West angled his head in my direction. "You're right. I do like all of that. But you forgot one thing." I scanned his face, searching for a clue. "I like *you*, Golden Boy."

Ugh, the man was infuriating. Had probably never been told no in his life. But that was too bad. I wasn't some toy he'd been given to play with—although he'd been really good at it.

I gnashed my teeth together and blew out a breath. "What part of 'goodbye' did you not understand the last time we spoke?"

"The *bye* part." His eyes flashed with mischief. "I got the *good* because, well, I'm good at a lot of things. But bye? I don't really hear that a lot."

I rolled my eyes. "Well, brace yourself—you're about to hear it again."

The three-minute buzzer went off just as I was about to stand, and a loud round of applause filled the building as Edwin waved and moved off the stage. As the audience settled and the host stepped back up to the mic, I took that as my cue to get the hell out of there. But as I moved to step by West, he took my hand and looked up at me.

"Where are you going?"

I pulled my arm free. "Away from here. Goodbye, West."

About to brush by him, I was shocked when he got to his feet, blocking my path. "No. Don't do that."

I arched a brow. "Well, I'm not going to spend the night sitting here with you."

He put his hands up in surrender. "Okay, I hear you. You were here first. I'll go and find somewhere else to sit."

My eyes narrowed as I looked around the crowded space. There were no seats, no floor space, and even the balcony was full tonight. He'd have a tough time finding anywhere else to enjoy the show, but that wasn't my problem. I wasn't going to feel guilty he'd have to stand shoulder to shoulder with some stranger. He was the one who'd decided to show up here tonight.

"Good." I gave a clipped nod and retook my seat, and as West slipped out of the aisle and disappeared into the throng of people, I allowed myself to breathe.

God, how was it that he could affect me this way? It was like the second he was near, everything else faded until all I could focus on was him. But now I could at least try to enjoy the rest of the show. The idea that West would actually stay seemed highly unlikely. So I settled in and waited for the next slam contestant, more than happy to believe he'd dipped out for the night.

The crowd chatted amongst themselves as the host conversed with the judges off to the side of the stage, and I took a sip of my soda, relaxing now that the danger had been removed.

Danger. That was the exact warning West should come with.

Danger to my body.

Danger to my mind.

And danger to my heart.

"Exciting news, everyone!" The host rubbed her hands together and smiled out at the audience. "Someone signed up to fill one of the final spots, and guess what?"

"*What?*" they boomed back.

"He's fresh meat."

Everyone let out an ear-blistering cheer, catcalling and wolf-whistling their enthusiasm for the newbie poet, something they no doubt viewed as encouraging. But if that had been for me, it would've sent my ass running.

The host held her hands up and gestured for everyone to simmer down, then turned to the side of the stage and motioned for the next contestant to join her.

I lifted my soda to take another sip, and when the spotlight shifted to the shadows and West stepped onto the stage, I almost sprayed my drink all over the person in front of me.

What the fuck?

"This here is…" The host covered the mic and leaned over to West, and then nodded. "*Mr.* LaRue. So fancy—"

Oh God, just kill me now.

"The rules are, as always, new or not, three minutes. You speak. We judge. And hopefully don't send you crying. The mic's yours…sir."

West winked at the host, bold bastard, then, cool as you please, moved in behind the mic as though he'd done this a million times before.

Of course he was comfortable up there, in the spotlight in front of a room full of strangers. Probably thought he'd win by just standing there. Which made me wonder: *He does know he has to speak, right?*

"Evenin' everyone."

West leaned down into the mic, his sparkling eyes dancing over the crowd as I sank down in my seat, hoping against all hope he wasn't going to—

"I'd like to dedicate my poem tonight to JT." He brought his other hand up to shield his eyes from the spotlight. "He's here tonight, right over there."

Everyone in the café turned in their seats, their eyes all locking on to me like lasers. I was going to kill him. The first chance I had, *I was going to kill him.*

The buzzer went off, and West gripped the mic and waggled his eyebrows at me. "My piece tonight is called 'Douchebag Prince.'"

I groaned. *Sweet mother of God.* Who knew what was about to fly out of West's mouth? Did I even want to know? All I knew was that I'd do anything in that moment for the ground to open up and swallow me whole.

"There once was a prince"—West pointed to himself—*"who lived in a castle.*

Who, it turns out, was no prince but kind of an asshole."

My eyes popped wide as people started to boo, but West merely shrugged and kept right on.

"He let his arrogance and desire for petty revenge

Overrule all common sense when challenged by friends:

To enter into a deceitful plot, where a wicked bet was waged.

All he had to do was corrupt an innocent, then go on his merry way."

Holy shit. He was laying it all out there. I could feel the questioning eyes bounce between me and West, but all I could focus on were the words coming out of his mouth.

"'Easy,' the prince said, 'I can do that,' without any worry at all.

*Because never would he guess the innocent in question
would be the one to make him fall.*
Fall head over heels. Fall flat on his ass.
Fall the second their eyes met in the King's class.
But fall he did as soon as he saw,
*Those beautiful brown eyes and a face he'd slay dragons
for.*"

My breath caught in my throat as West turned the full force of his attention on me. As if no one else was in the room. Like nothing else mattered but me and finding a way to get through.

"*But the prince was determined; he never lost.*
This time would be no different, except for the cost.
Because never did he think he had the ability to find
Someone who adored him not for his money but his mind."

West smiled as he broke our connection to tell the crowd, "He also adored my body, but that didn't rhyme."

Everyone started to laugh, and damn it, so did I. West was making it impossible to ignore him—not to mention stay mad—as he slipped right back into his poem like the natural he was proving to be.

. . .

"The innocent was sweet, his love golden
But his heart and trust the prince had stolen.
Hurt and betrayed the innocent lashed out,
Telling the prince to 'Get the fuck out!'"

West pointed dramatically to the side stage exit, making the audience laugh. Then he lowered his arm and took on a serious tone.

"The prince left, dragging his pride out the door.
But what good would that do him, when his heart was broken on the floor?
He needed a way to prove that he had changed.
A way to make the innocent look at him again."

West's eyes came back to mine then and the apology swirling in his had my breath catching.

"The prince tried to apologize, but that wasn't enough.
He even braved the queen, to prove he was tough.
But in the end the most honest thing he could do
Was lay his heart on the line and let the innocent choose.
Could he ever forgive the prince after what he'd done?
Or would the prince grow old knowing he'd lost...the one?"

. . .

When West delivered his final line and stepped aside to take a bow, the crowd let out booming applause and started to stamp their feet. The thunderous sound kept time with my pounding heart as I smiled, and when West winked at me, a tear slipped free.

Shit. I was crying.

I reached up and swiped the tears away, as happiness washed over me, filling me with hope and possibilities, then the audience turned my way and started to cheer.

My face burned, but I didn't care. I only had eyes for West, who was looking at me with a question on his face that I already knew the answer to.

I was out of my seat and heading down the aisle toward West as the wolf whistles continued. His eyes widened slightly when he realized what I was doing, but then he jumped off the platform, his long legs eating up the space between us.

My heart raced, closed to bursting, as we rushed toward each other.

"JT," West said, "I—"

I didn't give him a chance to finish. My hands were on him, cupping either side of his face as I slammed my mouth to his. West didn't hesitate—he wrapped both arms tight around my waist, kissing me back with an intensity that made my knees weak and set off explosions behind my closed eyes.

Around us, the cheers and shouts grew louder, but West and I were in our own bubble, devouring each other with a passion like it'd been more than days since we'd been apart. Like we never expected to touch each other again.

I pulled back, breathless. "You're absolutely insane, anyone ever told you that?"

He gave a smile, tightening his hold on me. "Among many, many other things. You okay being associated with someone like me?"

"I think I'm up for the challenge."

"Wanna bet?" As soon as the words were out of his mouth, he cringed. "Too soon?"

"Depends—what do I get if I win?"

West lowered his head and nipped at my lower lip. "Anything you want, Golden Boy."

I slipped my tongue between his lips, moaning as I wound my arms around his neck, and connecting myself to him any way I could.

West was here, in my arms again, and all the ugliness that had been between us was now gone. I wasn't the kind of person to hold a grudge, and was a full believer in second chances. So if anyone deserved a chance to redeem himself, it was the man who'd just stood up on stage and given over the power, showing that he did, in fact, have a vulnerable side.

"I want the poem," I whispered against his lips.

"Hmm?"

"If I can manage to put up with you, then I want to hear that poem at least once a month."

West chuckled. "I think the staff here might get sick of hearing it."

"Who said anything about performing it here?"

"Oh, now you're talking."

I grinned against his lips and rubbed my body up against his. "There's good acoustics in the shower—"

"My bedroom."

"Mhmm. I'm sure it would also sound wonderful up on your rooftop deck. I don't care where you say it, but you, *Mr.* LaRue, are going to give me what I want."

West pressed a hard kiss to my lips, then grabbed my ass, squeezing it tight.

"Get a room!" someone shouted, and West waggled his brows at me.

"Who needs a room when there's a second-floor balcony?"

I laughed, shoving at his chest as I shook my head. "I think we've got too many eyes on us to make that happen tonight. Besides, it's a full house."

"Damn. It's a good thing I brought a backup, then."

When I gave him a curious look, he laced his fingers through mine and started back through the crowd to the exit. As we passed, people clapped West and me on the shoulders and grinned. I had a feeling he could get used to that stage, which made another thought pop into my head.

"How the hell did you write all that?" I said. "I'm so impressed. You're a natural."

"I might've...had help. Like, a lot of help."

I side-eyed him, smirking. "Who did you pay to write it for you?"

"Me? Pay someone off? I'm offended you'd think such a thing." He grinned as he held open the front door for me to go out first. "Caleb helped me for free."

"Caleb? No way. He hates you."

"Exactly. You don't think I'd say some of that shit about myself, do you?"

My jaw almost hit the ground in disbelief, and West shrugged.

"I figured we should try to play nice now since we have something in common."

"Something?"

"Someone."

"Wow, I'm shocked. Remind me to thank Caleb next time I see him."

"Fuck Caleb. Actually, don't. I was the one up there performing it, remember? If you're going to thank anyone, it should be *me*." As we stepped out onto the sidewalk, West tugged me toward him.

"Trust me, I will never forget what you just did in there."

West brushed his lips against mine, sending a shiver through my body that I felt everywhere.

"West?"

"Mmm?"

"Take me home, and I'll thank you for the rest of the night."

West grinned and clicked his fingers in the air, and wouldn't you know it, the prince's carriage—a limousine —drew to a stop on the curb.

"You didn't expect me to take the train on my own, did you?"

I chuckled as West opened the door for me. "No, I didn't. Okay, Prince Charming, guess we better get in before this turns into a pumpkin and we're stuck in the East Village."

West feigned a shudder, but the smile on his gorgeous lips grew. "My castle or yours?"

thank you

Thanks for reading Infamous Park Avenue Prince!

Ah, those cocky Park Avenue guys. We couldn't resist diving into the world of rich Manhattan troublemakers and watching them fall for men they shouldn't.

Want more? You'll see all the guys again soon, including West and JT, in the next standalone in the series:

Insatiable Park Avenue Prince

Hmm... Which Prince will be falling this time?
Our lips are sealed. ;)

Join our reader group for all things BrElla (Brooke + Ella) books!

The Naughty Umbrella

also by ella frank

Blind Obsession

Veiled Innocence

PresLocke Series

Co-Authored with Brooke Blaine

Aced

Locked

Wedlocked

Fallen Angel Series

Co-Authored with Brooke Blaine

Halo

Viper

Angel

An Affair In Paris

Lust. Hate. Love

Elite Series

Co-Authored with Brooke Blaine

Danger Zone

Need For Speed

Classified

Dare To Try Series

Co-Authored with Brooke Blaine

Dare You

Dare Me

Truth Or Dare

Malvagio Series

Co-Authored with Brooke Blaine

Forbidden Mafia Prince

Sinful Mafia Prince

Standalone Novels

Co-Authored with Brooke Blaine

Sex Addict

Shiver

Secrets & Lies

Wrapped Up in You

All I Want for Christmas...Is My Sister's Boyfriend

Jingle Bell Rock

Once Upon A Sexy Scrooge

also by brooke blaine

South Haven Series

A Little Bit Like Love

A Little Bit Like Desire

The Unforgettable Duet

Forget Me Not

Remember Me When

Hate to Love Series

Bedhead

L.A. Liaisons Series

Licked

Hooker

P.I.T.A.

Romantic Suspense

Flash Point

PresLocke Series

Co-Authored with Ella Frank

Aced

Locked

Wedlocked

Fallen Angel Series

Co-Authored with *Ella Frank*

Halo

Viper

Angel

An Affair In Paris

Lust. Hate. Love

Elite Series

Co-Authored with *Ella Frank*

Danger Zone

Need For Speed

Classified

Dare To Try Series

Co-Authored with *Ella Frank*

Dare You

Dare Me

Truth Or Dare

Malvagio Series

Co-Authored with *Ella Frank*

Forbidden Mafia Prince

Sinful Mafia Prince

Standalone Novels

Co-Authored with *Ella Frank*

Secrets and Lies

Sex Addict

Shiver

Wrapped Up in You

All I Want for Christmas...Is My Sister's Boyfriend

Jingle Bell Rock

Once Upon a Sexy Scrooge

about ella frank

Ella Frank is the *USA Today* Bestselling Author of the *Temptation series*, including Try, Take, and Trust and is the co-author of the fan-favorite *Fallen Angel series*. Her *Prime Time series* has been praised as "highly entertaining!" and "sexy as hell!"

A life-long fan of the romance genre, Ella is best known for her steamy, heartfelt, M/M romances.

If you'd like to get to know Ella better, you can find her getting up to all kinds of shenanigans at:

The Naughty Umbrella
(Facebook Group)

And if you would like to talk with other readers who love Ella's character's from her Chicagoverse, you can find them **HERE** at
Ella Frank's Temptation Series Facebook Group.

Want to stay up to date with all things Ella?

You can sign up here to join her newsletter and get a FREE ebook.

about brooke blaine

Brooke Blaine is a USA Today Bestselling Author best known for writing romantic comedy and M/M romance. Her novels lead with humor and heart, but Brooke never shies away from throwing in something extra naughty that will scandalize her conservative Southern family for life (bless their hearts).

She's a choc-o-holic, lives for eighties bands (which means she thinks guyliner is totally underrated), believes it's always wine o'clock, and lives with the coolest cat on the planet—her Ragdoll/Maine Coon mix, Jackson Agador Spartacus.

Brooke's Links
Brooke's Newsletter
Brooke & Ella's Naughty Umbrella
www.BrookeBlaine.com

Made in United States
North Haven, CT
04 October 2023

42365366R00275